Tobsha Learner was born and raised in England and has lived in both Australia and the USA. She is a playwright, novelist and also writes thrillers under the nom de plume TS Learner.

Please visit her website at www.tobshaeroticfiction.com or follow her on twitter @Tobsha_Learner.

*Also by Tobsha Learner:*

Quiver
Yearn

# TREMBLE

Sensual Fables of the Mystical and Sinister

## TOBSHA LEARNER

PIATKUS

First published in Australia in 2004 by HarperCollins*Publishers* Pty Limited
A member of the HarperCollinsPublishers (Australia) Pty Limited Group
First published in Great Britain in 2012 by Piatkus

A CIP catalogue record for this book
is available from the British Library.

Internal design by Michael Donohue

ISBN 978-0-7499-5905-0

Printed in Great Britain by Clays Ltd, St Ives plc

Papers used by Piatkus are from well-managed forests
and other responsible sources.

MIX
Paper from
responsible sources
FSC® C104740

Piatkus
An imprint of
Little, Brown Book Group
100 Victoria Embankment
London EC4Y 0DY

An Hachette UK Company
www.hachette.co.uk

www.piatkus.co.uk

For J.

# TREMBLE

# Contents

# The Root

Dorothy leaned back against the coarse wicker chair and watched the afternoon sunlight fall across the wall of the cottage. It was the last days of spring and already she could detect the heavier fecundity of August steaming up through the soil.

She stretched out her solid but shapely legs and caught a glimpse of her reflection in a window. The face that stared back at her was pleasantly attractive. Dorothy's most distinguishing feature was her complexion. She had classically pale Welsh skin with heavy dark eyebrows, and her eyes, ringed with thick black lashes, were somewhere between grey and blue. 'The colour of threatening weather,' her ex-lover used to call it. Above them, her dark hair stood up like an errant haystack. It was the face of a woman in her mid-thirties. Dorothy had no illusions, she knew she looked her age.

'I hope you like nettle tea,' Great-Aunt Winifred sang out. A whiff of a dank smell, not unlike horse manure, drifted out from the kitchen.

The old lady placed a steaming cup of tea in front of Dorothy and sat down, her sharp face a road map of wrinkles with two mischievous brown eyes buried below a strong brow.

'Is it medicinal?' Dorothy asked nervously, hoping for a syrupy nectar that would ease the constant heartburn she'd been plagued with ever since she'd given up the London flat, the married lover and the secure job in the archival department of the British Museum. A job, she'd realised, that had little to offer except a state pension upon retirement.

Winifred Cecily Owen gazed critically at her great-niece. At ninety-nine years of age she found that anyone under the age of seventy irritated her. They seemed to have lost the art of self-reliance and, worse than that, the art of happiness. She was convinced they had replaced it with an insatiable need to be entertained. Winifred's generation had been far less demanding. They were simply grateful to have the woods and the streams, the local dances at the nearby army barracks, and to repeat the life rhythms of their parents and grandparents. Why did everyone want so much these days?

The Owens had lived for over four hundred years in a tiny hamlet outside the Welsh village of Llansantffraid. The family had an uneasy relationship with the villagers, who, in all truth, had barely tolerated their outlandish behaviour over the centuries.

Generations of Owen women had gloried in their spinsterhood. Every decade or so, one chosen woman would run off only to reappear pregnant, as if blessed by an immaculate conception. And generations of local preachers, vicars and holy men had despaired. They were outraged at the complete lack of guilt the women displayed, as if it were their right to behave in such an ungodly manner, and branded the women witches, spreading the rumour that they were worshippers of Rhiannon, Cerridwen and Arianrhod — the three great goddesses of Cymru — and that their coven lay hidden in a cave in the foothills of North Wales. But despite the rumour, none of the clan of Gynia Mwyn was ever arrested, imprisoned or burned at the stake and so the uneasy truce continued through the ages.

In truth it was a symbiotic relationship. The villagers needed the Owens to provide greater drama than their own petty squabbles and intrigues, while the Owens needed the anonymous sperm donations. Even Dorothy herself had never known her father.

Dorothy was the only Owen, ever, to have left the hamlet and been allowed to return. There had been one who had left before her — her mother's cousin who had emigrated to Australia. The cousin, whose departure was seen as a betrayal, had never been spoken of since. Dorothy herself had barely been forgiven. Her great-aunt blamed the cinema. Edith, Dorothy's mother, had been a flighty, over-imaginative creature who had seen *The Wizard of Oz* at an impressionable age. Winifred was convinced that if Edith had given her daughter a Welsh name, Dorothy would never have wandered. As it was, Dorothy had fled for London at the age of sixteen and had found herself an apprenticeship at the Imperial War Museum. It had taken her another eighteen years to find her way back to Wales.

'You home for good then?' Winifred ventured, reading a fatalism in the slump of her niece's shoulders. The girl had a body, the aunt noted, that seemed prematurely resigned to ageing.

'For a while. I have an interview at Shrewsbury Castle; they're looking for a curator for the museum.'

'The castle! That's a terrible place! I don't know why you would want to work for the English — a mean treacherous race who slaughtered your ancestors!'

Dorothy restrained herself from pointing out that it was the very same race that kept the village's souvenir shop and weekend cottages thriving, preventing it from becoming yet another ghost town. Still, it was the local English weekenders with their four-wheel drives who would regularly pull up outside Winifred's cottage to point out the witch to their restless nose-picking kids. She watched as the nonagenarian poured the tea from a huge silver pot, hands trembling. Winifred's long paisley dress was more reminiscent of the 1960s than an ancient sorceress's gown. It had probably been donated by the local thrift shop; and besides, what witch would get her food delivered by meals on wheels? Certainly not one with any dignity, and dignity was what her ancient relative exuded from every cell of her gnarled body. No, what Great-Aunt Winifred was suffering was the persecution every happily single woman suffers: the predictable social condemnation of her independence and childlessness. Dorothy reminded herself of what she'd learned during a university course on feminist history (with a strong Marxist slant): spinsters are a threat to patriarchy. As she grasped the china cup, she contemplated the possibility of elevating her great-aunt to the status of heroine.

'Still single?' Winifred went straight for the jugular.

Dorothy's noble contemplation plummeted to the ground; her great-aunt had an unerring capacity to sniff out anyone's Achilles heel. The young woman blushed and nodded. Feminism aside, she still found it hard not to feel stigmatised by *that* word.

'Nothing to be ashamed of; we Owen women have a long history of going it alone. One day I'll show you how. They don't call me the Merry Spinster for nothing. Now drink your tea, it'll make your breasts grow.'

Sipping at the scalding brew, Dorothy put the last comment down to approaching dementia. Great-Aunt Winifred was, after all, ninety-nine. It was then that she noticed the knitting bag at her aunt's feet. A mangy sack woven from hoary greenish thread, it was almost indiscernible against the moss-covered slate that paved Winifred's courtyard. Suddenly it jumped, as if something were trapped inside. Dorothy looked again — the fabric definitely seemed to be twitching. Was she hallucinating? Could it be the nettle tea? She glanced back at her aunt, who smiled serenely but not without a certain smug innocence. The bag jumped again, this time unmistakeably.

'What's that?' Dorothy pointed to the bag, ensuring there could be no ambiguity. Aunt Winifred pursed her lips, indicating a grievous invasion of privacy.

'Harold. He's a family heirloom — you'll be getting one when I die. And that's all I have to say on the matter.'

She gazed blankly up towards the sky. Faking senility, Winifred had discovered in recent years, was an extremely useful ploy. Besides, she knew what the girl needed, even if Dorothy herself didn't.

Meanwhile, Dorothy's imagination took off, soaring right out of the courtyard and up over the grey slate roofs of the village. Witches have familiars. I'll probably get to inherit some flea-bitten stray kitten, or worse still a toad, she thought. The bag twitched again.

Dorothy looked away politely, trying to steer her mind away from the guilty observation that she was projecting onto her aunt the stereotype of hag. It was politically incorrect, and she hated being politically incorrect. Peter, her married ex-lover, had often accused her of being too self-conscious, too aware of making the acceptable move.

Ironically, that was how he'd manipulated her into bed in the first place, playing on her initial rejection of him because he was married. Well, that and her astonishment that he found her desirable. Physical attraction was not something Dorothy had ever associated with her unfashionably buxom body. She wore her shape like a crucifix, blind to her own inherent splendour. There was history in her bones and a stoic grace in the sway of her hips that spoke of Boadicea. A very Celtic sort of beauty.

Dorothy settled into her new job within a couple of weeks. Although far humbler than the Imperial War Museum, Shrewsbury Castle had its own stately grace. Situated on a hill overlooking the town of Shrewsbury and the border counties (known as the Marches to the Welsh), the fortress had been built to ward off the fierce Welsh tribes who had ventured into England. Originally medieval, it had been rebuilt in the fourteenth century and fortified again in the seventeenth century, and little now remained of its Norman origins.

Dorothy's office was an octagonal room at the back of the ticket booth. Most of her fellow workers were volunteers; she was one of only two paid staff. Part of her job was to classify the immense collection of historical objects donated to the museum, which ranged from medals to souvenirs picked up on the battlefield. The classification process gave her the illusion of control. It felt therapeutic to sort through the vast pile of medals, each one a minutia of history, as if giving meaning to her own personal chaos.

In the village Dorothy noticed that the name Owen seemed to evoke both dread and a slight hint of envy, especially from the long-suffering wives. As soon as it was known that she was Winifred's kin, people began to shun her. One woman in the supermarket openly referred to her great-aunt as that 'crazy old lesbian'. She even mentioned a live-in girlfriend during the war, but when Dorothy confronted her the housewife became suddenly vague. 'You don't look like an Owen,' she muttered, turning to the frozen peas.

Dorothy found she didn't mind the isolation; there was a certain solace in her exile. It appealed to the martyr in her and somehow legitimised the indulgence of her grief over the loss of her lover. She took to conjuring up less attractive memories during solitary walks through the nearby mountains and woods, as a means of finally exorcising him: the large white hairy belly that flopped over his trousers; his arrogance; the way he constantly criticised her and then expected her to counsel him

17

about his marital problems. She also began to rely more and more on her great-aunt.

Winifred had insisted on setting Dorothy up in the little house adjacent to her cottage, furnishing it with the meagre pieces Edith had left after her death. Winifred cherished having a relative to confide in again, and many a night Dorothy found herself trapped in front of her aunt's gas fire, listening to yet another tale of the Gynia Mwyn and their extraordinary female lineage.

The ancient spinster was busy herself. She had decided to dedicate the next few months to putting her affairs in order, as she was convinced that she would die at the end of summer. As befitted a woman who loathed the English, Winifred was a staunch anti-royalist and was determined, to the point of death, not to be a recipient of the Queen's obligatory telegram on her hundredth birthday.

⊂≥

At six o'clock on a cold wet late-summer's morning, Dorothy was woken by a loud banging on the front door and the news she had been dreading.

The church organist stood there, clutching the morning papers over his head.

'Get decent, girl, your great-aunt's decided to die.'

Dorothy pulled her raincoat over her flannel nightdress and rushed through the heavy drizzle to Winifred's cottage.

Winifred lay in the nineteenth-century brass bed, her skin pulled taut and transparent across her bones. She was arguing with the local vicar. 'No, Keelan, I will not make my last confession. I've got nothing to atone for and the Lord himself can testify to that.' Her head fell back against the pillows, the effort of speech exhausting her.

'You've not made an appearance in church for over twenty years.' The vicar, a large florid-faced man with a well-known drinking problem, was insistent.

'I beg to differ,' Winifred snapped back. 'I have *never* stepped into that heathen place of superstition!'

The vicar barely controlled his temper. 'There you go, blaspheming on your deathbed! That's enough to send you to the wrong place right there, if you get my meaning.' He leaned back, quaking with anger. He was determined to be the first to convert an Owen, even if it killed her in the process.

Dorothy sat quietly at her great-aunt's head. She noticed that Winifred was clutching her knitting bag against the yellowed lace bed coverlet.

'Pagan I am, pagan I die. It's what you've all been accusing me of for decades anyway. Oh, the hypocrisy! It's enough to hasten my end, and I'm not due to die until four o'clock.'

She turned her face blindly towards her great-niece. 'Dorothy, is that you?'

'It is.' Dorothy tentatively reached across and took Winifred's hand into her own. The flesh was so withered it felt like the claw of death itself.

'Tell this self-appointed social worker to piss off so I can get on with the delicate act of passing over,' the old woman hissed.

Dorothy ushered the vicar into the hallway. 'Father, it might be better ...'

'I should have known she'd react that way. They're a stubborn bunch of heathens, the Owens. I'll be praying you don't go the same way.'

Propelled by a rush of familial loyalty, Dorothy pushed the tenacious cleric out into the rain.

Back in the bedroom her great-aunt was humming the 'Internationale' under her breath. For a moment Dorothy thought she might have fallen into total dementia. But then Winifred's eyes fluttered open.

'Come here, child, it's almost time. The goddess will come for me on the hour.' She clutched at Dorothy's skirt.

'Auntie, don't say that.'

'Enough with the bullshit.' With a supreme effort Winifred held up her knitting bag. It jiggled slightly in the candlelight.

'This is what I'll be leaving you.'

Dorothy's eyes widened with apprehension as she braced herself for a hedgehog or, worse still, some endangered rodent, like a pygmy shrew, when Winifred reached dramatically into the bag and pulled out a withered root. Dorothy tried hard to conceal her bewilderment.

'It's lovely,' she muttered in an unconvincing manner.

Ignoring her niece's lack of enthusiasm, the old woman dangled the vegetation proudly. It hung like a limp turnip. Dorothy peered closer. It looked like a large twisted stem of ginger and was covered in strange reddish hair-like roots.

Winifred pressed it into Dorothy's hand. 'Never betray the mandrake,' she gasped. Then, as the grandfather clock chimed four, she died, her bony hand still fastened around her niece's wrist.

❧

They buried Winifred's ashes at her favourite spot on the riverbank, according to the complicated instructions she had left in her will.

'Unconsecrated land,' the mourners whispered knowingly to each other as Dorothy got down on her hands and knees to place the strange pewter casket into the damp black earth.

The local men's choir broke into a Welsh folk song — Winifred had specified no religious music — the tenor voices swelling and floating up with the evening mist. Above the funeral proceedings hovered a single black raven. Dorothy looked up at the bird, then down at the rushing water. A wave of loneliness swept over her. Now she was the only one left, the last of the clan.

A middle-aged woman dressed flamboyantly in a long silk dress approached her. A ravaged face that must once have boasted a handsome beauty peered out from under an enormous hat. She took Dorothy's hand and drew it towards her bosom.

'I knew your great-aunt. She was one of the circle. One of the ancient ones. She's up there now,' she whispered dramatically, pointing to the contoured disk of the rising moon already visible in the steely sky. 'Up there, riding with Arianrhod on a great white mare toward Caer Arianrhod to join her sisters. One day you too shall inherit the mantle.'

The woman released Dorothy's hand and, with a studied swish of her skirts, turned and walked across the muddy embankment towards a waiting BMW. Dorothy noticed several of the parishioners crossing themselves as the stranger cut across their path.

⤳

Later that night Dorothy sat on her narrow single bed and watched the shadows cast by the fire dancing across the wooden roof beams. The silence was profound. She reached across and picked up the mandrake root from the cherrywood table beside the bed. She slowly turned it in her hands. What does one do with a mandrake root? Cook it? Eat it? Plant it?

She held it up to her face. A strong musk radited from it, strangely animal, even familiar. She tried to think where she knew the scent from, but the memory kept escaping her. She turned it upside down. The root had feathery offshoots that looked as if they belonged in soil.

She went downstairs and searched around for a flower pot and some potting mix, then planted the root carefully, treating it like a bulb, making sure that the tip showed just above the soil. She left the pot on the kitchen table, went back upstairs and fell asleep after listening to a debate on the radio on the pros and cons of fox hunting. She dreamt of nothing.

The next morning she was woken by a tickling under her nose. She sneezed and opened her eyes. An invisible hair kept stroking her cheek. She sat up, glanced at the pillow and screamed out loud.

Curled up comfortably in a little indentation in the pillow lay a penis — in repose, one might say. Dorothy was transfixed. Her brain whirled madly, trying to absorb the illogical and surreal sight of an unattached male organ asleep.

She took a few deep breaths, trying to regain control, and looked away, but her eyes inevitably crept back to the sight. The penis still lay there, curled with an air of conceit. In fact it seemed to be waking up; disbelievingly, Dorothy watched it grow tumescent before her very eyes.

It was about six and a half inches long, uncircumcised, with long black pubic hair. With a shudder it flipped itself onto its shiny heavy testicles and waddled towards her, now unmistakably erect. Dorothy shrieked, leapt out of bed and onto a chair. The penis — moving like something between a rabbit and a small dog — also leapt off the bed and onto the carpet where it waited hopefully at the foot of the chair. They had reached an impasse: Dorothy, too terrified to move, and the penis, standing pert before her, a little too eager to please. They stayed like that for a good ten minutes. Until the phone rang.

'Don't you dare move!' Dorothy yelled. With a timid shudder the organ waddled a few inches back on its balls. She tentatively climbed off the chair then bolted down the narrow wooden stairs and grabbed the phone. It was her employer, Mr Carrington, concerned that she hadn't arrived at work yet.

'I'm having some difficulty with a small animal ... a rodent — no, not a rat exactly ... I'll be in late.'

Dorothy put the phone down, her heart still thumping in her throat. Behind her she heard a gentle thudding. She swung around; the penis was hopping down the stairs towards her. There was something pathetically vulnerable about the way it launched itself blindly off the last step, flying through the air to land with a painful bounce on the Persian rug she'd inherited from her aunt. Her aunt! So this was what had been twitching in the knitting bag. Now she understood why Winifred was known as the Merry Spinster.

The penis inched forward and rubbed itself against Dorothy's bare foot. She pulled back immediately, but then a perverse curiosity made her stretch her foot back towards the expectant organ again. It felt silky, the touch of that velvet skin deliciously familiar. She was reminded of those stolen afternoons, lying back in the motel bed, stroking her lover into submission. She closed her eyes and allowed herself to be caressed.

It was not an entirely unpleasant sensation. The penis rubbed itself backwards and forwards like a cat; Dorothy could practically hear it purring. The clock in the hallway chimed ten. She'd promised to be at work in half an hour. The organ flopped itself seductively over her foot and appeared to look up at her. What was she going to do? She couldn't leave it alone in the house.

She reached down but the penis slipped out of her hand and darted behind the sofa. Dorothy spent a good fifteen minutes catching it. She wrapped the wriggling member up in a sock and hid it in her underwear drawer. As she drove off she prayed that it wouldn't leap out and give the cleaner a heart attack.

Walking along the High Street, Dorothy got wolf-whistled at fourteen times. Astonished, she gazed at herself in the reflection of a shop window. She was wearing jeans and a threadbare sweater with holes in it. She looked like she always did; what had changed that was causing this sudden male attention?

Even her boss, Mr Carrington, who must have been at least seventy-five, commented on how good she was looking. Another colleague dropped two Georgian swords onto his toes when Dorothy bent down to do up her shoelaces. At lunchtime, when she walked into the bank, every male set of eyes swung around and stared.

Dorothy was bewildered. For a woman who was used to being invisible to the male sex, it was incredibly disorientating to be suddenly not just visible but apparently extremely desirable. Then a frightening thought occurred to her. Maybe, in some perverse way, this male attention was connected to the penis. As if its manifestation had suddenly imbued her with a powerful pheromone.

That afternoon, convinced she was being betrayed by some terrible scent, Dorothy spent forty minutes scrubbing her armpits in the women's toilets. When she finally emerged, flushed and stinking of tar soap, water still staining her armpits, Mr Carrington, worried about her mental state, sent her home early.

On the way back she was followed by a police car. The inanely grinning policeman pulled up beside her and complimented her on the originality of her car. Dorothy gazed at him in disbelief; she drove a blue Honda sedan. A moment later a cyclist fell off his bike because he was staring so hard at her. Then, at the petrol station, the attendant lost concentration and dribbled petrol all down the side of his trousers.

For the first time in her life Dorothy began to consider the advantages of being plain. Relieved to reach the sanctuary of the cottage, where a solitary cow grazed in the field next door, she checked the horizon for any visible male, then bolted to the front door. Inside, she exhaled. At last she was alone — well, almost.

≈

The only way Dorothy could describe how she lived with the penis for the next couple of weeks was ... well, like dog and mistress. It followed her everywhere like a love-struck puppy, hopping up beside her on the couch to watch television, getting tangled in the wool when she was knitting, perched precariously on the soap dish while she bathed.

At first Dorothy barely tolerated the intrusion then, slowly, she started to appreciate its steady vigil. She even found herself listening out for the pitter-patter of those heavy balls thudding gently on the carpet.

'You've always wanted a pet,' she said to herself, in a futile attempt to banish the thought of any possible sexual exploitation on her behalf. Not to mention the idea of her aunt ever having used the poor creature in *that* manner.

Poor creature? She peered across the room. The penis was lying on its side in front of the fire, trying to look as innocent as a sex organ could. What kind of sorcery had conjured such an organism? Dorothy was fairly well read on such matters: investigating myth and legend had been part of her training as a historian. She knew of the Golem of Prague, but never had she come across anything like this. For one hideous moment she entertained the thought that perhaps it had been cut off a dead man. She kneeled on the carpet and took a good long look. The penis didn't display any scars. She sat back in relief. She dreaded to think what other skeletons lay in her great-aunt's cupboard.

The next day at work she consulted an archaic dictionary of definitions entitled, *Esau's Book of Devilry, Everything the Mere Mortal should know about Magick*. She looked up mandrake root.

*The mandrake root is a curious plant that is found
growing at the foot of the gallows. It is said to spring
from the seed of the ejaculation of the condemned man
at the moment of death. It hath been harvested
bounteously by both witches and sorcerers in their
spells ...*

The alchemist Esau went on to describe the bulbous and forked
appearance of the mandrake and to summarise the inherent evil
the root personified. There was even an illustration beside the
floral calligraphy: it showed a curious twisted bulb that
resembled a crucified figure.

'Not a bit like my mandrake root,' Dorothy concluded. 'I
mean, how can a thing imbued with that kind of self-parody be
evil?' She closed the book angrily. 'Witches be damned.'

Perhaps Great-Aunt Winifred the sorceress had got it wrong.
Maybe Dorothy's penis hadn't sprung from a mandrake root at all,
but was a twisted manifestation of her own sexual frustration. Or
even an extreme form of penis envy. Dorothy sank into a deep
reverie, depressed by the possibility of looming psychosis.

'Ms Owen?'

Dorothy found herself gazing into the remarkably handsome
face of a tall blond man. His eyes were green and blue, seeming
to change with the light like those of a knowing cat. He had
strong eyebrows and straw-coloured hair that framed a long face
cut diagonally by curiously strong cheekbones, as if an exotic
gene had found its way into what was otherwise a classically
Anglo-Saxon countenance. The nose was diminutive and neat,
almost feminine, while the mouth spoke of obstinacy (a thin
upper lip) offset by the sensuality of a ridiculously full lower lip.

Each stared at the other for an interminable time, both
sensing a kindred attraction.

'I ... I ... er hope I'm not disturbing you,' he finally
stammered, awestruck by the sexual luminosity that surrounded
this rather plain woman.

'No, not at all. I was just researching a family heirloom.' Before
Dorothy had a chance to cover the book he glanced down.
'Damned strange heirloom,' he said, reading the title upside down.

She pulled the book away from him and drew herself up to her full height. 'You are?' she asked formally.

He extended a deliciously delicate hand; both smooth and strong and promising in its size. 'Stanley Huntington. I'm here to research my ancestor, Lord Cedric Huntington.' Stanley, allowing his fingers to linger a little longer than was necessary, was pleasantly surprised by the ripple of electricity that ran between them.

Stanley Huntington had come down from London to begin research on a book he'd been promising to write for years. An intense man of thirty-nine, Stanley had the air of the perpetual student; nevertheless he was ambitious. Now that he had finally finished his doctorate, an utterly useless thesis on the methods of medieval roof-thatching, Stanley had decided to pursue his great passion: to write the definitive biography of his famous ancestor.

Lord Cedric Huntington was sent by the king to destroy the notorious Welsh lord Llewelyn the Fierce. Llewelyn, from all accounts, was four foot eleven and ferocious, with a great mane of black hair. Determined to win Shropshire from the English, he was hated and feared by the local nobility and had already enjoyed several victories by the time Lord Huntington was commissioned to despatch him.

His aristocratic ancestor was, as Stanley described to Dorothy, a modern thinker trapped by the historical restraints of his time. A less generous description might have involved the word 'fascist'. Whatever the true nature of Lord Cedric Huntington, Stanley was a man in need of a hero and a hero he had found.

Dorothy spent the rest of the afternoon helping Stanley go through tomes of medieval battle accounts. The two of them worked together in the office where the archives were stored. It was hard not to bump into each other in that confined space, and again Stanley found himself strangely drawn to this dumpy awkward woman who kept apologising for the dusty chaos. She wasn't his usual type at all.

Whatever his failings as an academic, Stanley had never had a problem attracting women. His good looks and faint air of helplessness endeared him immediately to the opposite sex.

Promiscuous in a dispassionate way, he preferred to conduct three or four liaisons at once. His air of innocence was a powerful alibi and the women never guessed his duplicity, happy to believe him when he used his scholastic studies as an excuse for his absence. Consequently, his affairs had as much emotional impact on Stanley as the weather. But then Stanley had never been in love.

He cast a furtive look at Dorothy, who was bending over a yellowed map of the castle. Aesthetics were important to him and the librarian was anything but beautiful. Nevertheless, there was something extraordinarily compelling about her. Something he couldn't apply logic to, but it had been affecting his groin all afternoon.

'I've found it!'

Her voice jolted him back. He'd been deep in thought, wondering what she'd look like naked and spread-eagled across the small library steps folded away in the corner.

'Found what?'

'The record! Here!' She slipped on her thick National Health glasses and read aloud.

'The hanging of the traitor Llewelyn the Fierce was conducted by Lord Cedric Huntington, who took particular pleasure in prolonging the execution by partially reviving the Welshman before hanging him again. When the news of Llewelyn's final demise spread there was great mourning all over Wales.'

Dorothy, suddenly aware of ancient enmity between their two races, frowned. 'Lord Huntington sounds like a real sadist,' she volunteered.

Stanley edged a little closer then thrust a hand into his trouser pocket; the way she had lisped over the word 'sadist' had given him an instant erection. 'Sadism does not exclude greatness,' he announced grandly, the perfume of her hair driving him crazy. He tilted his face forward at an angle he knew was flattering. 'Say, what are you doing later?'

They went for scones at Dorothy's favourite tea-room. The seventeen-year-old waitress with orange dreadlocks and a nose ring, who normally made a point of ignoring Dorothy, was at the table in a flash. She simpered all over Stanley but Dorothy noted that he had eyes only for her. His attention was immensely flattering but she couldn't help feeling slightly guilty. She actually toyed with the idea of warning him that he might be attracted to her under a false premise. But as he leaned towards her, a blond lock of hair falling over those heavy-lashed eyes, she realised that she was far too fascinated to disillusion him, even when he embarked on an extraordinarily detailed and boring thirty-minute soliloquy about the beauties of medieval roof-thatching. In short, Dorothy was hooked.

Afterwards Stanley wanted her to take him back to her village, to sample 'the border culture' as he put it. Dorothy hesitated, which only encouraged Stanley further, his wide eyes wandering across her bosom as if he were caressing her already. Dorothy had been celibate for months and she was finding the way his fingers made love to the sugar container more than a little distracting. Prudence won in the end. She promised to meet him for lunch the next day.

Stanley walked her to her car. There was a slight sullenness in his step. He wasn't used to not getting his way immediately and he couldn't remember a time when a woman had interested him so profoundly. Perhaps it was her very ordinariness that attracted him. He pondered over the absurdities of lust — desire certainly fell where it wanted yet, try as he might, he could not banish the vision of her lying naked beneath him, preferably still wearing those rather old-fashioned glasses. That fantasy was enough to bring him to orgasm later that afternoon and keep him going most of the night.

Dorothy returned home in a state of considerable excitement. Was this love? Her racing heart, the dryness of her throat and the way she kept glancing at herself in the mirror, as if searching there for the mystery that he so obviously perceived in her, indicated the prerequisite emotional turmoil. Even the penis, trailing her around forlornly, seemed to sense a transformation it didn't particularly care for, as if somehow it realised in its blunt primordial head that perhaps it was no longer the centre of her attention.

Before going to bed, Dorothy sat at the walnut dresser she'd inherited from her mother and examined her reflection. She loosed her thick black hair and leaned forward to study her blue eyes and high forehead. She did possess a certain charm, but considered herself a little overweight. Pulling back the skin of her face, she noted with harsh objectivity the sagging of her cheeks and the thin wrinkle that ran down between her eyebrows. She reached for a tube of make-up.

The penis, perched between a black and white photo of Dorothy's mother in her girl scout uniform and a miniature plastic statue of the Virgin Mary, watched her with a slightly critical droop. She ignored it and smeared the pale liquid over her cheeks, then peered tentatively into the mirror. She looked like an amateur Noh actor. Was there any hope for a woman incompetent in the arts of feminine beauty, clumsy in her movements, with a second-rate degree in military history? There had to be something she could improve on.

Her eyes wandered back to the penis. It had inched its way across the dresser and was busy dipping itself into a pot of lip gloss. It toppled forward and got stuck, its tip in the pot while its balls dangled uselessly in mid-air. Dorothy laughed out loud. It resembled a bizarre Japanese erotic print she remembered seeing. Just then the obvious occurred to her: perhaps she could become a wonderful lover. She had something to practise with, even if it lacked the dimensions of a full-size man.

The penis fell over with a crash. It waddled blindly towards her, now wearing the lip-gloss pot like a ridiculous helmet. Dorothy's mind was made up.

In bed that night she reached across and picked the penis up from where it was curled in its usual spot on the pillow.

She ran it gently along her body, over her nipples and down across the soft skin of her inner thighs. It stiffened immediately. Then, with a kind of impatience, it shook itself out of her hands and took over.

The man who the penis was originally attached to must have been a wonderful lover, Dorothy concluded, lying back in a haze of bliss. That night she experienced pleasure she hadn't known she was capable of, relaxing in a state of near ecstasy as the organ prodded, probed, caressed and sort of licked her body for hours. It finally reached a shuddering orgasm of its own after Dorothy's fourth climax . . . or was it the fifth?

Now satiated, Dorothy found it far easier to distance herself from Stanley's advances. She cancelled on him twice and three times rang to rearrange dates. Her coolness surprised and excited him, it wasn't something that he'd experienced before. What had made her so mysteriously resilient to his charms? He thought she might have a hidden lover, but a few strategically placed questions debunked that theory. Maybe she just didn't like men? But he could tell from her sudden blushes, the way she walked beside him, her hips swaying, her body leaning towards him, that she found him attractive. Her elusiveness heightened the chase. Stanley was decided: he must have her.

They dated for four weeks. The budding historian swung between tortured frustration and masochistic anticipation. The daily proximity of Dorothy made every inch of his body throb. Baffled, he channelled his chagrin into his work, discovering within himself new depths of intellectual discipline. To his amazement he even started to see Dorothy as his muse. Finally, determined to ensnare her, he decided to recruit her as his editor. Dorothy was ecstatic. It was the first time anyone had acknowledged her creative potential. She threw herself into research.

As Stanley developed the outline of the book, he began to project parallels between himself and Lord Huntington. He imagined that he could see a faint resemblance between himself and his famed ancestor in the aristocratic arch of his nose, the high forehead, the intelligence behind the limpid blue-green eyes. But there was one aspect of his forefather's personality that Stanley did not wish to emulate. It seemed Lord Huntington had been universally hated, even by his own men, his legendary cruelty undermining any potential loyalty.

One fifteenth-century account scrawled in Latin by a local cleric described the pillage and destruction of a Welsh hamlet that, during the border battles, had unfortunately slipped over to the English. Lord Huntington had personally supervised the rape of the women and girls, as well as the beheading of all males over the age of ten. Even Stanley was nauseated as he ploughed through the account, pages of which appeared to be blood-splattered. It was becoming increasingly difficult to find any redeeming features in his heroic relative.

Meanwhile, Dorothy started collecting and editing material for Stanley to incorporate into the main work. He gave her the task of researching Llewelyn the Fierce — Lord Huntington's sole nemesis, until his execution. From all accounts Llewelyn appeared to be a Welsh Robin Hood, famous for his generosity to the common people, even those he conquered. Folklore rumoured that Llewelyn always offered the choice of Welsh nationality before he impaled anyone. He was also infamous for the number of women he had scattered throughout the Welsh foothills and as far east as Kidderminster.

His promiscuity fascinated Dorothy. He was described physically as a short, stocky man with a mane of thick black hair, yet there were records of his beautiful voice, and one eloquent mention of a wit that could charm even the crows from corpses.

There was also reference to Llewelyn's soulmate: a witch mistress of remarkable beauty, but rarely seen as she lived as a hermit. One witness, a woman who ran an alehouse near Bangor, described how she had seen Llewelyn flying naked with his sorceress on Allhallows Eve, twisting and turning in the light of a full moon, his hair standing straight up like the mane of a lion.

Dorothy was enthralled. She searched in vain for more information. All she could find were two facts: that Llewelyn's mistress had been considered a heretic by her peers, and that she was definitely Welsh.

Over the next couple of months Stanley planned his strategy. He would convince Dorothy of his sincerity, then seduce her and maintain the relationship for as long as her research skills were needed. It was callous but practical; he couldn't envisage taking her back to London. There was no way she was presentable to any of his friends and he certainly could not take her to his literary club. He had his reputation to think of. Dorothy had her skills; wife of an upwardly mobile historian just wasn't one of them.

He took her to a demonstration of roof-thatching in a village outside Shrewsbury. They stood with a group of enthusiastic Japanese and German tourists waiting for a muscle-bound Yorkshireman to haul a bale of hay up a ladder. In the dappled sunlight, Stanley started a loud discourse on the history of thatching, describing the feudal implications. The tourists, hungry for any kind of information, listened intently and the Japanese filmed every one of Stanley's dramatic flourishes. As he finished they burst into spontaneous applause, and Dorothy felt a rush of pheromones shoot through the lower half of her body. She had never realised that roof-thatching could be so sexually stimulating. It seemed Stanley's strategy was working.

That afternoon they kissed. The proximity of Dorothy's voluptuous body was almost too much for Stanley to bear. She felt the length of him stiffen through her clothes and the faint outline of him pressing against her reminded her of the six and a half inches she'd left waiting at the gate that morning. Stanley's organ felt considerably bigger. Dorothy blushed; six months ago such a thought would never have occurred to her. But her nocturnal liaisons had imbued her with a sexual bravado that had surprised even herself.

Next Tuesday night, she thought, that's when I'll have him over. I'll cook something extraordinary and afterwards he will be so swept away by my lovemaking that he'll make a commitment to me there and then. She smiled, her eyes on Stanley's mouth which, she noted, held great promise. To hell with emotional caution. A lineage of wild women tugged at every molecule of her muscle tissue — Dorothy Owen was going to take a chance.

⬧

Dorothy got home later than usual that evening. As she was driving down the muddy lane that led to the cottage, an object flew at her car window, giving her a terrible fright. She swerved violently and screeched to a stop, inches away from a massive oak tree. For a second she sat stunned at the wheel, her eyes closed, waiting for her heart to crunch to a halt. It must have been a bird, she thought, or maybe even a bat. When she opened her eyes she was shocked to see the penis clinging to her windscreen wipers, shrivelled and trembling in a kind of desperate last stand.

Dorothy pulled on her gloves and climbed out of the car. The delicate skin of the penis was beginning to adhere to the frozen glass. She leaned over and breathed warm air on it to lessen the pain as she peeled it gently off the icy glass. The frozen organ rippled with pleasure; this was confirmation that its mistress cared. After another little puff of hot breath, Dorothy slipped it into her pocket to warm it as she walked to the house.

What was she going to do? She couldn't have a free-ranging six and a half inch penis flying around the cottage while she was entertaining the potential love of her life. How would she explain it away? Although she wasn't very experienced with men, she knew enough to realise that it was fatal to advertise the existence of ex-lovers. Or in this case, would it be ex-appendages? Perplexed by her dilemma she switched on the gas fire and, after wrapping the penis in a kitchen towel, left it to thaw out.

She would just have to hide it on Tuesday night. Perhaps in a large biscuit tin in the pantry. Or maybe in the fridge. Its metabolism seemed to slow down when it was cold, a bit like a lizard. It couldn't be that cruel to sedate a penis, could it? The last thing she wanted was Stanley to be confronted by this aberration which, for all she knew, could even be a manifestation of her own imagination.

⤳

Over the next few days the organ grew increasingly possessive. It was more demanding at night and took to patrolling the front door during the day, as if expecting an attack from an intruder. Dorothy was convinced that it sensed a potential rival.

By the time Tuesday arrived she was in a state of extreme anxiety. She took the day off work and spent the morning ploughing through recipes. In the afternoon she shopped for ingredients. She had abandoned her original plan to make roast lamb, deciding to be far more ambitious after discovering a recipe book of sixteenth-century dishes. This was one of Stanley's favourite eras, so Dorothy had gone for suckling pig with cloves and crab apples, with a quince and walnut tart to follow.

As she stuffed the piglet, the penis watched her from the mantelpiece, bent at an angle that somehow suggested vengefulness. Dorothy couldn't help but feel a little guilty. Don't be ridiculous, she told herself, it's a dispossessed organ. It hasn't got a brain or a heart. A penis is not a man, just as a man is not a penis. She became so confused by what sounded like some perverse Cartesian debate that she put cherries into the stuffing instead of prunes and then forgot to glaze the piglet with honey before putting it into the oven.

Maybe it can read my mind, or at least sense my mood, she thought. As if to prove her right, the wayward member hopped towards the cake mix, and was just about to plunge into it when Dorothy caught it mid-flight. 'Naughty! Naughty!' She shook it angrily. 'That's not for you, that's for Stanley.' The penis quivered and Dorothy thought she detected a low growl of discontent, but conceded it might have been the wind in the rafters.

⤙

That night Dorothy prepared carefully, putting on the evening dress she hadn't worn since her fateful last date with her ex-lover. It was a tight-fitting blue velvet with a plunging neckline. Peter was a breast man and had insisted on dictating what Dorothy should wear; something she'd secretly resented. There is a satisfying symmetry in plotting to seduce another man while wearing an ex's favourite dress, and Dorothy, in front of the mirror, fastening her mother's pearls around her neck, felt in control of her emotional destiny for the first time. And that, frankly, was as exciting as waiting for Stanley.

He was due in half an hour and she still hadn't worked out what to do with the penis. It had been behaving very oddly, whizzing around the house like a frenetic wind-up toy. It had already made a hole in the lace curtains and dive-bombed one of her favourite vases. Dorothy had been forced to tie it to her bedpost, where it now sat, twisted up in ribbon like a macabre birthday gift. There was no doubt in her mind. She would have to lock it up for the night and pray that Stanley wouldn't discover it.

She sprayed herself with her favourite perfume (Chance by Chanel), slipped on her four-inch heels and untied the struggling penis. She marched downstairs and found a biscuit tin. She carefully placed the organ inside and, after pacifying it with a few strokes, slammed the lid on and secured it firmly with some old string. She placed the tin in the pantry, shut the door and waited for a moment. All was silent.

It must have gone to sleep, she concluded and, with a sigh of relief, fortified herself with a small glass of Benedictine. Stanley was due in ten minutes and she was horribly nervous.

Stanley was late. He paused on the threshold, relishing the moment. At last conquest was in his sights. He smiled and flicked a leaf off the shoulder of his cashmere sweater. He had always known she would succumb in the end. They all did, sooner or later. He adjusted his crotch, sniffed his armpit to check whether he had been too lavish with the cologne, patted the condoms in his back pocket, then tapped softly on the wooden door. Dorothy opened it even before Stanley had finished knocking. Just as he imagined: she was waiting, hot and aching for him.

With a flourish that he liked to think of as regal, he presented her with a large bunch of lilies. Dorothy accepted them graciously, quelling her disappointment. She secretly considered lilies a little funereal. Stanley, oblivious to the nuances of the moment, pulled her towards him and thrust his tongue, which tasted faintly of liquorice, into her mouth. 'Let's eat first,' she murmured and disentangled herself.

Dorothy was just beginning to relax as they sat down at the kitchen table she'd decorated with her mother's best linen. Stanley lit the candles. The appetiser — a crab and soba noodle salad — was received with great acclaim and Stanley, genuinely surprised by the sophistication of Dorothy's cooking, found himself reconsidering the possibility of marriage. In the light of the candles, her pearls glowing against her ivory skin, Dorothy looked more than presentable. His friends might even find her accent romantically rustic. The historian and his Welsh muse — it had a nice ring to it, very Ted Hughes. Stanley was toying with this delightful thought when a sudden loud knocking came from inside the pantry.

Dorothy looked up fearfully. 'It's the plumbing,' she announced loudly, trying to drown out the sound. 'It dates back about a century, wretched thing.' She continued to eat as if nothing had happened.

Stanley was just wondering why she found pipes so frightening when the knocking started up again. 'Just ignore it, it'll stop in a minute.' Dorothy glanced desperately at the pantry.

'Funny place for pipes,' Stanley volunteered, then gagged on a piece of crab as the possibility crossed his mind that it could be vermin. 'It's not rats, is it?' he ventured, his face now a couple of shades paler.

'Look, if it makes you feel better I'll go and bang on them. That usually helps.'

Dorothy got up and walked over to the pantry, let herself inside and carefully shut the door behind her. The biscuit tin leapt an inch off the shelf as the penis struggled to get out. She eased off the lid.

'Okay, this is it! If you don't start behaving yourself I'll lock you away for good,' she whispered to the bulbous tip that was poking out. The penis pulled back and curled sulkily against the waxed paper that lined the tin. Dorothy put it inside a picnic basket then placed two bags of flour on top of the lid for good measure. Breathing deeply to regain her composure, she returned to the kitchen.

The smell of burning pork skin was detectable. She ran to the oven and pulled out the baking dish. The roast piglet looked magnificent.

'Decidedly feudal,' Stanley announced cheerfully, dismissing the whole rat incident as he helped her carry the dish to the table. He was touched by her culinary efforts; he hadn't felt so honoured in years. At last here was someone who not only had an inherent understanding of his greatness, but was willing to be midwife to it. This is a woman with ambition, he conceded as he watched the succulent meat fall away from the carving knife, a good cook, a great editor and a meticulous researcher. A woman a man could marry

He found himself staring at her mouth. It was captivating in crimson, and he wondered what else she might be good at. Good cooks were often good lovers and the pig did look delicious.

Her cleavage bulged up over the velvet; the abundance of her flesh would be a new experience for him. He felt himself stiffening under the table and tried to distract himself by staring at the toasted hair running along the pig's skin. It was difficult.

The second course went smoothly. Even Dorothy acknowledged that the cherries in the stuffing gave the dish a sophisticated Asian flavour, a subtlety she convinced Stanley was deliberate. More importantly, there was silence from the pantry. Dorothy stopped glancing at the door every three minutes and finally began to relish the triumph of the meal.

They had drunk a bottle of good French wine and all that was left was the dessert. Stanley, conscious of his tightening belt, pushed his chair back from the table and suggested that they pause. He never liked making love on a full belly, and he was determined to give a performance that matched Dorothy's culinary skills. They moved to the living room to sit in front of the fire.

Dorothy's head was spinning from the wine and little shivers of excited anticipation kept running up her thighs. She sat herself primly on the couch. Stanley, brandy in hand, settled his long limbs on the floor in front of the gas fire and contemplated her ankles, which, to his relief, were not that thick.

He began caressing her legs. Dorothy shut her eyes. Stanley's touch was light and tender. He had the technique of a professional, his strokes achingly delicious. It's now or never, she thought as the moment stretched and stretched until she was frightened it would snap and evaporate, leaving them with only the possibility of friendship. Ignoring the rising panic that comes with the chance of rejection, Dorothy Owen gathered all the courage of her ancestors and, reaching down, took his face in her hands.

They were in the middle of a lingering kiss when, from the corner of her eye, she saw something dart across the carpet. The trail of flour left no doubt. Luckily Stanley had his eyes shut, for the next thing she saw was the spectacularly white-dusted penis leaping up onto the settee like a flying ghost. With her lips still on Stanley's mouth, she pushed against him in an attempt to prevent him seeing the maverick organ.

Enraged, the penis hopped onto one of the arms of the couch. It paused, arching towards them with a discernible frown twisting its cleft tip. Then, without warning, it dived under Dorothy's raised skirt.

Dorothy squirmed and Stanley, taking her discomfort for pleasure, thrust his tongue further into her mouth. Meanwhile, under her skirt the penis started to probe blindly up between her thighs. Dorothy couldn't help herself — she jumped.

'Ow!' Stanley grabbed his swollen lip. Dorothy had inadvertently bitten down.

'Sorry, I got carried away.' She tried to sound casual while clamping her legs together in an effort to catch the offending member.

Stanley smiled crookedly. He liked a touch of pain; this woman really did have potential. 'Go right ahead, just be careful you don't draw blood,' he murmured, then moaned dramatically to encourage her further while trying to run his fingers up her legs.

Dorothy pushed his hand away while pulling his face into another kiss. At the same time she was attempting to keep the infuriated organ trapped between her thighs. It was a feat of extraordinary coordination, requiring a certain twist of the pelvis which Stanley mistook for passion.

Finally, with a wriggle, Dorothy managed discreetly to remove the penis while retaining her composure. 'I just have to go to the bathroom,' she said, stepping over the puzzled Stanley, carefully hiding the irate penis in her sleeve. Stanley leaned back. There was mystery to this woman, he surmised, and Lord knows he was ripe for a little mystery.

The mysterious woman stood in the bathroom, flour smeared across her very expensive nylon tights. She had plunged the penis into a sinkful of warm water and it lay there now, luxuriating in her distress. Furious, Dorothy had a sudden impulse to flush it down the toilet — but what would the authorities say? They'll probably trace the organ back to her and accuse her of dismembering a man. She was near to tears. There was only one thing left to do. On her way through the kitchen she stopped by the fridge and threw the errant body part into the freezer.

'Are you okay?' Stanley murmured. He was standing in shadow by the kitchen doorway, his hair dishevelled, shirt loosened to display his copious chest hair, lips thrust forward, totally aware that he looked irresistible. Dorothy jumped, then covered her fright with a studied languidness.

'Fine, I was just checking if I had any ice-cream, you know, to go with the quince tart.' She hoped that he wouldn't notice the flour marks on her velvet dress.

'I don't want any dessert. I want you.' The words were meant to sound seductive but they came out in an awkward squeak. In an attempt to conceal his unexpected nervousness, Stanley buried his face in her hair. Immediately a loud rattling started up from the freezer. For one hideous second Stanley wasn't sure whether the rattling was the sound of his heart or was actually external. Before he had a chance to make up his mind, Dorothy was hustling him upstairs to the bedroom, desperate to get him away from the freezer. She propelled him up the narrow wooden staircase, clasping his buttocks in front of her like an ascending beacon.

Stanley, taking her cue, delightedly assumed that lust had got the better of caution. When they reached the bedroom the two of them tumbled to the floor. Velvet and corduroy entangled in a steam of perfume and cheap cologne. It promised to be a very English coupling.

Suddenly sobered by the very real weight of Dorothy's flesh, Stanley sat up and began to unzip her dress with disturbingly professional ease. Dorothy felt him encircle her and lift her breasts out of her dress. He pulled slowly at her nipples. She stiffened immediately. It is this, she thought, this feeling of being encompassed, of being embraced, that I have missed so much. It was a sensation that a mere six and a half inches, however adventurous, could never hope to achieve.

Surrendering herself, Dorothy swung around and kissed Stanley, her fingers plucking at his shirt. She ran them through his chest hair and across the groomed abdominal muscles towards his groin. He groaned and arched up, making it easier for her to unzip and release him. Stanley's penis sprang out in its full grandeur. It was the part of him that he was most proud of; he was a well-endowed individual. Dorothy's eyes widened in wonder. He was at least eight inches, she estimated. After all, she had recently developed an expertise in these matters. Running her fingers across the soft skin, she brought him to her lips and was amazed at the difference, both in texture and scent.

Somewhere above her Stanley was groaning. The experience was doubly pleasurable for he had never assumed that this rather dowdy archivist would be a good lover, never mind an imaginative one. As he watched her head bob up and down he decided that he would definitely ask her to marry him. He was nearly forty and, if he was brutally honest with himself, he couldn't remember any other woman showing this much enthusiasm for at least a year.

He was close to orgasm. Time to give her some pleasure, he surmised, especially if she was to be Mrs Huntington. He pulled her up to his mouth, then traversed the whole length of her body with his tongue, finishing by sucking her toes — a nifty little trick he'd learned from a Korean au pair girl. He then moved further up, parting her gently with his fingers. Stanley always felt that cunnilingus was the mark of the evolved male. Besides, it made them remember you, even if it was only one night. It was therefore with immense satisfaction that, somewhere above him, he heard Dorothy scream with pleasure.

Stanley played both her orifices with his fingers; feeling her contract, he was determined to bring her to a second climax. He gave her a moment to catch her breath then hoisted himself over her. She lay there, gazing at him, her eyes great glistening pools of blue-black lust. Resting on one arm, he gathered up one impressive breast and filled his mouth with the erect nipple, nipping her gently, orchestrating his caresses until she was swollen to his touch. Then, when he could feel her moistening, he hauled himself up and rested the tip of his large cock at the very edges of her nether lips. Dorothy thought she might die from pleasure or scream again with delicious anticipation, so badly did she want him. He manoeuvred both her legs over his shoulders and, with a cheeky smile, entered her so slowly she could feel every inch of him.

'This is for England,' Stanley said softly.

'And this is for Wales,' Dorothy replied in Welsh, throwing him on his back to ride him like the true witch she suspected she might be.

Meanwhile, downstairs, something burst out of the freezer.

Afterwards they both lay sprawled across the bed, thoroughly satiated. Dorothy, every cell in her body released, fell asleep immediately while Stanley lay there lulled by the comforting sound of her soft snore. His body felt astonishingly relaxed. There was something wonderfully wholesome about making love to Dorothy. Maybe it was just the satisfaction of the kill after a long hunt. Maybe it was love. Stanley oscillated between these two meditations as he slid into a dreaming half-sleep.

He dreamt that they were at their wedding. Dorothy, in a long silk wedding dress, floated above him as they proceeded down the aisle. The way her black hair snaked around her head was disturbingly pagan. He could see himself walking beside her, two foot below, clutching at her hand which hovered tantalisingly above his own. The stone church looked medieval: wooden beams crossed the ceiling while coloured light filtered in from the oval stained-glass windows.

Stanley glanced sideways at the congregation. He was shocked to see that it consisted of farm animals. A pig sat in the front row wearing a cassock. It seemed to be laughing at him. Behind the pig sat a donkey, sober in a doublet and hose, while beside him a goat in a jerkin was doubled over in amusement. Absorbed in the dream, Stanley failed to hear the bedroom door creak open.

The floating bride and now fearful bridegroom continued moving down the aisle. The preacher, standing at the altar, had his back to them so Stanley couldn't see his face. Inexplicably panicked about the protocol of arriving at the altar with a floating bride, Stanley tried to pull Dorothy down but she remained out of reach. A great sense of failure at not being a proper bridegroom filled him. He wanted to run but found that his feet were strangely frozen to the floor.

Just at that moment, outside the dream, he felt what must be Dorothy's hand gently stroking his arm, trying to wake him up. Struggling in sleep he couldn't respond. The caresses continued, the touch felt velvety and oddly familiar. He wasn't sure whether it was her fingers or the heel of her hand. The massage travelled further up his chest, towards his neck and face. Stanley desperately wanted to reach out, to wake up and touch her, but he just couldn't shake off his drowsiness.

In the dream he started to run towards the altar, yelling, 'Preacher!', but the sound kept coming out as 'Peach!' Stanley felt increasingly inadequate. It was a very unpleasant sensation. It suddenly occurred to him that perhaps he wasn't worthy to be Dorothy's husband. He peered up at the roof; to his horror Dorothy had disappeared. Terrified he swung back to the altar.

The preacher slowly turned around. From under the hood the craggy face of an old man peered blindly at him with goat's eyes. Stanley screamed, waking himself from the nightmare. At that point the penis, which had been stealthily and silently working its way up his body, leaped into Stanley's open mouth.

The academic's eyes widened in absolute horror as he recognised the shape and taste of the disembodied organ. Gagging, he tried to grasp the member that was writhing and pounding its vengeful way deeper into his throat. Now blue in the face, Stanley desperately pulled at the testicles bouncing against his chin. The organ would not budge.

The last thing Stanley felt was the contraction of his lungs as he struggled to catch a last gasp of air. Still Dorothy snored on. Even the flailing of Stanley's arms in his death throes failed to wake her.

It was a glorious morning. Dorothy felt the sun on her face before she even opened her eyes. Images from last night's lovemaking flooded her body so sweetly that for one moment she feared she had imagined the whole thing.

She reached out and felt for Stanley. Her hand hit the top of a cold and clammy thigh.

Stanley's body lay across the sheets. His eyes were rolled back in their sockets. White foam and spittle covered the lower half of his face. His jaw was stretched open in a hideous grimace and his lips were wrapped around a gnarled old root, most of which was plunged down into his throat. Dorothy recognised the mandrake immediately.

'Miss Owen, you have a visitor.'

The prison officer, a stout cheerful woman in her late fifties, waited patiently as the penitentiary's newest inmate tidied herself up. She was a demure spinster-type, the officer had noted, polite and well spoken. Not your usual murderess. She looked more closely at the inmate: mid-thirties, not exactly a beauty but she had something enchanting about her. Never mind that there were rumours about her being a witch. As far as the officer was concerned, if all witches were this nice she'd trade in the rest of the nasty-minded inmates and start a coven.

Dorothy allowed herself to be led to the visitors' reception area. Prison food and lack of exercise had made her simultaneously both thin and flabby, yet she still carried herself with resolve. She saw herself as having surrendered to fate but not resigned to it. She found this an oddly comforting thought, but it had still been a horrific six months since Stanley's death.

One of her troubles had been finding a lawyer who believed her account of his death and was prepared to create a plausible defence. In the end she'd settled for a retired judge who had a fascination for the occult. His defence had been rambling and practically incomprehensible. In contrast, the prosecution had selected a glamorous female lawyer who kept using catch-phrases like hysteria, sexual psychosis and projection. The alluring prosecutor caught the imagination of the jury, the press and the public, portraying Dorothy as an obsessive determined to both seduce and destroy a man higher in status than herself, who would most likely abandon her eventually. Obsessives had been celebrated that year in popular psychology and the media leapt on the case with ill-concealed joy. Dorothy was labelled 'The Root Murderess' and all kinds of lewd hypotheses on the sexual foreplay that preceded the murder appeared in the newspapers.

The prosecution won easily. Dorothy got a life sentence.

'Probably end up being twenty years if you're a good girl, then you can sell the story, get it optioned for a movie and become a millionairess,' her lawyer told her cheerfully, slipping her the card of his publisher as he left.

Dorothy had discovered that there was a monastic aspect to prison life that suited her. She found that by imagining she was incarcerated in some medieval castle she was able to deal with the vicious hierarchy amongst her fellow inmates. She even had a room with a view, a sweeping panorama of Dartmoor's bleak landscape. It was here, sitting on the bench in her cell, that she found she had all the time in the world to contemplate her previous life.

They arrived at the screened-off visitors' section and the prison officer sat her down. A few minutes later a tall dark-haired woman, immaculately dressed in a tailored suit, appeared. She sat down opposite with silent poise and reached towards Dorothy, picked up her hand and began stroking it. Dorothy was too stunned to react.

'You don't recognise me but I was at your great-aunt's funeral.'

Her accent jolted Dorothy's memory. She had been Winifred's one friend, the enigmatic stranger who had claimed that her great-aunt had been one of the ancient ones, a follower of Arianrhod, the goddess of time and karma. Dorothy pulled her hand away sharply. 'What do you want?' It was hard to keep the resentment out of her voice.

'The mandrake root, do you still have it?' the woman whispered conspiratorially. The prison officer, standing beside the door, pretended not to hear.

'They confiscated it as evidence, then returned it later. It's stored in a safety deposit box at the Abbey National bank in Tunbridge Wells.'

'Good. I think both your aunt and I owe you an explanation.' Her voice was mesmeric. Dorothy felt as if she was being hypnotised into listening.

'I am also an Owen; in fact, your second cousin once removed. Like yourself and Winifred, I have never married. Most of us don't, preferring to take the mandrake as husband instead. This tradition has gone back for hundreds of years. It all began with the hanging of Llewelyn the Fierce.'

Dorothy shuddered, struggling with a suffocating sense of history being cyclical. 'The same Llewelyn that was hanged from the walls of Shrewsbury Castle?' she ventured, finally finding enough saliva to articulate.

'The very same, executed by the vile tyrant Lord Huntington. They left Llewelyn hanging there for three nights and three days. By the time Gwen Owen came to claim his body the crows had already picked out his beautiful black eyes.'

Dorothy's blood ran cold. 'Gwen Owen? Was she ...'

'...Llewelyn's mistress — yes, child, she was. An extraordinary human being and a wondrous sorceress. When she came to that cold wall and stared upon the body of her only love she did not shed one tear. Instead she swore to avenge herself on all future generations of Huntingtons, even if it took centuries. She then bent down and looked for the patch of earth where poor Llewelyn must have spilt his seed as he died. The mandrake root was already growing at the foot of the gallows. Gwen cleared the soil around it and harvested it carefully, gently pulling the root away and placing it beside her breast. From that day onwards Llewelyn's mandrake root was handed down the Owen line. So you see, your mandrake root was just carrying out its destiny, taking revenge on a Huntington. Its actions were the culmination of the very reason for his existence. Gwen finally had her revenge.'

The woman paused and reached into her handbag for a peppermint.

Dorothy tried to control the tears welling up in her eyes. 'A man died!'

In refusing the offered mint, Dorothy knocked the tin from the woman's hand. Peppermints flew everywhere. The woman ignored them. Her face softened and she stroked Dorothy's hand again.

'Winifred should have warned you. But she was just thinking of your happiness.' She peered down at Dorothy's hand. 'You have a profound future, your magic lies in the Word.'

'So how is all that information going to help me now?'

'It won't, but write the story anyway. It's time we Owens were immortalised.' She left with a swirl of her long skirt.

Dorothy watched her go. Behind her, framed by the barred window, a fleeting shadow flew past. Set against the gathering night sky, it might have been a wild black-maned man entangled in the arms of his laughing mistress; then again it might not.

# Rainmaker

The tumbleweed twisted in the hot breeze as it rolled down Sandridge's main street. It caught on the bleached stone steps of the church then, as if disgruntled with the breaking of its flight, curled around a bent Coke can.

The tightly knit farming community was in its thirteenth month without rain and the wheat crop, visible beyond rusty barbed-wire fencing, was withered and sparse.

The gas-station owner, a sceptical man in his mid-fifties, looked up from his caramel milkshake and out through the window of the diner. Across the street the thin-faced widow everyone knew as Gracie was already peeping out from behind her nylon curtains. They both watched as a brand new Ford Bronco, gleaming in the sun, turned into the main street. It was the first visitor the farming community had seen for months, and this was a town that distrusted strangers.

The Ford Bronco itself was unremarkable, except that it was pulling a 1960s Airstream trailer. The silver oblong with its curved corners shimmered like a forgotten prop from a sci-fi movie. But it was the design painted on the side that made it particularly bizarre: a gaudy rainbow arching up into a grey cloud from which a shower of rain fell in glistening blue dashes. The word RAINMAKER stretched proudly above it in calligraphy of purple and gold.

Jacob Kidderminister pulled up outside the town hall. Same tedious routine, same flat-topped buildings and same size place, he thought, reading the sign that proudly declared the population of Sandridge to be: *Five hundred souls and growing*. Somebody had scrawled *'white'* between the words 'hundred' and 'souls'. Jacob shook his head in disgust. If there was one thing he detested more than drought it was racism. 'Welcome to paradise,' he said to himself bitterly.

Just then a huge turkey vulture emerged out of a nearby tree and flapped its way lazily across the road to perch on the signpost. Hissing, it cocked its head towards him. Jacob wound down his car window. 'Hello, Mr Birdie,' he said.

The creature looked him straight in the eye, giving Jacob the uncanny feeling it was reading his mind. Suddenly it turned in the direction of a tree on the other side of the street. Jacob followed its gaze, to see dozens of starlings sitting silently on the branches staring back at him. Immediately the hairs on the back of his neck rose — he had never seen so many starlings during a drought. He had the strong impression the birds had been waiting for him. The turkey vulture flew off. With a great rustling of wings the starlings lifted from the tree en masse. In a plunging arc the bird of prey flew in the direction of the church, the starlings following in a tight swooping cloud, and all disappeared into the belfry.

Jacob studied the church. A brick wall with curled barbed wire along the top ran around it; a decidedly unChristian sight. In the wall stood a large iron gate bearing a notice reading: *The Aryan Fellowship of Jesus, Oklahoma*. The bile rose in the back of Jacob's throat; he'd come across the Aryan Fellowship before, in a town a hundred miles west. They were a nasty bunch of bigots and Jacob had been forced to flee after they'd nailed one of his coyotes alive to a cross. Every cell in his body pulsed with the desire to run. But as he squinted up at the bell-tower, the way the sunlight caught the edge of the brass bell reminded him how there was beauty and hope in even the ugliest places. And, for the first time in his life, the rainmaker ignored his instincts.

He pushed back his long chestnut hair and rested his forehead on the steering wheel. He had the type of beauty that only becomes apparent after a few minutes; his sensual face had a satyr-like quality that oozed into the psyche like a subtle perfume. In other words, he was the kind of man that women found irresistible and men dreaded. At forty-six Jacob was at the height of his powers. But at this precise moment he felt anything but powerful. He was exhausted. He'd been on the road for twenty years, travelling from one settlement to another, one dustbowl to another, wherever he was needed — but in every place he'd ended up being run out of town. His was a thankless task, he thought, a gift that had become a curse.

Rainmaking was a talent he had been born with, one that had been handed down over generations. His father had been a diviner, famous for finding water in the most remote parts of the American wilderness. Jacob used to accompany the garrulous bearded man as he scrambled possessed over gullies and ravines, his forked branch twitching, often followed by a mob of jeering disbelievers. But those same farmers, real-estate developers, prospectors, would all stop in their tracks, gasping, hours later when the drill released a gushing spout of fresh clear water from exactly the location the diviner had predicted. Jacob could never understand why his father didn't stay and reap the rewards, financial or otherwise, the townsfolk offered him. It was only later, when Jacob was older and inflicted with the same gift, that he realised his father had been unable to dwell in one place. For as soon as the diviner found water, the restlessness would be upon him again and he was immediately summoned by another drought. It was a slavery which had held Jacob's family in bondage for generations.

Moon, the silver-grey coyote sitting beside him, whimpered. They'd been driving for ten hours straight and she was desperate for some exercise.

'Okay, girl, I hear you. Let's say welcome to what is gonna be home for a few weeks.' And with world-weariness evident in every aching muscle, Jacob pushed open the door and climbed out.

He stood staring at the cloudless sky for a moment then wiped the sweat from his hands on his creased leather pants and sauntered up to the door of the town hall. It was locked. He turned to look down the street. Although there was no one visible, he could feel hidden eyes burning holes through his shirt.

'Go on, stare as much as you like, for I am the alchemist and your world will never be the same again,' he muttered defiantly, then realised that he was completely devoid of inspiration. Sighing deeply he tucked a business card under the door's brass handle and whistled for the coyote.

The Ford Bronco headed over to the empty trailer park at the edge of town. Preacher Williams watched it go, staring after it from his office alongside the church. A thin-lipped man, who wore his misery in the stoop of his shoulders and hollowed cheeks, the preacher had a particular hatred of anything that smacked of handcrafted faith, cults or sects. He had convinced himself that devilry, a corruption of the human soul, had seeped slowly but undeniably into the last half of the twentieth century and now into the twenty-first. It was a global corruption from which he was determined to save his corner of the world.

'Rainmaker indeed,' the preacher muttered and reached for the phone, the wine-coloured star-shaped birthmark on the top of his hand becoming visible for a second.

Chad Winchester, sitting high up in a tractor in the middle of a ruined dry field, heard his cell phone ringing but couldn't remember where he'd placed it. Understandably the florid mayor was distracted — Abigail Etterton, wheat farmer and the most glamorous widow in the state, had his erect penis in her mouth. Chad glanced tenderly at Abigail's beautiful mouth sliding up and down his glistening organ. They'd been lovers for over two years and there had been many occasions when he'd considered divorcing his wife. Political astuteness, however, always overrode the exigencies of love. He moaned quietly, deeply regretting his ambition in that instant. Sandridge was a fiercely religious town and his wife, Cheri, cheerleader of Sandridge High 1976 and head of the Wheatgrowers' Wives Association of Oklahoma, was a popular woman. But a woman who had never achieved orgasm, and not for want of trying on Chad's part.

His own climax was proving uncharacteristically elusive, not helped by the ringing cell phone. The thought that it might be some disaster he should deal with gnawed at the edge of his mind.

'Oh, for Christ's sake, you might as well answer it,' Abigail remarked from between his legs. Embarrassed, Chad tucked away his rapidly diminishing penis and reached for his cell phone.

The rainmaker looked out of the window of his trailer. When he'd parked it in the dusty trailer park the place had been empty. Now, the locals had started to gather in bunches. There were two sprawling Mexican families, their children chasing each other with handfuls of black dust. There was the gas-station owner, holding a pitchfork in one hand, glaring at the trailer as if he were expecting battle. Next to him, six young farmers, obviously brothers, lounged over a brand new tractor. From their high cheekbones and strong features Jacob guessed they were of Germanic descent. Finally, there were the women.

'All women have their own beauty, if you look at them long enough,' Jacob observed, fascinated by the way one, who looked like a librarian, moved her hands in fluttery gestures. Next to her was a buxom blonde matron in a hat. Obviously an official's wife, Jacob thought, assessing her body with the practice of a connoisseur. 'Or how about the virgin aching for experience?' he murmured, gazing at the gauche schoolgirl in the short skirt who rubbed her legs together like a restless colt.

'Gals, I'm here for you. I am everyman. I will fulfil your every fantasy while none of you, not one, will ever be able to move me.' He smiled painfully. 'I am as arid as the land I've come to liberate.' The declaration made his heart suddenly ache.

He pulled the shutters down, overwhelmed by an exhaustion that was spiritual rather than physical, and leaned wearily against the wall of the trailer. Stuck to the refrigerator were photographs of his four ex-wives and an article torn from *Life* magazine about a horrific British murder involving a vegetable root. Jacob had a fascination for bizarre murders and the description of the Welsh spinster murderess had captivated him. One day he was going to meet her. Smiling at the thought, his eyes wandered to a pink garter embroidered with the name Charlene that hung on the fridge door handle.

Jacob pulled it off and sniffed it. Sometimes he wondered whether he had a heart at all. He'd reached his mid-forties without ever being affected by anyone. It wasn't that he was shallow — at least he didn't think so — it was just that he had a constant sense of emotional distance, as if he were experiencing the world from the bottom of a deep clear well. The women he'd been involved with — and there had been hundreds of them — all fell in love with the idea of rescuing him from the shimmering depths of his aloofness. They would caress him, nurture him, lie down for him, dance, weep, shout and moan, but he remained untouched by any of them. And now, nearly half a century old, Jacob had abandoned the idea of love altogether. The best he could hope for was the secure feeling of being wrapped up tight, losing himself in yet another sexual conquest. The sensation made him forget his mortality, his loneliness and fears. But the feeling inevitably passed the moment he reached orgasm and then the remoteness would rush in, stronger than before.

He sat down at the fold-out formica table and poured himself a whisky. He then pulled out a stopwatch and pushed down the tiny knob at the top. Ten minutes, he thought, and then they'll come knocking.

~

Cheri Winchester, the mayor's wife, still sported her hair rollers. The sun had dried her curls into stiff rivulets but she was too distracted to notice. 'Applefort called in a rainmaker after three years of drought and they say that it worked a treat,' she remarked to her best friend, Rebecca, who ran the local cultural centre which consisted of a sole dusty exhibition dating back to 1954 when Sandridge won the prize for the cleanest town in the south west.

Rebecca stepped closer and peered at the caravan across the fence. 'Dangerous voodoo. Dreams destroy people's lives, you mark my words.' She pursed her lips, remembering her own broken hopes — a fiancé who died in the first Gulf War and with him any chance of Rebecca escaping spinsterhood.

'Oh, Becs,' Cheri ventured, 'you know I believe in collective hope.' Rebecca squinted at her; sometimes Cheri's quirky ideas irritated her intensely.

'Surely if we all pray together we can make a little rain fall?' Cheri blushed, the boldness of her statement leaving her on shaky ground.

'Amen.' Stefan Kaufmann, one of the six handsome brothers, smiled sexily at her. Cheri smiled back, then to her dismay heard her husband's car approaching.

Chad's silver Lexus skidded to a halt. The crowd swung around. The mayor, perspiration already staining the armpits of his blue shirt, climbed out from behind the wheel. Bill Williams, the preacher, whose pale body never seemed to sweat, even in this scorching heat, tagged behind. The crowd parted as Chad strode through, his showmanship at its peak. The preacher scuttled crab-like beside him. Jeremiah Running Dog, sheriff, second-largest landowner and head of the local Lions club, followed them. A bulky man in his late sixties and weighing over three hundred pounds, he was feared for his unpredictable temper. Jeremiah moved at a leisurely pace, but if one looked closer the coiled muscles at his neck betrayed his apprehension.

⤳

There were three sharp taps on the aluminium door. Jacob finished his whisky. This was how it always started: the men of the town would make the first approach. Drought reduces people to the most basic of emotions, he mused. Dignity dissolves after the seventh month. There is something about a dearth of rain that flattens the hope out of all men, yellow, white, green or black. He knew he could predict the reception he'd get from any small town official just by plucking a withered blade of the local grass and rubbing it between his fingers.

He stood up and stared into the mirror by the door. He slicked back his hair, adjusted his silk shirt and practised a smile. He still had trouble relating to the handsome man who looked back at him, always incredulous that all the heartbreak he caused had left no mark on his face. The pristine features suggested the morality of an angel. 'If only they knew,' he whispered and stepped out of the trailer.

The three town representatives stood waiting. A gasp of expectancy rippled through the crowd as Jacob paused in front of them. The sunlight transformed the rainmaker's hair into a blazing dark red halo. From the neck up he looked like Jesus; from the neck down like the devil, with his loose scarlet shirt and silver pendant of a satyr visible against his oiled chest. Smiling at the crowd he bowed elegantly, sending a quiver through the women.

The mayor decided to take charge. He cleared his throat and announced loudly, 'We don't like hawkers here, or strangers for that matter.'

Jacob leaned down and caressed his coyote with his tapered hands, his ring, its sapphire the blue of water, glinting in the sun. Eventually he spoke: 'I heard there was a drought.' He lifted his face and the searing indigo of his eyes pierced Chad Winchester with a terrible longing for the sea. For a moment the mayor wondered if he wasn't affected with the same drought madness that had caused Jeremiah's thirty-five-year-old son to leap to his death into the town's empty dam the summer before.

'A drought,' Jacob continued, 'which is breaking the backs of animals and the hearts of men.' His resonant voice boomed around the field and caused the body-hair of the crowd to collectively stand on end.

Sensing the disturbance the sheriff moved forward. 'What can you do?' Jeremiah demanded, rolls of fat clinging to his sweat-soaked shirt. He tried not to stare too hard at the glinting pendant, which only added to the obvious sexuality of the man.

As Jacob walked towards them the immensity of his presence made the men involuntarily step back. The rainmaker was at least six foot five and the Cuban heels gave him another three inches.

'I can make it rain, for weeks if I choose. I can make this ground bear grass. I can turn all your crops green again.'

'Spoken like a real con artist,' the preacher muttered. He scanned the mesmerised crowd then turned back to Jacob. 'What are you after, mister? Money?' Mockery tinged his voice.

'I have my conditions. Money ain't one of them,' Jacob replied, his perfect teeth gleaming. He noted the glint of hatred in the preacher's eye and remembered the Aryan Fellowship sign.

'So if you're not after money, what are you after?' Jeremiah stepped between the two men.

Jacob twisted his sapphire ring. This was the moment when his intuition was really tested. The code of honour his lineage had bred into him obliged him to be truthful, but it was a truth that required diplomacy.

'You have to understand that water is an element. It needs to feel welcome. There is an emotional aridity in this town which has driven the rain away. For it to return, it needs tenderness, affection, love ... sex.'

A ripple of excitement ran through the crowd at the word 'sex'. Preacher Williams breathed in sharply, sounding like a wounded bullfrog. Jeremiah surprised himself by remembering his own secret Cherokee beliefs, next to him Chad thought about Abigail, and how the air around her often seemed moist with her juices.

Unperturbed, the rainmaker continued. 'There are frictions between living souls that create an ether of invisible fluids. These fluids attract the rain clouds — they operate as a kind of magnet.'

Jeremiah, now acutely aware of his own schism between Cherokee and Christian and feeling uncomfortably compromised, spat into the dust. 'Cut the bullshit. We're not interested in your methodology, we're only interested in results and what you're asking for them, boy.' The last word rang out with condescension.

Jacob paused for a second, then: 'What I want is one of your women.' He tossed out the sentence as if it were the most casual of requests.

The crowd began to murmur. Chad raised his hands and hushed them. He turned back to the rainmaker. 'What for?'

'The only way I can induce rain is to make love to one of your women,' Jacob repeated slowly.

The crowd broke out in an uproar. The preacher let out a great screech of indignation; Jeremiah had to forcibly hold back one of the Kaufmann brothers; while Chad stood frozen in the midst of the commotion, paralysed by the realisation that his personal equilibrium, both political and sexual, was under threat.

Jacob retreated to the trailer. 'I strongly suggest you consider my proposal,' he said to the mayor before slamming his door.

Ignoring the jeers audible through the thin walls, he poured another whisky. 'The seed is planted, now I just have to watch it grow,' he said. Satisfied that events had been set into motion, he curled up on his bed and fell instantly asleep.

Outside, the preacher glared in disgust at the silver trailer as the crowd dissipated, wandering back to their lives. Cheri went to the hairdresser to rescue her hair. Chad drove to his office to meet with the town veterinarian who had more reports of dehydrated cattle. Rebecca strolled back to her bookshelves, secretly appalled at the small throbbing between her legs.

❧

While Jacob slept he dreamed the shape of the settlement. It was his way of marking out his territory. Propelled by the image of himself carried in the minds of Sandridge's residents, he shot high above the roofs of the town to float in the cloudless sky. He loved the sensation of disembodiment, as if his physical self had dispersed like a cloud of invisible droplets. He was nowhere and everywhere.

Below him he could see how people's emotions stained their lives like colour. The old widow's grief, a dark blue-grey hue that seeped across her kitchen table as she sat staring out at the empty fields. Jeremiah, standing in his stable and remembering his dead son as a boy, his memory streaming pale mauve from his hand onto his shivering horse.

The beast glanced up knowingly at the rainmaker's invisible hovering spirit. Jacob smiled down at the stallion and continued his journey, floating along Main Street, past the town hall, past the doctor's surgery, past the diner with its tin walls glinting in the sun, past the bell tower of the church.

He paused at the church. From his position in the sky he sensed a most marvellous presence. Fascinated, he moved closer.

*Who are you?* The words manifested as clearly as sparkling icicles and hung in his mind as strongly as his own voice. A strange new emotion gripped him as he realised the presence was female. Before he could answer, the shimmering was hidden from him by an ugly darkness. It fell across the light and enveloped it. *Help me!* she cried out, her pain almost ripping Jacob's head off.

'I have no power in this form!' he replied, panicking, pushing against his own skin, trying to transform spirit into muscle.

Whoever it was beneath the darkness struggled and then lay still. It was like watching a hawk tear apart a rabbit. Horrified,

Jacob tried to bring himself awake but found that he could not. Instead his dreaming pulled him closer to the violence below. The barriers of brick and mortar melted away and, looking down, he recognised the preacher, his thin pale buttocks pounding against a girl pinned beneath him. The air filled with the sound of screeching birds. Several starlings and an owl flapped wildly around the room, swooping and attacking the preacher, who paused only to beat them off with his arm. Transfixed, Jacob could not look away; it was both a terrible and an extraordinary sight, for the girl had the most exquisite soul he had ever experienced.

When the coyote nudged the rainmaker awake he was sobbing. Jacob touched the wetness in wonder, unable to remember the last time he had cried. He lay on the expensive Belgian bed linen, dread clawing at the pit of his stomach, the beauty of the young woman troubling him in an entirely new way.

He opened the door of the trailer and sat for a time on its steps. The coyote began a long desperate howl at the sun. As Jacob watched a line of fire ants divert around the cracks in the burnt earth, he started to wonder whether there wasn't a seam of heroism in his soul after all? Who was she? What was her connection to the preacher? Why hadn't he seen her with the other townsfolk? Trailing his finger in the dust he found himself haunted by the thought of seeing her again. The question was — how?

His reverie was broken by a loud screech. The turkey vulture watched him from the top of the fence, its eye a swivelling raisin in the plucked anger of its head.

The sun shone and the drought continued. A dozen more of Jeremiah's cattle keeled over, the tarmac began to melt and crack along the edges of the main street, and Chad was obliged to reduce water rations to one shower a week. It was miserable. The townsfolk despaired; three more farmers committed suicide; and several families packed up and headed east. But still the rainmaker continued to camp at the edge of town.

Jacob had taken to sunbathing on the roof of his trailer, naked except for a leather thong. His long lean body was like a panther's. Reflected countless times in the mirrored surface of the trailer, he was an erotic deity filling the sky. Many of the women found themselves watching him. Each secretly found time to spy on the rainmaker as he applied coconut oil to his glistening flesh in languid studied gestures, his massaging fingers promising a sensual knowledge that made them tremble in anticipation.

As he lay there, the sun heating his flesh, he sensed the rising hostility of the menfolk. The drought would go on, for as long as he let it. This was a fact as true as his knowledge of the woman the preacher kept hidden. The image of her had begun to possess Jacob and he found himself conjuring impossible schemes: he would use the rain to distract the preacher and then he would rescue her. His mind whirled dangerously as the sun fried his skin.

The outrageous nature of Jacob's demand had swept through the town and was debated at the bar and at every fireplace. One precocious seven year old even wrote a school essay about him. The whole community was in a fever. Publicly the town closed its ranks and condemned him; privately opinion was divided. The men wanted rain and the women ... Well, the women had begun to want the rainmaker.

Cheri Winchester, the mayor's wife, found herself dreaming of swimming naked with the bronzed stranger. One morning there was actually a little moisture staining the sheets, as if her body had retained and then released a liquid trace of the slow salty dance that haunted her nights. While in other beds, in other streets, other women twisted around those muscular limbs in somnambulant passion like ballerinas underwater, to wake disappointed, their bodies still clenching around a void, beside their sleeping husbands.

At the book clubs and knitting circles the women's vitriol knew no bounds. At the same time they blushed, terrified that the others might guess how they had been occupied during the night.

'Have you seen the way he struts up and down in that thong? He might as well be buck naked!' the postmistress hissed through her false teeth and dropped a stitch.

'You've got to admit, he's a fine-looking fella,' replied the mayor's mother, a well-preserved sixty-seven who wasn't above a little sexual dalliance herself.

'I wish he'd lose the thong, then we'd be able to judge his wares, turkey neck and all!' cracked the school teacher, and the whole knitting circle, whose combined ages totalled over five hundred years, burst into raucous laughter.

~

Jacob managed to strike up a friendship with the postman, an irrepressibly cheerful Latino who delivered the mail on a huge Harley Davidson with a racoon skull strapped to the handlebars.

'So tell me about the preacher — has he got a woman?' the rainmaker asked casually.

'No, man, that unholy bastard lives alone. And I'll tell you something else, ever since he moved into his house no one has been inside and he has it rigged up like a castle. High security — I'm telling you, the guy is one nasty gringo.'

Through the iron gate Jacob could see the bell tower rising up from the neat brick church. Under one of the eaves, hidden in the shadows, was a diamond-shaped barred window. It fascinated him. He turned in the direction of the preacher's house and scanned the building, the tendrils of his intuition curling like invisible smoke across the walls. Regardless of sensing the girl's presence, he couldn't locate her.

On the other side of the brick wall the preacher sat crouched over his desk composing his sermon for the week. Its theme was the dangers of charlatans during times of natural disaster. Despite the dryness of his every-day speech, Bill Williams was a powerful orator. He had a certain charisma and his smooth manners were attractive to sectors of the ravaged rural community. His thinly disguised racism provided a convenient scapegoat in hard times. Three African-American families had left the town since his arrival; there had been an incident where masked men had severely beaten a young Mexican boy; and a 'KKK' had been burned into the wooden walls of the local schoolhouse. Neither the sheriff nor the mayor had been able to catch the perpetrators. It was as if the town had closed ranks in a great wall of silence. Bill Williams relished such support. He knew the town officials were secretly frightened of him and he was determined to undermine their power.

As he wrote, a flock of finches nestling in the desiccated tree outside his window burst into song. Without turning around Bill Williams knew that his daughter had entered the room.

'It will be ready to type in half an hour,' he growled, then, mistaking her silence for sullenness, he turned. Bill's daughter was as exquisite as he was ugly. At twenty she had the kind of beauty that sucked the breath away like a sudden punch to the diaphragm. Long curly dark hair, cascaded down to her waist. She had deep brown eyes that shone violet in a certain light. Their slanted length and heavy lids gave her an oriental appearance and heightened the impression of remoteness. She had an angular face softened by youth, but the sharpness of her cheekbones emphasised her fragility. On closer inspection a buried intelligence spoke of a wisdom far beyond her years — which was just as well, for Miranda, the preacher's daughter, could not speak. She was mute, and had been since birth.

If Preacher Williams had one defining secret in his life it was this: the existence of a daughter who, to his great chagrin, resembled her mother so exactly that every time he looked at her he experienced the same intense mortification he'd felt on the one occasion he'd faltered morally.

It had been his first job, in a poor neighbourhood in South Chicago. In those days he had been a shy, awkward youth. His father, whom he adored, had lost his job as a storeman to an immigrant and drank himself to death by the time Bill was thirteen. The boy, whose sensitivity had already made him a target for the local kids, sought refuge in books, particularly the Bible. He soon discovered that if he voiced the racist fears of his community and spiced them up with some religious polemic, he gained a captive audience. It was heady stuff for an adolescent who'd had little love and no respect up to that point in his life. It was only a matter of time before he became a lay preacher and then joined the Aryan Fellowship.

Late one night he came across a young African woman who had been hired to clean the church. As she bent over the pews, polishing the brass rails, the preacher couldn't help noticing how shapely her behind was, how high her bosom. The poor girl had barely realised that he was standing behind her when suddenly his pent-up anger and frustration exploded. He grabbed her, covered her mouth with his hand, and raped her. Afterwards, too terrified to speak, she fled, leaving the preacher drenched in shame, his trousers still around his ankles, curled up on the stone floor like an aberrant child.

Months passed and he'd almost forgotten the incident, until one night a pale brown infant appeared at the foot of the altar, wrapped up in an African shawl. As he looked into the baby's face, she reached up to him, revealing an identical birthmark to his own in exactly the same place on the top of her tiny hand. There could be no doubt. Terrified that his secret might be revealed, the preacher hid the baby in his car. As he drove around aimlessly he thought about all the places he could abandon the baby, but the fear of that telltale birthmark exposing him as a rapist as well as a hypocrite forced a momentous decision. He took her home that night and placed her in a cardboard box for a crib, vowing to keep her hidden from the world.

The baby never cried, and as the child grew older he realised, with a certain amount of relief, that she was mute. Finally he named her Miranda, after Shakespeare's heroine, deluding himself with the notion of himself as her Prospero.

He looked at his daughter now, sensing a change in her. She was staring at the window that faced the main street. He followed her gaze and, to his intense irritation, saw the rainmaker walking on the other side of the street.

Watching his grace Miranda thought of sunlight catching the top of the ocean's waves, which was puzzling as she had never seen the sea. So that's him, the girl thought, the one I felt approaching over the desert, her heart racing with recognition.

The preacher pulled the blinds down with a snap. 'If I catch you looking at that abomination again, I'll blacken the windows in your bedroom for a week,' he threatened, grabbing her wrists. She nodded silently and he let go.

63

If he had been more observant, he would have noticed that, as she walked out of the room, her hips undulated with the exact same rhythm as the rainmaker's distinctive gait.

❧

The church was packed. Sweat poured off the over-dressed parishioners, running in rivulets under the women's hats, staining the backs of the men's crisp white shirts, collecting in beads across the children's faces. Condensation started to drop from the ceiling. No one noticed; they were all leaning forward in concentration, gathered there for one reason: to hear the preacher pass judgement. Word of the rainmaker and his terms had spread to the more isolated farming communities which, in better days, used Sandridge as a market for their cattle and wheat. There were faces the preacher hadn't seen for years, except at funerals and weddings. Even the local hermit, the most famous misanthrope in the state of Oklahoma, had turned up. The church had never been so crowded.

At the back, a row of bachelor farmers sat on the low pews. As they knelt heavily to pray, dust from the burnt fields puffed up into miniature clouds above them like momentary halos. The wooden kneeling boards groaned with their weight. The preacher lifted his arms into the silence that resonated with collective despair as the entire congregation, from infants to great-grandmothers, prayed for rain.

Hidden in an archway behind the altar, concealed by a curtain, sat Miranda, her face pressed against the wooden divide.

Look at him, how can he call himself a holy man? she thought, all the fear and hatred of her father rising up. If I could, I would shout these walls down. Oh, rainmaker ... do you hear me? Do you feel me pressed against you? She shut her eyes and wished him closer. Between her knees lay her manacled wrists.

The preacher blessed the congregation, coughed, then began his sermon.

'And the weak should be wary of the charlatan, for he shall lead them into a corruption of the spirit, into a falsehood of

64

faith.' He glared at the gathering, his eyebrows bristling. 'And there is a charlatan amongst us, an unclean man, a man not of our race, a man who is the very personification of evil for he seeketh to corrupt this town!'

A farmer in the front row clutched at his heart, old Shirley Kelly lost her false teeth, but caught them with her handkerchief, while Hank Thurson, the diner owner, found his thoughts turning to his accountant.

'I speak of the so-called rainmaker!' the preacher thundered, his voice echoing through the church. 'A man devoid of spirituality or humanity, a man who has demanded the most disgusting of payments — human flesh — the bodies of the respectable wives and daughters of this fair town!'

There wasn't a woman in the building who did not feel a delicious spark of anticipation run down her thighs at the preacher's indignant words.

Behind the curtain Miranda's eyes flew open. The rainmaker needed a woman for his magic. If it could not be her, then let him feel her as he made love to other women. Despite the scratches across her breasts and the marks of a whip on her back, Miranda took stock of her own strength. There was no doubt in her mind: Jacob was there for her alone.

'Preacher! You are wrong!'

The whole congregation swung around. Standing at the back of the church was the rainmaker. Dressed immaculately in a white Armani suit, with mirrored shades that reflected the worshippers, he looked like a modern-day saint.

'What kind of holy man are you?' he challenged. 'A man whose spirit has atrophied into a wizened semblance of humanity! How can you claim that it is I who is lacking in spirituality? I am a miracle-maker! All I need is belief … and a woman who is willing to moisten the very air with her sighs.'

Immediately thirty women consciously locked their knees to prevent themselves from leaping to their feet to sacrifice themselves for the greater cause.

'Carnality is not spirituality!' spat the preacher in response. 'You, sir, are the devil incarnate, sent to destroy these people! Leave this town! There is no place in Sandridge for foreign con-men!' he screamed, transported by the conviction that he was administering divine justice.

The church erupted into chaos. Four of the Kaufmann brothers advanced upon the rainmaker, who remained strangely unperturbed. He had become distracted by the image shining at him from behind the altar. Invisible to others but crystal clear to him, it was a vision of Miranda. In his forty-six years he had never seen a woman so complete in her beauty and suffering. Incredibly humbled, he dropped to his knees.

'You see how he is struck down! Struck down by the Holy Spirit itself. And the Almighty shall smite down the disbeliever!' Bill Williams screamed. The choir of the Aryan Fellowship of Jesus burst into a country and western rendition of 'The Battle Hymn of the Republic'.

Still on his knees the rainmaker looked up. Some assumed he was praying, but Jacob was studying the sun, the heat of which he could feel through the roof. At his silent command the temperature shot up five degrees and a crack appeared in the roof, through which sunlight streamed down illuminating him like a saint. Several women screamed. The preacher gestured and two of the hefty Kaufmann brothers hauled the rainmaker to his feet. As they dragged him out the door, several pious female parishioners couldn't help noticing how long and shapely his legs were as they trailed behind him, feet bumping across the stone floor.

Outside, Jacob lay in the dirt. He had never been happier, this was what he'd been waiting for: a woman who shared the same powers as he, a soulmate who was not bound by time or physicality, but who traversed the laws of nature. He had to rescue her; they belonged together.

Infused with an inspiration he hadn't felt for years, he got up and dusted himself off. The Kaufmann brothers watched suspiciously until he had disappeared from sight. Satisfied, they went back into the church. A moment later Jacob emerged from behind a small hillock and darted around the back of the building. Finding an open window, he eased himself through it, landing silently in a storeroom.

*I am here.* Her words rang in his head as soon as he was

inside. Her presence radiated so strongly Jacob felt like he was standing beside a blazing fire.

*Through the door and behind the curtain on the left.* She guided him until he found the concealed archway. In the background the preacher's voice droned on. Holding his breath Jacob pushed the curtain slowly aside.

She was standing next to a chair, her back to him, the curves of her body visible even through her shapeless cotton dress. She was tall, almost as tall as he was, with long tapering legs, a high waist and high buttocks. She looked like the willowy Nubian woman he'd seen in photos or woodcarvings. Silently he moved up behind her and placed his arms around her. Without turning, she leaned back against him, arching her face against his. Her scent was extraordinary: a heavy musk that reminded him both of the sea and of the waxy cactus night-flowers he'd seen in Mexico. Instantly aroused, he twisted her around and looked into those violet-brown eyes.

'When the women come to me, it will be you who I am loving, and then, when I have freed you, it will always only be you and I,' he whispered, the only spoken words between them and the only time he had uttered such words to any woman. Her luminous eyes gazed into his and for a moment he was gripped by a novel sensation — fear of rejection. Then she smiled sadly and he realised she was mute.

'What's your name?' he whispered. She caressed his face with her fingers, tracing his mouth in wonder. It was then that he saw her chains and the seeping raw skin on her wrists.

'Miranda?' It was the preacher's voice. Terrified, the girl pushed Jacob back towards the storeroom, gesturing wildly that he should leave. But just before he stepped away, she pulled him to her and kissed him. For the first time in his life Jacob felt his heart contract.

⁓

It was a horribly hot night. The rainmaker lay wide awake. Even as a man whose life had been shaped by impulsive emotions and visions, he had always felt in control. Now, he was losing that control and part of him was petrified. Outside a twig broke; he listened for a second, then decided it was the coyote on one of her nocturnal scavenges. He turned over but found that the image of Miranda remained pressed against his burning eyelids.

The mayor's wife paused, frozen in the moonlight. She was wearing nothing but a Victoria's Secret camisole under Chad's old parka. The sound of cicadas was intense, the incessant buzzing blocked out most other sounds. All she could hear was the thudding of her own heart.

Cheri hadn't been able to analyse the sensation that possessed her when she woke beside her sleeping husband. She had arisen like a somnambulist, slipped on the camisole and walked silently out of the back door to find herself gliding down Main Street like a ghost. An invisible rope of a thousand glistening tingling threads pulled her along, tugging at each nipple, sucking at every part of her long-neglected sex.

'I'm not in command of my actions,' she repeated to herself, trying to take some comfort in the mantra. 'I am under a spell,' she muttered as she quickened her pace towards the caravan, a silver zeppelin under the moon.

'At the very least,' she concluded as she arrived at the trailer's doorstep, 'this is the kind of sacrifice only the mayor's wife should be expected to make for the greater community.' And with that consoling thought, she knocked softly.

Above, a tawny owl which had been following her progress with great curiosity, hovered for a second, its beady eyes watching as she stepped into the van. Perching carefully on top of the vehicle, using its claws to balance, it made its way to the window.

It wasn't exactly the woman Jacob had been hoping for, but he'd always nurtured the philosophy that womanhood was elemental and, as such, the individual manifestation wasn't really so important. He smiled at the mayor's wife, a voluptuous woman whose vital juices, he assessed with one glance, were long overdue for liberation.

I dedicate this lovemaking to you, Miranda — he sent the thought to his captive lover as the matron fell into his arms in a timely swoon.

As Jacob carried Cheri over the threshold, a light flickered on in Rebecca's bedroom across the road. Sandridge's cultural ambassador wasn't one to leave anything to hearsay. Meanwhile, hanging upside down, its round feathery face pressed against the window, the owl's eyes widened.

The mayor's wife lay across the quilt, her eyelids fluttering. 'I'm here,' she murmured coyly, 'I'm here to make ... rain.'

But Jacob's hands had already lifted the hem of her camisole, were massaging their way up her thighs, touching her in a manner she had not thought men capable of. 'I hope you appreciate the sacrifice I'm making,' she managed to say between gasps, as he caressed the secret part she'd spent many a wasted night praying that Chad, in his clumsy fumblings, might find.

'I'm here for the town,' she screamed as Jacob buried his face in her sex.

As he worked his tongue, the rainmaker conjured up gargantuan clouds that gathered on a night horizon, rolling cumulus, decorated with silent flashes of lightning that twisted magically into Miranda's hair blowing wildly around her face as she smiled at him.

As he caught Cheri's clit between his lips, he imagined the trees bending in a stormy wind. Swaying, they transformed into the dusky arch of Miranda's naked back.

Meanwhile, over at the diner Hank Thurson's barometer swung to *Humid* for the first time in over a year and the weather vane atop the town hall burst out of its rust to spin wildly.

With her legs pinned to the bed, Cheri had no choice but to surrender. A spider web of ecstasy ran from nerve end to nerve end. Experiencing sensations she hadn't known existed, she clutched at his hair, pulling violently. The pleasure was so intense she thought she might faint, but still the rainmaker held her down, pausing only to bite gently at her inner thighs in brief respite before fastening his mouth again to her sex. Above the trailer, storm clouds gathered. The owl shook her feathers.

Cheri cried and moaned. Deep within her the rainmaker felt all the trapped disappointments, the sorrows of missed opportunity, the tedium of mindless duty building like a massive tidal wall. Maestro that he was, he took his time, allowing the longing to subside for a moment, only to build it up again, knowing that the higher the wall, the greater the outpouring.

Miranda, Miranda, he thought over and over, sending her every shiver of pleasure he felt. He intensified his lovemaking, calling on all his prodigious abilities, blowing, licking and teasing every nerve end to the point of explosion.

Finally, when he sensed he had brought Cheri to the brink, he raised himself high on his hands and plunged his heavy sex deep into her. Finally Cheri understood the true function of the male organ. As Jacob thrust into her she clutched at his buttocks, shocking herself with loud guttural cries, wanting more and more. Recognising her urgency he quickened his pace. The tsunami rose and rose until it filled Cheri's mind, then broke, flooding her with glorious, unadulterated pleasure.

'Ahhhhhhhh!' she screamed, her first ever orgasm rippling through her like an epiphany. A second later Jacob followed, his body trembling violently. In the bell tower, Miranda, her pelvis raised up in bliss, twisted in ecstasy at exactly the same moment.

Suddenly the residents of Sandridge were woken by a huge peal of thunder, and the owl flew off in the direction of the church.

✲

It rained and rained and rained. In the early hours of that first day the townsfolk came out and danced under the heavy droplets of water, their naked legs and arms splashed with black mud which had been dust for so long. Jeremiah, shaking with relief, went to his son's grave and thanked God and the great buzzard — talisman of his people — his tears mingling with the rain.

Only the mayor, a heavy sleeper, slept through both the thunder and the pelting of the rain. It was Cheri, rosy and flushed, who shook him awake three hours later to tell him the fireman wanted his permission to ring the church bells as the outraged preacher had barricaded himself in.

Chad, although drowsy, still noticed the strange new aura surrounding his wife. Others might describe it as happiness, but he put it down to her exhilaration at the breaking of the drought. Again he congratulated himself on having had the sense to pick a woman who excelled in her duties as the First Lady of a god-fearing farming community. Chuckling to himself, he dusted off his raincoat and pulled it on over his pyjamas.

'I wonder who the woman was?' he remarked to Cheri as the Lexus pulled out of the slippery driveway. Cheri blushed, but as usual Chad was too preoccupied with himself to notice.

~

The preacher had been awoken not by the thunder but by a sudden chorus of nightingales. When the beautiful but piercing cries filled his bedroom he leapt to his feet and, dragging a great flannel robe over his shrunken frame, flung open the window and peered out. He didn't notice the trembling raindrops bursting over his bald pate; the sight before him was so frightening and so lovely that his heart jolted against his chest. He wondered for one brief moment whether he had been blessed with a visitation, but then as he looked closer he recognised Miranda.

She was dancing nude in the rain, her body contorting like a snake to its own music. At first he thought that she was being attacked by a flock of birds, but as he looked closer he saw that the nightingales hovered around her, each holding a strand of her long black hair in its beak, each whirling madly like a demented dervish. A lone owl sat on a branch above, as if it were conducting the whole event.

'Witchcraft!' the preacher cried out and rushed outside, throwing his coat over her and bundling her back into the house. After pushing her into the dingy bedroom and bolting the door, he sat at his desk, shaking with rage and terror. It was then that he heard the fireman banging on the door, demanding that the church bells be rung.

~

71

Chad stood on the back of a fire truck in front of the church, heedless of the pouring rain. He held a megaphone in one hand while his other arm lay draped around Cheri. It was a posture he felt conveyed family values and leadership. The mayor cleared his throat, the wet, elated crowd hushed into silence and Chad began. 'This is incredible! It is truly a miracle! God has blessed Sandridge!'

A great cheer went up. Overwhelmed, Chad squeezed Cheri's arm for effect; he was a strong believer in exploiting the moment.

'I don't know who we should thank,' he said, gesturing towards Jacob's trailer, 'the rainmaker, or the woman who chose to make the greatest sacrifice of all!'

At this Cheri blushed again. Her flushed cheeks went unnoticed by the men, but several women looked knowingly at each other. Rebecca leaned over to whisper into the ear of the beautician.

Chad continued, oblivious to the flame of gossip which was spreading like wildfire through the women in the crowd.

'Instead, I suggest we give thanks to the Almighty Himself!'

Obediently the townsfolk followed Cheri Winchester's example as she bent her head to pray.

The second night Jacob was visited by the fireman's wife; the third night the beautician practically pounded down the door; the fourth night he was frightened the van might actually tip over as the schoolmistress vigorously rode him. On the fifth night Rebecca drank the miniature bottle of whisky she'd been saving for Thanksgiving and marched over to the trailer park. The rain did not stop. Exhausted, Jacob stayed in his trailer.

He was thinking of one woman only. With each new conquest his desire for Miranda became more urgent. Between the sessions of lovemaking he started taking long walks around the church, marking the time the preacher locked the iron gates, where the wall was lowest and any other information that he might be able to use. On his second trek around the perimeter he noticed the owl following, flying from tree to tree.

'You're with her?' he asked. The owl, as if in response, flew nearer and perched on the handle of an abandoned plough.

'Tell her it will be soon. I will send her a signal.'

The owl cocked its head then flew off to the belfry. As Jacob watched, slowly a plan manifested.

⁓

Miranda leaned against the bars of the diamond-shaped window. The owl was just visible as it zigzagged towards her through the pelting rain. It landed on the window sill then squeezed itself through the bars. Hooting softly it shook the rain from its feathers.

Miranda held out her hand. The owl leapt onto her arm and walked up to her shoulder. Tenderly it rubbed its head against her cheek.

*Have you brought me a message?* she asked. The owl, clicking with its tongue and hooting, told her that the rainmaker would come for her before the next full moon.

*Are you sure? What about the other women?* she ventured, wanting the reassurance she already sensed.

*Don't waste my time*, replied the owl crossly. *You know it is you and only you he makes love to. He has a plan and they are part of it.* Then, upon seeing a scurry on the other side of the room, the owl swooped down to catch a mouse.

⁓

The heavens had been opened and the rainmaker was paid a thousandfold for his moisture-inducing efforts. The women couldn't get enough of him. Their nocturnal visits to his caravan became so frequent that they started to pass each other in the now muddy field that was the trailer park. Each woman discreetly ignored the other as they crossed paths, hair concealed by headscarves, ludicrous sunglasses wrapped around elated faces. Some even wore false eyebrows, false moustaches and wigs.

Their cries of pleasure pooled in the crevices and corners of the trailer, eventually gushing out of the windows and straight up into the overcast sky, triggering a new downpour every time. It was perfect alchemy. Soon Jacob was rendezvousing with every female over the age of sixteen and under the age of seventy-two and the pharmacy had run out of every known method of contraception.

But with every seduction Jacob felt his heart become a little more hollow. For the first time in his life he craved one woman and one woman only. Although he was able to envisage her image with each new caress, and although he knew that she was trembling in unison with him, it wasn't enough. 'One more week. When the water rises another four inches I will make my move,' he calculated, trying desperately to stem the gnawing void he felt inside.

His only comfort was her ambassador. He started giving the owl gifts to take to her: a pale green glass marble he'd won as a child; a locket containing a crystallised droplet rumoured to be the last tear shed by Marie Antoinette before she was beheaded; and a fragile shell from the North Sea whose echoes had a mysterious Irish lilt that rang out from its spiral depths.

Early each morning the bird arrived at the belfry where Miranda was incarcerated. It would drop the gift at her feet, perch on the end of the rusty brass bed and, in low hoots, give her Jacob's messages — descriptions of where they would flee to, where they would live once he'd freed her. He told her about a beautiful island down in the Mississippi Delta where he had grown up. There they would build a house, grow fruit trees and, most of all, be safe. He even told her that he wanted to have a child with her. 'The loveliest child in the world, who will be able to make rain and talk to the birds; a child made from a rainbow,' he said. As the owl talked, Miranda's eyes would widen with Jacob's dreams. Soon, she thought, soon he will come for me.

From her window high above the town she could see the silver trailer. She imagined it lifting up into the sky and flying away, leaving only a glittering arc. Then they would be on his island, where she would have a voice as exquisite as the nightingale's.

Meanwhile, the preacher's congregation dwindled. A week after the first rain had poured through the bell tower and dripped onto the altar, only twenty worshippers sat in the pews. At first Bill Williams attributed the absence of his parishioners to the frantic mending of field boundaries and riverbanks, but when his most devout followers — all of them female — stayed away in droves, he became suspicious.

The preacher made his way to the library, determined to gatecrash the knitting circle. When he arrived he found a group of rosy-faced, happily chatting women, each glowing (obscenely, he thought) with an extraordinary sense of wellbeing. Worse were the nauseatingly generous compliments they paid each other over the clicking of their knitting needles. Bill Williams was shocked to his very core. If they weren't all over the age of menopause he would have sworn that they shone with the ruddy glow of pregnancy. Even more disturbing was the wall of silence that sprang up when he asked if anyone had seen the rainmaker.

The preacher stumbled out of the building to be confronted by a mass of migrating frogs crossing Main Street to breed in the new canals running alongside the road.

'The man has got to be eradicated, he is human vermin,' he muttered as he plucked one particularly amorous amphibian from his bald head. He turned and marched towards the mayor's office.

When the preacher had finished his tirade, Chad glanced outside. Although the rain eased during the day, it always came down in heavy squalls from about 7 p.m. every night. Interesting, the mayor thought, not quite able to pinpoint why this observation should be so disturbing, and whether he should associate it with his mistress's sudden reluctance to see him. The world was not what it had been, and neither were the women in the town, he concluded. As he watched a cow struggle through the stream that had once been Main Street, he wondered about the rain's disastrous commercial impact. It was then that he decided to call a meeting.

～

The husbands, sons and brothers of Sandridge crowded into the town hall. Not one woman had been invited to the meeting. As the last farmer wiped his mud-encrusted boots and squeezed into the space a hush settled. The men turned to their elected leaders with tense faces. Chad suddenly felt nauseous with nerves. Jeremiah, noticing that the mayor had paled, nudged him in the ribs.

'Er ... I'm sure that everyone here is in agreement that ... er ... the rain has to stop,' the mayor ventured.

A murmur of support rippled through the crowd. Chad took courage from the notion that these men might be businessmen first and husbands second.

'Good,' he continued. 'Therefore, the question is ...' His voice trailed off.

'Louder!' some smartass yelled from the back of the hall.

The mayor cleared his throat. 'The question is ... whose woman is sleeping with the rainmaker?'

The farmers looked perplexed, then angry. Their glances began to slide in the direction of their neighbours.

'Well, it ain't mine!' one middle-aged farmer shouted. 'My Shirley's never been happier. Why, the other night she begged me for it! And I'm telling you, that was a first!'

Another, a young beanpole of a man with a squint, leapt to his feet. 'He's right. Mine wanted to try a new position last week and ... it was kinda wild!' he concluded triumphantly.

The oldest farmer in the district pushed himself up with the help of his walking frame. 'Agnes and I made love for the first time in twenty years. I dunno what came over the old gal but she was hot for it all right. Nearly damn well killed me,' he declared, hands shaking.

Suddenly every man in the hall started to shout out descriptions of the amorous adventures their wives, girlfriends and lovers had submitted them to since the rains. It was bedlam, but one thing was for certain: the women of Sandridge had never been more sexually adventurous, nor happier, in any man's memory.

Jeremiah pounded the table with a judge's gavel. The commotion stopped instantly. Pushing Chad aside the sheriff stood up. 'I don't give a rat's ass as to who the woman is — we have just gotta make sure this damn rain stops before it ruins all of us!' he shouted.

The preacher seized his opportunity and, springing to his feet, yelled out, 'The rainmaker is to blame for all this! He is evil! He is the devil in disguise! I say we pull him in!'

Immediately a delegation of muscled farm hands volunteered to drag in the sex-crazed wizard.

'The sex-crazed wizard is already here.' Jacob's sardonic voice rang out from the back of the hall. His eyes were dark-ringed with exhaustion, his hands trembling.

'Who is she?' Chad demanded.

'Which one?' Jacob retorted and smiled sweetly, at which fifty outraged husbands rolled up their sleeves.

'There is nothing I can do to stop the rain. What is given freely is impossible to take away.' And with that he calmly left the hall.

Four miles away, the dam, now full and brimming, absorbed its last raindrop and collapsed, sending tens of thousands of gallons of water cascading through the town. The water gushed down Main Street, swishing up against the brick wall surrounding the church. It flooded through the iron gate and found a weak spot in one of the church walls. Slowly it began to erode the stonework.

The next morning the local telephone and internet services crashed due to over-use. Every female resident had been issued with an ultimatum: one visit to the rainmaker would mean expulsion from the community.

All over town wives, mistresses and daughters, having been cut off from their girlfriends stared glumly at silent phones, while outside their men struggled with sandbags in a desperate attempt to hold back the floodwater. Some unfortunate women sported black eyes, others lovebites; several had split lips — all injuries inflicted by their men with the same desperate intention: to wipe the mark of the rainmaker from the bodies of their women.

That night Jacob taped a sign to his door with one word written on it: OUT. He drove to the other side of town and left his car parked outside the motel as a deliberate false lead. Carrying his rock-climbing gear in a backpack he doubled back. On the way he noted that the preacher's Volvo was parked outside the mayor's office. He crept up to it and jabbed the two front tyres with his hunting knife. *That will keep him there for at least another hour*, he thought.

The rainmaker followed the path of a creekbed now swollen with water. Moon, the coyote, ran before him, a silver shadow darting from bush to bush. Neither of them were frightened of the rushing floodwaters. Water was Jacob's element and he was totally in command of it. But he was not in control of love, and this was what occupied him as he strode through the darkness.

*I can sense her entirely*, he thought, stunned by the clarity of his perception. Encouraged, he tailed the owl who flew in front of the coyote.

The creek joined with the floodwater and led him to the gap in the churchyard wall where the waters had broken through. Jacob stepped into the grounds thanking the rain gods. The coyote followed; finally they were both on the other side of the forbidding wall. For a moment the rainmaker froze, suspicious that it had been too easy. Then, exhilarated by her proximity, he turned and saw a light shining in the bell tower.

The owl flapped her damp wings and swooped up towards the belfry. A second later Miranda stepped forward into the light and Jacob could see her framed in the window. His heart jumped and his mind stretched out, up through the dripping branches to curl its way through the barred windows and across her lips.

*I'm here, my darling, it won't be long now.* His silent reassurance hung like smoke in the rain. Her answer came back, as lyrical as wind chimes, *Be careful, it's too quiet.*

Nervously Jacob glanced around; there was no light on in the house or the church.

The owl landed on Miranda's shoulder. She held out a key; the bird flew back through the rain, towards Jacob. Swooping low it dropped the key at his feet. The rainmaker unrolled his mountaineering equipment, took out a rope and swung it up to hook onto a support fifteen feet up the tower. Slowly he began to make his way up, sinking each foothold into the mortar between the stones. He was halfway when a bullet whizzed past his head.

'Keep climbing and I'll kill you!' The preacher stood at the bottom of the tower, rifle raised. He fired another bullet which grazed Jacob's left shoulder. The next embedded itself into a heel of his heavy climbing boots.

Miranda gasped.

This is it, Jacob thought, preparing to die. At least I will perish pursuing something worthy.

Instead he found himself tumbling through the air to land heavily in the soft mud. He lay there for a moment, stunned, convinced that he had broken at least two limbs.

The preacher strode over and rested the snout of the rifle against his forehead. 'I could kill you now and the Lord would thank me for ridding the world of one more piece of vermin. Now git!' he snarled.

Jacob lifted himself up painfully. He wasn't scared of the preacher and he wasn't frightened of dying. He looked up at Miranda, who shook her head, telling him to go. He touched his heart then his lips, sending the gesture her way.

'You got one minute before I shoot!' The preacher pushed the rifle into Jacob's ribs.

After silently pledging to Miranda that he'd be back, Jacob limped through the iron gate. He'd almost reached the motel to pick up his car when he realised that her key had fallen out of his back pocket.

As soon as Jacob was gone the preacher ran up to the belfry. Miranda was already cowering in the corner.

'Bitch!' The preacher undid his belt. 'You are nothing more than an animal on heat!' His belt whistled through the air and landed with a crack on Miranda's flesh.

*Hit me! You can never touch me now!* she screamed silently. *I am loved, and I will be saved!*

He whipped her over and over until she sank into unconsciousness. Dragging her to the bed, he wrapped a heavy chain around her ankles and wrists.

'I am saving you from the beast. He will soil you and take your soul,' he whispered, weeping as he tied her down. The owl, perched on a rafter above, gave silent witness.

The next morning Jacob lifted the gauze bandage he'd stuck over his wound. He'd been lucky, it was a superficial graze. He leaned over the mirror lying flat on the kitchen table. If the bullet had been any lower he would have been killed.

Outside, a starling swooped down and settled on a cherry tree whose naked branches had suddenly become studded with pink flowers. The bird cocked its head and looked through the window at the unhappy man. Then it began to sing. Soon, other starlings circled the tree.

At the church Preacher Williams was busy mopping the floor. The water had crept in under the door and got halfway up the aisle before he'd rushed in and discovered a small plaster statue of the infant Jesus floating on its back clutching an empty packet of Marlboros. As he pushed the mop he imagined he was prodding the rainmaker's tortured corpse.

A rustling from the bell tower caused the preacher to look up. She must have woken, he thought, and wondered whether he should go up and unchain her. No, let her suffer a little longer, he concluded. A little pain was always educational.

If he had bothered to walk outside and turn to the belfry, he would have seen that his attempts to confine his daughter were, at best, cosmetic. Miranda had managed to loosen the chains so that she could sit up and look out of the window. She gazed over the flooded fields — a patched quilt of brilliant green and blue. But it wasn't the revived land that caught her attention; it was a small dark cloud that appeared to be heading towards the rainmaker's silver trailer. The intense concentration with which she stared at it gave the impression that she herself was directing the flock of starlings as it wheeled and plunged through the sky.

⤫

The rain continued to fall. From his office Chad looked out towards the trailer park. Why was it still raining, he thought bitterly. What else could he do? No woman had been seen entering the trailer for over forty-eight hours nor had the rainmaker left. It was a mystery. There was only one option left: he would have to enlist the support of Cheri, something he'd been avoiding ever since she had tearfully confessed to him that she had been the first to visit the rainmaker. And that now, having achieved the orgasm that had been so elusive throughout their marriage, she wished to file for divorce — a move which would spell political downfall for Chad. Being an elected representative of the people is so damn difficult, he thought, and wondered whether it was too late to revive his football career.

⤫

'I swear by my allegiance to the Wheatgrowers' Wives Association of Oklahoma that I have not had congress with the rainmaker in the past four days, nor will I in the near future. I realise that this is for the greater good of the farming community as well as my marriage. So help me, God.' Her voice barely audible, a stout farmer's wife on the wrong side of fifty finished the pledge. The other women crowded into the health centre burst into encouraging applause. The farmer's wife sat down, adopting a fierce scowl to disguise the fact that she was about to burst into tears.

Cheri Winchester, holding a microphone, strode through the crowd like a TV evangelist on a mission. 'Now I know this is difficult, I know many of us have tasted pleasure like never before, but our livelihoods are at stake! This is an emergency! The rain still falls. There is a Judas amongst us, and it is our responsibility to root her out!'

The women erupted into another round of applause. Endorphins surged through Cheri as the possibility of a shimmering new future began to unfurl in her mind.

'Now who will be next to open her soul?' she continued dramatically.

Rebecca clutched the edge of her seat. Her life before her sexual encounter with the rainmaker had been like a black and white nightmare, arid and repetitive, devoid of joy. Could she return to that? Torn, she swayed, then sprang to her feet, sobbing uncontrollably. 'Take me!' she cried. 'Cleanse my soul!'

The crowd yelled encouragement and Cheri, staring at the elated face of her friend, suddenly realised with absolute clarity what her bright new future was to be: politics. But outside the rain kept falling.

That night Jeremiah stood beside his patrol car, clutching a silver hip flask as he prodded the sodden ground with his boot. There was more water now than mud and he was deeply worried. He looked up at the moon; it was almost full. At this time of year they should be preparing to harvest. He'd thought of arresting Jacob but he was convinced the rainmaker was connected to some new-fangled criminal cartel. 'Probably Islamic terrorists,' Jeremiah muttered to himself and spat on the ground.

He flicked open his pocket watch. It was nearly midnight and, as far as he was concerned, the rainmaker hadn't left his trailer in two days.

Jacob sat on the floor in the centre of the trailer, meditating in the moonlight that filtered through the clouds. He focused on one elusive image: Miranda, free in his arms. His heart was hollow with longing. He hadn't eaten in two days and he knew that if he was to save himself he should really leave town.

The whisky was making Jeremiah drowsy. Tired of the incessant drizzle down the back of his collar, he climbed into the car and turned on the heater. He stared out of the rain-blurred window; the silvery blob of the trailer became smaller and smaller until it disappeared completely as he fell asleep.

A second later the flock of starlings hovered above the trailer. Their shadow fell across Jacob's face. He didn't have to open his eyes to know that he'd been summoned.

Magic is something we often don't recognise until after the event. Perhaps this inherent elusiveness adds to the mystery. The terrible truth is that magic and tragedy are sometimes interchangeable. Jacob Kidderminister was painfully aware of this as he climbed out of the skylight and onto the roof. But, as we all know, foreknowledge is defenceless in the face of love. Surrendering to the inevitable, Jacob opened his arms wide to the sky and allowed the birds to fasten themselves to his arms. A second wave of starlings lifted up his legs and then the flock took flight, carrying the prostrate lover across the fields to the preacher's daughter.

The starlings took him to the top of the tower. As they hovered there Jacob reached out and grabbed the huge bell. For a second he dangled precariously, his arms wrapped around the curved bronze circumference. 'Please, please, don't make a sound,' Jacob prayed, hoping that the metal tongue wouldn't clash against the sides. Miraculously it didn't. Carefully he rocked himself so that the bell tilted towards the floor of the belfry. When it was safe he dropped down. He crouched, waiting.

*I'm here, below you.* Miranda's voice sounded clearly in his head. Jacob ran his hands across the floor, searching. He found what he was looking for — the edge of a trapdoor. He lifted it and there she was. Her hair matted, blood still staining her shoulders and face.

'What has he done to you?' Shocked, Jacob spoke out loud. He jumped down into the room and in an instant she was in his arms, touching his face, his hair, covering him with kisses.

*None of it matters now that you're here*, her mind sang to him, *and we will be free*. Her mouth drank him in, and Jacob realised that it *was* possible to desire with one's heart and soul. So this is love — this blinding feeling of familiarity and, at the same time, of mystery, this sense of coming home, his mind rambled, forgetting that she could think with him.

He pushed open her dress and kissed her scratches. Her breasts were high and round; she pushed them against his chest, longing to experience the sensations he had sent to her through the bodies of other women. He stared down at her, momentarily overwhelmed by the contrast between the delicacy of her body and the violence wrought upon it.

Very gently, as if he were caressing the air itself, Jacob ran his fingers across her skin, reading the quivering nerves beneath. He circled the dark nipples that covered most of her small breasts; she felt like a child beneath his large hands. He cupped her hips, the fragility of her gleaming like ivory. Her pubic hair curled out; a lush thick black bush startling against dusk of her thighs. Carefully he played her until he knew that every millimetre of her thirsted for more. It was only then that he buried his face in her breasts and collapsed for a second, overtaken by an intense sensation of fear and excitement. Projected desire became reality and with it came the crushing intuition that in all beginnings there is inevitably an end, but with her he did not want the moment to finish but, impossibly, to stretch on for ever.

And so, with all the courage of a man who finds himself suddenly free-falling against all the knowledge he has armed himself with, Jacob took her flesh into his mouth. He drank a path down her body in hungry kisses — until he was buried in the very core of her. She tasted like honey, she tasted like the sea he knew as a boy. And the beauty of her would have shamed the most exquisite orchid.

He made love to her with his mouth until she was writhing and then, very gently, he placed himself between her legs and eased himself into her. All the while he held the gaze of those mauve-black eyes, losing himself deep in the colour until he forgot who he was and who she was, and, wrapped in an intimacy he had never experienced before, a profound burden lifted from the top of his head, a writhing knot of fear that unravelled and evaporated above him with each delicious thrust.

Squalls of rain lashed the steeple and the flock of starlings sheltered beneath the bell, silently ruffling their feathers. Outside, under the grey sky, the owl swooped and circled in a wild frenzy of joy.

Jacob's lovemaking grew faster and faster as Miranda gasped in pleasure, until finally, reaching that moment when all perception melts, both were caught in shuddering ecstasy together.

Afterwards she lay in his arms, tracing the tear that ran down one of his cheeks. *Is this what the island will be like?* she asked silently.

Jacob kissed her bruised wrist. 'It will be like this every day and every night. We will spend our days on a small boat winding our way through the Delta, fishing for catfish and crab, and then at night, after we've eaten, we'll lie in front of a fire and I'll hold you in my arms and you'll know that nothing terrible will happen to you ever again.'

Miranda shut her eyes and saw them standing together in front of a wooden house on stilts. Jacob is kissing the side of her face as she squints up at the sun. In her arms is a baby, a light-brown laughing infant.

⌇

Two hours later the sheriff was woken by an ear-splitting peal of thunder. The sky lit up with a display of lightning that made him wonder whether the military base a hundred miles away had exploded. The rain grew heavier. Yet at dawn, everyone in Sandridge was jolted out of their sleep by a sound they hadn't heard in weeks — silence. The rains had stopped. A second later the sun broke through the clouds and the ground began to steam.

People ran out of their houses screaming with joy. Delirious farmers danced in the fields, wildly shooting guns into the sky.

Men kissed their wives and forgave everything. Only one man stayed in the shadows of his house: the preacher.

~~~

Now that the rains had stopped no one took much notice of the silver trailer that stayed parked at the edge of town. Everyone was too busy fixing fences, reviving their crops and fattening their livestock. Everyone except Rebecca.

Following her pledge, she locked herself in her bedroom and cried straight through three boxes of tissues and three showings of *Sleepless In Seattle*. Afterwards, after drinking another miniature bottle of vodka, she went down to the cultural centre, logged on to the internet and entered a chatroom entitled 'Hot spinsters over forty'.

Walking home, heartened by a very lively conversation with Mr Big of Massachusetts, she noticed Moon the coyote waiting patiently on the doorstep of the trailer, looking starved and bedraggled. Rebecca suddenly realised that the rainmaker hadn't been seen for over a week. She approached the canine, murmuring tender words of encouragement. The bitch lifted her head and looked at her with liquid eyes that spoke of terrible loss.

Rebecca surprised herself by picking up the starving creature. With the beast cradled firmly in her arms, she headed towards the sheriff's office.

At the same time Abigail Etterton was watching a small flock of starlings hovering over an indiscriminate patch of flooded ground. It wasn't the birds themselves that disturbed her so much — after all, the rain had brought up thousands of worms — it was the fact that the night before she had seen a gathering of nightingales suspended over that same patch of ground. And nightingales, as all good countrywomen know, are solitary birds. What was it about that particular part of the field, she wondered.

Just then she noticed a figure dressed in a long black robe picking its way across the pasture. As it drew closer she realised it was the preacher. Not seeing her, he stopped just short of the birds and, with a shocking guttural cry, began to fling stones at them. Very unChristian behaviour, Abigail thought, wondering about the sanity of the minister.

She was about to call out when she heard one of the farm hands shouting her name — her favourite mare was foaling. Abigail wiped her hands and ran towards the stables, forgetting all about the birds and the preacher.

☞

The search party drove down every dirt trail and poked into bushes; they peered into the shimmering dam and contemplated dredging it. They combed through the waving fields of wheat and ransacked barns ... until the sheriff called the search off. The rainmaker was missing, but not before he'd done his job and, besides, it wasn't as if he was a local, Jeremiah rationalised. One week was a respectable time to spend looking for a stranger, especially one who had gone out of his way to seduce all the womenfolk in town.

The sheriff had his deputy pin up notices declaring that Jacob Kidderminister had left voluntarily due to family circumstances and in the rush had left behind his trailer and his possessions. No one questioned the law enforcer's assessment.

The water receded; Rebecca adopted the coyote; the Kaufmann brothers towed away the silver trailer to sell for recycled aluminium; and life went on.

The preacher resumed his sermons and gradually his congregation trickled back. But Bill Williams appeared a destroyed man. The stoop was more pronounced, the thin lips were curled in a permanent sneer of disapproval. But what was most noticeable was that the old fire and passion had completely disappeared from his preaching. During one sermon, delivered in a barely audible whisper, he fell into loud sobbing. Embarrassed, the organist petered into discordance and the congregation began to snigger.

The subject was raised at the knitting circle. The postmistress (who had flown into Dallas for a face-lift since the incident of the rainmaker) put down her needles. 'I say he is losing his wind,' she declared defiantly.

The other women rattled their knitting needles in agreement.

The mayor's mother spoke up. 'Why don't we swap him for a young sexy one? You know, one of them that talks in tongues. You never know, he could turn out to be a useful contributor to the mental health of the women of this town, just like the rainmaker!'

The room dissolved into giggles.

~≈~

The rivers became streams again, frogs returned to the wetlands and the wheat rippled fatly under the hot sun. Life was bursting with fecundity. Bill Williams recovered and slowly the fervour began to creep back into the Sunday sessions at the small church — with one difference: he never mentioned race again.

All returned to normalcy. Except the townsfolk seemed to take more joy in their everyday tasks, as if the drought and the floods had given them a greater understanding of the vulnerability of life.

And so it was that the mayor and his mistress again found themselves in Abigail's back paddock, with Abigail's face buried between Chad's legs. The mayor, having just reached orgasm, pulled her up and gazed into her eyes. He had never felt more emotional. Divorce proceedings were underway and Cheri had already begun her campaign trail to run against him in the next council elections. All of which Chad was treating with supreme equanimity. He was in love and had reached a momentous decision. He was going to ask Abigail to marry him.

He'd barely got the words out when she emitted a loud scream.

'Hey, I didn't expect that kind of reaction,' he muttered, crestfallen, but then noticed that Abigail was pointing to something in the field. He turned and gagged on a wave of nausea.

Beneath a tree in which a flock of starlings were roosting, sticking up out of the mud were two human hands entwined. One, fragile and dark, was obviously female. The other was large and white. Twinkling on its index finger was a large sapphire ring, which Chad instantly recognised.

They lay tied to a rusting brass bed, his muscular body curled around her darkly luminous flesh. It was a posture of infinite tenderness, a petrification of the moment when two people collapse into each other in love. The dead couple, miraculously preserved, were raised out of the earth like a glorious classical statue suspended in its own time bubble. The stunned onlookers removed their hats in respect, lowered their eyes in hushed shame. The silence was broken by a lone nightingale that perched itself on the bed frame and burst into song.

Jeremiah, in an attempt to hide his clenching heart, adopted an air of professional detachment. He pointed to a single bullet wound visible in Jacob's back. 'I would say that one bullet was responsible for both the deaths, having passed through the male's body and into the female.'

He paused, visibly shaken by the clouded gaze of the dead girl who, despite her black skin, looked vaguely familiar.

'Who is she, by the way? Anyone here know?' He turned to the small group of farm hands and officials who had helped drag the bed from beneath the mud.

The youngest Kaufmann brother, the shyest, spoke up. 'I don't know who she is, but she's got the very same birthmark as the preacher on her hand. Why, I've seen that mark a thousand times!'

The men all leaned forward to look. There it was, as clear as day, a star-shaped wine-coloured mark.

By the time the sheriff and the mayor reached the church, word of the double murder had spread across town like a virus. The officials pushed open the iron gate with some dread. Jeremiah hated homicide cases. Luckily he hadn't had to deal with many, but they were enough to scar a man's soul for life.

By the time they reached the door of the church the two men sensed something was amiss. The door was wide open, the altar smashed, the plaster hands of the Lord Jesus had been hacked off.

As Jeremiah bent down to pick up one of the miniature hands, a creak came from the belfry above them.

~≈~

The preacher's body hung from a rafter beside the huge brass bell, suspended by a metal chain. The body slowly swung around and the darkened, swollen face came into view. It was ravaged, pecked to pieces. On the floor below lay a single owl's feather.

# Echo

The tramp stank of piss and some unmentionable human filth Gavin couldn't even bear to imagine. His leathery face loomed out at the property developer from under the canopy of snaking vines that still clung to the decaying wooden verandah.

'Forest come un twisty up your soul, you have nothing, boyo, seep into yer DNA then zap! Dead meat scum.'

He spat what looked like the last of his teeth at the property developer's feet. Gavin, a big-boned man, who moved with the lolling grace of an individual who knew his own strength, was not a sentimentalist. He was also convinced that everyone was responsible for their own destiny and that poverty was quite likely contagious. He stepped back and regarded the squat, ragged figure with open disgust.

'Get the fuck off my site before I arrange for the Salvos to come and pick up a corpse, comprende, you psycho schizo? I'll give you the grace of ten minutes to fuck off, starting from ...' Gavin pulled up the sleeve of his Zegnitti suit, chosen especially because it was woven entirely out of synthetic fibres, and studied his Gucci watch, 'now.'

The old man clutched a battered leather medicine bag to his chest. His matted locks crawled with lice; his eyes, kaleidoscopes of crazed delirium, fixed unerringly on Gavin. He lunged forward and tugged at his suit, his stench washing over the developer in a nauseating miasma.

'I know. Forest talk through concrete. Forest crack roots into your skull. Believe. You must.'

Gavin's patience snapped. Pulling his sleeve away, he grabbed the collar of the tramp's filthy coat and hauled him to the edge of the vacant lot. The vagrant's legs, blue-veined sticks, knocked against the broken bricks that were scattered over the thick undergrowth, but he still clutched the medicine bag to his chest.

The property developer reached the gate, kicked it open and dropped the itinerant. He fell heavily, rolling to rest in the gutter.

'You cursed. You no longer living. Flitter, flitter,' the old man muttered, blood mixed in with the spittle flying from his mouth, his skinny arms held above him as though he was expecting to be kicked.

His leather bag had split open to reveal ten green cuttings inside. Incongruously their roots were all neatly bagged like scientific specimens. Thinking they might be marijuana, Gavin leaned down. At closer inspection the plants looked odd, like primitive facsimiles of plants he would normally recognise. Great — a fucking environmentalist, he thought, some old hippie who's lost his marbles.

'Catch you here again,' he said, jabbing his finger in the tramps face, 'and my boys will have your balls.'

With that he slammed the gate. By the time he reached the wooden shed he'd had erected that very morning — a sentry box for his site manager — Gavin had managed to forget the encounter. At least, he thought he had.

At forty-three Gavin Tetherhook was an impressive individual, both materially and physically. A staunch atheist, he prided himself on being self-made. He had grown up with his younger brother, Robert, on a sugar cane farm in northern Queensland and defiantly called himself a country boy. The Tetherhooks had been sugar cane farmers for five generations, until the 1970s when the sudden influx of cheap American sugar sent his father broke in less than two seasons. Devastated, his father had gone out into the cane field, strung his clothes over the unfurling tender-green leaves to make a tent, then sat, stark naked beneath it, weeping into the furrowed dirt. His two sons had found him six hours later, his exposed feet burned raw from the midday sun. The farmer had never recovered mentally, leaving Gavin's mother to sell up and rescue what she could after the bank had been through.

The family was forced to moved to a cheap boarding house on the outskirts of Tully, a frontier town famous for being one of the world's top locations for UFO spottings and for its marijuana crops — two facts not entirely unrelated.

After months of complete silence Gavin's father eventually secured a job as a coach driver while his mother turned to religion for solace. The stoic fifteen year old, determined to haul himself out of the never-ending cycle of poverty and resignation, apprenticed himself to a builder of dubious reputation involved in the first local real-estate boom. Meanwhile his thirteen-year-old brother Robert began increasingly to depend on Gavin for the guidance his father was now utterly incapable of. It was a role Gavin relished and soon the two boys were inseparable.

Gavin's first job was to assist in the harassment of long-term residents who were reluctant to move, harassment that involved dog turds through letter boxes, mysterious fires and the odd knee-capping. It was terrorism that got results. By the age of twenty, the last vestiges of morality erased from his personality, the entrepreneurial youth had purchased his first house. He bought his second at twenty-two — a shack which he demolished to create a parking lot. A year later he broke with the builder and set up his own property development company; six months after that he bought out his employer.

Yep, Mr GP Tetherhook Esquire was an impressive man. So Gavin reminded himself as he adjusted his balls then zipped up in the men's toilets at the Brisbane RSL Club after lunch, the day he had evicted the tramp. If it wasn't for the divorce, he thought, tucking a thick grey lock behind one ear, if it hadn't been for that fucking little bitch upsetting his wife, he'd have a perfect record financially *and* emotionally.

Cathy. He still couldn't say her name without a ripple in his stomach walls which he vaguely understood to be grief. Cathy, his wife, mother of his three children: Aden, twelve; Irene, nine; and Jonathan, four. Their names were imprinted on him like an epitaph.

After checking behind him for witnesses, Gavin leaned against the wall of the urinal, momentarily overwhelmed by the sense of failure his divorce evoked. The marriage had been part of the plan, part of the vision he had of himself at fifty: wealthy and retired, with his groomed blonde wife glistening beside him for ever. Gold Coast mansion, private yacht, sons he could take fishing. Now that fantasy had evaporated overnight. Bugger them. Bugger them all.

Gavin steadied himself then stood up straight: six foot four inches of fairly well-maintained male flesh. He hadn't gone to pieces; he hadn't suddenly developed cancer like his mate Wayne did after his separation. No, he was okay, he still looked good. So maybe he was drinking a little too much, and fuck knows he was over the promiscuity, however exciting it'd been at the beginning. Now it was just the money, the golden scaffolding, that kept him upright, that kept him *hard*.

Whistling defiantly he rinsed his hands and stepped out of the bathroom, leaving the door swinging.

The structure was going to be a ten-storey block of service flats — chic units to maximise the constant stream of businessmen and tourists that passed through Brisbane. Gavin had waited until the dip in the housing market then bought the heritage bungalow in Fortitude Valley before auction after checking he could cash in a few favours with the local member to fast-track a planning permit.

It was a formula that had worked over and over and, as Gavin leaned against the iron scaffolding and gazed across the Brisbane River from the fifth floor, he felt a familiar roar of adrenaline, almost akin to a sexual rush, sweep through his body.

Maybe it was a reaction to the devastation the natural world had inflicted upon his father, combined with a hatred of the oppression and tyranny of a farmer's life as he battled the unmanageable — the weather, the seasons, the lack of rainfall. Whatever the cause, the idea that he had conquered nature in a way his father had never even imagined thrilled Gavin profoundly.

This obsession against nature manifested in a variety of ways. First there was his choice to wear only synthetic fibres. Gavin went to extraordinary lengths to purchase the latest fashions in fabrics that incorporated nylon, polyester or artificial silks. The property developer loved the scratchy sensation of polyester against his skin, the way his nylon sheets caught at his toenails, the unnatural way his body heated up under them. Then there was his tenacity in annihilating all vegetation on his construction sites before they began building. He was notorious for it, and fiercely proud of the fact that he was the prime target of the local environmental movement. Finally, his abhorrence of nature and his desire to control it translated to his sexual aesthetic. In the early days of their marriage he had demanded that Cathy removed most of her body hair. He loved combing the neat pubic triangle of fine blonde hair once his wife's long-suffering beautician had imposed some order onto Cathy's otherwise unruly bush.

Lately, since the divorce, he'd found himself going further, demanding that his young mistress rid herself entirely of body hair. The imposition of hegemony upon her body gave him the illusion of order — something he craved increasingly since his departure from the family home and routine.

Not that Gavin Tetherhook was going to admit that to himself, let alone anyone else. He pulled his mind back to the present: prime real estate at prime prices. The slogan was pounding out a rhythm in his mind — *Prime real ...* — when suddenly the scaffolding collapsed and the ground rushed up to meet his falling body.

'You were lucky, mate,' his site manager told him as he hauled him to his feet. 'Thirty-foot drop and you land on a pile of sand. Broke yer fall real nice, eh?'

Dazed, Gavin blinked into the sun then brushed the sand from his trousers. 'I think I might have blacked out for a second or two,' he replied slowly, squinting as the blurred landscape pulled into focus.

The property developer ran his hands across his body feeling for pain. The knees seemed all right, his back ached slightly around the shoulders where he must have landed, and there were two large bruises already beginning to form on his forearms, but apart from that everything seemed normal.

'Want a lift to the hospital? They could run a few checks.'

Remembering that he'd failed to insure the site for work-related accidents, Gavin shook his head. 'Nah, I'll be right. Now what were those alterations you wanted me to look at?'

⤸

Later that night, in the sterile comfort of the brand new apartment — part of an investment block called Bridgeport he was about to launch onto the market — a refuge since Cathy had thrown him out two months ago after discovering he was having an affair — Gavin stripped off his clothes and stood heavily naked in front of the full-length mirror in the bedroom. Raising his arms above his head he rotated slowly looking for further injuries. Nothing; just the familiar triangle of chest hair that curled thickly up from his belly, fanning into two grey wings that encircled his nipples, and the comforting weight of his cock resting against his thigh. He sucked in his stomach and glanced critically in the mirror. There was no doubt he was a good-looking man, a man who could still turn heads, a *masculine* man.

In acknowledgment of his approving eye his penis began to harden. Life force — nothing to be ashamed of, Gavin thought. But he couldn't help remembering Cathy's face in the throes of orgasm, an image from the golden days of their marriage — his hands tracing the line of fine blond hair that ran from belly button to pubis; the sound of her laughter — girlish, not yet tainted with cynicism.

Recently he'd suffered a deluge of such memories, as if time had decided to play a cruel trick on him, bending back on itself like a lewd female contortionist. In reality he and Cathy had slipped into an antagonistic celibacy after the birth of their third child.

Gavin had loved his wife, still loved her, but the insidious loneliness had stifled him as she turned away from him night after night. She made him feel fallible. Human. Male. A sperm bag. In his darkest moments he hated himself for his weaknesses.

'You never know what you've got until you've lost it,' he reminded himself. Then, determined not to free-fall into depression — something that seemed to happen increasingly lately — he grabbed a dressing gown and headed into the bathroom.

It was a magnificent triangular room set into the corner of the apartment. Gavin had hired one of Queensland's top interior

98

designers to do the fittings and it was resplendent with spa, bidet and sunken bath. Sinking into the steamy bathwater the property developer tried to remember what the theme was meant to be. The curved golden taps reminded him of exotic belly dancers. Then there were the Arabic tiles whose mosaic patterns covered the bathroom floor. Harem, that's right — a bathroom fit for a sultan. A strange choice he had thought at the time, recalling the immaculately groomed homosexual interior designer who had proposed it. But Gavin had approved it anyway and the outcome stank of luxury, a perfect foil to the rest of the apartment which echoed the pristine transitory world executives liked.

He stared out of the ceiling-to-floor windows. From this height he really was the king of the castle. The apartment was on the thirtieth floor and looked over the whole panorama of downtown Brisbane. Gavin had deliberately left the steel vertical blinds open. The idea that he might be visible to any office worker working back late in the building opposite excited him.

His hand crept down his thigh and wrapped itself firmly around his cock. Three strokes later and he was in the middle of an orgy featuring two of his personal assistants and a very cute schoolgirl he'd spotted at a bus stop several days earlier. Groaning, he settled further into the warm water and submerged his ears, allowing the aquamarine roar of the water to blank out all other sound. The landscape he chose for his fantasy was the empty floor of a parking lot, with his Merc, a toy he'd bought for himself for his forty-fourth birthday, parked in its centre.

Gavin liked hard surfaces. To reach orgasm he had to be in an environment where everything that encompassed him was man-made. The three objects of his fantasy lay draped across his Merc like unwrapped Christmas presents. The two women — one a slim blonde in her mid-twenties, the other a buxom brunette in her late thirties — held the tall curvy schoolgirl between them, spreading her thighs wide. The women's breasts and shaved genitals had been sprayed with a kind of edible PVC — a recurring motif in Gavin's fantasies. Gavin, dressed in his tightest, most expensive suit, strode up to the Merc and buried his head between the struggling young girl's legs, breathing in the pungent smell of pussy and rubber. Nibbling, he began to tear off tiny strips of the PVC with his teeth. The image of his mistress's glistening child-like slot crowned with the pink bud of its clitoris appeared at the corner of his fantasy like a floating mirage. Feeling guilty about avoiding her phone calls, Gavin consciously dismissed the vision and the hovering vagina vanished instantly. He pulled the last rubber strip from the girl's genitals and began tonguing her. Above him the other two women were sucking the PVC from each other's breasts. The moaning grew louder and the schoolgirl pulled him up to her flushed young face. Smiling mysteriously she turned and magically straddled the bonnet of his car, her arse spread high and wide. In a flash he was upon her, his fingers sinking into her creamy flesh. The next second he found himself thrown across the soft fake-leather driver's seat. It reclined the full one hundred and eighty degrees as one girl sat on his face while another straddled him and he caressed the third with his fingers. His breath grew faster, the quivering of climax building up behind his balls and eyes.

Suddenly the grotesque face of the tramp leered over one girl's shoulders. Feeling himself instantly wilt Gavin tried to will away the hovering image. The man gestured lewdly and his blackened hairy face faded. Again the property developer was in the grip of his orgy. The encircling tight movements of his hand quickened as nipples, long and hard, brushed tantalisingly across his lips and the smell of hot rubber, faint diesel fuel, the way the schoolgirl's full arse had splayed over the Merc's hard metallic bonnet all culminated into a quickening montage that finally sent his seed spurting.

Gavin sat up and opened his eyes. His sperm was a creamy ink blot etching its way through the water like white coral. He watched, fascinated — as he had been all his life — by his own emission. Is this where we begin and end, he wondered, in a shivering moment of forgetting. Such thoughts were the nearest he ever got to introspection.

Sighing, he let the last remnants of tension lift from his weary body, then lathered himself down with a loofah, and stepped out of the bath.

In the building opposite, a watching office cleaner reached her own climax with a sudden squeak. Then, as the yawning silence refilled with the buzzing of fluorescent lights and the distant ringing of a fax machine, she pulled down her drab wool skirt and, sighing wistfully, lifted the industrial vacuum cleaner to continue her cleaning.

Leaving a series of damp footprints on the tiled floor, Gavin sat heavily on the toilet and allowed his penis to fall between his legs. After relaxing, he managed to urinate. As his water tinkled down he gazed across the tiles. It was then that he noticed the footprints.

At first he thought there must be some error, some optical illusion. For instead of the unmistakeable outline of a man's foot, he saw something else. Something that, as he stared closer, terrified him more and more.

The footprints were not that of a man. Bigger than his own foot they appeared to belong to a creature whose three elongated toes extended into long sharp claws. The heel had disappeared altogether, in its place the third toe. Every footprint was identical.

Dizzy, Gavin sat back on the toilet seat. He wondered whether he hadn't been concussed by the fall after all. He closed his eyes, waited for a moment, then slowly opened them. The footprints, although rapidly evaporating, remained the same — undeniable glistening evidence that sickened him with its *wrongness*, its perversity.

Deciding that the best course was to assume the prints were simply a trick of misplaced body weight and water helped by the strange shadow thrown by the line of pretentious lights fitted at floor height, Gavin reached for the medicine cabinet. He swallowed some sleeping pills and headed for bed.

～

*Flitter, flitter*. The beating of enormous feathery wings filled his mind and he sensed the shifting of the air around him by their massive sweep; not birds' wings but something finer — insects' wings. Welcoming the drowsiness of the drug as it slithered through his veins Gavin pushed himself further down into the mattress, aching for oblivion. The noise grew louder. His internal vision blinked into life. He was looking down the length of his own naked body but the angle was wrong. It was as if his neck was two foot long and floating twelve inches above his torso. Pinned there, unable to jerk his way out of the nightmare, he was chilled to the bone.

Suddenly his body hair began to grow, new tufts sprouting on his belly, the skin of his hips, the underside of his elbows. The growth accelerated, and thick black hair massed in dark patches, covering his body like a colony of frenetic ants. He watched horrified, paralysed, as the spiralling hair just as rapidly thinned to fine white tendrils that snaked across his flesh, tips wavering blindly like a speeded-up time-lapse film of plant roots growing. *That's what they are, roots.* With the thought barely formed Gavin realised that the 'roots' had all curled downwards over the sides of his body and were burrowing into what appeared to be the spongy bed of a marsh.

He woke with a nauseating jolt, opened his mouth to breathe and realised that he was choking. His mouth was full of a mushy pulp, full to the back of his throat. Gasping he opened his lips as wide as they could go and reached in. He pulled out a leaf and then another and another. Each unfurled as he dropped it onto the doona cover.

He stared at them then picked one up. Holding it up to the morning sun he saw that it was like no other leaf he had ever seen. Long and thin, like a fern frond, with delicate seed pods or fruit that resembled tiny cones hanging from the end. A fruit-bearing leaf? It didn't make sense. Convulsing, he coughed up the last leaf, which flew across the bed and stuck like a lump of green chewing gum to the shade of his bedside lamp. The light stuttered and in a moment he was waking again, this time really waking, curled around a pillow, his eyes gummy and his mouth malodorous. Something about the awaiting day hung over him ominously.

Swinging his legs over the edge of the bed, he held his aching head in his hands and tried to remember. Ah, that's right. Cathy, her lawyer, the mediation. That explained the nightmare —

some unconscious fear of being buried? Kids' stuff. Trust him to be so literal.

A sharp stinging on his back broke his chain of thought. He turned to the mirror — across his shoulders ran three long scratches. Seeping slightly they resembled claw-marks. An image of the footprints from the night before glistened suddenly before him. Panicking he pulled back the sheets to see whether something had scratched him during the night. There was nothing; just the polyester sheet, innocently wrinkled. Slightly cheered Gavin tried smiling but found that his mouth was too gummy. Disgusted with his ageing body he stood and threw the curtains open.

⁂

'My client would like to point out that her self-esteem has been seriously undermined by her husband's actions and, since the onset of his affair, she has required psychiatric help at great expense.'

Cathy's lawyer, a woman in her early thirties with sensible spectacles and a profile you could cut glass with, reached over and squeezed Cathy's hand maternally. Maybe not quite maternally, Gavin noted, wondering whether the lawyer wasn't in fact a lesbian. Cathy, resplendent and silent in a beige Versace suit and D&G sunglasses she had neglected to remove at the onset of the meeting, rewarded her solicitor with a very slight smile. Cold bitch, Gavin thought, then was dismayed to realise that he still found his estranged wife desirable.

'Well, my client would like to point out that if his wife had sought psychiatric help before the marriage began to deteriorate we might not be sitting here now.'

'That is irrelevant.'

'I don't think that withholding sex for four years is irrelevant if we are talking about self-esteem. My client is a normal full-blooded male —'

'If he'd needed to have sex he might have chosen to have it with an individual who was not a close associate of Mrs Tetherhook!'

103

'The young woman in question was Mrs Tetherhook's Pilates teacher not a close associate.'

Frustrated, Gavin leaned forward and slammed his Schaeffer pen onto the walnut veneer. 'Look! This is not a fucking dick-pulling competition, let's cut to the chase.'

He swung around to Cathy who remained icily impervious.

'What is it that you want? And no fucking bullshit — I'm footing the bills of both these morons.' He paused, fighting the desire to rip his wife's sunglasses from her face.

They all waited: Gavin, his lawyer, his wife's lawyer. Barricaded behind her shades which glinted like the sectioned eyes of a huge blowfly, Cathy remained silent. Then, her half-inch long pale pink nails barely touching the paper, she pushed a folder across to her lawyer who flicked it open with a frightening efficiency.

'My client wants half your assets, full custody of all three children, a guarantee that you will cover all school and college fees as needed, plus full expenses of any holidays. You will be allowed weekend access to the children — that is, Sundays. Finally, she wants her name exclusively on the Bridgeport development.'

'But I only used her name for tax purposes!'

'As I understand she is currently part-owner. Now she wishes to be complete owner.'

'Never!'

'In that case we have no choice but to proceed to court. However, my client wishes to point out that it could be detrimental to both your finances to undergo an independent government assessment of your assets.'

'You fucking bitch!' Gavin lunged forward only to be pushed back by his lawyer, an otherwise jovial man in his late fifties.

Cathy removed her sunglasses for the first time. She stared at Gavin, her eyes devoid of emotion. 'I don't think you understand. I am genuinely inspired by the development of Bridgeport; I have been from the very beginning. It means as much to me as I know it means to you.'

She smiled slightly and Gavin found himself wondering whether there wasn't a sadistic streak buried deep within the woman he'd thought he knew. He got up heavily and walked over to the window. Bridgeport. The rounded wall of the tall building glittered in the afternoon sun. It had been a vanity project, the one investment Gavin knew wasn't going to make him money. Instead it was a bid to immortalise him in the history of Queensland landmarks.

It was a piece of architecture that appeared to defy the laws of physics. A triangular wedge with an adjoining curved wall; a lyrical sculpture that soared up into the humid Brisbane sky, gloriously contemptuous of the predictable rectangular buildings surrounding it.

It was the curved wall, a magnificent wave of reflective glass, that really gave the building its distinctive edge. The initial stages had begun before September 2001 and Gavin had managed to hold on to the project despite the deluge of global disasters that had followed the World Trade Center attack, from the stock market crash through to SARS. There was no way he was going to hand it over to his ex-wife now. Bridgeport was his passport to legitimacy, his homage to Brisvegas.

Standing there Gavin became aware of a faint vibration beneath his feet. For a second he wondered whether there was actually a train going under the building but then the tremor grew to a palpable quiver. The others appeared indifferent: Cathy and her lawyer were in the middle of a whispered conference, while his own solicitor was hunched over a file, his bulbous nose and weathered face puckered in disapproval. They hadn't noticed anything; could it just be him?

Panicked, Gavin looked back outside. Everything appeared normal, the glittering façade of Bridgeport reflecting back nothing but the calm blue of the sky.

Still the feeling grew that something was terribly wrong. It seemed to Gavin as if the light itself was glaring back at him in defiance. Simultaneously he became aware of a loud rustling, as if an invisible wind had entered the room. Gavin steadied himself against the window ledge, praying that the others would not notice the colossal wave of internal panic that had him pinned.

The rustling, like rats scratching at a thin wall, got louder, assaulting one side of his brain then lunging to the other. Gavin's knuckles whitened as he clutched at the window ledge. The sound accelerated to the amplified cacophony of a thousand leaves rattling in a hurricane. Suddenly a massive gush knocked him to the carpet.

'Nothing but an excess of ear wax.'

His doctor folded up the ear stethoscope and leaned back in his swivel chair giving Gavin a quizzical look. 'Everything else seems normal — blood pressure, heart rate, lungs.'

Gavin stared mournfully at the whitened band of flesh where his wedding ring used to sit. This was what he had been fearing: a verdict of physical normality.

'Given the traumatic nature of recent events in your life ...' the doctor ventured.

'Give me a break, doc. I've been through way worse than divorce in my time.'

Ignoring him, the doctor doggedly continued. 'I wouldn't rule out the possibility of a panic attack.'

'A panic attack?! But I wasn't even panicking. It was the sound, that awful loud rustling; I felt like a moth caught up in a wind tunnel ...'

'Look, I haven't entirely ruled out a physical cause. I've written a referral for a CAT scan — just in case — and here's the number of a good friend of mine, a psychologist who specialises in both divorce counselling and panic attacks. One often heralds the onset of the other.'

The depressed property developer tried to distract himself by counting the number of houses he'd bought and sold as the sleek car purred its way through the streets. Panic attack. It made him sound like a real mental case — Jesus, he'd be the laughing stock of the company if it got out to his employees. He'd managed to convinced Cathy and her battle-axe lawyer that it was an inner ear infection. Last thing he wanted was them claiming he wasn't mentally fit to have even weekend access to his children.

The opening bars of Beethoven's Fifth interrupted his train of thought. He picked up his mobile and checked the incoming call. It was Amanda, his twenty-three-year-old mistress. He switched the phone off. That was the third time she had tried to reach him that day. In all truth, Gavin had never felt this unsexual in his entire adult life. It wasn't just the divorce — although the unexpected sensation of loss had caused part of him to retreat — it was also the fact that open access to Amanda was, to his surprise, a big turn-off. She was far more alluring as a clandestine liaison. As soon as he'd been thrown out of the family house and moved into his own flat she had transformed from the mysterious creature whose perfect youth and flattering receptivity had originally captivated him into a needy harridan whose insecurities seemed to multiply by the day.

Besides, the last time they'd been together he'd failed to get an erection — a fact that had secretly festered inside him ever since. It was natural to feel vulnerable given the circumstances, Gavin reminded himself, trying to remember if he'd ever felt this way before. Maybe once: the day his father sat the family down and announced that he had lost the farm. The burly farmer had actually broken down in tears. The sight had so shocked his two sons that later they made a pledge with one another never to weep publicly themselves.

The Merc screeched around the corner and up the ramp into Bridgeport. As soon as the car entered the artificial greenish light of the car park Gavin felt better, as if he was sheltered within a great concrete womb of his own making. It was only on the way to the elevator that he remembered the car park had been the scene of his erotic fantasy two days before. Perhaps there was some potency left in him yet. Cheered, he entered the elevator whistling.

~

He decided to double his dose of sleeping pills. After an accompanying glass of whisky, he left a message on Amanda's land line telling her he couldn't see her for a couple of weeks.

Afterwards he slept like a baby, floating in perfect drug-enhanced dreamless slumber.

In the morning he woke groggy but invigorated. He leapt out of bed and even managed a few of the yoga stretches Amanda had taught him to ward off backache. He was in the child's pose in front of the full-length mirror, staring in admiration at his firm buttocks and long muscular thighs, the comforting weight of his testicles resting against his heels, when he noticed the strange dust. The sole of each foot was covered in a greenish powder, as if he'd been standing in a dried-up river bed. Where had it come from? He'd only just taken off his perfectly clean nylon socks.

Sitting up he examined himself. Trapped under his toenails was more of the mysterious dirt and also under his manicured fingernails. He shuddered, repulsed. It looked like algae. Thinking back he tried to work out where he might have picked up the dust during the day. Nowhere. The itchy feeling of being unclean made his stomach lurch.

He ran to the shower and scrubbed himself until his skin was wrinkly and bright red. Standing under the high-speed shower nozzle he let its luxurious pounding wash all misgivings from his mind. Nothing had meaning, just this, the immediacy of physical pleasure. He was okay. He wasn't just going to survive; he was determined to flourish.

His pager went off in the other room. Gavin stepped out of the shower and, still wet, walked into the bedroom. A trail of shiny footprints followed him, each one a clear outline of an alien claw with three toes.

～

'She's a beauty but she's a bugger to drive. It's all this semi-computerised bullshit, you have to be a fucking genius to operate some of the equipment nowadays.'

Gavin's main project manager, a Pacific Islander named Murray but nicknamed Shortstuff due to the fact that at five foot four he was the shortest Islander anyone had even seen, gestured to the mammoth crane. The name *Stella* was painted in scarlet calligraphy on the side of the operating cabin.

They were on Gavin's third building site — a considerable tract of land that was to be a new housing development west of the Brisbane hills. They'd already cleared the site, despite some local protest over what had been described as an endangered wetland. 'The Kellen wetlands? Give me a fucking break — a bloody swamp more like,' Gavin had scoffed before giving the order for several tonnes of sand to be dropped on the area before they levelled the ground.

Relishing the memory, Gavin stood in a hard hat and shades looking up at the crane that arched into the blue like a beautiful giant steel praying mantis.

'Let me have a go.'

'Boss, I don't think that's a good idea. You know what the men are like about the boss — you've got to be superhuman, eh? Can't have that illusion shattered.'

'I'll be right. I've got my operator's licence and the model I used to operate is only a couple of generations before this one. The basics have got to be the same.'

Ignoring Shortstuff's warning he hoisted himself up into the cabin. 'Mind if I ride the bitch for a couple of minutes?' he asked the operator, who was leaning across the controls a cigarette stuck precariously to his lower lip.

The operator threw his cigarette away, grinned shyly, then swapped seats with him. Gavin's hands hovered over the miniature thicket of gear sticks and brakes almost as if he was saying grace. A giddy excitement overtook him. He glanced out of the window — they were a long way up. He'd forgotten the exhilarating feeling of being the nerve centre of this massive machine that could destroy as well as create. He reached for one of the handles.

'Wrong one, boss. Try this to get her moving.' The operator shifted a lever and the crane began to slowly shift, the enormous tread rolling forward over the compacted earth.

'I know what I'm doing,' Gavin hissed, determined not to lose face. He reached for one of the control sticks and the arm lifted, the over-sized trowel swinging up from the ground. 'I used to operate one like this about fifteen years ago. Jeez, it was a buzz,' he shouted over the roaring engine. The operator grinned, a gold tooth flashing at the edge of his mouth, but fearing more reprisals stayed silent.

The crane moved out towards an open area of the site. There was a lone tree marring the skyline. Pushed over at an angle, it clung to the earth in mute protest. Gavin aimed the crane straight for it. 'Let's get rid of this fucker!'

He pushed down the accelerator and the crane lurched forward, squashing bushes and gliding effortlessly over lumps of buried debris.

Just before they reached the tree Gavin went to lift his hand but found that it was glued to the gear stick. Mystified, he struggled, his right hand clamped around the accelerator. The crane was picking up speed; the herculean arm swinging dangerously from side to side threatened to topple it.

'I can't move my hand!' Gavin screamed. He pulled with all his might but the hand remained stuck, as if the palm had somehow fused with the machine.

The horizon jolted with the motion of the rolling tread, sky and ground threatening to collide with each new lurch. The operator, clutching at the side of the swaying cabin, stretched across and with an almighty shove managed to push Gavin's hand off the accelerator. Reaching for the brake he pulled the crane to a slow rumbling halt against a slope. It groaned then leaned at a forty-five-degree angle.

There was a violent stillness. Outside a flock of cockatoos flew up squawking with indignation. The two men, pinned by their seatbelts, contemplated the burnt-red diagonal of the earth. Gavin lifted his hand. In the centre of his palm, branded into the skin, was the neat outline of a leaf — a simple fern-like frond ending with the delicate outline of a seed pod. Shaking visibly the property developer held out his arm.

'Do you see that? Do you see it?' he asked the operator whose olive skin was still blanched with shock. He looked down at the hand blankly then back up at Gavin, his features settling into a rigid caution.

'No, boss, I see nothing.'

'What do you mean? Can't you see that ... that mark?'

'Boss, I'm telling you, there's nothing there.'

Gavin looked back at his palm. The brand was entirely visible to him; he ran his fingers across it — unmistakeable; a lifted ridge rough to the touch. He thrust his hand back under the operator's nose. 'Feel it.'

'Feel what, boss?'

The operator glanced anxiously across the site. In the distance he could see other workers running towards the crane. He wondered whether he should try to placate his employer in case he'd become suddenly mentally unstable.

'Just feel it. I have to know.' Gavin's voice was choked.

Tentatively the crane operator reached out and, fearing there might be hidden homosexual tendencies in the burly man sitting next to him, very lightly touched his palm.

'Feels totally normal to me. Maybe you just froze — you know, nerves. Happens to a lot of blokes when they haven't driven for a long time. It's only natural,' he said carefully.

Gavin, normally such a controlled man, seemed to collapse into himself, his shoulders slumped, his face liquefying as if he was struggling not to cry.

'Don't worry about it, mate, we're still upright, no harm done,' the operator added softly, the status dissolving between them.

'Mr Tetherhook to you!' Gavin jerked himself upright. 'Mention a word of this to the others and you're out of a job, understand?'

The crane operator nodded curtly. A second later Shortstuff was at the door, helping Gavin down.

Back in the safety of the Merc, the property developer pulled on his driving gloves and left them on all day, despite the 40-degree temperature.

Later that day, when at last the air began to cool and the evening sprinklers were throwing out their incessant rainbows, Gavin headed to the State Library. There, under the fluorescent lights, still wearing the gloves regardless of the severe itching at his wrists, Gavin scanned the shelves of the Natural Sciences section. It was the middle of the school exam period so the place was packed with groups of adolescents restlessly trying to focus while the air jumped palpably with pubescent hormones. Irritated by the bursts of giggling and deliberate rustling of paper Gavin fought the urge to scream.

Finally he located a book on Australian flora. He scanned the room, looking for a place where he wouldn't be spotted by anyone else. There was a single empty desk behind the Theology section. Once seated he stealthily slipped off his gloves. He kept his palm turned downwards as he flicked through the pages with an uncomfortable sense of furtiveness, as if he were viewing pornography.

He found a diagram of a leaf that vaguely resembled the strange foliage on his palm. Slowly, heart racing, he turned his hand over. Yes, it was still there: a perfect imprint. Hidden behind the raised book he held his palm against the illustration. It didn't correspond with the image at all. Disheartened, he turned page after page until he came to a chapter on the prehistoric flora of Australia.

Under the sub-heading *Triassic Period of the Mesozoic* was a drawing of a fern with cone-like seeds attached to the end of its main leaf. It was called a Dicroidium. The imprint on his palm was very similar except the seed pods looked more jagged. Staring closely at his skin, Gavin realised each tiny section was a hexagon.

He tore the page out and slipped it into his breast pocket, then put the gloves back on and exhaled. Somehow, by defining the image he felt he had regained a level of control.

Outside he walked straight over to the Queensland Museum. It was a Thursday and he knew it would be open until eight. At reception he asked to be put through to a staff member who knew about palaeontology. The receptionist, a round woman in her fifties squeezed into a plastic stool, her abundant flesh rippling out of the sleeves of her blouse, blushed as she recognised the property developer from the social pages she scanned religiously every morning.

'Mr Tetherhook,' she stammered. 'Stanley Jervis is our resident palaeontologist. I'll call him immediately.'

They both stared at the rough pencil sketch Gavin had made of the footprints. Stanley Jervis — a clean-cut individual who looked like a corporate version of a Scientologist — snorted suddenly in ridicule. 'Saturday sent you, right?' he barked derisively.

'Saturday who?'

'Saturday Honeywell. Oh, come on, mate, this whole thing stinks of those madcap conspiracy theories of hers. You can't believe the number of times I've had to sit through one of her dumb diatribes. She even implicated the museum in one of her crazy theories — something about repressing information about coastal erosion. We had to let her go after that. Now she's one of those radical greenies.'

'I don't know any Saturday, and I certainly wouldn't know an environmentalist. Do you know who I am?'

'Should I?'

'Yes, you fucking should. I sunk twenty thousand into the renovation of this building.'

'Tetherhook . . . Gavin Tetherhook, the property developer?'

Gavin nodded, staring him out. The palaeontologist swallowed, his protruding Adam's apple bobbing like a buoy.

'I shouldn't imagine property developers are usually given to these kinds of delusions . . .'

'I'm not asking you to pass judgement. All I want is a description of what kind of animal, primordial or otherwise, could have made those prints.'

Jervis looked at the sketch again then at the illustration of the leaf.

'This,' he pointed to the leaf, 'looks like a Dicroidum, very common in this area during the Triassic period of the Moszoic. As for the footprint, the fauna around at that time included three-toed theropods. They were bipedal nasty carnivorous dinosaurs with particularly sharp curved claws at the end of each toe.'

The scratches on Gavin's back tingled suddenly.

'Any chance you could give me a contact number for this Saturday of yours?'

'Sure, but I'm not sure she's going to be pleased to hear from you.'

'Why?'

'You're the bloke that developed the Kellen wetlands, right?'

Gavin nodded, remembering the wave of public condemnation he had incurred — an outrage he hadn't calculated into the overall costs of the development.

'Saturday Honeywell ran the campaign to save them,' Stanley Jervis said a trifle smugly.

Great, Gavin thought ruefully, funny how things come back to haunt us. He wondered if it was a side-effect of living a long life or one of ruthless ambition.

⁓

Standing behind a glass partition, the radiologist watched the large feet covered by white nylon socks slowly disappear into the humming apparatus. Inside, the light filtered in at Gavin's feet, but the tube he lay in was illuminated as well. The machine droned as the CAT scan edged its way slowly down his body and radio wave after radio wave painlessly and invisibly deciphered each section of his brain.

Gavin attempted to distract himself with thoughts of the immediate future: the next meeting with Cathy; his legal position; making love with Amanda and the disturbing possibility of further emotional involvement. But he couldn't keep his mind from the notion of cancer. Could he have a tumour? Surely not. The doctor didn't think any of the symptoms indicated a brain tumour — there had been no headaches, no blurring of vision, just the infernal hallucinations. He had to be okay, he would be okay ...

The machine stopped suddenly and the radiologist's voice came through a speaker, tinny and distant. 'Now that wasn't so bad, was it, Mr Tetherhook?'

'I'm fine.'

'Good. You'll be out in a nanosecond.'

The bed he lay on slid forward smoothly. Gavin, hating the vulnerability of being prostrate, swung himself back onto his feet.

'Now if you sit here for five minutes I'll print out the results, but from what I could see on the screen everything looks absolutely normal.'

Normal. He inadvertently glanced at his palm — the outline had faded slowly over a period of twelve hours and finally disappeared leaving nothing, not even a rash. Regardless of circumstances, Gavin had decided he would not go to a psychologist. A pragmatic man who had always regarded therapy as an indulgence for people who hadn't grown up with priests, he was convinced that whatever was bombarding him with these visual and aural hallucinations was too real to be explained as a psychological reaction to his divorce. No, the CAT scan was the last physical check — and if anything else manifested he planned to take more radical action.

The radiologist looked up from his screen.

'Just as I thought, totally normal, both hemispheres showing absolutely no sign of lesions or tumours. I'll have the scans sent over to your doctor in the next week, Mr Tetherhook. By the way, I love that new building of yours, Bridgeport. It really is stunning.'

Gavin stepped out of the hospital doors. *Normal, I'm normal* — the phrase ran through his head like a new marketing campaign. *Gavin Tetherhook, property developer supreme, was recently vindicated in his fight for full control of the Bridgeport development after a long legal battle with his ex-wife Cathy Tetherhook*. Gavin could see the headlines now, could see himself post-divorce: independent, handsome, healthy. Hell, he might even start the Pilates class Amanda had been nagging him about to combat the middle-age spread that had started to thicken around his hips. Yep, the vision of the yacht was coming back: himself on deck with his kids, but this time with wife number two — blonde, groomed, but a good fifteen years younger than wife number one.

His reverie was interrupted by his mobile vibrating with delicious intimacy against his thigh. He reached into his pocket and checked the number. Amanda again, as if she'd intuited his sudden change of heart. He almost answered then changed his mind. Let her wait, he'd ring later that night.

He reached the car which he'd parked under a jacaranda tree. As he bent to pull open the door he felt an unexplained chill. The hairs prickled at the back of his neck. Resisting the immediate instinct to look behind him he ran his gaze across the ground. The car and the pavement surrounding it was enveloped in a bizarre shadow that seemed to have an emerald tinge to its darker parts. Gavin froze, his hand still on the door handle, trying to muster up the courage to look up. The shadow had the jagged outline of something vast, something organic ... It was wrong, terribly wrong.

Clutching at his polyester jacket, desperately seeking comfort from the synthetic weave that caught at his fingernails, Gavin took a deep breath in and looked up.

The jacaranda tree was small — there was no way it could be casting a shadow of such magnitude. His heart suddenly racing Gavin leapt into the Merc and sped off. He bent over the wheel, eyes glued to the road as the car swallowed the tarmac faster and faster. For one horrific moment he thought the shadow had followed him like a massive hovering bird but just then the car drove into sunlight. It flooded the plush interior like sudden comfort. Three blocks later Gavin pulled to the side of the road and wept.

'She's a live wire is old Saturday Honeywell, that's for sure. But she's the best man for the job, there's not a palaeobotanist in the country that can match her expertise.'

There was a pause at the other end of the line. Gavin could tell that his colleague — a civil servant in the Ministry of Planning and Environment who specialised in land clearance and contra-deals with corrupt developers such as Gavin — was wondering what the hell a notorious anti-environmentalist like himself wanted with a radical botanist.

'Found something, have you? Cause if it's of national significance you're gonna have to fess up. Times have changed, there's a lot of green dollar now in native flora.'

'Don't worry, Jeff, I'm not hiding anything.' They laughed together and some of the tension crackling along the phone line dissipated. 'It's a private matter, nothing the ministry need worry about. By the way, how *is* that charity of yours getting along?'

After Gavin put the phone down he made a note to donate a couple of thousand dollars to the Barrier Reef Foundation — unspoken barter for the ministry to leave him alone for a few more months.

Saturday Honeywell's phone number stared up at him, her name round in his mouth. Wishing for the impossible he evoked an image of a svelte scientist with her hair neatly scraped back, indicating a pragmatism he anticipated would anchor his fears for ever rather than the typical ratbag environmentalists he was used to dealing with.

He felt a twinge in his balls. It reminded him that he hadn't had sex for over a month. He gazed out of his office window across the river that snaked lazily through the city. Perhaps he would see Amanda that night — what harm could it do? It might even take his mind off his growing anxieties. He shouted to his assistant to put a call through.

They lay across his fake satin sheets, Amanda's long torso arranged perfectly as if she was conscious of the way her body fell. Gavin was convinced that she was: everything Amanda did seemed calculated. The twenty-three year old was almost as tall as he, an ex-gymnast and an aspiring model. Amanda taught four Pilates classes a day, except on Sundays when she practised Ashtanga yoga in the morning and rode a horse in the afternoon. In other words she had absolute control over the lithe small-breasted body that lay like a reclining python beside Gavin's own naked body. Feeling a little vulnerable about his thickening perimeter, the property developer pulled up the sheet.

'Why cover up? You're beautiful,' Amanda purred in that irritating little-girl voice she adopted whenever they'd had sex — only in this case they hadn't.

'Don't patronise me,' Gavin replied then immediately regretted his harsh tone. It wasn't her fault he was distracted. In truth he'd never fully engaged with his women, even his wife. He could never relate to descriptions he'd read in books about the emotional surrender men felt at falling into the body of the woman they loved. He was always a little removed, as if his consciousness was floating above his body, a small helium balloon jerked along by his galloping penis.

Gavin looked at Amanda's rippling abdominal muscles that undulated towards her naked pubis ... perhaps his eye *was* too cold, too critical.

'Did you notice?' Amanda purred. Gavin glanced at her again, wondering if he'd missed a body piercing or a new haircut.

'The total Brazilian, silly!' she giggled, pointing to her crotch. 'I did it for you — not a hair left.'

'It's okay,' he grunted, wondering if he should raise the question that hung over them, thickening the air like humidity.

Amanda rolled onto her stomach and faced Gavin's back. The three scratches had already begun to form thin white scars. Could they be war wounds from a secret lover?

'Gav, how did you get those?' She ran her cool fingers across the bumpy ridges.

Panicking slightly Gavin searched wildly for an explanation.

'New suit I had altered — silly bugger of a tailor left a pin in. Why?'

'There isn't anyone else? I mean, if there was you'd tell me, wouldn't you?'

He kissed her shoulder. 'Baby, of course there isn't. I promise. Listen, I'm sorry about ...' He couldn't bring himself to actually say the words. Under the sheet his flaccid penis lolled against his thigh like an accusation.

'It's okay, I know it happens a lot to men your age,' Amanda murmured, curling up under his arm. Spoken like a true twenty-three year old, Gavin thought, fighting the urge to run from the room.

'Yeah well, it's never happened to this man before.'

'It's the divorce, it must be really stressful,' Amanda continued, unaware that she was moving in a very dangerous trajectory. She'd tried everything — fellatio, blowing on his balls, a full body massage, even tickling — but he'd failed to grow

118

hard, and frankly she was feeling a little demoralised herself. Maybe he'd stopped finding her attractive. She sneaked a look at herself in the full-length mirror opposite — was that possible, she wondered.

'You don't love me any more,' she whined, her guard slipping. An uncharacteristic tiny pool of sweat began to gather in the hollow of her hip.

'I do, baby, I do,' he answered automatically, already calculating ways of getting rid of her before nightfall. She was so perfect with her immaculately plucked and waxed eyebrows, her manicured fingernails clipped to just the right length and varnished mauve. Originally he'd been attracted to her because of the boyish figure that seemed to defy its own femininity with breasts that were hardly there, hips more reminiscent of a young boy's than a woman's, a body that still dominated over nature and the onslaught of gravity. She was always impeccably clean, never seemed to perspire, and her scent was a very faint lemony fragrance that didn't even hint at the fruity earthiness that even his pristine wife exuded at certain times of the month. In short, Amanda seemed unnatural and this was precisely what Gavin had loved about her. But now? Now he couldn't even get an erection.

'Mandy baby, look, I'm dealing with some very big issues right now — you know, men's stuff I can't really share. But listen, remember that holiday I promised you — New Orleans? We'll go there in the summer. In the meanwhile, let's take a break from each other for a couple of weeks while I get sorted, eh?'

'You're not leaving me, are you?' She sat up suddenly and her blow-dried raven hair shiny with product — Gavin had always loved the slightly chemical smell of it — slid around her shoulders, just like a television commercial.

'No, I promise. I just need to get some distance to really be able to give myself to you.'

He wondered how she'd believe such bullshit, but Amanda, looking at him with wide black eyes, seemed to hang on his every word.

'I understand. Men are like that,' she said. 'I read about it in that American book. They need to retreat into their cave and then they spring back at you like a ball at the end of a piece of elastic. Well, Gav, I'm here for you when you're ready to bounce back,' she announced with a very serious air.

Just to bounce up would be good at this point, Gavin thought darkly, and reached over to hand her back her clothes.

⟨⟩

Saturday Honeywell's house was one of those large Queenslanders encircled by a wide wooden verandah. Balanced precariously on stilts it looked as if it hadn't undergone any renovations since it was built, which, Gavin judged, must have been a good hundred years ago. He pulled up the parking brake and rested his head on the edge of the car window. The block was substantial: it could hold two residential apartment buildings with parking if you knocked the house down and extended as far as the fence boundary, he noted, already calculating the profit margin.

He got out and steeled himself. It looked far worse than he'd imagined. He had been hoping that Ms — God, he hated it when women called themselves that — Ms Honeywell might be one of those neat scientists who pride themselves on their organisational skills. He had tried to console himself with the thought that he might finally have located someone he could feel safe confiding in, but this — this fecund jungle, this obscene waste of good building land — was almost too much to bear. He hitched his trousers up and walked heavily towards the front gate. There were the remnants of a large vegetable patch with a few struggling ears of corn and several bean plants. The rest had gone to seed and been left to sprawl across the garden path, some hardy offshoots even climbing up between the wooden slats of the verandah, which, he noted, was in a state of irredeemable disrepair.

The front door had a brass knocker in the shape of a turnip root. Obscenely twisted it looked suspiciously turd-like. Gavin, thoroughly revolted, had to shut his eyes as he lifted it to knock. The heavy banging resounded through the wooden house.

Immediately several dogs began to bark. Gavin heard the patter of tiny paws then the unmistakeable clunk of human feet. Three minutes later the door was flung open.

'Nah, the place is not for sale.'

A mass of red hair, small suspicious piercing blue eyes and some kind of green and gold bandanna flashed before him then the door was slammed in his face. Determined, he knocked again then shouted through the copper letter slot that looked disconcertingly vaginal.

'Ms Honeywell!? I'm not a real estate agent! I need to talk to you, it's urgent! My name is Gavin Tetherhook —'

The door was flung open again, catching Gavin still bent to the letter slot.

'*The* Gavin Tetherhook?'

Saturday Honeywell stood with her hands on her hips, her ample figure swathed in a black cotton kaftan embroidered with the stars of the southern hemisphere and a local indigenous slogan which, translated, read *Fat white rich woman* — a fact Saturday was ignorant of, but had she known would have found vastly amusing.

A fog of patchouli, stale sweat and coconut oil (Saturday marinated her hair in it once a week) almost knocked Gavin off his feet. From her lower lip hung what appeared to be a rolled-up vine leaf, the 'cigarette' emitting a strong smell of cloves. The palaeobotanist exhaled a lungful of smoke in Gavin's face. The property developer stumbled back, then, recovering, drew himself up to his full height. He was dismayed to see that Saturday towered over him by a good inch — which made her six foot five.

'The one and the same,' he said curtly and handed her his card. He was further disgusted by her grimy fingernails, all of which appeared well-chewed. 'What's that?' he asked, pointing at the thing she was smoking, 'pot?'

'Unfortunately not. It's a beedie — a clove cigarette very popular in Indonesia,' she replied, staring down at his card. 'Well, fuck me dead.' She looked back up at Gavin, a withering appraisal that seemed to him to encapsulate both strong disapproval and wry humour. 'The enemy was demeaned to visit the Indians, so to speak,' she continued. 'Do you know who I am?'

'Yeah, Saturday Honeywell, palaeobotanist.'

'And head of the committee to save the Kellen wetlands. Why the hell would you be visiting me?'

'I need help.'

Surprised, she smiled slowly, already calculating the ways she might take out her revenge on the property developer, who, after all, had been the bane of most of her professional life. She looked more closely at the immaculately groomed man standing before her. He was better looking in the flesh than in the photos, she observed ruefully. One of those genetically blessed individuals with an obvious penchant for control, but there was a slight fragility behind the eyes, an anxious knotting of the hands that betrayed a hidden vulnerability that made her hesitate for a moment, curious about what could be disturbing such a bastion of confidence. Then the memory of Gavin's flushed smug face adorning the front page of the *Courier-Mail* after winning the right to develop the Kellen wetlands floated into her mind.

'You? Don't make me laugh.' She began closing the door again but Gavin had already placed his foot in the doorway.

'Please, I'm desperate.'

'No way — desperate?'

'It's an issue I have no understanding of, a supernatural issue. Stanley Jervis of the Queensland Museum said you might be able to help.'

'Supernatural? You're joking.'

'I wish I was.'

Saturday paused, reappraising the situation. If he was genuine and there was some problem, the knowledge of such a vulnerability could be very useful the next time Mr Tetherhook decided to develop an environmentally sensitive site. Concealing her revulsion she held open the door.

≈

The lounge room was lined wall to wall with books whose only organising principle seemed to be by dint of association, so that the feminist tome *Women Who Run With The Wolves* sat next to

*Mother Dog* — *A Treatise on the Matriarchy of Wolves*, while *The Autobiography of Alice B Toklas* nestled happily next to *Alice's Adventures in Wonderland*. A dusty Victorian tome lay on the floor, its leather cover embossed with the intriguing title of *The Orgy* — *Pompeii's Hidden Glory: A catalogue collated by Mr Alistair Sizzlehorn Esquire*. Gavin took heart, perhaps Ms Honeywell wasn't as politically correct as he'd feared.

If you could judge people by the way they filed their books, Ms Honeywell's life had a frenetic but semi-logical order, Gavin thought refusing the offer to sit down as every surface appeared to be covered with grey balls of cat fur. The felines responsible lounged regally on every available surface, six all counted, moggies of varying sizes. The cats watched Gavin with a supercilious arrogance bordering on outright disdain. Not that Gavin cared; he was too busy trying to ignore the fact that Ms Honeywell evidently preferred not to wear underpants, a detail made obvious by the way she had collapsed into a huge battered leather armchair, her kaftan riding up to her knees. Oblivious, Saturday Honeywell stared at her bête noire, who, until this moment, she had assumed had no idea of her existence.

'Oh, for God's sake sit down!' she barked, concealing her own nervousness with aggression, an unfortunate characteristic which had not helped her popularity amongst her fellow botanists.

'Sorry, but I'm ...' Gavin floundered, the darkened crevice between Ms Honeywell's legs hovering at his peripheral vision like some horrific demon whose face he dared not look into.

'Allergic to cats? I thought so, you look like the type who thinks his shit doesn't stink! Erasmus — hop off!'

Saturday threw a large tome at what Gavin had thought was a statue of a large cane toad. The amphibian in question — indeed a huge horny cane toad of some vintage — croaked angrily then sprang off the wicker rocking chair he had been squatting on and bounced wetly into the recesses of the shadowy room. The cats remained unconcerned, Gavin observed.

'Erasmus, in case you didn't know, was a great philosopher, the early father of humanism — not that you would care, being the local embodiment of the Anti-Christ and everything that places profit over people,' Saturday continued smugly.

Gavin perched himself delicately on the edge of the rocking chair, his feet firmly planted before him as ballast.

'Now listen, girlie,' he began, his patience snapping.

'Girlie! I'm forty years old, mate. That makes me a woman, which you'd know if I sat on your face — not that you'd ever get the pleasure!' she fired back.

Momentarily stunned by the image, Gavin leaned back. Immediately the rocking chair tipped in a deep lunge, sending him into a rocking motion that instantly diminished his status further.

'I'm not here to have a bloody debate about eco politics, feminism or some ancient codger who liked people, I just need to talk to an expert!' he bellowed, rocking violently out of control.

'Shouldn't you be talking to an exorcist rather than a botanist?'

'Well, it's both a supernatural and environmental problem.'

'Impossible!'

'Is it?' Gavin's challenging tone made Saturday soften.

'What have you got to show me?'

'This.' The property developer finally managed to steady himself and, with a dramatic flourish, pulled out the illustration of the leaf he'd stolen from the library. Saturday glanced thoughtfully at the held-out page, then snatched it, lifted to her nose a pair of huge red-rimmed spectacles hanging off a chain around her neck and peered at the image.

'So it's a Dicroidium, a rather common plant from the Mesozoic era some 225,000,000 years ago — what's this got to do with you?'

'I've got this dumb idea that this and some other very strange shit is somehow all coming together and attacking my mind … well, my senses really. So if you picked up that phone right now and called mental health services I wouldn't blame you,' he finished, his feet firmly anchored back on the frayed rug with the immortal phrase *Yes, I am Woman, hear me roar* woven into it.

Saturday Honeywell leaned forward. To Gavin's immediate relief her kaftan fell back over her knees. She reached across and took one of Gavin's hands between her own. Somewhere in his shocked mind Gavin dimly registered the fact that her hands were the same size as his.

'You poor little man,' she said in a voice Gavin decided to interpret as sincere — which was exactly the effect Saturday intended. 'You really are being haunted.'

And for the first time in over a month Gavin felt that at last he had found a confidante.

They sat in front of the computer screen in the corner of the lounge room. Saturday's technology was surprisingly up to date and, as Gavin watched her fingers dance across the keyboard, it was evident to him that she lived up to her reputation as one of the country's top palaeobotanists. She had carefully noted down every single encounter he described into a notebook covered in cane-toad skin, quizzing him on various minutiae: the precise sound of his aural hallucinations, the places they occurred, circumstances leading up to the event. All of which was immensely reassuring to Gavin. Maybe he wasn't insane; maybe there was a genuine reason, even some natural phenomenon, that would explain everything away he thought hopefully as he scrutinised her every keystroke.

He perched close by on a stool she'd pulled up for him. Her curly locks, which radiated out like the epicentre of some storm, presented a curious enigma for Gavin. Normally he hated messy hair on a woman, particularly when it was as defiantly unruly as this. But somehow, as the not unpleasant drone of her voice listed all megaflora of the Mesozoic era, the whorls of each curl proved a source of fascination.

'What I'd suggest, looking at the body of evidence, is that we create a panorama of the Mesozoic forest on the computer and see if we come up with anything you recognise. How's that sound, Gav — I can call you Gav, right?'

Gavin's concentration snapped back; he liked the way she said 'we'. It was always 'I' when he talked about work, but her 'we' felt warm and maternal. It made him feel *safe*.

'You can actually do that?'

'Sure, I designed some software myself: *Honeywell's worlds* — not very original, I know, but I've got several enviros that cover that period.'

As she leaned forward and slipped a disc into her zip drive Gavin couldn't help but notice her pendulous breasts that hung completely unfettered beneath the thin cotton. She'd have a figure like one of those early caveman goddesses, he thought, remembering a history project his daughter had brought home one night. Then found himself wondering if she had a lover and, if so, whether it was a man or a woman.

'No, I'm not gay,' Saturday said out loud, eyes on the screen as she worked her way through a variety of landscapes. Gavin, unable to help himself, emitted a small gasp.

Saturday chuckled. 'Relax, I'm only telepathic when it comes to myself and sex.'

As if on cue a pager bleeped somewhere in the room. Saturday reached into the desk drawer and pulled out a mobile phone that looked as if it had been designed last century. She glanced at it. 'There you go, that's the ex now.'

She thrust the mobile at Gavin. *Mercury in retrograde, your Taurean moon is under threat, can I come around tonight? Scorpio rising x* ran across the screen.

'Scorpio rising! It always is with him!' Saturday broke into another of her throaty chuckles. Gavin winced, the memory of his own impotency looming uncomfortably.

'Bloody idiot can't do a thing without checking the charts. Fucking voodoo. I threw him out last week; he has no scientific discipline whatsoever. Text back an emphatic *No*, will you?'

Obeying, Gavin rejected the botanist's anxious suitor but, taking pity, used only one exclamation mark.

Saturday finally settled on an image, the screen darkening as a speed-up evolution thickened the landscape. 'Have a look at this,' she murmured. Gavin moved closer, surprised at how vivid the colours were on the screen.

The primordial forest had a heavy canopy and minimal sun filtered through to the forest floor which was alive with primitive-looking ferns and vines.

'There's your Jambadostrobus.' Saturday moved the mouse so

an arrow pointed to a tall pine-like tree. 'It would fruit only at the top — impressive, eh? Like that leaf of yours producing seed pods attached to each individual leaf.'

Gavin peered at the screen; the thick foliage made him shiver. There was something obscene about the abundance of spiralling vegetation tumbling and curling over itself in an attempt to secure more light. It was familiar, but it was not the landscape he'd been plunged into.

'How would the forest sound if I was standing in it?' he asked, praying he didn't sound too crazy.

'You wouldn't be. There weren't any humans, at least not as we know them, at this time. Just shrew-like mammals that were probably tree-dwellers.'

'What about the theropods?' he persisted. A slow blush crept up from his collar as he remembered the footprints, their steamy outline evaporating slowly in his mind's eye. His fingers closed on a fossil that sat on the desk. Saturday firmly took the rock away from him. The property developer was looking increasingly distraught; one knee jerked involuntarily and there was a stretched look to his face that Saturday had initially thought was stress but now recognised as fear. Interesting, she thought making a mental note, hallucinations involve misplaced delusions of grandeur.

'Nasty flesh-eating buggers that scampered across the forest floor,' she said aloud. 'You wouldn't want to meet one on a dark windy night. As for the sound, who knows? Looking at that canopy, you're not going to get a great deal of rustling, certainly not a roar, unless you're perched right at the top or hovering above. If anything there would probably have been an eerie silence below.'

'Then that's not it!' Gavin, exasperated, stood up and began striding around the room, running his fingers through his hair over and over as he fought the sense of vertigo that failure brought.

'It looks wrong. There are elements, but it's not right, I know it!'

'But it's a beginning, Gav.' Watching his fallen face and the way one of his eyebrows was twitching from nerves, she couldn't help but take pity. 'Don't be so male about this. This isn't one of those linear problems you can solve just like that; you have to take a holistic approach. It's like a prism, something to be understood from many angles simultaneously. We know one thing: it's a forest, a landscape, that is haunting you, right?'

Gavin nodded like a little boy, his hair standing up in tufts. Finding it difficult to breathe he loosened his tie and undid his top button. He hadn't been so dishevelled in years.

'Now we just have to locate where it is and when,' Saturday continued, wondering whether she shouldn't be video-recording the conversation.

'You believe me, don't you?' Gavin whispered, crumpling into a beanbag in the corner.

'Put it this way, Gav — I believe in Gaia, in Goddess Earth as a living organism, and frankly if she were going to pick on anyone, it would be you.'

∞

Stepping off the back porch, the property developer followed Saturday through the plethora of ferns, feral gardenia bushes, flowering gums and fountains of reeds, his eyes drawn to her great arse wobbling in front of him. The air was thick with jasmine and the fruity smell of freshly turned earth. The palaeobotanist reached a small clearing, a band of luminous green in the overgrowth. She bent and tore a flowering branch off a low bush.

'Here, take this — sage. Smoke your apartment, smoke your office, smoke your fucking Merc — it might help ward off any more visitations, you never know.'

Dubiously Gavin took the offered herbs. He held them at a distance, acutely allergic to flowering plants. 'Thank you,' he said, his voice already turning nasal before he sneezed violently.

As they picked their way back around the side of the house a craggy stone head suddenly loomed up at him. It was the face of a man, entirely covered by the leaves of a tree that seemed to be growing out of the centre of his face, branching out just above the bridge of his nose. Startled, Gavin leaped back.

Saturday grinned, taking a secret delight in the property developer's terror. Now he knows how it is to be bullied, she thought.

'Isn't he magnificent? The original stands in Bamberg Cathedral. Thirteenth century, you know, a hangover from the pagan worship of the Green Man.'

'The Green Man?'

'The Celtic god of Nature.'

Gavin stared at the face. The darkened eyes, fringed by the curved edges of the leaves like winged eyebrows, glared out in accusation and terrified him. And the more Gavin stared, the less he was able to shake the sensation that somehow he knew the man.

'Is that what you think, that I'm being persecuted for my sins?' he asked, the formal wording of his question strangely appropriate for the Gothic atmosphere that pervaded the house and its surrounds.

'Hey, I'm an agnostic, a floating voter. But one thing I do know is that an observed particle will behave in a certain way because it is being observed. In other words, if you believe in something it exists — and fear can only empower it,' she finished, embellishing her words with an ominous tone. As if affirming her statement, a pear suddenly dropped from the tree to the ground.

⋙

His wife stood at the lounge room window. She was wearing a dress he recognised from the summer holiday they'd taken a year ago. He remembered the crisp smell of starch rising up from the linen mixed in with the scent of her suntan oil. Gavin had wanted her then. But, smiling softly, she had removed his hands from her body, a gesture that had sliced through his heart. However, he'd shrugged it off blithely, bellowing for his children to join him for a swim.

There they were now: Aden had grown since the last time he'd seen him; the shadow of manhood pushing out his wrists and making jerky his loping strides. His daughter, Irene, sat on the kitchen counter swinging her legs. *My baby*, Gavin thought,

129

remembering the moment the obstetrician had handed him the crumpled girl-child, her alien sex twinkling up at him as he gazed at her in stilled amazement.

He rested his head against the steering wheel. He was parked across the road, the car thinly concealed by the row of trees in the front garden. His daughter looked so determined, sitting there. That one's got my drive, he thought, every muscle contracting with longing. Just then the four year old was lifted into view as his brother swung him up playfully. Would they ever forgive him? Did they even really know him? he speculated, remembering all the times he'd worked back late, all the times he'd been absent even in their presence, the flurry of mobile calls, the constant distraction of ambition burning up his attention. What had all that useless activity led to — this moment of complete solitude? Burying his head further into his folded arms he wondered whether the holidays they'd spent together, the gifts of guilt he'd lavished upon them, had secured their love. Doubts sprang up and twisted into themselves. What was he becoming? Something he'd always feared: his father, his broken father.

He started up the car and accelerated away from the kerb. Inside the house Cathy caught a streak of ruby as the Merc passed. Pursing her lips she pulled the blinds shut.

Was he rewriting history already, Gavin wondered as he sped through the streets of Fortitude Valley. Was that what loss was — a remapping of memory? An attempt to imbue the banal with meaning? Would he ever rid himself of the insidious sensation that he was constantly living in the past tense? Would he ever return to living in the moment instead of mourning what was gone and, more importantly, had perhaps never been?

Furious with the deluge of self-indulgence he moved into fifth gear and watched the speedometer notch up to a hundred and ten. If he drove fast enough could he burn out this haunting, revert to the secure successful man he was before?

The sudden scream of a police siren jolted him out of his reverie.

The razor ran up the side of his thigh, black hair and shaving foam building up under the blade. Gavin washed it clean under the running tap. Dispassionately he watched the last of his body hair spiral down through the steel grid of the plug hole. It had taken him four hours to remove the hair from his chest, his shoulders, his legs, arse and toes. His testicles he'd shaved then used some cold-wax strips Amanda had left in the bathroom cabinet to pull out the last vestiges of stubble. Now they hung a little forlornly, unrecognisable in their shiny chicken-skin nudity. But the cleansing had been worth it. Gavin felt new, strong and strangely innocent which was exactly his intention. Now nothing could invade his mind or his body.

He was going to drive the demon from his life. The shaving was part of it — an act of purification to ritualise the smoking of his apartment. It had seemed the only solution.

He stood in the bathroom stark naked except for the wavy grey hair on his head. Apart from the rawness of his shaved flesh he looked remarkably unchanged, there was no indication of the turmoil going on under the skin. In wonder he placed his hand on the mirror, over his reflected chest. When he pulled away the imprint left on the glass was of a three-pronged claw.

Gavin vomited violently into the toilet. His legs trembled uncontrollably as bile ripped from the base of his gut. He felt like weeping. Moving slowly he stepped into the waiting bath.

The hot water was immediately comforting. He lowered himself down until his head was covered. Underneath, all was a muted echo, a world of dull thuds and the thumping of his heart against his eardrum. Then it started ... a thin whistle that slithered over all other sounds, increasing slowly in volume. *Go away*, he prayed, his lungs squeezing through lack of oxygen. *Go away*. But despite his prayers the rustling grew louder.

He opened his eyes underwater: a dull greenish light filtered in from above — the canopy of a forest. A dark figure stared down at him from beneath matted hair. Terrified, Gavin sat up bolt upright, water streaming down his face and chest. The bathroom was quiet, pristine, completely normal. Gavin got out, his heart racing, and pulled the plug violently. As the bathwater drained away it left behind a sheen of green algae.

~

He'd had the smoke detectors turned off. The last thing he needed after being booked for speeding was the police turning up to find a well-known property developer striding around his own apartment minus body hair stark naked and clutching a bush of burning sage. Jesus Christ, he thought, what was he becoming?

Shivering slightly, he bound the branches of the sage tightly with wire, then held the bundle over the gas flame of the stove. They flared instantly. Gavin pulled them away and blew the flame out. Sure enough the bush began to smoke as the embers ate their way down the stems.

Holding the bush high he went to the main fuse box and switched off all the lights. Now the apartment was illuminated only by the amber glow of the smouldering plants and the city lights outside. Gavin walked slowly around, waving the bush carefully to make sure the billowing smoke filled all corners of the apartment.

In the office block opposite the cleaner switched off her vacuum cleaner and watched in amazement as the man she had taken to fantasising about walked gracefully through the flat opposite, his skin illuminated a soft pink from the burning torch he held above him. He was naked and, oddly, seemed to have lost his body hair. Was he a member of one of those newfangled religions, she wondered. There was something sacred about the way he was moving. A practising Catholic, she thought it might be a sin to watch the pagan rites of another even if she *had* appropriated him for her own erotic life. Switching the vacuum cleaner back on, she stoically turned her back.

The sage gave off a sickly sweet smell. The whitish fog sank to the ground, curling along the carpets, then rose steadily as Gavin walked backwards and forwards. He wondered if he should be chanting. The only thing that came to mind was the anthem of the Broncos. Determined, he sang it over and over like a hymn.

Reaching the bedroom he inched along the bed, making sure he didn't catch sight of himself in the mirror opposite. The smoke spilled languidly from the stems and across the bed, covering the shiny sheets with a pale mist.

Turning to go into the lounge room he caught a glimpse of his reflected feet at the edge of his gaze. They appeared to be covered with long matted fur and caked in a brownish sludge. Stunned, Gavin immediately blotted the image from his mind. 'Go away, begone,' he muttered over and over — a line he remembered from a horror film he'd seen as a child. 'Go, go, begone.'

An old man's head suddenly manifested out of the smoke, leering up at him and mouthing the words *flitter, flitter*, his face a translucent death mask. The tramp again.

Shrieking, Gavin dropped the smouldering sage and ran full pelt into the balcony door. His body hit the glass like a bullet. The door shattered into a thousand glittering pieces that rained down with a tinkling sound. The property developer fell through onto the balcony, cracking his head on the floor. He lay curled like a foetus. Tiny glass splinters ran down one side of his body; catching the city lights they shimmered like miniature daggers. Beads of blood pooled at each tip.

Rain began to fall in heavy tropical droplets — a hot summer shower that increased in tempo until it drummed against the glass and concrete. Still Gavin lay motionless, his unconscious mind tumbling like an injured hawk.

Scarlet began to thread itself through a viscous mass of grey; sensation ran like trickling sand across his wakening nerves. The grey shifted to a copper haze with a lip of sunlight. Gavin blinked and his eyes cleared. Groaning, he flexed as feeling flooded back into his bruised limbs. He opened his eyes and found that he was staring at the sunrise framed by the steel balcony wall and the edge of the concrete floor.

The sun rose, a lazy orb that disappeared behind the frosted glass. Somewhere someone coughed. Shocked Gavin sat up, then realised it had been himself. There were pinpricks of heat down his chest and left arm. Dispassionately he pulled out one of the splinters and watched the blood roll down his shaven arm, now prickling in an angry rash.

He stood and hobbled back into the flat. The phone rang. Ignoring it he went straight to the bed and lying carefully on his intact side fell asleep.

*'Gavin, this is your irate lawyer speaking. Where are you? You were due in court this morning — your failure to appear has meant an automatic transfer of ownership of Bridgeport to Cathy. Sorry, mate, there was nothing I could do. We can contest but you have to ring me. I'm beginning to get worried.'*

*'Boss, this is Shortstuff here. You haven't turned up to work for over a week now. I've been covering for you but I don't know how much longer I can hold out. There are papers to be signed, and I need your permission for some new orders. Ring me, boss . . .'*

*'Gavin, this is Amanda here, I miss you. Ring me, I love you. You can come out of the cave now, truly. Ring me. Big kiss, your baby.'*

*'Dad, it was my birthday on Tuesday and you didn't ring. Mum says it's because you forgot and now that you have your own life you don't care, but I don't believe her. Ring me, it's Irene and I'm ten now in case you did forget.'*

❧

*Flitter. Flitter.* He thought it was the ocean. Or maybe the sound of a ceiling fan sinking lower and lower until it felt close enough to cut off his head. Then he realised it was his phone. There was blinding pain, the light was dazzling, but he was awake. He reached over and knocked the phone off the hook. A female voice sounded out, tinny in the mute room, then came the bleep bleep of the dial tone. Gavin lay still for a second, gathering his strength. Apart from an itchiness that ran across his body like an infra-red map joining heat point to heat point, he felt good, strong. He now knew what to do.

He stepped out of the car. He was naked beneath the polyester shirt and trousers and the shaving rashes smouldered on his skin like bubbling tar. Determined not to scratch, he clutched at the digital camera slung around his neck; he usually used it to photograph his properties but now he was going to use it like a gun. Like a fucking gun.

It was hot. Summer had blossomed without him noticing. The thick air pressed against his temples and the wind-borne pollen irritated his sinuses. He walked across the road towards the vacant lot. Shortstuff had been busy — the area had been cleared except for a pile of rubble and bush at the very back. Gavin unlocked the gate. It was Sunday and the place was silent except for a flock of parakeets who chirped and squabbled in a line of trees across the road and the 5:17 Qantas flight to Sydney roaring overhead. In front of him stretched a sea of concrete.

Gavin kneeled, pressing down with his thumb. The cement was slightly soft. Poured about a week ago, he thought. He stood; there was no sign of *him*. No abandoned medicine bag, no tattered coat.

'Where are you?' Gavin bellowed. The parakeets scattered like confetti as his voice bounced back. 'Hello!'

Nothing but silence and the distant sound of a lawnmower. What if he'd gone? What if he couldn't find him? What then?

The heat rose from the concrete, rippling the air. Normally Gavin relished moments like this, the smell of hot tar, wet concrete and newly welded girders filling him with exhilaration at being the conqueror, the emperor of steel. Today he was just panicked.

A hot breeze blew a dried palm leaf across the bare ground. The movement caught his eye and suddenly he saw a footprint set distinctly into the concrete. He recognised the three clawed toes immediately. Above that print another one, then another, a whole string of them winding their way towards the back of the lot.

It is a definitive moment in a man's life when his conscious will is jettisoned for something more primal, more instinctive, when the prehistoric brain hijacks civilised thought. Such a moment can change a man's life, although at the time it may feel as arbitrary as a missed phone call or an accidentally deleted email. Caught in one of these moments Gavin slipped off a shoe and sock and pressed his bare foot down hard beside one of the footprints. The imprint he left was identical. At last something real; evidence.

Carefully he took a photo, squinting into the viewfinder, one shoe off, one shoe on. Image captured for ever, he slipped his shoe back on and followed the track of footprints. It arced in a semi-circle, as if the creature had paused mid-flight then decided to change direction, as if being chased. The trail ended at the pile of rubbish at the back of the lot. Gavin stared at the mountain of trash in front of him, his protective layers shearing away one by one until it felt like the back of his head had been peeled off and he could sense every trembling leaf, the shiver of every blade of grass, the humming vibration of communication wires buried in pipes six foot under his feet. The tramp was very close. Gavin could swear he heard breathing, heard him whispering *flitter*, *flitter* so softly it was barely a tickle against his eardrums.

He examined the pile — broken beer bottles, plastic concrete bags, wattle branches with dying blossom, the rusty wheel of an ancient bicycle and something else ... something staring up at him through the spokes. What was it? A lump of moss? A decayed tree stump? As he stared harder the object's features swam free-form to compose themselves into an image too shocking for his mind immediately to assimilate. But as he blinked again, Gavin could see exactly what it was: the head of the tramp coated in a strange lichen, the eyes two blackened lumps of jelly hooded by wings of green moss, the mouth open in screaming accusation, vegetation fringing the withered meat of the lips.

It was a face Gavin had seen before — on the stone statue in Saturday's garden, the Green Man from Bamberg Cathedral. The two heads were identical, except this rendition of the demented knave of Nature had once been alive.

Gavin pulled the bicycle away to reveal the rest of the tramp's body, still huddled within its ancient parka. The cloth fell open with the movement, exposing blackened skin that had begun to split, showing the desiccated muscle beneath. There were two distinct marks on the old man's chest, one above his heart.

Gavin knew it immediately: the same imprint of a leaf that had appeared on his palm. Gavin lifted his camera. A moment later his knees gave way to a terrible trembling.

⋙

'Saturday! Saturday!'

Saturday Honeywell was crouched in a deep ditch, carefully brushing down a layer of fossils. Part of Boral mining corporation, the limestone quarry was massive and located some ten miles out of Brisbane. Saturday had been called in when one of the stonecutters unearthed a vast cross-section of stratification: layer upon layer of fossils.

Oblivious to everything around her Saturday was immersed in the world she was bringing back to life with the fine hairs of her brush, each stroke pushing the dust aside to reveal another feathery leaf etched into the lime, tendrils still arching out towards a sun that had shone over 200,000 years before. She prised the stone from the wall of the ditch, squatted back on her haunches and flipped the magnifying glass that was strapped to her forehead over her eye. She peered down at the lapidification.

Gavin leapt off the back of the jeep that had given him a lift out to the ditch. He stood silhouetted for a moment against the wheel of one of the tractors, his head barely reaching its hub.

'Saturday!' he bellowed again.

'The hippie chick?' one of the workmen asked. Gavin nodded. The workman grinned a gold-toothed gappy smirk and pointed in the direction of an open cut marked with flags.

Ignoring his leer Gavin began to stride then broke into a full pelt towards the ditch. He reached the edge and peered down.

The sun divided the space into a chequerboard of dazzling white and blue shadow. At first he didn't see her; she was kneeling in the shade of the cut side that plummeted down about sixty feet.

'Saturday!'

She looked up, hand shading her eyes, then pointed to a ladder leading down the side of the quarry. In his polyester suit now creased with grime, Gavin climbed down as fast as he could. It was instantly cooler in the shade.

'Fuck, you look terrible!' Saturday shoved a flask of cold water at him, unable not to feel sorry for the man. Gavin drank thirstily, then looked at her, eyes glittering dangerously.

'I found something I want you to look at. Real evidence!'

'Listen, Gav, I read about your wife. Looks like she stands to get the lot, that can't be easy —'

'Saturday, I found him! I found the tramp!'

Saturday assessed the man in front of her. A nasty rash crept up from the neck of his shirt and extended as far as his earlobes. He didn't appear to have any eyebrows and at the ends of his trousers his naked feet, covered in mud and greenish mould, were bruised and bleeding.

'You've been missing for over a week. Your mate from the City Council rang me looking for you; reckon he was frightened I'd chopped you up and fed you to my worm farm. Where have you been?'

'I've found something and I need your help. Now.'

He stared at her, the desire to touch her battling with his fear. If she'd lost faith in him he knew he was doomed.

'Hey, you've caught me between the Mesozoic and the Palaeozoic, my most favourite place in the world . . .'

'Please.'

He grabbed her dust-covered glove. Sighing, she bent down and picked up her tool bag.

'Evidence? What kind of evidence?' Saturday muttered as she pushed open her front door.

She was still dressed in dusty dungarees and desert boots. Gavin couldn't help noticing the sweat stains etched in two great patches under her thin cotton tee-shirt. Saturday unhitched the dungarees, letting them drop to her waist as she pulled off the headscarf dusted white with limestone. Braless, her prominent nipples were completely visible under the fabric. The rolls of flesh rippling down to her waist ballooned out under the denim.

She crossed to the stove and put the kettle on with a slam. She was irritated. Access to the quarry was limited and it was important to catalogue the fossil find as soon as possible to ensure the site got a protected listing. But Gavin had looked so forlorn, so desperate, she hadn't been able to help herself.

Vulnerable men were her weakness. She was for ever picking up the recently divorced, the bereaved, or simply the lost, all of whom were drawn to her warmth and reassuring bulk. Sometimes she wondered whether she wouldn't be better off abandoning the search for a man who actually wanted her for herself and just opening up an orphanage. Where had her plans for discrediting the property developer gone? The irony was, now that he seemed bent on a path of self-destruction all she wanted to do was save him. Was it a genetic flaw or some kind of evolutionary paradigm she would never be able to escape?

Saturday gave Gavin a suspicious penetrating stare then walked up to him. Gavin could feel the warmth radiating from the vast expanse of glistening olive skin — a mixture of sweat, coconut oil and something far fruitier. He traced a droplet of sweat as it ran from the edge of her armpit down the underside of her arm. Suddenly he knew what he had to do, recognised the act that would earth him, would give him back his strength to battle whatever it was that was trying to destroy him. He lifted her arm and ran his tongue down her skin. Saturday froze in shock. Gavin, amazed at himself, tasted the salt at the tip of his tongue and his pheromones launched a full-frontal assault on any remaining rationality.

He yanked up her tee-shirt. Her brown nipples seemed to stain the whole of her humongous breasts, orbs veined and covered in a multitude of thin white stretch marks. They hung down to her waist. Overwhelmed by the desire to topple this mountainous body and penetrate it there and then, Gavin buried his head in the soft pendulous flesh.

'Gavin, please, this will ruin my credibility as a serious environmentalist. Frankly, it would be more acceptable to sleep with the head of the National Party,' Saturday whispered hoarsely, fighting the waves of desire that swept up from her groin. In lieu of an answer he lifted his head and pulled her into a deep penetrating kiss. She tasted faintly of chamomile tea and garlic. Much to Gavin's amazement he didn't mind — in fact, the very humanness of her excited him even more.

Standing at full height he had to lift his chin slightly to reach her mouth. He had never felt this equal with a woman in his life. She stood with her eyes closed, tongue on tongue, tasting him with short flickers, working her way up to a full sucking — a kind of mini-orchestration, as if just letting him know what she was capable of. At the receiving end of her tongue Gavin felt all that defined him evaporate away. He wanted this. He wanted her. He wanted to drown in that avalanche of flesh, to lose his particularity, his need for control, his fear.

He pulled up his shirt and pressed against her, nipple to nipple. The size of her was overwhelming. He had never been with a woman who was both wider and taller than himself. He lifted her hands and placed them on his rock-hard cock.

'Well, thank God you're to scale,' she said and laughed, a full-throated sexy gurgle.

Inspired, Gavin wrapped his hands around the cheeks of her massive arse and tried to hoist her up onto his hips. Instead, overcome by her weight, he stumbled backwards and fell flat on the ground, pulling her down with him. Saturday landed across him, winding him considerably and miraculously missing his erect penis and testicles.

They lay on the kitchen floor like a bizarre starfish. Watching critically, one of Saturday's six cats turned up its nose and walked off in disgust, tail twitching as if to indicate what ridiculous creatures humans were.

Gavin was in bliss; a breast was pushed against his cheek, another against his ear. Courageously and utterly undeterred he lifted it and searched for the nipple, almost blinding himself with half an inch of erect tissue in the process. God, this feels good, he thought, sucking down hard. Somewhere in the distance he heard Saturday groan.

He rolled her over onto her back and, with a powerful tug, managed to pull off her dungarees. The ginger pubic curls extended as far as her navel and a great pale roll of belly hung over her pubic area. He pushed it up. The swollen lips of her sex were a vivid slash against the tightly swirling hair. It was like the mouth of Mother Earth herself, a great moist cavern. He pressed his mouth against her and filled his lungs with her pungent scent.

'Keep going like that and I'll come way before you,' Saturday murmured and yanked him by the ears back up to her face. 'Besides, I want you inside of me,' she finished, then bit into his lip deliciously. She reached down and freed his cock. Her grasp was firm, knowing. None of the tentativeness of Amanda's touch. Saturday caressed him as if his flesh was her own, making him grow harder, bigger, than he'd ever felt before. She reached further down and cupped his burning balls. Her hands were deliciously cool. Gavin let out a long sigh; it was as if he'd come home.

'Jesus, Gavin, you're like one long plucked chicken. What happened?' Saturday gazed at the ugly rash that extended from his groin to his chest.

'I cleansed myself, made myself pure.' His voice thickened as her strokes telegraphed quivers of ecstasy down each thigh. She hesitated for a moment, wondering whether he was mad, literary or merely poetic. She decided to gamble on the latter.

'You're one crazy bastard.'

Without answering he slipped his fingers into her and searched for her clit. He found the hard button and started caressing it, pulling until it grew between his fingers. Watching her face as he pleasured her he catalogued its features: the heavy-lidded eyes, a blue the azure of dusk, he thought; the blemished pores showing that she must have had a troubled adolescence; the sunspots that peppered the round cheeks; the crinkling at the corners of the eyes as she smiled back at him, humour threatening to burst from her. Every living flaw excited him. She was the embodiment of Nature. She was his catharsis. The seduction of her would be his liberation.

Saturday's breathing grew faster; a slow flush flooded her skin until it seemed almost as red as her hair which spread around her like an angry cloud. Removing his hand she pulled him far up above her so that he straddled her chest. Then lifting her breasts, she placed his cock between them and pushed them

141

together so the flesh tightened around his penis. Close to losing control he began rubbing backwards and forwards, then, worried about the political correctness of such a gesture he peered down at her face.

She smiled back at him, a slow wicked grin as if she knew exactly what he was thinking. 'Faster,' she commanded, cupping his balls.

He obeyed, resting his weight on his knees, but although the dominant nature of such a position would usually excite him, at this moment he found it did not. He wanted to please *her*, to see the wave of orgasm sweep across those broad features, to hear *her* cry out. He turned his body and took her sex into his mouth. He closed his eyes and drank in the scent and taste of her until she permeated every pore. Meanwhile Saturday ran her tongue down his shaft, glorying in his girth, his hardness. Both of them quickened, close to climax.

Gavin paused for a moment, resting his cheek on the soft expanse of her belly. Suddenly he felt something rubbing against his foot. Arching down he peered across the length of their bodies. One of Saturday's dogs — a diminutive mutt that looked like a cross between a Jack Russell and a Chihuahua — evidently inspired by the human activity had mounted Gavin's leg and was busy humping his foot. Horrified, Gavin rolled off Saturday and kicked the enthusiastic beast away.

Saturday cracked up laughing. Gavin, sobered, looked at her then began to smile, eventually breaking into a deep chuckle himself.

The palaeobotanist rolled herself to sitting, her body wobbling as she threw back her head with laughter. Watching her breasts shake made him want her again. He slid over and began kissing her wildly, from her belly to the tip of her nose, then, pushing her back down onto the ground, he entered her finally.

He hoisted her legs over his shoulders and thrust into her hard. There was so much of her he was engulfed, her tightness and wetness catching at him as if her very cunt was sucking him into the core of her. This was it. His floating critical eye was closed, his body was jerked into *now*, the present tense, for the first time in his life. With an almighty rush, the emotional fused with the sexual. His quickening triggered her own and as he began to orgasm she followed a few seconds behind, and they both came yelling, sending hissing cats flying to all four corners of the house.

～

'Jesus, Saturday, that was fucking marvellous.'

Lying nestled in the crook of her arm he had never felt more relaxed in his life, as if after holding his breath for forty-three years he'd finally exhaled. One huge erect nipple dominated his horizon; snuggling down into the soft flesh he felt like a child. Saturday, for once, was silent, staring up at a damp patch on the ceiling — a leak she'd failed to fix a summer ago. Secretly she was frightened, attuned as she was to the tremors that still ran like an underground earthquake through the very stratification of her body. She didn't want to fall in love. Not with him — a man whose politics were as abhorrent to her as Hitler's. Besides, she was convinced she was merely a curio, an interesting diversion for Gavin. Why would a man like him want a woman like her, she couldn't help thinking as she looked at the toned abdomen, the chiselled profile curled into the crook of her shoulder.

Her vagina involuntarily contracted, the shape of him still echoing deep within her. She could have him again now, and if there was one thing Saturday hated, it was needing a man. There had been a time in her life where she deliberately did not come, having realised that when she orgasmed she let men in emotionally, and immediately there was a kind of fatality to the way the relationship — comradeship was how she liked to think of it, being an active socialist — played itself out from then on, invariably ending with the man leaving her. She'd be buggered if she was gonna let some man hurt her again now, especially someone she had always regarded as the bane of the Queensland environmental movement. This wasn't just sleeping with the enemy, it was sleeping with the devil.

I think I must love her, Gavin thought, his eyes half-shut, dozing against the soft warm breast, her armpit hair tickling

143

his nose. I'll dump Amanda and move in Saturday, he concluded, wondering how her naked bulk would fit with the pristine trimmings of the apartment. She'd look great in a grey silk dress, low-cut, with those enormous breasts jutting out, he imagined. His mind rambled on until he had the palaeobotanist squeezed into black vinyl as a familiar fetish re-emerged.

Distressed by this new train of thought, Gavin opened his eyes. A large daddy-longlegs was tentatively making its way across the wooden floorboards. He stared at the tiny body swaying precariously on its spindly legs, as if amazed at its own gravity-defying design.

Gavin hated spiders, their hairy legs, the way their silk spilled so effortlessly out of their rears like slippery excrement. But as he watched the insect daintily tip-toeing across the floor he realised that at this moment he loved this particular arachnid. In a sudden epiphany he saw the spider as it viewed itself: a fearless hunter perched high over its terrain; the lion-king of a microscopic world that existed as a constant invisible below human eyes. It was then Gavin realised that he knew exactly how to solve the riddle.

His meditation was rudely interrupted by a large tabby who pounced on the defenceless creature and carried it off in its mouth, eight thread-like legs whirling madly, fringing the cat's jaw like a demented beard.

⮌

'Saturday, I need to blow an image up. Can you do that here?'

Excited, Gavin strolled naked around the kitchen, his penis lolling against his thighs. Saturday, wrapped in a purple tablecloth and smoking a beedie, speculated whether his behaviour might be the onset of a bi-polar disorder, then less reverently wondered if Gavin'd be up for another bonk. She finally decided that the best action would be to humour him. She stubbed the beedie out. 'I have a scanner that can do the job, assuming it's a photographic image.'

'Perfect.'

Gavin found his jacket and pulled a pile of photos from the pocket. He laid them out carefully on the scarred wooden table and waited while Saturday looked.

'Jesus! It's a corpse! Where did you get these, Gav?' A new tone of fear ran through her voice. To reassure her, Gavin put his arm around her waist. She pulled away.

'Don't worry, I didn't kill him. Nature did — or whatever it is that's after me.'

'What do you mean, Nature? Where's the photo from? Some morgue?'

'I found him, on one of my sites, but that's irrelevant. I want you to look at the face. Recognise it?'

She peered closer. The features looked barely human under the thick velvety covering of moss and grey lichen. Dispassionately she wondered how the lichen could have sprouted so quickly on a decaying body; under normal circumstances it would take decades to get such thick growth.

'It's your Green Man, Sat, that German critter in the garden.'

'Personally I can't see the resemblance,' Saturday murmured, although she noticed that if you tilted the photo at a certain angle there were some similarities. He was obsessed she concluded; perhaps it was cumulative guilt, some kind of subconscious remorse. But she couldn't imagine Gavin regretting anything.

'But what about that strange vegetation sprouting over his face, what do you think that represents?'

'Some kind of unusual decay. It would have needed very bizarre weather to produce that.'

'Blow it up.'

'What?'

'Magnify a section ... I have an idea about something.'

The photo filled the whole of the computer screen. Saturday highlighted a portion and pulled it away as a separate window.

'How far can you magnify before you lose detail?'

'About 400 per cent. It's not quite state of the art but it's close.'

Her fingers raced across the keyboard as she spoke, magnifying the image again and again, until all that was visible was the moss itself, magnified four hundred times. It looked like a forest.

The few hairs left on his body rose with the chill of recognition. 'That's it,' he whispered.

'There must be something wrong — moss doesn't normally look like that close up. It doesn't have —'

'Branches? Trunks? Leaves?' Gavin's voice grew shrill with hysteria. 'Can't you see that it isn't moss — it's a forest, *the* forest . . . that horrible parallel world I've been trapped in.'

'Will you calm down?'

'Saturday! Don't you see? He's been murdered, and it was he who warned me at the beginning . . .'

Saturday peered closer. The magnification did look like a forest, but not any forest that she knew of.

'Okay, say we do work from the premise that it is a forest — I don't recognise the vegetation. It's neither prehistoric or contemporary, although it probably looks vaguely more contemporary.'

Gavin sat down heavily, his head in his hands.

'Say it is a warning. Say it's not from the past but the future . . .' he murmured.

'Now you're really losing the plot.'

'Can you add in environmental factors — like weather, pollution?'

'Of course.'

'Pull up a contemporary rainforest — one that would be appropriate for now, in this area.'

Thinking he'd gone crazy she followed his instructions, reverting to the computer modelling she used as a base program. A recognisable rainforest filled the screen, a canopy of Queensland vegetation with a thick undergrowth of ferns. She glanced across to check that the telephone was within reach, comforting herself with the thought that she could always ring the police if necessary. Gavin was beginning to look more and more maniacal.

'1.6ppm of carbon dioxide, that's the eight-hour average for the Brisbane CBD. Times that by fifty.'

She punched in the equation: the forest sprouted more leaves, the trunks extended spine-like into the sky which had darkened to a dirty grey.

'Take the greenhouse factors and treble them ...'

The horizon darkened again and the evolution process speeded up, tendrils winding like blind snakes up tree trunks, the undergrowth thickening to an impossible density.

Gavin froze. 'Stop it there.'

The image on the screen stopped moving. Gavin held up the printout of the magnification of the tramp's face. It was a perfect match.

'No.' Saturday swung around in her seat, her whole body quivering. 'No, it's not possible, Gavin. It's just coincidence, an optical illusion. It just isn't scientific — even you must know that.'

'But, Saturday, you've seen what's been happening ... I would have thought you of all people —'

'— would have what? I'm a scientist not a mystic.'

She picked up the photo of the old man. 'How do I know that you didn't kill this guy then have some strange mental breakdown where you concocted this whole scenario to justify the murder?'

Gavin looked at her in horror as her hand crept towards the phone.

'You *have* to believe me. There's no one else, no other witness ...'

'Witness? I'm not a witness. I've seen nothing to convince me of the reality of your haunting, except some reportage and now a photo of a corpse.' She lifted the phone. 'You've got ten minutes to get out of the area then I'm phoning the cops.'

He stared at her, barely comprehending her words. He couldn't believe that she would do this to him after making love, that she hadn't felt the overwhelming connection as he had.

'But we made love ... I thought you understood ...'

'Just go. Go now!'

Gavin picked up his polyester suit and bolted for the door.

He waded through the thick undergrowth, driven by a dulled sense of purpose. He stank of piss and some unmentionable human filth, but had become so accustomed to it he could no longer smell himself. He'd been living in the vacant lot for as long as he could recall. His mind was a blank beyond the moment he had found himself lying on the rubbish tip, familiar faces now reduced to ghostly circles as his memory evaporated into fog.

In the distance he heard the sound of a vehicle pulling up, the thud of a car door. He wasn't frightened. Other human beings were shadows that passed beyond the wall that separated his world from theirs. He lived in a forest, the forest of the future.

His toe hit something sharp; he bent down to find that he had cut himself on the edge of a rusty tin. A piece of newspaper lay nearby. The headline across the top of the article read: PROPERTY TYCOON DISAPPEARS. FOUL PLAY SUSPECTED. WIFE GETS ESTATE BY DEFAULT. He tore the paper in half and wrapped it around his bleeding toe. The crash of footsteps interrupted him. Someone had broken into his world.

The old tramp smelt of urine and centuries of decay. His leathery face loomed at the young property developer from under the canopy of thick serpentine vines that still clung to the decaying wooden verandah.

'Forest come un twisty up your soul, you have nothing, boyo, seep into yer DNA then zap! Dead meat scum. You cursed. You no longer living. Flitter, flitter,' Gavin muttered, then spat at the developer's feet. There was blood mixed in with the spittle.

The young man, meticulous in his dress and his business acumen, reared back, convinced that both insanity and poverty were contagious.

Great, a fucking environmentalist, he thought, some old hippie who's really lost his marbles.

# Virgin

She stood at the prow of the ferry as it rode up the crest of a wave and plunged down the other side, up another and down again, relentlessly ploughing towards the island visible on the horizon. The Aegean Sea, she thought, taking a deep breath of the salty air that was tinged with diesel.

'Islands of myth and tragedy,' she whispered into the breeze as white limestone formations appeared on the shore. She could almost see Io, the maiden, suspended in her flight from the amorous Zeus disguised as a bull. Above a rock pool Medusa stared at an army of fossilised lovers and there was Dionysus, clutching a bunch of grapes, facing in the direction of Athens.

The sea winds filled her lungs with a pounding vitality, the churning water below was an unbelievable turquoise and already she could feel the Greek sun burning her skin. She didn't care. This was life, uninhibited, vibrant. Finding it hard to contain the growing flutter of excitement hidden beneath the grey flannel she crossed her arms.

'The nun, she's not bad, eh?' A Greek sailor nudged his friend, who cuffed him on the head, warning him to keep his cock holy and his mind clean. But still the sailor stared. The nun was youthful, in her late twenties, with pale skin and startling green eyes. A strand of strawberry blonde hair crept out from beneath her traditional habit; tossed by the wind, it twisted with a sensuality of its own. The young man peered closer. It was hard to tell what her body would be like under the robe, but the outline of her bosom was prominent, suggesting a voluptuousness. There was about her a certain self-consciousness and assailability that enabled the sailor, a seasoned authority on women, to guess correctly that she was a virgin. What he would never guess was that her name was Clarissa Metahue and she had lost her faith several months before.

She was twenty-six years old and had been a sister of the Benedictine order for over six years. A priest had set up a recruitment centre at the private Catholic girls' school she'd attended and Clarissa, convinced that the Virgin Mary had appeared to her as a child, had taken the priest's interest as a reinforcement of her secret calling. Amazed by the resilience of her own courage Clarissa had chosen a spiritual vocation over Adelaide University. Her choice had almost destroyed her staunchly atheist father, a banker with far more conventional ambitions for his only child. The summer she announced her intentions he had threatened to disinherit her, then tried to bribe her into a university place, and when that failed announced that he expected her to pay back every single cent he had invested in both her childhood and education. He only relented when Clarissa's mother convinced him that if this was a phase the girl was going through, the last thing he should do was to alienate her.

Nevertheless, fleeing his disapproval the novice had taken a position in an impoverished suburb called Taperoo, near Port Adelaide. There she ran a centre for single mothers, many of them heroin addicts with histories of abuse. It was a baptism of fire for a middle-class girl from a prosperous home. But she learned to love her job and, despite the ongoing frustrations, the triumphs that tenacity can bring — until she became involved with a small Aboriginal girl called Ruby from the Nunga community. Full of intelligence and energy, the five year old would entertain the depressed women with her babbling humour and mimicry. She was the progeny of a local musician — her mother had died from a drug overdose complicated by diabetes — and her twenty-year-old father, dreadlocks to his shoulders, would drop Ruby off at the centre in the morning and sometimes fail to collect her at night.

Clarissa let the child sleep over at her cramped one-bedroom house on the edge of the estate. Lying together in her bed they would use shadow play on the wall to invent an imaginary world both of them could escape into, a world where the local social worker became a witch with snakes for hair, where trees walked, postboxes sang and where the cracks in the pavement led to strange paradises; a dream world full of Ruby's laughter and Clarissa's misplaced adulthood.

Inevitably the nun found herself fantasising about motherhood. Lying there she imagined her dedication to Christ as a beautiful white marble path sweeping before her, shaping her whole life, a clear plan that was entirely comforting until the warmth of Ruby's body became a painful reminder of the childlessness this dedication entailed.

At the end of that winter Ruby was diagnosed with leukaemia. Six months later she was dead. It was a slow, anguished death, and somewhere between the child's terrible pain and the bitter grief of her young father whispering doubts crept into Clarissa's daily meditations, her anger turning to quiet despair as her prayers proved useless. No humane God would have allowed this to happen; no thinking deity can condone such suffering, she found herself reasoning.

One morning she woke up and found herself pinned to her bed by an overwhelming sense of vertigo. It was only when she had coaxed herself into standing upright on trembling, mistrusting legs that she realised her illness was not physical but spiritual. Clarissa Metahue had lost her faith.

Her Mother Superior visited the community centre on her annual pilgrimage and instantly recognised Clarissa's malaise. After a lengthy interrogation, she announced that she was going to send the young nun to an isolated convent overseas famous for its restorative powers.

It was set on a high cliff on a tiny Greek island which lay next to the most eastern island of the little Cyclades, Donousa, and was known only as the little brother of Donousa. One of the most remote outposts of the Catholic Church surrounded by the Greek Orthodox denomination, the convent was over four hundred years old and had been founded by a pious wife who had accompanied her knight en route to the Holy Crusades.

Clarissa, numb with grief, packed that same day. After changing planes at Heathrow for Athens, she eventually found herself standing on the deck of the ferry in a place that was already another world.

She felt the heat of the man's gaze on the back of her neck and blushed. She glanced quickly at his taut figure. The muscles in his naked back rippled like an undulating washboard as he flung the rope to a waiting sailor at the dock. Clarissa never seen a naked man. And oddly, she had never felt any great rush of desire. Her sexuality was completely dormant and she justified her moment of voyeurism now as objective curiosity. It was

153

difficult to miss what one had never experienced, and secretly Clarissa was thankful to have avoided the machinations of passion, especially after witnessing the abuse the women in the community centre tolerated — all justified, she thought, by a nebulous co-dependency they insisted on calling 'love'.

The boat drew up to the wooden dock. Brightly coloured fishing boats were beads of bobbing colour against the pale limestone. Behind them, the small shops looked as if they had frozen somewhere in the fifteenth century, an illusion broken only by the odd neon sign, antiquated themselves with their flashy 1970s graphics.

The walkway was lowered and the sailor watched the nun gingerly pick her way across carrying a battered suitcase. What a waste, he thought then forgot her completely.

The holy woman stood beside a high sun-bleached wall that seemed to grow out from the very edge of the cliff face. Dressed in a pale blue habit she was almost invisible against the sky, her face a floating oval of tanned wrinkles, her eyes black slits of knowledge. The pious impression was only slightly offset by the state-of-the-art Nike runners that peeped from under the hem of the neatly ironed robe.

Leaning on her walking stick she craned her head to watch the Australian woman, uncomfortably perched on a donkey, make her way up the side of the steep hill. The abbess chuckled deeply. At ninety she had a wicked sense of humour. She could have sent the convent's car — a donated old Jaguar — to meet their visitor, but had decided to test the fortitude of the newcomer instead.

'Welcome! Welcome!' she yelled. 'I trust the journey wasn't too arduous.' She hobbled towards Clarissa, grinning broadly, and held out her ringed hand for her to kiss.

Clarissa tentatively squeezed the wrinkled hand then looked around her. The view was spectacular. The sea crashed at the bottom of the cliff a couple of hundred feet below, while a swirling ball of gulls circled hungrily, waiting for shoals to be swept in by the breaking waves. The call of an eagle caught her attention; it was a lone black cross floating effortlessly on the wind.

'I like to think that this altitude brings us closer to God, my dear, and I hope that after a time you too will come to share my sentiments.' The abbess watched her closely.

Clarissa's superior back in Australia had obviously spoken to the Greek woman, who suddenly winked at her. 'I hope so, I honestly do,' the nun replied carefully, conscious of the awkwardness of her position.

'You speak perfect English,' Clarissa commented as they walked through the crumbling medieval gates into a courtyard which blazed with flowerbeds planted in an Arabic geometric pattern and was surrounded by cloisters.

'I am one of the few, I'm afraid. I hope you won't be too lonely. Sister Evans told me that you had considerable community experience.'

They continued through the quadrangle, into the shade of a vine-covered trellis that ran above the doors of the stone cells which served as the nuns' sleeping quarters.

'Five years in one of the poorest suburbs in Australia,' Clarissa replied as they entered the spartan room which held a single iron bed, a desk with a portable radio sitting on top and the obligatory wooden crucifix on the wall.

'Perfect,' the abbess replied. 'We serve a small community down in the village. It is a backward place and the women have many problems they can share only with us.'

'But I can't speak Greek,' Clarissa interrupted, visions of wildly gesturing peasants flooding her mind.

'Even better.' The old woman patted her hand and left.

The next day Clarissa was driven down to the village that nestled at the foot of an extinct volcano beside the small harbour. She was introduced to Pater Dimitri, the local priest. A rosy-faced man in his mid-fifties who walked with the bounce of the perpetual enthusiast, Dimitri was in charge of the white-washed church. He walked her through, showing her with obvious pride the garish locally carved crucifix with lurid blood oozing from the feet and hands and thorn-pierced forehead.

'Every year on Saint Barbara's day we have the holy relic procession. We bring her down from the convent in a cart, parade her through the streets and every woman comes to be blessed,' the priest declared grandly, breathing a noxious mixture of garlic and peppermints over her.

He also told her about the villagers; how, behind the facades of the brightly painted houses lay real poverty, with many of the families barely able to afford to send their children to school. After fourteen most of them worked on the fishing boats or beside their mothers at the factory. Any extra cash came from tourism, but these islanders were deeply religious people who didn't care to have their beaches polluted with naked German backpackers or their cafés invaded by loud sunburnt Englishmen. They had placed an embargo on the pleasure cruises that stopped off at many of the other islands; consequently their economy had stopped growing. The main medical authority on the island was a herbalist who was rumoured to be over a hundred years old. To see a conventional doctor one had to travel to nearby Donousa. It was as if time itself had been frozen. Many of the women, even the younger ones, still wore the traditional headscarf and modest long-sleeved blouses. There was one satellite dish, perched awkwardly on top of the main café, but it was used solely to watch soccer matches or the Eurovision song contest. The locals studiously avoided any coverage of international news or politics. They were a closed, superstitious clan determined to cling onto tradition.

Later he took Clarissa to the cannery where the village women worked, twisting thin sheets of tin into cans for the sardines their husbands caught in the bay. The cannery was little more than a glorified shed with an aluminium roof and hardboard walls. In one corner squatted the cutting machine; it looked as if it dated from the 1950s. An enormous woman dressed in a black frock, her hair covered by a scarlet stained bandanna, studiously fed the machine with long strips of glittering tin, her huge forearms shining with fish oil. There were two other machines spitting out the bent metal that made up the sides of the cans while another punched the pieces together, pushing them along a conveyor belt to collect like shimmering waves at the end of a table where women of all ages sat ladling sardines into the cans. The smell — a concoction of fish, perfume and sweat — was overwhelming. The women, chatting brightly amongst themselves, seemed immune to both the noise and the stench. Their gestures, automated from years of practice, had a mechanical beauty that juxtaposed strangely with their animated faces, their lips splitting like fruit in laughter. The workers themselves resembled some arcane grouping, and reminded Clarissa of a Rembrandt painting she'd seen — a Biblical gathering of worshippers, the luminous features of adolescents peeping over the heads of wizened matriarchs, the young mothers still supple with an olive beauty. Hope and misery traced across all their faces.

On a wall Clarissa noticed a board wallpapered with postcards from all over the world: family who had escaped to become migrants now living in far-off places like Canada, America, South America, Australia. With a pang of patriotism Clarissa noticed a postcard of the Sydney Opera House sandwiched against one from Yellowstone Park. Another, from Brisbane, showed a bizarre montage of a giant koala clutching an ultra-modern tower block with the word 'Bridgeport' emblazoned across it. Clarissa recognised the building from an article she had read in the Qantas magazine on the flight over.

She stood lost amongst the noisy machines, shyly turning from one face to another, uncertain about whom to approach.

'Hello, you holy sister,' a kid said cheekily, looming out of the shadows, his face smeared with sardine oil. 'I am Georgio, your official translator. Any problems, these women will tell me and I will tell you in English. Yes?'

The boy sat down next to her. A bell rang and the machines stopped. Instantly the factory was filled with the sound of the sea. The women lovingly covered the machines with brightly coloured cloths, kissed the plastic statue of the Madonna which stood at the base of the largest piece of equipment, then politely formed a queue in front of Clarissa and Georgio.

There was Maria, whose husband was a philanderer; Effie, who didn't want a seventh child but who also didn't want to offend God; and an octogenarian called Sofia, who claimed that her dead husband had been sexually harassing her in her dreams. 'I didn't want him when he was alive and I don't want him now!' she squawked, sending the other women into great peals of laughter.

Clarissa suggested natural birth control, emphasised the importance of communication with the men and lastly the sustaining power of prayer. But she struggled, trying to sound authoritative as she talked about the omnipresence of God. The village women, infinitely more experienced in matters of life, love and death, stared sceptically at the pale Australian nun who sweated under her habit. They could smell the festering doubt. They could see the disbelief in her eyes as she blessed them with trembling hands. But as obedient Catholics who respected their Mother Superior on the mountain, they crossed themselves anyway, consoling themselves with the thought that miracles could come in many guises.

At the end of the afternoon Clarissa, exhausted, stood up on shaky legs. Georgio, seeing that she was about to faint, rushed out and brought back a bowl of ice he'd stolen from the storage unit at the back of the factory. The ice stank of fish but Clarissa didn't care. She pressed the cubes to her neck and forehead. It felt delicious. Just then a beautiful girl, her aquiline features half-hidden by a headscarf, approached the nun timidly.

'Please, please, I can't have baby. I must. For four years I have been married, no children. Please?'

Clarissa looked at Georgio questioningly.

'She is ... infertile. You bless her and she will have baby, yes?' He indicated the girl's abdomen. Clarissa glanced at her; her black eyes were full of blind faith. Suddenly the nun felt nauseated by the responsibility of creating false hope.

'Tell her I can't help. She should see a fertility expert on the mainland.'

Clarissa turned away; Georgio grabbed her sleeve.

'No! She has seen one. You are her last chance. God will fix her. Please, she is my sister,' he pleaded.

Wearily Clarissa laid her hands on the young girl's stomach.

'Holy Mary, mother of God, please bless this woman, make her whole and able to bear a child,' Clarissa muttered feeling like a total fraud, then added a few words in Latin for effect. The girl was close to tears as she covered the nun's hands with kisses.

⟡

Weeks passed quickly, more quickly than Clarissa would have thought possible in a place where time was measured only by the changing of the light and the seasons. She adapted to the spartan routine of her fellow sisters, to the simple food, to the ringing of the convent's bell four times a day calling the nuns to prayer. She even started to learn a few words of Greek. But her faith remained dormant. If anything, the harsh realities of village life were a daily reminder of human endurance not spiritual enlightenment. Her doubt grew like a secret canker and at night, in desperation, she turned to her original love: mathematics. Using the one computer at the convent, she began to study quantum theory on the internet, searching, as it were, for physical evidence of a God who perhaps hid his existence in the minutiae of life itself. She felt like an alchemist trying to work out how many angels would fit on the head of a pin. She felt like a fraud and she found nothing to exorcise her doubt.

The harvest season arrived, Saint Barbara's festive day drew nearer and Clarissa was swept into the preparations for the procession of the holy relic. It was the main annual event for the village and many came from nearby islands to attend. The convent's founder, the wife of the crusading knight, had been given the relic by another pious knight on the day he came to tell her that her husband had been killed in Jerusalem. On that very same day the newly widowed woman had discovered she was pregnant.

The relic was kept in a vault deep within the convent and was brought out only once a year. Whenever Clarissa asked precisely what part of the saint had been preserved, the sisters politely but firmly changed the subject. All she learned was that the relic attracted mainly female worshippers.

The Mother Superior decided that the guardian of the relic that year was to be Clarissa. It was a task considered to be a great honour, she sensed from the jealous reactions of her holy sisters. Daunted by the prospect she pleaded with the abbess.

'With all due respect, I don't think I'm the right choice. I don't know the local customs, I'm an outsider and I'm too young,' she argued, looking up at the abbess from her kneeling position.

'That's exactly why it should be you. You are the embodiment of purity, even if you're not aware of it. I know Saint Barbara would have approved.' The abbess smiled wickedly.

'But . . .'

Clarissa was interrupted by a wave of the hand. 'No buts, I have decided. However there is one condition.'

'What's that?'

'You have to promise me that you won't touch the relic itself. It can be dangerous,' she announced solemnly.

'Dangerous how?'

'Don't ask, just promise.' The abbess looked her straight in the eye.

Clarissa, knowing that she had no choice, nodded slowly and was ushered swiftly out of the room.

Saint Barbara's day arrived and Clarissa, dressed in a special white habit with a scarlet cowl — a tradition which symbolised both purity and the rejection of depravity — sat perched on the ceremonial carriage as it wound its way precariously down the mountain side, pulled by two blinkered donkeys. The float was a farm cart disguised with lengths of embroidered velvet. White Madonna lilies, a cascade of veined trumpets, were piled high on it, next to bowls of polished eggplants and grapes — the phallic vegetable and purple fruit a gesture of acknowledgment to the earlier pagan gods of Pan and Dionysus. In the middle of this glistening cornucopia, raised on a wooden platform, lay the holy relic itself. Contained within an ornate medieval glass casket, encrusted with semi-precious stones and woven with gold filigree, the relic was barely visible.

To Clarissa, perched above it on a cane chair sprayed gold to resemble a throne, the sacred artifact looked rather like a withered, flesh-coloured prune. It was already midday and the scent of lilies was sickening in the heat. She swayed from side to side as they descended the narrow mountain path. Two priests walked in front of the cart solemnly waving thuribles of burning incense, followed by four choirboys chanting in Latin. Along the way stood lines of hopeful supplicants, throwing stems of wild lavender and murmuring prayers. Red-faced and hot, they had waited for hours in the sun, fanning themselves with pine branches. Lemonade-vendors walked up and down hawking their wares.

Dizzy, Clarissa forced herself to sit upright, trying not to forget that she was supposed to be a representative of God. But under the white habit she felt horribly human. She urgently needed to urinate and the scarlet cowl cut into her forehead. It's all so barbaric, she thought, all these people worshipping a piece of cow's flesh a medieval pedlar sold someone as a holy relic. What has this got to do with real faith? And when am I going to reach a toilet? These and other unholy thoughts crowded her mind until the heat burned away everything else and she fell into a state of blank meditation as she rocked back and forth with the motion of the cart.

They arrived at the town square where four extremely handsome fishermen waited — all bachelors, dressed in their Sunday best, hair slicked back, shirts white and gleaming. Ranging from seventeen to thirty they had been voted the most beautiful men of the village by the women of the island and three of its neighbours. The shortest was blond with green eyes; the next black-haired with blue eyes; and the other two black-haired with black eyes: the full genetic representation of conquerors from the Byzantine through to the Ottoman. Smoothing their oiled hair, white teeth flashing like eager racehorses, they preened themselves proudly as the cart drew near. Amid wolf whistles and shouts of encouragement they each hoisted a corner of the platform onto their shoulders. Then, muscles bulging like knotted ropes, they carried Clarissa and the holy relic slowly through the cheering crowd and into the church.

Once inside the nun thankfully climbed off the throne and, after a quick visit outside to the sectioned-off hole in the ground that functioned as a toilet, took her place beside the encrusted casket now placed in the centre of the altar.

The pilgrims shuffled through the tiny church — the old, the blind and the diseased, the unemployed and the poor — all barefoot and meekly hoping for a miracle, their faces transformed by bliss and belief as they touched the casket. One mother held up her howling four-year-old boy, uncovered the stump that finished just above his knee and pressed it gently against the glass lid. Clarissa, made tense by what she perceived as obscene futility, leaned forward expecting to catch the angry child's flailing arms, but to her surprise he immediately fell into silence, his scowl replaced by sudden amazement.

By the end of the day Clarissa's white habit was grimy with dust. The last devotee was ushered out. Pater Dimitri locked the church then led the nun into the room behind the altar that functioned as an office and laid out a feast of fresh fish, bread, salad and figs. Clarissa was too numb with fatigue to speak, but slowly the food and accompanying retsina revived her. She glanced through the open door towards the casket. It looked innocuous, like a jewel case from some fairy tale.

'What exactly is the relic?' she asked. Pater Dimitri, who was already on his fourth glass of retsina. chuckled.

'They haven't told you?'

As she shook her head he laughed even louder.

'The holy relic is the withered nipple of Saint Barbara.'

'Are you serious?' Shocked, she glanced back at the glass.

'Of course,' the priest answered sternly. 'It is of the divine and has performed many miracles since they took it from her body.' And with a wink, he tossed down the last of the retsina.

↦

Clarissa lay next to the altar on the uncomfortable camp bed covered by goats' skin, keeping vigil. Outside she could hear the sound of the waves lapping against the stone pier. Somewhere a dog barked and nearby a donkey brayed. It was comforting. She imagined the village night had sounded like this for centuries.

Images of the past floated through her mind: her father ecstatic with joy when she was accepted at Adelaide University; Ruby's frightened face staring up at her, tubes writhing from her fragile body; her closest girlfriend looking horrified when Clarissa told her she was joining the order; her father teaching her to play chess when she was ten ... Images of family, community, all now lost to her. Outside a cat wailed; in the rafters above a bird rustled. Clarissa rose from the bed and walked over to the holy relic.

Moonlight streaming through the stained glass window made the casket glow blue and emerald. Could it really be dangerous? she thought, strangely attracted to the engraved inscription on the glass lid. Holding a candle above her head she leaned over to get a closer look. She recognised the words as Latin. Beneath the cloudy glass sat the nipple. Clarissa peered closer. The areola was visible, a dark wine colour surrounding the nipple, which was collapsed and shrivelled. Fascinated, she wondered whether the nipple had ever been an object of lust, imagining that perhaps a man had once caressed and sucked on that sad piece of flesh. Guiltily she crossed herself for the blasphemy.

She had to get a closer look. As if in a trance she ran her hand across the casket's surface. It's just a box with a stage prop inside, she thought, nothing more dangerous than the trick rubber fingers I used to buy as a child. She dared herself to go further. *Go on*, a voice kept saying inside her. *At least open the lid*, it urged.

To her surprise it opened easily, as if the hinges had been recently oiled. Now she could see the appendage more clearly. It looked as if it had been neatly cut away from the breast and was bigger than she had thought. 'The breast would have been large, with a dark smooth areola and a long nipple,' she said out loud, trying to muster a detached medical tone in an effort to exorcise any guilty feelings. The image of the full breast floated before her and briefly settled across the carved features of the suffering Christ. Now feeling incredibly furtive she couldn't stem the flood of possibilities that ran through her mind. I wonder what it feels like? Should I touch it? What would happen if I did?

If it were fake then nothing could happen to her. If it were genuine and she saw no result it would finally prove to her that there was no God and then she could free herself. On the other hand, perhaps touching it might restore her faith. It was all so confusing and yet the nipple was so tantalisingly close … one little caress, surely it would be harmless.

'No one would know,' she whispered out loud. What did she have to lose?

She placed one finger delicately onto the relic. It had the same texture as a piece of old leather. As Clarissa had suspected, she felt nothing — no great revelation or spiritual bliss. Just a slight clamminess and mild revulsion.

Disappointed, she closed the lid and retreated to the camp bed. As she lay there she couldn't help but reflect on how much easier life would be if she could believe in miracles like the pilgrims she'd seen that day, their faces luminous with hope. Then the night, a comforting black envelope smelling faintly of camphor and stale incense, closed in on her and she surrendered to sleep.

She spent the next day receiving another endless line of optimistic supplicants. At dusk the convent's Jaguar waited for her in the town square. As Pater Dimitri walked her towards the car a blind man stepped out of the shadows. Stumbling slightly he blocked their path, his face tilting as he sensed the people in front of him. Suddenly he placed a hand on Clarissa's stomach and, in a high-pitched voice, shrieked some words. Dimitri pushed his arm away and hurried Clarissa to the car. Although the incident had only lasted a couple of seconds Clarissa found it very disturbing.

'What did he say?' she asked nervously.

'Nothing,' Dimitri replied with forced casualness.

'If it was nothing then you can tell me,' she persisted.

'"He's coming", that's what he said. You see? The man has mental problems.'

'Who did he mean by "he"?'

'I really have no idea. Stavros is our local idiot prophet, some people listen to him, some don't. Forget it happened, please.'

But on the way back up the mountain Clarissa couldn't erase the image of the man's face, the ferocity of his features as he made his prediction. *He's coming.* Who? she wondered. Who would be visiting me in this remote spot? Her father, perhaps? The idea of her father arriving at the dock in his suit and holding the ever-present mobile phone seemed absurd. No, it had to be someone else, someone she didn't know yet who had searched her out, chosen her ... for what?

I'm a fool to take the babblings of the local village idiot seriously, she told herself, grappling with her new-found cynicism and a yearning still to believe.

⌒

Clarissa continued counselling the village women, but her lack of faith spread like a cancer. Every morning she found it harder to drag herself out of bed and kneel on the freezing chapel floor with the other sisters. When she gazed up at Jesus' face she no longer felt the rush of inspiration. 'What is it all for?' she murmured under her breath.

In the midst of her anguish she failed to notice that her period didn't come that month, or the next or the next.

One morning she checked the calendar and realised that she hadn't bled for over four months. She wondered if she was anaemic; remembered reading that a change in diet or even a change in drinking water could alter the menstrual cycle. She vowed to concentrate on improving her nutrition. Yes, the change in diet had to be the cause. Relieved she spent the rest of the day on a fishing boat with Georgio.

For the next few weeks she cut down on dairy products and daily forced down a local meat dish. Her stomach grew swollen, but when the end of the month came still Clarissa hadn't bled. That day at the cannery she kept imagining the onset of period pains but nothing happened. In the evening she wept with frustration.

The next day she decided to visit the island's herbalist. He lived in a cottage sandwiched between the bakery and the tannery. The scent of freshly baked bread competed with the sickening stench of tanning fluids and Clarissa thought she might throw up as she ducked through the low doorway. The décor looked as if it hadn't changed since the sixteenth century and the tiny room was more like a cupboard, with hundreds of bunches of dried herbs hanging from the ceiling. Nailed to the wall next to the long wooden counter, next to a 1956 calendar featuring Sophia Loren in a spotted bikini, were several shrunken goat and sheep heads. Clarissa reeled back in disgust.

'So, holy woman, what can I do for you?' The herbalist spoke in a strange American-accented English. He barely reached her shoulders and his face was so wrinkled that it was difficult for Clarissa to see whether he was smiling or frowning.

'I'm ill, I have problems ... down below.' She placed a hand on her womb awkwardly.

He looked her up and down, then sniffed reflectively. 'I can see, even with my eyes. Lie down on the counter, I will tell you what is wrong.'

Clarissa swung herself up onto the long table and lay down. With her habit draped over the sides she felt a little like a giantess trapped in a mouse hole. In an effort to ward off panic she stared up at the ceiling and watched a lizard stoically crawl across the wooden roof beam towards a struggling moth. Please make him not a total fraud, she prayed to herself, trying hard not to feel ridiculous.

The ancient herbalist climbed up onto a stool and pulled down two dried chicken claws from the wall. He hobbled over to the table and waved them slowly over her stomach, mumbling an incomprehensible incantation under his breath. Finally he laid the claws carefully in a cross across her abdomen then produced a tuning fork from one of his pockets. He banged it against the wooden bench, placed it end down next to her and listened to the high-pitched note for a few seconds. Suddenly he clapped his hands as if to disperse the air above her.

'Get up,' he said brusquely. While Clarissa rearranged herself, he concocted a mixture of herbs, pouring a little from one jar and then a little more from another until he had created his own foul-smelling blend.

'I have seen this condition only once before, when I was four. The victim, she too was the attendant to the holy relic. Maria Stelopolis, that was her name. A beautiful woman.' He paused for a second. 'You touched the nipple, didn't you?' he asked, not unkindly.

Startled, Clarissa tried to gauge his reaction but there was nothing judgemental in his tiny buried eyes. She started to stammer but silencing her he pushed the jar of herbs towards her.

'I cannot promise I can stop what has begun, but this tea might help. You must drink it each day before the sun is in the sky and twice on a full moon.'

'What happened to the other woman — Maria?'

'I cannot remember. My mother took me to the mainland and I was not here to see the results.'

'You must have heard something?'

'It was over ninety years ago. I tell you, I can't remember!' His face closed over and she could tell that he was lying.

~

For a week she drank the tea every morning before dawn. Its flavour was what she imagined horse piss might taste like and the only effect it seemed to have was diuretic. As the days passed Clarissa waited anxiously for her period to appear, but nothing happened except that she continued to gain weight.

Her distress did not go unnoticed. One morning the nun woke to find the abbess perched on her bed. She was so frail that she seemed to float above the sheets.

'You have lost your faith,' the abbess said softly. Clarissa looked at her in surprise.

'Your Mother Superior told me all about it.'

167

'I don't know, I'm not sure what I feel any more.' She turned away in embarrassment, unable to hold the abbess's gaze.

'We have a retreat, a special place where the sisters may go for periods of solitude. I have been there myself. It is a cave by the sea.'

On reading the expression of dismay on Clarissa's face the abbess smiled. 'Oh, it's not that bad! It's fully equipped with electricity. It is a beautiful place to be alone and reflect. You are at one with the elements. It's magical — trust me, I know. Anyway, I'm giving you no choice; my driver will take you there tomorrow.'

She exited in a cloud of lavender water and flurry of pale blue skirts.

Clarissa climbed out of the car and helped unload her bags — two suitcases, one full of books, the other clothes — and a tray of potted seedlings. They were some herbs and several bulbs she had planted to remind herself of Australia.

The retired soldier who chauffeured for the convent peered at the sea and the rocks then back at the Australian woman.

'You gonna be all right?' he asked gruffly in broken English, thinking she was too pretty to be a nun.

Clarissa looked at the mouth of the cave. It had a yellow door neatly built into the stone wall. Wild lavender, thyme and fennel grew down the side of the cave and onto the grassy outcrop in front of it. A small cove fringed with spotless white sand lay below. It had rock pools into which the sea crashed.

'We Australians are survivors,' she said and smiled.

He grunted and insisted on showing her where the nuns kept a lobster pot in the ocean, explaining how she should pull it up once a week to either eat or free the unfortunate crustacean inside. There was also an oyster bed, mussels that could be picked off the rocks, wild onions and garlic growing further up the grassy slope and a lone peach tree planted by a nun two hundred years before. Although Clarissa had brought plenty of supplies the driver was still reluctant to leave her alone in this remote spot.

'Here,' he said, holding out a mobile phone, 'this is for you to use in an emergency. The Mother Superior said you should keep it with you at all times.'

'No, thank you. I don't think I want the temptation of talking to people.'

The driver ignored her and pushed it into her hand.

'You take it, if you don't I lose my job. I have been told to collect you in four weeks.'

Shaking his head he walked back to the car. All English are pig-headed but the colonial English are most pig-headed, he thought as he carefully manoeuvred the ancient Jaguar back up the grassy slope.

Clarissa slipped off her sandals and walked down to the beach. The soft grass felt delicious under her feet. She reached the sand, stripped off and waded into the shallows naked. She lay down and allowed the gently lapping sea to roll over her body, lifting her up with every wave. For the first time in her life she felt safe, as if her physical self was melting into the water, extending like a thin film that stretched over the surface of the sea, then the oceans, then over the very skin of the world itself. Total safety, total surrender. Perhaps it is Nature that is divine; the thought curled at the edge of her mind like a whisper, almost indiscernible from the scented breeze that carried across from the beach, brushing against her closed eyelashes and cheeks.

It was later, after a simple meal of fresh crab, bread and salad, that she noticed the tray of seedlings. They had grown at an extraordinary rate — the basil, which had barely been visible, was now six or seven inches tall and covered in leaves. Even the bulbs had shot up, several bearing buds just about to burst into bloom.

'It's not possible,' Clarissa said out loud; she'd only planted them the day before. Could she be mistaken? No, there was no way — she'd planted the seedlings herself, using the dry scrubby soil she'd scooped out from the convent grounds. She couldn't imagine that thin earth being particularly fertile. So why were the plants growing at such a phenomenal rate?

As she walked back to the kitchen table she became aware of how heavy her body felt. She stood up and lifted her smock, running her hands over her belly. She seemed to be swelling visibly. Was she growing as well? Coincidence; must be some kind of weird optical illusion, she thought, then carefully measured herself with a piece of string, tying a knot to mark the breadth of her waist. After another glass of wine she finally fell asleep watching the dying embers of the open fire.

⤳

In the morning, half-awake, she turned automatically and was shocked to discover she had grown so large that lying on her side was impossible. She glanced across at the plants: the tulips had already blossomed and were beginning to die, while the basil had gone to seed.

Maybe whatever's wrong with me has speeded up as well! If it's a disease it could be spreading unnaturally fast. The thought that she might have picked up some parasite upon her arrival on the island filled her with horror. She reached for the mobile phone but accidentally knocked it to the floor where it broke on the tiles.

Panicked, Clarissa struggled to her feet. What was she going to do now, miles away from any medical help? She glanced around the cave and noticed a small pile of flares neatly stacked in the corner. She picked one up, it was damp with mildew. They were all useless. No flares, no phone and no transport — she was trapped.

'Clarissa, be rational.' The sound of her own voice echoing slightly against the cave walls made her feel even more lonely. Determined, she continued, 'Don't panic, perhaps the swelling will start to go down by itself.'

To double-check that it wasn't just her imagination she pulled the length of string from the mantelpiece and tried to wrap it around her waist. It didn't even join. She was bigger, far bigger.

Repulsed by her body she threw on a loose dress then realised that she was ravenous. Like a crazed woman she pulled out the supplies of sardines. Her hands shook with hunger as she ripped three tins open and emptied the contents onto a hunk of bread. She crammed the food into her mouth, hardly chewing, desperate to appease the gnawing sensation that radiated out from her centre.

With oil dripping down her chin she eased herself into a chair. The weight of her stomach pushed against her bladder and made her legs ache. And still she was visibly expanding.

'Well, if I'm still eating I can't be that ill, right?' Anyway, what could she do? The nearest road was at least ten miles away and she couldn't imagine finding the strength or the agility to walk there.

'Trust in God' would be the advice she would give to a village woman in the same situation. Trust in God. But where was her faith? Desperate, she lowered herself onto her knees and began to pray. Suddenly a curious sensation made her sit up. Her stomach actually jumped slightly, then again.

She froze, terrified. Whatever was inside her belly was moving. Perhaps it was a parasite, wriggling through her organs up towards her heart. She looked around wildly, trying to get some sense of reality. She noticed a series of charcoal marks crossed off on the whitewashed wall. Written neatly alongside each row were dates and names of women. Nuns, she guessed, who had stayed here before. It was a crude calendar. She peered closer; some of the dates went back to the sixteenth century. Suddenly she noticed the initials *MS* carved into the wall: *MS 1904*.

Of course! MS stood for Maria Stelopolis, the other woman who touched the nipple, the one the herbalist remembered! No wonder he didn't know what had happened to her — she probably came here and perished! Never to be heard of again. For a second Clarissa wanted to weep, imagining herself, curled up, dying alone at the entrance of the cave, miles from anyone.

'Get a grip,' she told herself. 'This cave is real; women have stayed here before and survived. I'm going to recover from whatever's happening to me. I will!' She took a deep shuddering breath and forced her heartbeat to slow down. Then she was overwhelmed by another bout of extreme hunger. Again she was driven to the table, this time with an insatiable desire for cheese. In half an hour she'd consumed half her supply of fetta. Finally she was forced to drag the bed over to the kitchen table which she had covered with fruit, olives, bread and yoghurt. She spent the rest of the day lying on the bed, cramming herself with food. She continued to swell at a rapid rate. By late afternoon she'd abandoned her loose dress as it had grown too tight and had wrapped herself in a sheet.

Outside, the shadows grew longer. Clarissa walked heavily over to the fireplace. She lit the pile of driftwood balanced precariously over the mound of coals then turned on the lamp. She had just made her way back to the bed when she was gripped by a terrible cramp. It lasted for about five seconds then disappeared. Minutes later she was seized by another shocking pain. It went on for hours. With each new wave of agony she swore that she would make herself crawl outside and just scream for help, but then the pain would abate and she could do nothing except gather her strength to deal with the next surge. There were times when she thought the agony would kill her, would split her in two like a peach being ripped open, but as the night progressed she slowly sensed a shift within her body.

The first light heralded the dawn. With a mighty effort Clarissa pulled herself to her feet and squatted, acting on pure instinct. She screamed — one long howl at the top of her lungs — and pushed down hard. To her complete surprise a baby shot out of her vagina and onto the bed. A bluish-red colour, scrunched up, with a cone-shaped head it was obviously a boy and obviously alive. Clarissa collapsed back onto the bed in shock.

This isn't happening to me. This ... alien thing couldn't possibly have come out of my body, she found herself thinking. Alien it certainly looked, covered in a whitish gunge with the deep red corkscrew umbilical cord still attached, spiralling out of her. She had another contraction and the placenta followed. She lay there for a moment, legs sprawled, her thighs covered with blood, adrenaline surging through her body. The whole event felt like some extraordinary dream and part of her expected to wake up into a reality she would recognise — not this ... this pulsating landscape of blood and confusion.

172

She looked down. She was still bleeding profusely so she grabbed the sheet and stuffed it between her legs. It was then that she heard a little whimper that sounded like a cat. Clarissa's heart jolted. 'My child,' she said as blissful astonishment washed over her.

She turned towards the baby. His arms and legs kicked wildly in the air and it was obvious that he was trying to open his eyes. She wiped his face and nostrils clear of the toothpaste-like muck he was covered in, then wondered about the umbilical cord.

'You've been at a birth, remember? C'mon, Clarissa,' she said out loud in a desperate attempt to clear her brain of the hormones that had left her functioning in a thick fog.

'Peg it, that's it ...' She reached out and pulled a couple of small metal clamps off the fuse box near the bed. She pegged one either side of the cord and cut it in the middle with a kitchen knife.

The baby opened his eyes and looked at her. It was an extraordinary feeling — that she had produced this thing, this whole other being, out of what? She put her hand over his skull. He was warm, alive, she could feel the life force beating through him. This was no dream. Suddenly the adrenaline left her. She lifted the baby up to her breast and placed a nipple into his mouth. He began to suck immediately. Exhausted, she fell asleep.

She woke five hours later and to her utter amazement the baby was already the size of a three month old, robust, beautifully formed, with thick black hair and almond-shaped eyes of a curious green colour. Why is he growing so fast? Clarissa wondered. He must be influenced by the same phenomenon that affected me and the seedlings. The baby gazed up at her with his huge eyes, which also seemed uncannily wise. Other than that, he looked completely normal.

She sat up. She felt remarkably fit. With the use of a mirror she checked her vagina. She knew she had torn but the skin had miraculously healed itself. And already her figure was almost back to its usual size.

Why wasn't she frightened? Was this sense of contentment hormonal? Or was she under some strange influence that dulled all normal emotional reactions? Still groggy, she tried analysing the events. She remembered years ago she'd read that there had been one or two reported cases of so-called virgin birth. One was the rare occurrence of the embryo of an identical twin becoming trapped inside the body of her sister, and when fully grown the sister had given birth to her twin.

It seemed ridiculous to attempt to apply any scientific rationale to the birth or the acceleration of every natural process in and around the cave. It seemed she had only one choice: to accept the phenomenon. But that would require the faith she knew she still lacked.

The baby smiled at her. At least he seems happy, she thought, gathering the child into her arms. The clean milky smell of his hair made her heart clench. She carried him over to the bowl. There she washed him carefully, examining every inch of his flesh for any faults. He was flawless.

'You're beautiful, however you came to me,' she told him then realised that she hadn't given him a name. She tried to think of all the Biblical names that would fit and decided to call the boy Joseph, because it felt as if he had come to her from a dream.

'Joseph,' she said out loud and the baby reached up and touched her cheek with his hand. As he touched her his fingers extended another quarter of a centimetre. Impulse made her place the baby's hand in her mouth. She could feel the flesh growing, millimetre by millimetre, with each beat of the child's heart. It was an astonishing sensation. She pulled his hand out of her mouth and stared at his body. It was like time-lapse photography. She could see his arms and legs lengthening, the muscles developing, unfurling beneath the skin like roses. She checked her watch, timing his development: he grew two centimetres in less than three minutes. Clarissa was stunned. Suddenly the baby starting urinating, his pee shooting up like a miniature fountain. That was real enough, even for her. Laughing, she wiped him clean.

As she washed him down Joseph stared up at her. 'You know exactly what's going on, don't you?' she asked him, and to her fascination the child seemed to nod. He was now the size of a one year old, his beauty blinding.

She cleaned herself and put on a fresh white tunic she found in the cupboard. Her breasts were heavy again with milk. Amazingly she felt better than ever; the birth seemed to have renewed her health not depleted it.

Joseph crawled across the floor of the cave. It was hard even to believe that he actually existed. She needed concrete proof, evidence that he wasn't just a projection of her own mind. Suddenly she remembered that she had packed a digital camera. She ran to the bed and pulled out her suitcase. Throwing clothes around she searched frantically and found it buried under a pile of stockings. Joseph pulled himself up by the table leg and took his first steps. As he walked clumsily towards the door she aimed the camera at him.

She sat down on the floor and stared at the image. The background was crisp and in focus, but the child's outline was blurred, as if the speed of his growth kept his molecules in constant motion. But he was there in the image, evidence that something extraordinary had happened.

You're real, she thought, her eyes welling up with tears.

The child smiled and, wobbly on his feet, walked over. He rested his little torso against her then reached up and grabbed one of her full breasts. With a knowing look, he fastened his mouth on her nipple and began to suck. Her pleasure was disconcerting and intense. She sat back and let him take his fill. She felt his gums grow hard as he literally began to teethe while still on the nipple.

'Ow!' she exclaimed as he nipped her. She pulled him away and wiped the milk off his mouth. 'How am I ever going to explain you?' she pondered as Joseph played with her hair. 'No one would believe me if I told them I was a virgin. They'd think you were the result of a secret love affair and accuse me of breaking my vows.'

She imagined the headline in the Adelaide *Advertiser*: LOCAL NUN GIVES BIRTH TO MIRACLE BABY! It made her smile. She couldn't even begin to imagine how her father would react, but one thing was for sure: he would never believe her. Perhaps no one need know the truth.

'Come on, time to be introduced to the world.' She picked up a blanket, tucked the struggling child under one arm then walked outside.

～

He sat next to her in the shade. Fascinated, he watched the sky and then the sea. He now seemed about five years old. His loveliness enthralled her. She couldn't help running her hand across the smooth softness of his back and buttocks. He was perfect. His hair had thickened and fell down to his shoulders. His face had lengthened and he now had the look of a boy rather than a baby. His mouth had become fuller and more pronounced as his cheekbones had sharpened. His skin tone had darkened giving him a Middle Eastern appearance. Clarissa could see none of her genes in him. It was as if he had sprung up biologically independent of her.

'I may have given birth to you, but you're nothing to do with me, are you?' she asked, expecting nothing but the seagulls to answer. To her immense shock he replied, but in a tongue she couldn't understand.

'Speak again,' she demanded and he did, this time with a longer sentence but still in a completely incomprehensible language. She pointed to the sky and he replied with one word. It sounded vaguely familiar.

'Wait!' She got up and ran into the cave, her heart pounding. She grabbed her English dictionary and a reference book on biblical languages. She returned and, panting, flung herself down beside the child who had grown another inch in her absence. She flicked through the book then pointed at the sky. 'Again,' she demanded.

Joseph gave her a glance that could only be described as both ironic and patient. He repeated the word. She looked at the open page. Yes, she was right! He was saying 'sky' in Aramaic. She ran her finger down and found the word for 'sun'. Carefully wrapping her tongue around the complicated sounds, she pronounced the word slowly. Joseph clapped in delight and pointed to the sun then leaned over and kissed her.

She sat back stunned at the sensation that had shot through her body at the touch of his lips. It hadn't been the kiss of a child, nor of a son, but of a lover. She looked at him and he smiled, a slow, wicked grin, then reached for the English dictionary. Could it be possible that his mind is fully formed? she wondered, uncertain whether she had just imagined the kiss.

She watched as he read, his features blurring ever so slightly as he continued to grow. It was like watching wind rippling through the leaves of a tree, the changes so infinitesimal that it was hard to pinpoint them exactly. The child flicked through the pages of the dictionary, his eyes greedily darting from one entry to the next, drinking in the book.

All of a sudden she was petrified about what this child would reveal as soon as he could communicate with her. What happens if he has been sent here by evil forces? she thought as all kinds of horrible scenarios began to crowd into her mind. What if he's here to destroy? Maybe even to kill me? She had never had a strong belief in the devil per se, but had seen enough inexplicable violence in her working life to believe that there was an essence of evil that existed beyond analysis, beyond judgement — it just was. Could he be of this essence? Medieval archetypes of Satan floated through her head: the horned grinning death-mask carved into the stone at the entrance to the church, a warning to all sinners. Had *she* sinned? Could this child be a manifestation of Lucifer? She panicked; there was nowhere to escape to, they were marooned in the tiny bay together.

'Don't be frightened,' he suddenly said in perfect English.

Clarissa screamed and ran into the cave. She slammed the door behind her and stood there, heart pounding. Through the window she could see the child's perplexed face as he ran across the sand after her. He stumbled and Clarissa gasped, all her motherly impulses on alert. To her confusion and relief he got back to his feet and continued towards the cave. Clarissa closed her eyes, torn between her maternal instincts and self-preservation.

There was a knock on the wooden door. 'Clarissa?' Joseph's voice was barely audible.

How does he know my name? Her thoughts whirled around madly.

'Clarissa,' he said again. 'I read your name inside the book you gave me.'

He read my mind! He's telepathic! Terror rattled her throat as the world fell away.

'I'm not here to harm you,' he whispered, knocking again, his hand pressed against the glass.

Not here to harm me. So he *has* been sent — but by whom? For what? She pressed herself against the wall.

'Please ...' He spoke through a crack under the pane, his voice sounding weaker.

She slid across and peered through the window. He was already taller but he was still a child; she could overpower him if she had to.

'Who are you?' she said, speaking through a small crack.

'Open the door. I need you.'

His plea made her melt. Before she had a chance to think rationally she found herself opening the door. Joseph was already ten years old.

'This was ordained. Tomorrow we shall talk.' He took her hand and led her back down to the sea.

They sat in silence watching the waves.

'I know everything about you, without words,' Joseph said eventually, his voice still a child's but the intonation adult. The intimacy between them inexplicably deepened. He stood up, as if to deliberately break the spell.

Clarissa, who had never experienced male nudity, couldn't help but be fascinated by the changing shape of his sex, which hung like a ripening fruit, thickening and growing against the now muscular length of his thigh. The shadow of hair was already visible across his belly. He caught her looking at him and arched his back, extending to his full glory.

'Am I beautiful to you?' he said, without a trace of arrogance, almost as if referring to himself in the third person. Clarissa, blushing, was shamed into silence.

Again Joseph reached for her breast. Not knowing how to react she froze as he bent down and began to drink hungrily. He nestled his head against her other breast and began to toy with that nipple, teasing it between his fingers. As she slowly came out of the hormonal fog of breast-feeding, she was shocked to realise that he was playing her nipple with his tongue. It was not the action of a child.

'Enough.' She pushed him off her, trying unsuccessfully to adopt the authoritarian tone of a mother. 'I'll get you something to wear, you can't run round like that.'

She gave him a pair of shorts and a loose tee-shirt. They were her size but she calculated that he would grow into them in a couple of hours. He laughed and twisted around as she pulled the clothes over his head. Dressed, he leapt out of her arms and ran into the shallows, splashing joyfully and taking delight in both the coordination of his limbs and the foaming water.

Clarissa watched from the beach, trying to convince herself that he would be safe. To her relief he swam like a fish, singing some haunting song in Aramaic as he floated on his back, rolling with the incoming waves. He is like a mythical figure, she thought. It seemed to her that he was a being more archaic than Jesus. Indeed, if he did come from God, which God? Her own, she assumed, since he had been formed in her, but why her of all women?

Joseph suddenly tilted his head as if he had heard something.

'What is it?' she shouted, but he gestured to her to be quiet. He stood, lifted his hands up to his mouth and made a curious clicking sound out to sea. Silence. He called out again. Suddenly the spine of a hump-backed whale rippled out of a swelling wave, a spout of water following as the whale returned the call. Joseph clapped his hands with joy and called out again. And again the whale threw a great spurt of water up into the sky, the majestic barnacled head emerging for a second, one beady eye cocked towards the dancing boy. Slowly it turned and dived back down again. The surface of the ocean closed and it was as if the creature had never been there. Clarissa looked back at Joseph. He stood there staring at the horizon and for a moment she saw sorrow break across his face.

❧

At dusk she fed him spaghetti, olives and fetta cheese followed by figs and honey. He paused before the huge plate of food, then grabbed handfuls of the pasta to stuff it into his mouth. She had to teach him how to use a fork and knife. He learned at lightning speed and she realised that he only needed to see anything once to master it.

After dinner he picked up a wooden flute lying on the mantelpiece and began to play. It was a complex melody embellished with sudden flourishes. As he played he danced, rotating his hips uninhibitedly as his feet drummed against the stone floor. He was dancing for her and Clarissa found the seductiveness of his movements both exciting and excruciatingly embarrassing. She covered her confusion by clapping along as he whirled, getting wilder and wilder with the exuberance of an adolescent.

He finished playing and threw himself down on the rug at her feet. There was the shadow of a moustache on his upper lip. His eyebrows had thickened, his cheeks had hollowed out, and despite having the skin of a boy he already had the bones of a man. A devastatingly handsome man. For a moment he watched her watching him, the fierce green of his eyes a beautiful but startling contrast to his olive skin.

'Clarissa?' he said, his voice now cracking with the hormones that were pumping through his body.

'What?' she answered softly, not wanting to destroy the moment.

'Lyrical, your name is lyrical,' he said, reaching across for her foot. 'Which comes from the Greek meaning senses, as in lyric, having the form and manner of a song.' He started to caress her foot. His touch was delicious; his massaging fingers sent a multitude of sensations up her leg to her groin. She involuntarily groaned; it was hard to pull her foot away but she managed.

'Remember, I am your mother,' she said with as much dignity as she could muster. Joseph looked mystified. 'Mother love is not the same as love between a man and a woman,' she tried to explain.

Then why did she feel so furtive, she asked herself. Was it because she desired him, or was it because she felt on some

180

strange level that she was denying him? And why did she feel lust now? She never had before.

She covered up her leg. It was getting dark and she was very conscious that there was only one bed. Joseph rolled onto his back and stretched luxuriously. He had all the physical splendour of a young colt, his narrow shoulders not quite a man's, his hips too narrow to cradle the bulge of his manhood.

'Why is mother love not the same?' He grinned.

Clarissa tried to ignore his erection clearly outlined under the thin material of his shorts. She was torn between intense curiosity and the terror of committing an unnatural act. His sensuality was so completely natural and without guile that she couldn't help but be swept up by it.

'It's late. We should sleep. If I give you a blanket will you be all right by the fire?'

He nodded reluctantly. He was now about fourteen, his hands dangling awkwardly at the end of his long wrists. She handed him the blanket and turned her back on him as she changed into her nightgown. But she felt him watching her undress, his gaze sweeping across her back like beams from a lighthouse. She played up to him, turning slightly, knowing that he would see the curve of a breast, the glimmer of pubic hair. Clarissa was appalled at herself; she was actually enjoying the tease. It excited her in a way she'd never experienced before.

Dressed in her flannel nightdress she spun around. He was already curled up in front of the dying embers of the fire. He studied her solemnly and the poignancy of his glance sobered her immediately. It was that terrible look of first love, of adolescent torment.

'Look, you can lie down next to me if you like, but that's all,' she said curtly and got into bed. Joseph leapt to his feet and dragged the blanket over. His breath was a sweet perfume drifting across her cheek.

⌖

The next morning she was woken by the sharp scent of rosemary. Joseph was squatting by the side of the bed. His white teeth gleamed as he held up a fish still thrashing the air with its tail. For a moment Clarissa didn't recognise the handsome man who leaned over her, then she remembered the bizarre events of the last two days. Struggling with the pervasive sense of disbelief that had never entirely left her, she sat up.

'Get up, it's breakfast time,' he said. He looked about twenty years old and had a short beard covering his face.

'I will prepare the food,' he called out as she dressed. She noticed that his English was now perfect without a hint of an accent.

'How did you catch the fish?' she asked as she pulled her dress on.

'I didn't have to catch them, they offered up their lives. They told me they would be honoured to serve me,' he replied without a hint of irony.

He placed the platter of fresh fish, bread and olives in front of her.

'Tell me, who are you?' she asked.

He sucked a bone clean and placed it carefully on the plate. He looked up, lines forming around his eyes.

'I am centuries old. I manifest only when I have been summoned.'

'But I didn't summon you. All I did was touch a withered piece of flesh!' she protested, trying not to respond to the curious tightening in her loins she felt every time she looked at him.

'Don't you believe I exist?' He reached out and caught her hand, holding it tightly.

'Yes,' she murmured, not certain at all.

'Clarissa, you summoned me — maybe not consciously, but part of you wanted me, wanted a sign.'

Surprised by his verbal sophistication, Clarissa glanced across to the fireplace. Lying next to the blanket was a pile of books he had obviously consumed during the night. One of them was Carl Jung's *Man and His Symbols*. He's probably got a complete grasp of psychoanalysis as well as contemporary philosophy by now, she thought, daunted by the prospect of dealing with a superior intelligence.

'Were you here before, with the other woman, Maria?' Clarissa pointed to the initials carved into the wall.

Without answering Joseph looked away; again a tremendous wave of sadness washed over him. 'We have a little time, not much, but a little.'

He stood, clapped his hands and executed a few flamenco steps.

'First the sea, then the sky, then the earth,' he announced enigmatically.

⁓

He took her swimming. Now fully grown and the same age as her, he stripped off his shorts and stood in the water naked, holding out his hand. She found it hard to look at him directly, so, wearing a thin petticoat, she advanced and averted her eyes. A wave pushed her over and he caught her, pulling her up against him. The muscular tautness of his body felt utterly foreign to her. She pulled away shyly and from the corner of her eye caught the proud arc of his erection. Again she found herself torn between intense shame and desire.

He grinned at her then turned towards the sea. He put two fingers in his mouth and whistled. A minute later a pod of dolphins appeared, playfully leaping through the ocean spray. Joseph whistled again, two of the sea mammals swam towards them. He waded towards one and, as it waited patiently in the shallows, straddled it and rode the beast, one arm held high, the other clasping its fin as man and delphis leapt through the waves. The image resonated with Clarissa; she tried to remember where she had seen it before, then it came to her: it was a motif she'd seen in a fresco in Athens. A boy riding a dolphin. So it had really happened, this ancient rapport.

'Come!' he shouted over the crashing waves. 'You ride too!'

Clarissa hesitated. The smaller dolphin, obviously female, hovered in the shallows, waiting for her. Again Joseph beckoned. What the hell — the whole thing felt like a fantasy and, as in fantasies, Clarissa assumed she was immortal. She waded out and cautiously hoisted one leg over the slippery but surprisingly warm back. The dolphin cocked her face up towards Clarissa as if to ask if she was ready. Clarissa firmly clasped the dorsal fin. And then they were off, speeding through the water. It was as if she were flying; the island became a shattered mosaic of sun, sea and waving olive trees. Exhilarated, she felt like a god, the power of the creature surging between her legs as they swam. It lasted a few minutes then Joseph threw himself off and dived into the warm water. Clarissa followed. The two dolphins stood on their tails and clicked a farewell. Joseph replied by making a similar noise in his throat and with a playful splash they were gone.

Clarissa floated on her back, her arms and legs spread. She relaxed and surrendered completely to the sea. Above her was nothing but the immense blue of the sky. All human frailty dissolved into meaninglessness.

After they'd dried off, Joseph led her towards a path that wound up the side of the mountain. They climbed in silence, with the song of the skylarks above them. Clarissa watched the straining muscles of Joseph's buttocks and legs. He now looked older than her, somewhere in his early thirties. But she noticed that in the last hour the ageing process seemed to have plateaued out. There was a new serenity to him, as if his form had stopped shifting and he was finally settling down. The path widened as it reached the top of the hill. Joseph leaned down and hoisted her up to the top.

Clarissa stood in the sudden breeze. She found herself looking across a field of wildflowers: wild lavender, asphodels, forget-me-nots, all carpeted the clearing which was fringed with pines. It looked like the rambling garden of an abandoned estate, cultivated grounds which had once run to the edge of the small mountain. She closed her eyes and breathed in the intoxicating scent. Joseph came up behind her and put his arms around her.

'I knew this place once, many centuries ago,' he whispered. Still with her eyes closed she turned and kissed him. He kissed her back, biting her lips and tongue gently. He ran his tongue down her neck as he pulled open her blouse. Cupping a breast in each hand he dropped to his knees and buried his face between them as he pulled down her skirt.

Clarissa opened her eyes and looked down at him. He was to be hers; this was a union she never even dreamt of. Yet she couldn't believe how natural it felt, to have this near-naked man kneeling at her feet. She gasped as his fingers found the part of her she herself had never explored. It felt as if he was splitting her apart and blowing all her secrets to the wind.

He began to caress her flesh, stroking her backwards and forwards. Clarissa weakened against him, bliss cutting through her in trembling waves. She clutched at his hair but still he continued relentlessly. He moved his mouth down to her sex. Clarissa was mortified with embarrassment. How could he be so intimate? How could he know how to pleasure a woman so? She closed her eyes again and surrendered herself to the intense pleasure, her knees buckling under her. He lowered her gently to the grass and parted her legs wide, nuzzling into her, his hand buried between her thighs. His fingers squeezed her breast as she writhed under his touch. She had never felt more alive, more at one with her physical self. It was as if she was about to break into throbbing blossom. She opened her eyes and saw the beauty of his sex pushing blindly against the grass. She reached down in wonder. Uncertain and trembling her hand fastened around the tip. What incredible softness, a velvet she had never imagined. She felt him tremble under her touch. Oh, the wonder of him expanding beneath her.

He brought his face up to hers and, musky with her scent, kissed her. She wanted him. She wanted him in her, to fill the emptiness inside. She wanted to believe in something. In this. The inherent naturalness of the act. The very beginning when there was the Garden, then Adam, then Eve. And then love. Hot, pulsating, primal and screaming. The guts of paradise, the hot salty stench of life and with it, finally, tragedy.

Joseph slowly entered her. The miracle of his flesh made her weep and gasp until she exploded into one blinding flash and she thought she would die with joy.

But she didn't. And afterwards, in the sudden silence, nestled against his damp shoulder, Clarissa realised that her faith had returned. Belief lay not in some abstract paternalistic figure in the sky, nor in the painted blood oozing from Christ's crucified feet or the muttering incantations repeated while kneeling on a cold marble floor, but in an elemental force that filled the sky, the sea, the soil, and every living cell that died, lived and was reborn. And so it was that the young nun became one with the angel she was sure she had not summoned.

She turned his face to her to kiss him. With a pang she saw that he was now ageing rapidly. Grey was visibly creeping through his hair, wrinkles had begun to eat their way across his skin.

'I told you we didn't have much time.' He smiled sadly at her.

～

She helped him down the mountain. Holding onto her shoulder, grasping a branch for support, he made his way painfully. His body had already started to buckle, his shoulders hunching over, the flesh of his chest shrivelling as his skin mottled.

By the time they reached the bottom he looked eighty years old. Clarissa lowered him carefully onto a flat rock by the sea. With an effort Joseph lifted his head and gazed at the horizon. The sun was already low in the sky.

'When the light goes so do I,' he whispered hoarsely before collapsing.

Clarissa ran to the cave and brought out a chair and a tape cassette player. She sat him down in the cane rocker facing the sea. Joseph was already speechless with exhaustion. Silently he kissed her hand. He was dying and there was nothing she could do. She switched some music on. It floated out majestically, rising and falling with the circling seagulls. Joseph smiled at her, his skin taut across his cheekbones, his eyes hollowed like those of a martyred saint. The sun was just above the horizon.

'Beautiful. Music of the gods,' he murmured and with visible effort reached for her hand.

'Do not mourn me,' he said. 'I am as ephemeral as your dreams, a shadow dancing on the wall of a cave.'

Clarissa kissed him and knelt. She held her rosary beads and administered the last rites. With tears streaming down her face she sat beside him and looked at the sea as she stroked his withering fingers.

The sun edged towards the horizon, lacing the darkening sky with pink and purple hues. Finally it sank below the edge of the sea. A moment later Clarissa heard Joseph breathe out his last breath and his flesh grew cold in her hand.

She laid his arm across his lap and forced herself to watch as his flesh putrefied on the bone. Soon the skeleton began to burst through the dead skin like a strange underworld fungus. The flesh became powder, the bones turned to dust. This is eternity, she thought, gazing not in horror but in wonder at the relentlessness of Nature.

It was nearly dark but the rising moon was enough to illuminate the cane rocking chair. Joseph's remains lay as a fine white dust which traced the outline of the living man. Clarissa stood and looked out to sea. She imagined she saw the faint silhouette of a whale's rippling back moving through the waves. A breeze sprang up. It lifted the dust and carried it across to the sea where it hovered, cloud-like, for a second and then scattered across the water.

Three weeks later Clarissa returned to the convent. As she walked towards her cell a voice cried out her name. It was the abbess. The old woman was standing in the graveyard attached to the convent, clutching a wreath of flowers.

Clarissa hurried over. As the abbess embraced the nun she immediately noticed her transformation. The young woman seemed softer, a new humility shone from her eyes. And she didn't shrink from touch as she had before.

'So the retreat was successful?' the abbess enquired gently.

'It was extraordinary.'

'Good. So all is as it should be,' the abbess replied as she laid the wreath onto a nearby grave. Suddenly Clarissa noticed the name inscribed on the simple tombstone.

'Maria Stelopolis!'

'Of course. She was my aunt, didn't you know? And she led a very full and happy life,' the abbess said without missing a beat, then winked at her.

That night, alone in her cell, Clarissa pulled out the photo of Joseph. The toddler was still visible, standing slightly out of focus in the illuminated cave. She propped the photo against the wooden crucifix and stared at it until morning.

The next day Clarissa went back to the cannery. At the end of the counselling session she walked out the back and was gazing across the small harbour when Georgio ran towards her, dragging his sister by the hand.

'Ask her,' he said to his sister, pushing her purposefully towards Clarissa.

'Bless me again, for I see that now you have the touch,' she said to Clarissa in Greek.

'Nothing has changed,' Clarissa replied in English, but the young girl leaned forward and looked closely at the nun. Over her shoulders she thought she could see the faint outline of wings, or could it be the sunlight behind her? Either way the childless wife was determined to bear the son she had promised her husband.

'Bless me anyway,' she said in English.

Reluctantly Clarissa laid her hands over the girl's womb then closed her eyes to conjure up an image of Joseph, his face smiling down at her.

⤨

Time passed and Clarissa threw herself into setting up a women's health-care centre on the island, raising funds and organising for a gynaecologist from the mainland to consult two days a month.

Then one day, as she was walking with Pater Dimitri through the town, she noticed that the village women were staring at her and whispering amongst themselves. Doors opened as she walked by and a small bunch of housewives gathered and followed her as she continued towards the church.

'What is it?' she asked Dimitri, nervous that she might have unwittingly offended the community somehow.

The priest turned towards the villagers. 'We shall see,' he said in a low voice.

One of the women, the butcher's wife, a strident creature, stepped forward. She approached Clarissa and kneeled in front of her. 'O, holy sister, bless me and cure me of my barrenness,' she murmured. The other women nodded in silent approval.

Pater Dimitri raised the woman to her feet. He spoke to her then turned to Clarissa. 'It seems you have cured Christina, Georgio's sister, of infertility. They say you have the holy touch.' He grinned then whispered, 'Even if you don't bless them, don't worry — faith manifests in many forms.'

Clarissa paused for a moment then reached out to place her hands gently on the woman's womb, and felt life flow from herself into others.

# The Snore

Aaron Solomon Gluckstein hurried along to the Fulton Street subway, his cumbersome body bent into the icy November wind blowing straight off the Hudson. His shoulders shook with unnatural urgency as he fought the temptation to look to his left and take in the gaping hole on the horizon visible since September 11 that year. May the Rebbe save us all, he thought as the ghost of his cousin rose up before him. Reuben Gluckstein had perished when the second tower fell. He was one of the volunteer medics who had worked for the Hatzolah ambulance — the ambulance service supplied by the Lubavitch community. Reuben's death had been a great jolt to Aaron's awareness of his own mortality, a vulnerability compounded by the trauma of the disaster that thrashed daily like a recurring nightmare in the souls of all New Yorkers.

'Armageddon would be a breeze after this shit,' Aaron muttered then looked behind him nervously. He'd had the sense of being followed, ever since he'd left the massive granite offices on Fifth, a prickly feeling that burned the back of his neck. A man in a brown anorak and jeans turned a corner sharply; Aaron wondered if he'd seen him earlier, when he stepped out of Safecom.

Aaron was a claims assessor for one of the biggest insurance companies in the United States. Having completed half a medical degree, before training as an accountant, he'd found himself naturally slipping into insurance. He'd worked for the same company for over twenty years and was considered one of their most loyal and reliable employees. Tenacious with regard to his cases, he was feared amongst lawyers, many of whom had lost against his evidence in court. And he was fiercely proud of his ethical record ... until today.

What could they do? Kill him? It was a throwaway comment, until he remembered the mysterious disappearance of a colleague several months before. Aaron tried to dismiss the churning fear that had suddenly transformed his stomach into an uncomfortable soup. Hinkel. What case had he been investigating? Aaron racked his brains, but the cold was numbing. Hinkel had been due for retirement; he'd talked about living in Taos, New Mexico, he'd even bought himself a rundown

193

hacienda, but it was strange how one day he suddenly just wasn't there. His desk had been cleared and made devoid of anything that had marked it as Hinkel's. Aaron had never heard from him again.

Come on, Aaron told himself now, this is the civilised world, shit like that only happens in bad films, surely? But his accelerating walk betrayed his fear. Sucking the wind in between his teeth, he tucked the file he was carrying further under his arm. As he descended into the steaming subway entrance he deliberately switched his thoughts to a pleasanter image: Miriam, his wife, waiting for him at home. Married for only one year, just to sound out the word 'wife' made Aaron, a corpulent man who tended to disguise his shyness with aggression, smile.

The tight-knit Lubavitch community at Crown Heights had all but despaired of seeing the only son of their oldest matriarch — ninety-year-old Myra Gluckstein — married. At fifty-two years of age, Aaron's timidity was legendary. It was rumoured he never took his clothes off in front of another person, even at the Mikvah in front of other men. Of Hungarian descent Aaron stood at six foot five inches and weighed in at twenty-five stone. He was blessed with a jutting chin and the kind of nose you could imagine leading an army, but Aaron seemed only to employ his testosterone for business. He was useless in the pursuit of women. He also displayed an unfortunate revulsion for women pursuing him — of which there had been many. After all he was a desirable male: a God-fearing Jew who took the Rebbe at his word, knew his Gemara backwards and his Mishnah off by heart and, most importantly, a man of means. In short, an honourable individual; a mensch. And an unmarried mensch living with his ninety-year-old mother in one of the largest brownstones in Crown Heights was naturally an attractive commodity.

By the time Aaron had reached thirty the community was rife with rumours that he was (a) maybe homosexual, God forbid; or (b) a virgin.

Luckily for him, by the time he hit forty most of the mothers had forgotten he was single at all. Even the widows had stopped pointing him out from the women's balcony at temple and the supply of loaves of fresh-baked challah ceased appearing on his doorstep. Aaron Solomon Gluckstein had become invisible ... until Miriam.

His meeting with Miriam was a secret arrangement Myra Gluckstein made for her son via the internet. The community had their own special website, www.mitmazel.com, for such needs. Peering through her bifocals the matriarch screened dozens of profiles until she arrived at Miriam. Myra stared thoughtfully at the black and white photograph of the mousy thirty year old whose dark eyes seemed cursed with the same painful shyness as her son's. The fact that the young woman listed poetry as her hobby and Rilke as her favourite poet clinched it for the older woman, who, in the 1930s had taught philosophy and European literature at New York University. She was still a radical atheist then, before Abraham Gluckstein seduced both her body and soul into Orthodoxy.

'If she likes Rilke she'll be a romantic, and if she's a romantic she'll see only what she wants to see, which, with God's blessing, can only be a good thing in the case of my son,' Myra, a pragmatist, muttered as she jotted down Miriam's mother's number in Chicago.

A week later the reluctant candidate flew to New York (only her second ever trip there); a month later Miriam and Aaron were married. And much to everyone's amazement, not least of all Aaron's, it turned out to be a union of great love as well as great bashfulness.

And so it was, on that bitterly cold evening in November, that Aaron Solomon Gluckstein found himself hurrying to the front door of his house on Union Street, Crown Heights. The warmth of inside shone through the stained glass of the door and the smell of roasting meat wafted out. He glimpsed the shadow of his wife busily passing by. I love her, he reflected, and his happiness caught in his throat like a tickle, an effervescent sensation that immediately evaporated at the thought of the file tucked under his arm. Aaron kissed his fingers then touched the mezuzah that hung over the front door for good luck.

Miriam gazed at the rotund figure of her husband as he leaned back content, the plate before him wiped clean of everything, even the gravy.

'And I thought I married an intellectual,' he said, smiling.

'An intellectual who could cook, of this I made sure,' his mother chipped in, perched at the other end of the table like a sparrow.

'Now don't get comfortable. We're due at the shriebel in half an hour — there's discussion group on tonight,' Miriam announced, already clearing away the plates.

Aaron, who was far less enthusiastic than his wife about the informal synagogues that had sprung up spontaneously in houses around the neighbourhood, sneaked a look at the file he'd left on the heavy oak dresser his father had hauled out of occupied Hungary some sixty years before.

Miriam, who noticed everything, followed his gaze. 'Oh, do you have to work?'

'No, but there's something I have to think about.'

'If it involves ethics you should come to the group — the topic is the issue of privacy and disclosure. I heard it from Jacov's wife. The women, I think, will be discussing the same.'

Aaron looked sharply at her as if she had guessed his own mind. Miriam smiled sweetly back.

'Come, you know I love to think of you as a philosopher.'

'And I you,' he replied, unable to resist the mischievous humour that played in her eyes. His mother cackled.

'You know, once my Aaron was so shy he never raised his voice, now he's a regular Trotsky. For the first time I realise he takes after me and not his schlemiel of a father,' she said, marvelling at the transformation the inhibited young woman had wrought in the great awkward hulk of a man. Perhaps two shy halves make one proud whole, she thought, and wondered when she should expect grandchildren.

Children were the last thing on Aaron's mind as he glanced once more at the ominous file. He knew that, were he to open it, the first page would be marked 'DO NOT DISCLOSE'. The face of his superior, O'Brien, loomed before him. A striking man, always immaculately groomed, there was something inherently dangerous about him, an unpredictability that glittered under the impeccably polite veneer. Had he seen Aaron that morning coming out of the archives department?

The image of Hinkel arguing behind the glass door of O'Brien's office suddenly flashed into Aaron's mind; an event he'd accidentally witnessed just days before Hinkel's disappearance. Hinkel had been gesturing wildly, like some silent, terrified clown, while O'Brien just stood there, his face an impassive mask except for his eyes. Those pale blue eyes that always reminded Aaron of Hollywood Nazis. It was hard to trust a man whose eyes were paler than his hair. What if O'Brien had seen him with the file? What then? Again, anxiety trickled down his spine to fasten itself around his stomach.

The shtiebel was in an attractive three-story brownstone sandwiched between the yeshiva and a community centre. Already the room was crowded with men in their formal black coats and yarmulkes. Ranging from twenty year olds barely out of religious school to forty-year-old patriarchs, the discussion group sat in a semi-circle in front of a radiator. A photograph of the leader of the Lubavitch community, the Rebbe himself, stared down at them, the face with its white beard, grey shock of hair and piercing eyes as familiar to them as that of the President. The chatter of the women in an adjoining room was audible through the thin wall. As with all activities in the community the sexes were segregated.

Aaron surveyed the familiar faces: Mr Farras, Adam Rosen, Jacob Lowenstein, his brother Moses, the young rabbi whose fervour was infectious and whose Sephardic name Aaron always found unpronounceable and forgettable, and then the usual flotsam that had drifted in — visitors from Israel, family from other states. The claims assessor positioned himself in the largest chair in the room; even then his mass sprawled out below the armrests and took up the space of two men.

'The issue this evening is that of disclosure,' the rabbi began. 'On many occasions as a rabbi you will face the dilemma of whether it is ever acceptable to break the code of privacy. As an advisor to the community, people confide in you but there are situations when you might consider it your duty to disclose information for ethical reasons. For example, if a woman confides in you that she is having an affair, do you tell her husband? Or the case in England now, where a rabbi is being sued because he told a man that his wife was not attending the mikvah. In an event like this, what does one do? In the Talmud we read how ...'

The fledgling rabbi's voice droned on and Aaron, contented by dinner and the heat of the radiator, struggled to keep his eyes open. As he began to doze off a car part floated across his vision; he recognised it immediately.

'... Should one conceal information for the greater good?'

At the word 'conceal' Aaron's eyes flew open. 'N-no, I think n-not,' he stammered, 'even if it means the demise of that individual, even if the short-term profit of the institution in question is in jeopardy, for surely it is b-better to act in the greater good even if that means demotion, b-bankruptcy, the end of your career.'

In the ensuing silence Aaron blushed furiously; he'd interrupted abruptly and out of context. The rest of the men searched each other's faces, confused. Aaron's close friend, Ira Weinstein, spoke up.

'I think what Aaron means is that, unlike Marx, the means justify the end. In other words, it is better to be a Judas to save a nation than stay silent to save a village.'

The rest of the group nodded politely, still not understanding a word of Aaron's outburst. As Mr Farras, a closet Darwinist, launched into a tirade about the evolutionary advantages of favouring individual survival over that of the collective, the claims assessor fell into a painful reverie.

Should he act on the contents of the file? For years he'd fought to defend the reputation of his company, and now this — a vital piece of information that entirely undermined not only his own stance but his confidence in the company itself. He had been lied to, used as a stool pigeon. How could they do that to a religious, morally upright man such as himself? His most secret fear, the idea that he was inherently naive against an ethically bankrupt world, rose up before him like a relentless black obelisk. They'd sought him out as a student, homing in on all that youthful gullibility, then exploited him ruthlessly. Aaron Gluckstein was a sucker. The fall guy. The fat buffoon in the corner.

This was the company that prided itself on its policy of placing people over profit. That was their byline; the phrase, *Let us cradle your life in our hands*, was printed on every insurance policy they sent out. Aaron had never felt less safe in his life. The deep-rooted cynicism of the act he'd uncovered made him shiver. Whatever the company's motivation, it was a profound betrayal and one that wiped out twenty years of unquestioning loyalty, but the real issue was: what should he do now? Now that he had in his possession a piece of information that could save thousands of people's lives and cost the company millions?

'Aaron?'

Drawn back into the moment Aaron looked around wildly. The young rabbi put his hand gently on his knee.

'I think it would help the group if you shared the specifics of the moral dilemma you were talking about? Because surely one cannot separate the needs of the individual from the community —'

'No, no, that would be impossible,' Aaron replied aggressively, suddenly fearful his mind might be read. He stood, pushing his chair back, his bulk suddenly filling the room. 'I'm sorry.'

He stumbled blindly to the back of the room then, without knocking, opened the door to the women's meeting. 'Miriam,' he said sharply, interrupting a heated debate on fertility cycles, the moon and religious law. He peered short-sightedly into the array of seated women, a jarring medley of colourful long-sleeved jumpers and headscarfs punctuated by several rather glamorous wigs. There was a flurry of activity as everyone turned to see who the audacious intruder was.

Worried, Miriam rose to her feet. 'Aaron, is everything okay?' she asked, aware of the whispered disapproval around her.

'Yes, but we are leaving now,' Aaron announced, indifferent to the women. Flushed, the new wife mumbled her apologies as she pushed her way past the seated matrons.

The rabbi stopped them at the front door and took Aaron's arm.

'I hope we haven't said anything to offend you? Normally you are so good at debate.'

'No, Rabbi, it's just that tonight I have no energy or patience to discuss philosophy. There is too much real life out there to worry about.'

Aaron stepped out into the street, the bluish air freezing his cheeks and beard.

'Come.'

Miriam, wrapped by now in a voluminous grey woollen coat and hat, whispered a quick apology and left the chagrined cleric standing in the doorway.

'May the burden he is carrying be lifted,' the rabbi muttered before closing the door against the wind.

Outside it had begun to snow. Aaron, in a bid to clear his whirling brain, took a few deep breaths of the icy air. What did it matter about the file? He had his wife and his family. Now slightly ashamed of his behaviour, he checked to see whether the street was empty — it was — then quickly brought his wife's hand up to his lips to kiss. Physical contact between men and women in public was a religious transgression, even between married couples, but Aaron couldn't control his affection. Miriam smiled back and they strolled together, like an established married couple should, relaxed and unworried by the swirling snow.

On Union Street Aaron noticed that a light was still burning in the window of Number 770, the great synagogue. Excusing himself and promising he'd be home ten minutes after her, Aaron left Miriam and ran across the road. The door was still open. Knocking the melting snowflakes from his shoulders Aaron entered.

He sat in the back row, fingering his prayer shawl beneath his black coat as he stared at the Torah, its scrolls encased in silver and gold locked behind the gates of the ark. Then, sighing deeply, he bowed his head and began rocking, mouthing a meditation given to him personally by the Rebbe himself before he passed over to the other side.

Five minutes later the claims assessor stood, astounded at the clarity that streamed through him. He knew exactly what to do; there would be no more agonising, no more arguing with himself. Cheered immensely by his new-found resolve he left the synagogue.

~

Miriam lay in bed waiting for Aaron to finish in the bathroom. She could hear him brushing his teeth, knew that after that he would step on the scales then sigh, then — if they were going to make love — he would splash on aftershave before unlocking the door and climbing carefully into bed beside her, as if frightened of waking her. She, of course, would be playing along, her heavy flannel nightdress pulled down below her knees; her hair, long and luxurious, now exposed for her husband's eyes and spread artfully across the pillow; her eyes pressed shut, pretending she is sleeping.

He was opening the bathroom door now; the floorboards squeaked as he attempted to walk silently across to the bed. Miriam sniffed quietly. Yes, there was the faint smell of aftershave. Immediately her heart quickened in excitement; she even imagined herself moistening at the scent. It was their signal, his first move in the elaborate game of courtship they'd built up over the year.

Both virgins, their first forays into lovemaking had been disastrous, a parody of clumsy gestures they'd gleaned separately from friends and clandestine glimpses at instructive magazines to which they had no proper access. Having grown up within the orthodox community, where sex was considered a sacred and spiritual communication between married people, they were both desperately timid. It was a naivety that was understandable, but a considerable hindrance to a practical knowledge of important working parts.

It had taken a week before Aaron was able to penetrate Miriam at all, his fear of hurting her superseding his desire. It was only when Myra found her daughter-in-law weeping in the corner of the dim bedroom one morning that she discovered their utter lack of experience. Myra, a pragmatist and ex-libertine, would have none of it.

'Oi gevalt!' the ninety year old had exclaimed after laughing a little then weeping a little. 'Such pleasure is sanctified by God! Look at the Song of Solomon! To worship your husband's body and he yours is not a sin but a spiritual duty. In fact, according to religious law if he is not pleasuring you there are grounds for divorce. But even Sarah and Abraham needed a little instruction.'

Grabbing the young woman's hand she pulled her up to the crowded bedroom at the top of the house where Myra had slept since the death of her husband some fifty years before. She pulled an ancient copy of *The Joy of Sex* from the bookshelf, dusted it off and pushed it into her daughter-in-law's hands.

'This you read, you learn, and then you leave it accidentally on purpose on Aaron's desk. If he asks, it is mine from my sinful days. Believe me, it will work.'

And so it did. A few weeks later at the mikvah, the bath attendant was prompted to ask Miriam why she was smiling so much.

'Because my husband has sent me to heaven at least five times this month.' A reply which caused the bath attendant, a sober woman in her fifties, to smile too.

In short, Aaron's clumsiness had been replaced by an enthusiasm tempered by a newly acquired knowledge he was happy to practise on his wife. No wonder Miriam now waited in the bed with such impatience.

She lay quietly beside her husband for a few minutes, anxious for him to make his customary move — a deft caress of her breasts beneath her nightdress — but nothing happened. Finally abandoning any pretence of submissiveness she reached across and touched his penis. It was limp.

'Sorry, honey, it's work.'

Miriam switched on the bedside lamp. 'Is it the file?'

He sat up, amazed at the intuition of women.

'You haven't read it, have you?'

'Of course not. I would never do anything like that without your permission.'

'I can't talk about it, not yet. But you trust me, don't you?'

'Always.'

'It's an ethical issue, there's a lot at stake. My job, the company's future, maybe even my life ...'

Startled, she sat up.

'Aaron! Stop being dramatic, you're frightening me.'

'I don't know, remember Hinkel? Hinkel made a noise about something, I'm not sure what, and then he's gone. Suddenly, just like that.'

'You think the company —'

'Shhh! I'm trying not to think anything at the moment. All I know is that when something's wrong the public have the right to know ...'

'But the company's never let you down before.'

He drank in her confidence, wishing he had more of her blind faith. She is younger than me, he thought, she is sheltered by the community. She hasn't experienced the world beyond, a cosmos that is morally ambiguous, that is complex in its judgement, but I love her nevertheless. Kissing her he felt a ripple of passion in his loins.

'Wake me early in the morning,' he whispered softly, as if he feared the Almighty would hear his lust, then he relaxed his morally conflicted bulk and in an instant he was asleep and snoring.

Aaron Gluckstein was famous for two things. One was his sneeze: allergic to dust, he would often fire off a series of ear-splitting eruptions which sounded like sudden sharp gunshots. The other was his snore. It was legendary: an incessant rumbling that began in the back of the throat, like a low growl, and built until it reached a pitch that caused eardrums to vibrate, set window-glass rattling and dogs howling. Oblivious to the suffering it inflicted, the snore continued to increase until it peaked suddenly in a high-pitched whistle, only to start the cycle all over again, all night through. Complex in its musicality it was the mother of all snores, the maestro of uncontrollable body noises, putting other physical faux pas such as burping, breaking wind and stomach growls firmly in the shade.

In another era Aaron might have had a lucrative career as a circus performer, Myra often told him. 'Aaron: the snore that shook a nation,' she would say, picturing an enormous striped tent with a handpainted sign with gold lettering, her son sleeping soundly in his pyjamas behind a veil of gauze watched by an amazed and adoring audience. Myra had even considered the possibility of matchmaking him with a deaf wife, so worried was she about finding any woman who would tolerate such a racket. When she had come upon the weeping Miriam a month after the wedding, Myra was terrified Aaron's new wife was going to announce that she could no longer tolerate his sleeping habits. To hear that her son was merely an incompetent lover was a huge relief — this she could rectify.

As for Miriam, the snore *had* been a problem. For the first week the poor woman had hardly slept, lying beside this colossus who transformed into a howling wind-box every time he fell asleep. Driven to the brink of exhaustion she took sleeping pills, but found that the snore penetrated even through the muffled dreaming the drugs induced, thus transforming the beating of an angel's wings into the roar of an approaching train, the gentle lapping of a phosphorescent sea into a screaming tempest.

After much deliberation and a visit to her favourite rabbi who had advised her to, 'Be like water around a rock: embrace the rock, accept it, then begin to erode it quietly', Miriam had decided that her only course of action was to incorporate the noise into her own rituals for falling asleep. And so Aaron's young wife from Chicago trained herself, like Pavlov's dog, not only to relax alongside her husband's snore but to love it and even expect it. Within a month she could not get to sleep without the accompanying orchestrated cacophony of whistling air and grunts. So now, smiling at the familiar rumble, she curled up against him and fell asleep.

⌒

She woke to find her husband's mouth between her legs, his tongue already creating a whirlwind of pounding pleasure that left her thighs trembling. Not wanting to arrive at what she shyly referred to as 'the top of Jacob's ladder' without him she pulled him up. Carefully positioning himself above her, he took his full weight onto his elbow and eased himself inside her. He was an expansive man in all matters and it always took a moment before Miriam's pain transformed itself into a mounting bliss.

Staring down at his wife, Aaron thought he had never seen such beauty. Pacing himself carefully to the growing blush that travelled from her neck up to her forehead, he increased his tempo until he too was tottering on the highest rung of pleasure. Miriam's climax began first; contracting, she cried out and her cries triggered his own. Deep waves of pleasure rippled from deep within his body, shaking his flesh and causing flashes behind his eyes. In a moment of spiritual revelation he realised it was the most powerful orgasm he had ever experienced. It was then that his heart exploded and Aaron realised he was dying. 'I love you!' he shouted and collapsed on top of Miriam. His huge heart gave one last thud then stilled for ever.

For a moment she lay there confused. Then, as Aaron's mass solidified into a profound weight that pushed her down into the mattress, she began screaming.

A storey above, Myra woke, dutifully screwed in her hearing aid as she did every morning, then wandered downstairs for breakfast. As she hobbled past her son's bedroom she heard a pitiful moaning. Pushing the door open she found Miriam, still pinned beneath her dead husband, sobbing in shock.

On the last day of shiva, the seven-day formal mourning period, Miriam and Myra ushered friends and mourners from the house, uncovered the mirrors, replaced the photographs of Aaron and gave the last of his clothes away to charity.

Dressed from head to toe in black with a heavy wig covering every strand of her light brown hair, Miriam collapsed in a chair. It was the first time she'd been alone since Aaron's death and, with the clarity that comes with grieving, it finally occurred to her that her life would never be the same again. It was a terrible realisation. As she reached for a piece of matzo — Miriam had dropped ten pounds in weight in under a week — she began to shake with fear of the void that had suddenly opened before her. What was she to do now?

'Continue living. This is what all widows do — believe me, I know. Tomorrow you will go back to your job at the kindergarten, then you will come home and we will eat, maybe take a little walk, go to shul and eventually the pain will subside. Time blunts everything.' Myra spoke as if she had read Miriam's mind.

The retired academic had aged twenty years in a week, her face collapsing further in on itself as if grief had literally punched her. Her eyes, which had always retained the mischief and flirtatiousness of her youth, had dimmed and she could hardly walk for the sorrow of losing her only child. Leaning heavily against the back of a chair the ancient matriarch pulled herself towards the table.

'Maybe God has blessed us; maybe you are with child?' Myra's face filled briefly with hope, but Miriam shook her head and squeezed down the sorrow that filled her chest for the hundredth time that day.

That night the widow turned back Aaron's side of the bed as she always did, wiped her face clean with cold cream, peeled off her wig and pulled on the heavy flannel nightdress he had given her as part of his wedding gift. As she reached into the cupboard for a new tube of toothpaste she noticed the bottle of aftershave tucked behind some towels. 'It is a small sin of vanity,' Aaron would say, smiling. 'God forgives us the small sins.' Remembering, Miriam opened the bottle. The scent immediately conjured up her dead husband. Furtively she splashed some behind her ears then breathed in. It was like he was holding her again in his arms. Carefully replacing the bottle she went to bed.

Her side of the bed was glacial. It was now December and New York City had plunged into its usual big freeze. Thankful for the woolly socks on her feet she stretched her limbs over to Aaron's side. It was strange not to bump immediately against his body. He used to take up three-quarters of the bed and Miriam found herself even missing the little slope his weight made which she constantly had to avoid rolling down. Sighing gently, grateful for her faith and her belief in heaven, where she would see her husband again, she began to drift off into sleep. And then she heard it.

It began like a low growl. Then grew to a rumble that shook the bed and rattled the window panes like an aberrant wind. Miriam recognised the sound immediately but, horrified, hoped she was imagining it, that somehow it was a trick of the mind. Regardless of her wishes, the sound grew louder. Terrified, she buried her head in the pillow, shut her eyes tightly and began to mutter a prayer her mother had taught her to ward off evil spirits. But the noise grew. Audible outside of her own head it was undeniably real.

Should I listen, Miriam wondered as the sound climbed to its shrill peak, culminating in the high-pitched whistle she knew off by heart. And if I do listen, will that encourage it? And what *is* it? Is it a dybbuk wanting to possess me? Or a manifestation of Aaron himself?

'Aaron?' she whispered, finding her courage, but the only reply was a truncated snort followed by a sound like air rattling in the back of the throat.

'Aaron,' she ventured again, 'is there something you're trying to tell me?'

But again all she heard were the sound waves rising and falling in the pattern Aaron's snore always followed, a sequence as familiar to Miriam as the shape of her own hands. Sighing deeply, she stared into the dark and listened for another hour until, lulled by the familiarity of the noise, she fell asleep. Meanwhile, on the other side of the room, the file, long forgotten, slipped out from behind the filing cabinet where Aaron had hidden it the night he died.

'I didn't sleep so well last night. What about you, dear?'

Myra, immersed in a voluminous yellow dressing gown that seemed to swallow up more of her flesh daily, sat at the head of the table and peered button-eyed at Miriam.

'Not so well,' Miriam replied cautiously, wondering if it was possible that the old woman had experienced the same phenomenon as herself.

'It was windy. The wind got into my bones. I had to switch the light on and remember why I was still living. It *was* the wind, wasn't it, dear?' She grabbed her daughter-in-law's hand with her bony fingers and squeezed it tightly.

'I don't know, Myra.'

Her mother-in-law's gaze did not falter. 'Sometimes they leave a shadow of themselves behind. Could be a stroll they took at the same time every evening, could be a favourite seat they sat in — it just takes a little time before the shadow fades. I loved my son, Miriam.'

Myra's eyes misted over slightly. Without another word she finished her matzo broth and left the table.

Miriam returned to work as usual at the kindergarten, but mourning had made her numb. The world began to stream past her rather than through her. Helping the little girls learn their Hebrew alphabet, she wondered how she would live her life now with the one element that had given it meaning gone. Her future as she had imagined it had been completely stolen from her. There would be no children, no more of the security she had felt in her husband's arms.

She looked around at the innocent faces staring intently at the blackboard. '*Abba*, *ima*, father, mother,' the children recited. Was it a sin to feel this empty? Surely life itself was a blessing, Miriam rationalised, trying to jolt herself out of sliding despair. Dreading the thought of returning to an empty house, she turned her face to the blackboard to hide her sorrow.

By the time she arrived home the events of the night before were weighing heavily on her mind. Myra had made a stew; they read a little poetry together then prayed. Afterwards the old woman retreated to her bedroom to surf the net for articles on Kant while Miriam retired to sleep.

The widow stared at the bed for a while. Could she have

imagined the snore? Having had no experience with ghosts, or indeed anything supernatural, she couldn't tell whether the room felt haunted or not. It was the same as it had ever been: Aaron's grandfather's clock ticking away on the desk; their wedding photo next to it, both of them staring out bashfully; her slippers tucked under the foot of the bed. Everything was in place, except Aaron himself.

It was with some apprehension that she pulled on her nightgown and took her place in the big cold bed. She left the bedside lamp on for a while, trying to concentrate on some bills her husband had left her to settle. Finally, when exhaustion pulled at her jaw and made her eyelids twitch, she switched the light off and settled down to sleep.

Again, it began. Very quietly this time, seeping up through the mattress to settle on the pillow beside her like a hovering mosquito. Miriam was too frightened to move. The buzz grew louder, rumbling to its crescendo, climaxing with the descant shriek only to subside again. Five seconds later it started all over again this time a good ten decibels louder, as if it were deliberately trying to get her attention. As far as Miriam could tell, it had remained geographically fixed in the one place, somewhere in the centre of the pillow, purring like a cat.

She lay there pondering what to do next. Hoping to find some physical manifestation of her husband's ghost she tentatively stretched her arm across the bed. Her fingers touched nothing — just a chilly patch of empty sheet. Half an hour later she was still wide awake. The snore was now filling the room like a pounding jackhammer. Suddenly, between snorts, Miriam heard another noise: the click of the door handle. Her heart jumped at the possibility that it might be Aaron, miraculously returning to retrieve his snore, but instead the unmistakeable rasp of her mother-in-law's voice sounded out.

'Oi! What a racket! Miriam, are you still alive in all this noise?'

'Yes, Myra, I'm still here, but what shall we do?' Miriam howled, bursting into tears.

The old lady hobbled across the room and climbed into bed beside her, on Aaron's side. Miriam, amazed by her mother-in-law's fearless audacity, waited for some reaction from the auditory spectre, but, undisturbed by Myra's presence, it continued snoring, not even catching its breath, so to speak.

'Do? We do nothing. I'm an intellectual; I don't believe in ghosts. Do you hear that, Aaron?' the old lady yelled, causing Miriam to clutch her arm in fright.

'Enough with the snoring!' she continued sternly. Suddenly the sound stopped. Pleased with herself Myra turned around to Miriam. 'You see, a good son always listens to his mother.'

But just as the last word left her lips the snore started up again, this time even louder. Myra stroked her daughter-in-law's hand absent-mindedly while she pondered the dilemma.

'This is what I think: both of us are suffering from phenomenology — a philosophy I read about on the internet. Aaron's snore exists only because we think we are hearing it. It is a manifestation of our own grief, nothing more. The snore does not exist outside of our minds — do you hear that, Aaron!?'

As Myra jerked her head to shout at the snore her hearing aid popped out of her ear. Plunged into sudden silence the amateur philosopher beamed smugly. 'You see, I was right. Now he is gone, just like that! Boof!'

Miriam steadied her mother-in-law's frail shoulder as she slipped the hearing aid back into the old lady's ear. As her hearing returned Miriam saw a glimmer of fear finally thread its way across Myra's wizened features.

～

They spent the rest of the night in the lounge room; Myra on the couch, Miriam on the fold-out. Miriam wore ear plugs and took two Valium (supplied by Myra) while her mother-in-law slept soundly without her hearing aid, a copy of Rilke's *On Love and Other Difficulties* resting across her shrunken chest, as if to ward off any other unwanted supernatural visitors. One storey above them the snore whistled on uninterrupted throughout the night.

In the morning they held a conference.

'Mother, I think we should go straight to the new Rebbe. He will know what to do. Maybe there was something wrong in the way we buried Aaron, God forbid. Maybe there is some rational explanation in the Bible.'

'The words rational and Bible do not go together. May God forgive me for speaking so ill of the Torah but you forget that I was both a scientist and an intellectual before I married Aaron's father, God rest his soul.'

A scientist? Miriam racked her brain trying to remember what her mother-in-law was actually qualified in while Myra hobbled over to a dusty cabinet and pulled out an ungainly reel-to-reel tape recorder that looked as if it had been designed in the 1950s.

'We will switch this on and see whether we can record the snore. If we succeed, we will have empirical evidence that the phenomenon exists outside our own minds,' Myra declared, comforted by the thought of logical action.

'And if it does?'

'*Then* we worry.'

'What about going to a mashpia?' Miriam ventured. A mashpia was a wise counsel — either a rabbi or simply a wise person.

'We would have to go to one we really trust. It would have to be Mordecai Bergerman. He is like family; besides, I have one over him — a little indiscretion that is only about fifty years old but he still sweats it.' Myra grinned cheekily, her false teeth slipping a bit.

And so it was that on the third night of the haunting Miriam and Myra sat up and recorded three unadulterated hours of Aaron's snore. The next morning they both went trudging through the snow to Rabbi Bergerman's house, Miriam laden with the antiquated tape recorder hidden in a backpack.

Rabbi Bergerman had been Myra's husband's best friend. At ninety-one he was a year older than Myra but, if Abraham had been alive, ten years younger than him, therefore Myra still patronisingly referred to him as 'the kid'.

'The kid is no schmuck, he'll know what to do, but the last thing we want is this getting out to the community. They think I'm a little meshuga anyways; next thing we know we'll be executed for being communist spies, just like the Rosenbergs,'

Myra whispered dramatically. She'd been talking the whole way from Union Street to Montgomery Street and Miriam guessed that she was nervous. But she also wondered for the first time what her mother-in-law's politics actually were, and whether Aaron's sudden death and now the haunting weren't actually sending Myra a little crazy.

They arrive at the ugly apartment block. Grey and oppressively rectangular it had been built at the height of the 1930s' depression. Rabbi Bergerman lived with his son, his son's wife, their twelve children, three grandchildren and one great-grandchild. The family owned practically the whole building but the rabbi lived in the top-floor apartment with three of his unmarried grandchildren. The place was chaotic, a living hell of screaming kids and indignant shouting women, but it was a hell in which Mordecai reigned supreme.

Mordecai Bergerman was already waiting for them at the door of his apartment, leaning heavily on his walking frame. He ushered them in, then, after looking quickly for spies along the corridor, he slammed the door shut.

'Looking as beautiful as ever, Myra,' he croaked hoarsely.

The old woman smiled flirtatiously back. 'Considering my loss.'

'My sorrow goes out to you, may God rest his soul.'

The old woman settled herself into a large leather armchair and rested her walking stick across her legs. She studied the rabbi.

'That's the tough thing, kid. God hasn't . . .'

'God hasn't what?'

Myra sighed. 'God *hasn't* rested his soul. Miriam,' she barked, 'play the kid the tape. Let's see what an authorised member of the rabbinical council has to say about this.'

Half an hour later Rabbi Bergerman gave a low moan. 'This is serious.'

'I know, kid, I know,' Myra replied, secretly pleased that Mordecai had listened so carefully.

'Do you think we have done something wrong, Rabbi? Do you think my husband's soul is unhappy somehow?' Miriam piped up anxiously, worried by the dark look that clouded the cleric's brow.

212

'His soul? Don't be stupid, I'm worried about *your* souls!' he thundered, slamming his gnarled fist upon the desk. 'Myra, how could you come up with such nonsense? A ghostly snore! Such a thing does not exist! What are you trying to do — make an idiot out of me?'

Myra sat still for a moment in disbelief, then leapt up furiously sending her walking stick flying. Miriam, worried that her mother-in-law might have a sudden heart attack like her son, rushed to her side.

'Mordecai Bergerman, who do you think I am to waste my precious time on such a schmuck as yourself? This is the ghost of my dead son!' she announced, tears welling up. Placing her veined hand ceremoniously on the ancient reel-to-reel she added, 'And this is his snore. Either you believe or you don't. Once ... you would have.'

The two geriatrics gazed steadily into each other's eyes for so long that Miriam began to fear that perhaps they had both slipped into some kind of empathetic coma. Then Rabbi Bergerman finally hauled himself up by his walking frame and moved painfully into the centre of the room.

'Oi, what I do for a beautiful woman. Okay, this is what I suggest. Tonight, very secretly, I make a visit to your house. I will spend the night in the bedroom of your dead son witnessing this ... this shemozzle! Then I will know if it is real or not.'

And so it came to pass that Rabbi Bergerman, aka the kid, secretly spent the night at the Glucksteins, having insisted on hobbling there alone at the unnatural hour of 1 a.m. so frightened was he of gossip.

Miriam welcomed the freezing rabbi into the house, defrosted him in front of the stove with a mug of hot chocolate, then guided the fragile cleric up to the first-floor landing and into the matrimonial bedroom. The two women made him comfortable behind the screen — some tent poles and a sheet — they had erected for the sake of religious decency down the centre of the bed.

The snore was already audible by now and working up to full throttle. It was twice as loud as it had been the first night of its manifestation and, frightened the neighbours might hear, Miriam had placed pillows and cushions over the windows.

Rabbi Bergerman sat on the other side of the thin sheet rocking himself in prayer; in one pocket he secretly fingered an amulet he'd bought from a kabbalist to protect himself against evil on such occasions. He was ... well, frankly, terrified.

He stole a glimpse at the outline of Myra Gluckstein through the thin sheet. He'd been in love with her for decades, from the moment she'd arrived at Crown Heights seventy years before — then a tiny community of a few houses — a petite but voluptuous woman who seemed all black hair, lips and eyes with an intellect that could wither a man in two sentences. And here she was, sitting a mere foot away in what appeared to be — and here Mordecai squinted very hard to make out more details of her blurred shape — a very alluring yellow dressing gown. A sudden snort from the snore jolted him out of his reverie.

'Rabbi!' Miriam whispered, 'what do you think? Could it be a dybbuk?'

A dybbuk? Mordecai pondered the question. He was not a kabbalist — in fact he had always actively opposed such superstition — but here was undeniable proof of the supernatural, or at least some freak of nature, but a dybbuk ...?

'How can it be a dybbuk, Miriam, when it has no body to possess?'

'Maybe it is looking for one,' Myra interjected, a sinister note in her voice. 'And naturally, being a male snore, it would be looking for a male body ...'

Horrified at such a notion the aged rabbi leapt up and ran from the room, forgetting his walking frame all together.

They caught up with him at the front door where he was fumbling with the ten locks Aaron had insisted on installing.

'Hey, kid, relax! I was only joking!' Myra pleaded.

Her daughter-in-law stepped forward. 'Please, Rabbi, you're the only one who knows. You must help us!'

Rabbi Bergerman turned slowly. The young widow was in tears and Myra glared at him as if he was the guilty party. There

214

was no way he could abandon the two women. Resigned to his fate he reached out for his walking frame which Miriam had brought from the bedroom.

'Okay, okay, I hear you. Enough with the tears already.'

&#8766;

They held council around the kitchen table while upstairs the snore continued to whistle around the room, poking at the cushions taped across the windows, seeping under the pillows on the bed and around the legs of the dead man's desk, as if it were looking for something. Which indeed it was.

In the kitchen Mordecai took the opportunity to lean closer to Myra. He could smell the face cream she had used for the past fifty years, the scent bringing back instant memories. Glancing down he noticed her ankles below the hem of the tantalising dressing gown — they were still good.

'Mordecai, concentrate!' Myra reprimanded him, thinking he was dozing off. 'We have a crisis at hand!'

The rabbi focused his attention. 'So, this is what I think. There are two ways to go here. One: I bring in a zaddik — a holy man — and a minyan — maybe I could find ten men who would keep their mouths shut, maybe not — and the zaddik could read Psalm 91 then order the snore out. That is the traditional way of dealing with a dybbuk. But as this is not a dybbuk, and the snore does not appear to be looking for a body to invade, this might not be the way to go.'

The rabbi paused and downed the glass of kosher wine Miriam had placed in front of him. 'Therefore, two: I suggest that you consult a kabbalist. Naturally it would have to be a Sephardic, as we have none in Crown Heights,' he concluded, avoiding Myra's piercing gaze, his hands now folded self-righteously in front of him.

'Is there anyone you know who we can trust?' Miriam asked anxiously.

Rabbi Bergerman looked around the kitchen then lowered his voice as if there were spies. 'It just so happens that I know a guy in Queens,' he whispered, his hand reaching into his pocket for the amulet and the business card he kept with it, just in case. 'You can page him now, he's on twenty-four-hour call. He's no schmuck, a very successful business-man.' Mordecai placed the elegant card with its raised gold lettering firmly on the table.

Meanwhile, upstairs in the bedroom, the file slipped a little further out from the back of the filing cabinet.

The next day at school Miriam received a phone call from the principal. The woman's voice sounded nervous and strangely tense as she asked Miriam to come immediately to her office. She had an unexpected visitor. Miriam put down the phone already imagining bad news from her family in Chicago, or some disaster she hadn't calculated on.

When the widow entered the office, the stranger had his back to her. He was tall, dressed immaculately in a suit that even Miriam could tell would have cost more than her entire wardrobe, and he was carrying a briefcase. He spoke before turning around to her; a gesture that Miriam found profoundly insulting.

'Mrs Gluckstein, you are very young to be a widow.'

He swung around and Miriam knew instantly that he wasn't Jewish and somehow (she couldn't tell how) that he was threatening. Oozing with insincerity he held out a hand gloved in expensive leather. Miriam realised that he was handsome and a good deal older than herself.

'Michael O'Brien. I was a colleague of your husband's.'

Miriam nodded, remembering Aaron's description of his superior — a TV Nazi, he'd called him. Originally it had been a joke between them — his complaints about the man's officious manner, his insistence on absolute order within the department — but recently, a few months before Aaron's death, Aaron's tone had changed when he mentioned O'Brien's name. A note of tentativeness had entered his voice, as if somewhere he'd realised that he'd underestimated the man's power and, perhaps, his malice. Miriam now looked upon the man himself, and determined to be neither intimidated nor seduced. Ignoring his outstretched hand, she smiled slightly; to shake it would be a breach of religious law. Mr O'Brien stared down for a second, then, realising, laughed awkwardly.

'Sorry, I forgot. Solomon explained a few things, but it's so complicated — it's difficult to remember all the etiquette.'

'Aaron, his name is Aaron here.'

'Funny, at work he was known as Solomon.'

'Aaron Solomon; Solomon was his second name.' Miriam offered the man a chair, upon which he sat with perfect grace.

'I am sorry for your loss. It must have been quite a shock —'

'Forgive me, Mr O'Brien, but you have disturbed me at work. Is there a problem with Aaron's estate or something? Because I thought it was all clear cut.'

'Oh it is, it is. Aaron's company shares will naturally become yours and his pension also. No, that isn't why I am here, Mrs Gluckstein.' He stared down at his perfect black leather gloves. 'No, I'm here because our department is missing a file.'

At this he met Miriam's gaze for the first time since she had entered the room. There was absolutely no emotion in his stare. A tremble swept through her body.

'What has this to do with Aaron?'

'I believe he may have taken it home with him the night before he died.'

'He mentioned nothing and I certainly haven't seen a file about the house.'

For years afterwards, Miriam would ask herself why she had lied at that moment. It was the first deceit of her life. Dismayed, she stood there, her words finite and, it seemed to her, slightly repugnant. Later she would surmise that it was Aaron's spirit guiding her and, perhaps, the kind of animal instinct that enables a man to cross a deserted road a second before a speeding car screeches around the corner. Mr O'Brien stepped towards her. Something about him made her feel like a rabbit caught in the gaze of a predator.

'You have to understand, Mrs Gluckstein, how important this file is to the company. Its loss could have a devastating impact. We know how loyal Aaron was to Safecom; he was, in fact, one of our most loyal employees. That is why we have assumed *up until now* that the misappropriation of the file was accidental. This assumption could change, with very unpleasant consequences for the settlement of Aaron's estate.'

'Are you threatening me, Mr O'Brien?'

'A righteous woman such as yourself? Don't be ridiculous. I am just making the gentle suggestion that you look for, find and return this file unopened as soon as possible. Otherwise I can't promise that someone else won't take over this inquiry, someone far less sympathetic.'

'What inquiry?'

'Good day to you, Mrs Gluckstein.' He tipped his hat and left.

❦

Claiming a migraine Miriam excused herself to her fellow staff and rushed back home.

The bedroom windows were still covered over and the room was dark. Miriam switched on the desk lamp and looked around. Nothing seemed amiss. She had cleared out Aaron's desk after the shiva and had found nothing strange; just the usual collection of odds and ends that defined a man's life: an old bar mitzvah photo with his father, several lotto tickets curled up with a rubber band, a thousand staples and unused paper clips, a rubber stamp from work and an unsent love poem to herself. His shocking verse had made her weep, then laugh, but there was no sign of a stolen file.

She sat at the desk, remembering her last conversation with Aaron about the ethics of the individual acting for the greater good. Had he been trying to tell her something about his situation at work? A deluge of memories came to her: Aaron coming back one evening from work uncharacteristically harassed and aggressive, shutting off from her when she tried to ask what was wrong; her waking in the middle of the night to find Aaron sitting outside in their small courtyard, staring up at the stars in just his pyjamas. Had he been troubled by something? Had O'Brien been threatening him in some way? Had this been a contributing factor to his heart attack? The thought made her shiver.

A sudden breeze slipped under the door, chilling her ankles, and the room seemed to give a little sigh. With a thud the file finally fell out from the back of the cabinet onto the carpet. Astonished, Miriam picked it up.

An hour later she closed the file and, shaking from head to toe, rushed to the bathroom where she splashed cold water onto her face. Her immediate impulse was to burn the file and rid herself of the responsibility of such a document. What was Aaron thinking? He must have stumbled upon it by accident, she rationalised; she couldn't imagine that he had sought out such information willingly. Not Aaron. But then why was he frightened? As a religious man, having found such information he would have felt morally obliged to ... do what? She stared into the mirror: she'd lost more weight over the past week and the nights of exhaustion showed, making her look like a haunted child.

What will I do now, she wondered, remembering Mr O'Brien's blank eyes. Picking up the file, she hid it at the very back of the last drawer in the filing cabinet. What she needed was time to plan.

Later that same evening the two women were interrupted at their meal by the front door bell chiming the HaTikvah. Myra froze, a spoonful of chicken soup held to her mouth.

'He's early. The kabbalist is early.'

Miriam checked the huge clock on the wall. 'Only by twenty minutes.'

'Twenty minutes, twenty minutes — that's a lifetime in some insects' lives.' Myra threw down her spoon. Undaunted, the doorbell continued playing the Israeli national anthem.

'You want I should let him in?' Miriam asked, worried about the neighbours.

Guessing her fears, Myra sighed deeply. 'Don't worry, I told the Fleischmanns he's your brother visiting from Chicago. I suppose we can't let the ignorant primitive freeze.'

Miriam waved her finger at her mother-in-law.

'Myra, you promised: no name-calling and none of this primitive stuff. He is here to do an important job.'

Myra nodded, but promising nothing went back to her soup.

Dressed in black leather trousers and an expensive-looking woollen coat, with amber worry beads, dreadlocks and a woollen beanie of some Middle-Eastern weave, the kabbalist looked more like an uptown drug dealer than a man of mystical wisdom. As Miriam opened the door he was speaking in fluent Hebrew on his cell phone, seemingly oblivious to the tribe of Fleischmann children gathered in a curious mass behind him.

'Hello, I'm Hillel from Queens,' he said in a thick Israeli accent, flicking shut his phone and smiling at Miriam. 'I've come about a haunting.'

'Shh!' Miriam said. She glared at the children who, not unlike herself, must have been amazed to see that Miriam's brother from Chicago was black.

'Jacob,' Miriam said loudly to the eldest, 'say hello to my half-brother Hillel from Israel!'

'Hello,' Jacob muttered shyly then scampered off, his siblings following like starlings. After checking the street Miriam pulled the kabbalist into the house.

She took Hillel's coat then led him towards the kitchen.

'Maybe you would like some refreshments, Rebbe?'

'Please, I am not a rabbi, Mrs Gluckstein, I am simply a kabbalist. But I do speak fluent Aramaic and am well versed in both the Zohar and the Mishnah.'

They entered the kitchen where a shocked Myra stared solidly at Hillel for a good two minutes.

'You know, I marched in the civil rights movement and I personally shook the hand of Martin Luther King,' she finally announced solemnly. Miriam blushed to the roots of her hair.

'Mother, Hillel is Israeli, a Yemenite.'

Myra's body language went from reverence to irreverence in a minute.

'Sorry, I mistook you for African-American. So, you are here to rid us of the snore. What hokey-pokey rubbish are you going to serve up — and more importantly, what do you charge?'

Hillel, who Miriam had noticed, was a charming man of about thirty, winked lasciviously at the old woman which won her over immediately.

'You see, these Sephardim know how to flirt,' Myra cackled loudly.

'If I succeed I charge, if I fail I don't. But if I do succeed there is one condition: that you allow me to publicise the case — anonymously, of course — on my website,' Hillel concluded.

Myra nodded imperiously and the kabbalist reached into his rucksack and pulled out a small lump wrapped in gauze. He turned back to Miriam, his face now quite serious.

'The possession is of an aural nature, I understand?'

'It is the loud snore of my dear dead husband.'

'And he has been dead for . . .?'

'Three weeks.'

As she spoke the kabbalist unwrapped the lump to reveal a moist mass of clay which he started to knead with his fingers.

Miriam continued, 'We sat shiva, he was buried according to custom, his grave is undisturbed as far as we know and yet every night, at the time Aaron himself would have gone to sleep, about ten or so, the snore starts up.'

'I have heard of weeping haunting a room,' Hillel mused, 'and I have dealt with several dybbuks, including one that was Ladino, but I have never had a snore before or a dybbuk that wasn't looking for a home to lodge itself into.' His fingers teased out two legs and one arm from the soft clay.

'What did your husband look like?' he continued.

'He was tall . . . not thin . . .'

Hillel created a head and another arm, then wrapped a belly around the middle.

'My son was fatter than that, believe me,' Myra chipped, fascinated by the quick-moving fingers that flashed across the small clay figure.

'His face?'

Miriam walked over to the dresser and pulled out a photo. She lay it on the table next to Hillel. He studied it then swiftly made a rough model of Aaron's features.

'You see, it is like this. The light of your husband's soul has been fractured into many pieces, and one of these pieces has been left behind in this world — this is his snore.'

He held up the tiny duplicate of Aaron. 'If I can incite the snore to enter this vessel, then I will bury it and the last fragment of Aaron Solomon Gluckstein's soul will be laid to rest. But first we will try more traditional methods.'

⌁

That evening Hillel checked every mezuzah nailed up over every doorway except, naturally, the bathroom. The ornaments, each of which contained a small section of the Torah, seemed intact. Muttering a Hebrew incantation he then ran an amulet — a clay tablet covered in ancient symbols — in a line across the bedroom floor from the doorway to the bed.

Finally everything was in place. Hillel glanced at the clock: 9.45 p.m.

Miriam followed his gaze. 'It will start any minute now.'

'I need you and your mother-in-law in the other room; a female body will be a distraction. But you can watch through the doors.'

Myra and Miriam squeezed into the small adjoining bathroom and waited. Sure enough, at the stroke of ten the snore began: an invisible breeze that ruffled the bedspread ever so slightly. But the kabbalist heard it immediately. Wearing a beaded prayer shawl over his shoulders and several amulets around his neck, he reached for his battered copy of the Zohar and turned to the appropriate passage. He began to chant in Hebrew, rocking backwards and forwards on his heels.

The snore continued to grow in volume, completely ignoring the kabbalist's mumblings. Soon it was almost impossible for Hillel to hear himself without shouting. Finally he yelled, 'Dybbuk, be gone!' Arrogantly, the snore continued its vibrational tirade without missing a beat.

Hillel stared at the empty bed in amazement. Never had he heard such a supernatural sound: it was bigger than the faint whisperings he'd once exorcised from a mortuary; it was louder than the human murmurings that had appeared mysteriously inside a dog; more resonant than the haunted deep freeze in Mr Kimmel's herring shop. The snore had a kind of bass beat that thudded against the eardrum and caused the chest to vibrate. For one surreal moment Hillel contemplated sampling the apparition for a rap artist he knew in the Bronx, but decided that would be too irreligious even for him. There was only one thing left before resorting to the clay doll and that was the shofar.

Reluctantly he pulled out the polished ram's horn which he kept wrapped in a handkerchief of silk. The twisted horn had first belonged to his great-grandfather over a hundred years ago in Yemen. The words *May this blow sound through Time like Light through Dust* were etched into one side. The shofar was normally used in the temple to herald Rosh Hashanah, the new year, and Hillel had been careful about misusing the sacred instrument. But it was the ultimate weapon in exorcism.

He gently unwrapped the horn and lifted it to his mouth. The plaintive note echoed around, blending with the guttural rumblings of the supernatural nasal emission. The snore stopped politely for a second then started up again even louder.

Exhausted, Hillel leaned against the bed. He would now have to use the most powerful magic he knew: the clay doll. He carried it ceremoniously over to the bed and placed the small facsimile, now doused in Aaron's aftershave and wrapped in his tefillah, on the dead man's pillow where it lolled irreverently.

Miriam, cowering at the bathroom door, couldn't help but be fascinated by the kabbalist's intensity. Myra, collapsed in resignation, sat on the closed toilet, her head in her hands.

'Three generations of rationalist socialists and it has come to this,' she said. 'For what did I become frummeh?' Nevertheless, worried for her soul, she whispered a quick prayer.

Hillel joined the women in the bathroom. 'Now we wait. Notice I have removed myself physically from the room; this will prevent the snore from entering my own body,' he confided in a scientific tone which was not the least reassuring to Myra.

And so it was that the kabbalist, Hillel Ben Shloechem, and Miriam and Myra Gluckstein found themselves squeezed into a tiny bathroom while the snore whirled around the bedroom like a demented djinn, finally hovering above the doll whose prominent clay nose and belly jutted out like a beacon.

Hillel held his breath, Miriam started praying while Myra moaned in disbelief as the sound pulsated in volume then suddenly vanished. A second later, a thinner more nasally version of the snore emanated from within the clay figure. Immediately Hillel ran into the bedroom and grabbed the doll. Miriam followed.

'What are you going to do?'

'Bury it, bury it immediately!' he shouted, thrusting the clay mannequin into his rucksack where the snore continued to purr like a bagged cat.

He ran out onto the landing, followed by the young widow, and down to the lounge room. There Hillel took out the clay doll and placed it on the coffee table where it lay snoring loudly. Miriam, on Hillel's instructions, filled a shoe box with lamb's wool (kosher).

'Now say something to put Aaron's soul to rest,' Hillel ordered, noticing for the first time that under the black wig and heavy clothes the widow was quite pretty.

Miriam whispered into the small clay button she assumed was the doll's ear. 'Aaron, I will make a moral decision for both of us, I promise.'

Unnoticed by either Miriam or the kabbalist, a group of neighbours — the whole Fleishmann brood plus the family from the other side of the house — peered in through the windows, their faces pressed eagerly against the glass as they struggled for a glimpse of the bereaved woman performing strange rituals with this so-called brother of hers, who was obviously not a blood relative and quite evidently a kabbalist.

At that point, the snore flew out of the doll and up the stairs, hovering for a few seconds on the landing. It whizzed passed Myra who was coming out of the bedroom, almost knocking her down, then zoomed straight back into its usual space where it settled happily around the filing cabinet. Miriam and Hillel followed, using their ears.

'There is some evil happening here that even I cannot cure!' Hillel cried out as he watched the pages of the day calendar on top of the filing cabinet spin around in the breeze of the snore.

Grabbing his rucksack the kabbalist bolted, dreadlocks flying. After struggling with the locks on the front door he had to push through the crowd of curious onlookers that had filled the front yard.

'Kabbalist! What is the trouble?!' they shouted, jostling to reach him. 'Is the old woman a sorceress?'

But Hillel said nothing until he collapsed an hour later into a seat on the last number three train. There, to his horror, a single faint snore came suddenly from deep within his chest.

The next day Miriam made a momentous decision. She took the illegal file from the filing cabinet and photocopied every one of its thirty pages. Then, after a hurried call to her mother, she posted the duplicate to her in Chicago, insisting that she promise neither to read it nor disclose its existence to anyone else. It was insurance for the widow in case the file should be stolen or destroyed. There was no doubt in her mind, after mulling over Aaron's anxious behaviour before he died, that both O'Brien and Safecom were not to be trusted.

She walked home pensively, and couldn't help wondering whether Safecom weren't trailing her somehow. She tried to place herself in Aaron's frame of mind during the last hours of his life. He must have been both petrified and deeply torn. Her husband had loved his company, had always spoken about his colleagues as if, after the community, they were his family. Safecom had recruited him in his last year of university and he'd always felt honoured to have been selected. Aaron had testified many times in court for the insurance company, believing entirely in both the morality and honour of his employers. He had even been elected employee of the month several times over. The discovery of the file must have been a huge shock to him; a perfidy of the worst kind for an ethical man. Whatever the risk, Miriam did not want her husband to have died in vain.

As she turned the street corner a small crowd gathered in her front yard came into view. Thinking that Myra might have died Miriam broke into a run.

She pushed past the queue of people to get into the house. Her mother-in-law was sitting on the top step in a wooden chair that was pushed up against the front door. 'You can't get in! You can't!' she was screaming to those assembled.

Miriam rushed to her side. 'Mother, what is going on?'

'Thank God you're here. Somehow the word is out. They all want to talk to their dead relatives — idiots!' The last was shouted at the bunch of onlookers who stood solemnly in their best clothes, men on one side, women on the other, as if they were attending a wake.

Myra turned back to Miriam. 'What can we do? They won't go. Oi! If the rabbinical council hears of this we're in big trouble.' Her wig was on crooked, her dentures were slipping and she looked exhausted.

The young widow turned back to the crowd. Some of the faces she recognised from temple: several widows; Mr Rubens who still mourned his wife thirty years after her death; Sara Rosenberg who had lost her entire family including twin babies in the holocaust; and young Rachel Schoff whose son had died of an asthma attack three months before — all searching Miriam's face for understanding.

Mr Rubens shuffled forward. 'Please, we promise not to cause any trouble, we just want to make contact. We know something supernatural is going on here. Aaron was a good man, a kind man, surely his ghost is too?'

'There is no ghost here, go home! This is blasphemous! What do you think the Rebbe would say about this if he was alive? God bless his soul,' Myra retorted before Miriam had a chance to reply. But the onlookers ignored her, their faces all leaning towards the young widow.

'Myra is right — there is no ghost as such. But you can stay if you like and see for yourselves,' Miriam answered, not having the heart to disillusion them entirely.

And so it was that the community's bereaved spent that night in neat rows on the floor of the bedroom and the landing. All listened respectfully, some clutching their stars of David in awe, others rocking and praying, as the snore whistled above them.

Within the week pilgrims were coming from as far away as New Jersey to listen to the miraculous snore, now rumoured to communicate all kinds of messages in the nuances of its grunts and gurgles, from financial advice from dead loved ones through to racing tips.

By the end of the week the snore had become audible at the end of the street and entrepreneurial vendors had sprung up outside, selling ear plugs and plastic effigies of Aaron's nose.

'Any day now that phone is going to ring and we are going to be summoned to the rabbinical council to be chastised and maybe excommunicated,' Myra announced grimly, pointing at the china 1930s' telephone she had placed ominously at the head of the breakfast table. 'Like the fall of Leningrad it is only a matter of time. And all over a stupid nasal phenomenon that has nothing to do with my son!' she finished, slamming the table with her knobbly fist.

But Miriam was too busy wrestling with her conscience to notice the burgeoning industry around her dead husband's affliction. Three times she'd gone to ring up the lawyers and three times her courage had failed her. What was she frightened of? It wasn't the possibility of losing her rightful inheritance from the company, although that was a factor; it was more the courage of initiating action for the first time in her life and having the strength to withstand the immense publicity and hostility such an action would incur. But surely the snore was urging her to act?

On Friday night Miriam and Myra relaxed, knowing that everyone would be at their family tables. They had just sat down to their own shabbat meal when the squeal of truck brakes sounded outside.

Miriam peeped through the curtains: a huge Fox News van had pulled up. Already a stream of camera men and crew were disembarking with armfuls of equipment.

'Gott im Himmel!' Myra exclaimed in shock, slipping into the Yiddish of her childhood and momentarily forgetting Aaron was dead, 'Wo ist seinem Mann?'

Still clutching a piece of herring Miriam rushed outside. An anchorwoman with immaculate blonde hair and an inch of make-up perched on four inches of heel that were slowly sinking into the Glucksteins' narrow strip of lawn.

'Miracles are everywhere, even in these grim and sad times,' she said into her microphone, smiling at a camera balanced precariously on the shoulder of a dishevelled man who, much to Miriam's disgust, had neither beard nor skullcap. 'We bring you a story of hope from here ...' the camera panned along the row of brownstones, 'the orthodox Lubavitch community in Crown Heights — a story about a miraculous snore that once belonged to one Aaron Gluckstein, who passed on only a month ago —'

'Get away! Get away!' Myra flew out of the house and hit the anchorwoman firmly on the legs with her walking stick.

The woman winced painfully as she wrangled her facial expression for the rolling camera.

'We seem to have a disgruntled resident with us right at this minute.'

Smiling bravely she thrust the microphone at the irate nonagenarian.

'What's your connection to the snore?'

'Connection? I am the mother. Now get off my lawn — you are breaking both religious and state legislation. This is private property plus it is past sunset — it is already the sabbath and you should not be working.' She thudded her walking stick dangerously close to the reporter who backed away a few steps.

'But, Mrs Gluckstein, is it true the snore has predictive powers?' the anchorwoman asked undaunted, experienced as she was in frontline reportage.

'Predictive? Don't be stupid, how can a snore tell you the future? It is what it is: wind blowing through nostrils.'

'Mother, I think it's time we went inside.' Miriam stepped forward. Immediately the camera swung in her direction. Appalled, she lifted a hand to cover her face but the anchorwoman's microphone jutted forward like a bludgeon.

'And here we have the younger Mrs Gluckstein. Mrs Gluckstein, I do believe you are Aaron's widow?'

'Please, you are disturbing the community on the sabbath ... We just want to be left alone ... please ...'

As Miriam pleaded with the crew there came a sudden roar from the top of the street. Everyone turned to see four elderly rabbis approaching, flanked by twelve tall bearded yeshiva students who looked more like religious henchmen — which indeed was what they were. The four elders, ranging from seventy to ninety-four, strode vigorously towards the house, their tallises flapping like ominous black wings. Hobbling behind them came Mordecai Bergerman, struggling to keep up.

Myra clutched Miriam's arm fearfully. 'I told you, the four horsemen are here. We are finished,' she said, cowering behind her daughter-in-law.

Even the camera crew backed off, intimidated by the sobriety of the approaching posse. 'Jesus, Mick,' the anchorwoman said to her camera man, dropping into a Bronx drawl, 'all we're missing is Charlton Heston. Get the legals on the cell and check out our rights.'

But before the camera man had a chance to flick open his phone the rabbinical council were upon them.

'You have five minutes to get out of Crown Heights before we smash your cameras and maybe even file a legal action,' the tallest and most handsome of the students murmured seductively to the anchorwoman who, unnerved by the combination of sex and violence, dropped her microphone in the melting snow.

Meanwhile the most powerful rabbi placed himself squarely in front of Miriam and Myra.

'Myra and Miriam Gluckstein, the council has discussed your case and this is our judgement. We give you one week, and one week only, to rid your house and souls of this abomination by whatever means necessary. If you fail to do so we will excommunicate you, purchase your property at cost price then board the house up until further notice.'

Myra reached out a hand but the rabbi had already turned his back on them and was marching back to his colleagues.

'That schmuck,' she hissed to Miriam. 'He will not even look into the eyes of a woman for fear of catching something terrible — like empathy.'

Behind them the camera crew were slamming shut the doors of their van. Blushing furiously Mordecai Bergerman hobbled up to Myra.

'Myra, I did what I could. I have argued with them for days but in the end there was nothing I could do ...'

'So what do you suggest now, kid? We option the movie, nu?' Disgusted, Myra walked back into the house.

❧

The next morning had the atmosphere of a wake. Myra, convinced they were about to be evicted, had already begun to pack up her most precious objects — huge piles of ancient books and papers well over fifty years old. She sat in the infamous yellow dressing gown, a photo of Abraham circa 1946 sticky-taped to her breast in case she forgot him in the rush, staring mournfully at the fried matzo and egg on the plate in front of her.

'So what is the point of eating? I might as well die now and save on the airfare to Chicago, assuming your mother will have us.'

'Let's not panic, I have a plan,' said Miriam.

'So what do you know that I don't?'

Later that morning Miriam locked the bedroom door, propped up a shirt of Aaron's with his photo perched in the empty collar, then sat before the effigy. She paused for a moment, staring into his deep brown eyes, then said aloud, 'Aaron, I know why you haven't left us; there is something you have left unfinished, something that I'm sure, had you lived, you would have had the courage to carry through. Well, darling, I'm going to do it for you. And may God protect both of us.' Fighting back the tears, she took a deep breath then rang the number of the first lawyer mentioned in the file. Amazed to hear from her he immediately made an appointment to see her and insisted that she take every precaution against personal attack and possible burglary.

'You don't know these guys, Mrs Gluckstein,' he told her, fear thickening his voice. 'They will stop at nothing. Already I've had two clients mysteriously disappear. What you have in that file

230

could destroy a corporation more powerful than half the countries in the world. Your husband would have known that.'

Trembling Miriam put down the receiver, then immediately wondered if the phone was tapped.

Two hours later she was riding the subway escalator up to Wall Street. Dressed in an elegant suit Myra had borrowed from a secular friend, her black wig exchanged for a chic bobbed one, her legs revealed in stockings from the knee down and wearing high heels, she was unrecognisable — which was exactly what Miriam wanted.

I am not being irreligious, I am not breaking the law, I am play-acting for a higher purpose, she convinced herself as she attempted to walk without stumbling in the high shoes. A handsome executive smiled at her — a Christian. For a second Miriam looked behind her, thinking the smile was for someone else, then caught sight of herself in a window. The woman in the reflection was beautiful. She wasn't hunched over in shyness nor covered from head to toe; she looked modern, confident — but she wasn't anyone Miriam knew. Breathing deeply to check her fear she looked at the street numbers and finally found the building she needed.

'You've read all of this?' John Stutton, attorney, placed the file carefully on the desk then looked at the young woman sitting in front of him. For someone so beautiful she seemed decidedly uncomfortable in her clothes and he had a sneaking suspicion that she might be wearing a wig. The possibility of cancer treatment floated through his mind.

'I have,' Miriam responded gravely.

'And you would be willing to testify in court, despite the enormous risk to both yourself and your family?'

'There is no family, just Aaron's mother, and I've spoken to her. She is fully supportive. Myra was a radical once, before she became orthodox.'

'That's right, Aaron Gluckstein was . . .'

'We are of the Lubavitch movement.'

231

Now the young woman's discomfort was starting to make sense to the lawyer.

'It must have taken some courage to make the decision to approach me. I appreciate it.'

'Not courage. I have strong reason to believe it's what Aaron would have wanted, still wants.'

John Stutton, a staunch atheist and confirmed rationalist, decided he didn't really want to go into the reason why the widow should have arrived at such a conclusion after Aaron's death. He was just grateful that, out of all the lawyers mentioned in the file, she had chosen him. Trying to underplay the tremendous excitement that began to percolate at the thought of the biggest opportunity in his career, the attorney walked to the window. Outside the street lights had begun to light up the city.

'You do realise that when this breaks — and believe me, it will break, Mrs Gluckstein — it stands to be one of the biggest law suits this country has ever seen? It will also be a victory of the small man over the corporation, a long overdue victory.'

It was here that John Stutton, an unemotional man in his late fifties who had been fighting Safecom for over two decades, began to lose control.

'You have to understand that I have clients who have lost sons, daughters, spouses — all deaths that could have been prevented if this...' he pushed the file forward, 'if this information had been acted on.'

'I lost a husband, Mr Stutton.'

'Well, maybe now there's a chance to get a little bit of him back,' the lawyer concluded smugly, thrilled with his own rhetoric. The young widow couldn't help but wonder what the attorney would say if he knew that little bit had already come back, although not in a way he could possibly imagine.

Miriam returned to the house to discover the place ransacked. Tables and chairs had been overturned and papers fluttered down the staircase like disorientated doves. Myra's two Japanese

232

carp (almost as old as she was) were flapping on the carpet, their bowl smashed, along with several vases. Miriam stood in the middle of the room stunned, wondering whether the chaos could somehow be an imagined extension of her own recently disturbed life. A book, splayed and broken-spined on the edge of an overturned chair tottered and fell to the floor. The thud brought her back to reality. Safecom, it had to be. She ran up to the bedroom.

As she'd suspected the filing cabinet was on its side, contents spilled everywhere, and Aaron's desk drawers had been pulled out and emptied. She scanned the contents quickly — the thieves hadn't actually taken anything. What they were after was now safely in the hands of Stutton, Stutton & Jobain. Below, the front door slammed.

'Oi vey!' Myra shouted. Miriam ran back out to the landing to see her mother-in-law clutching at the wall for support.

'We have been robbed and desecrated!' she yelled, holding her two dead carp up to heaven. 'Enough with the misery! When is it going to stop, tell me this, you sadistic schmuck!'

Realising Myra was addressing God, Miriam took her to the kitchen and sat her down. She gave her a sedative.

'Take this and then you sleep, okay? We'll deal with the mess in the morning.'

'Sure, as if life is always that simple,' the old lady muttered cynically but allowed herself to be led to bed like a lamb.

As soon as Myra was safely tucked up, Miriam called John Stutton who immediately sent a security guard over.

'Mrs Gluckstein, these people are playing very serious hardball. They're not going to be worrying about religious etiquette when they break your door down in the middle of night, therefore I suggest you don't worry about it either.'

The security guard arrived within twenty minutes: a huge Latino with the friendly name of Jesus Hosé Mandelis. Deeply religious himself, he insisted on staying by the front door, even when gratefully consuming the snack of chopped liver and bread Miriam made up for him. She couldn't help be relieved by the fact that along with a collection of crucifixes and evil-eye charms, he wore not just one gun but two and seemed to keep in constant contact with a network of fellow security guards all over NYC via his pager.

Finally, exhausted, Miriam collapsed onto her and Aaron's bed, still fully clothed, still surrounded by the pandemonium the intruders had left. It was only as she was drifting off to sleep that she realised Aaron's snore was far fainter than before.

'So you approve,' she whispered, smiling, before curling up on his side of the bed.

⤛⤜

The next morning at Stutton, Stutton & Jobain, John Stutton recorded Miriam's statement and warned her that she would be expected to make an affidavit in front of a judge. then he ushered in a middle-aged couple. The husband, his face a road map of twitches, seemed incapable of meeting Miriam's eyes. The wife, a tall, thin dried-up stick of a woman clutched at her handbag as if she were drowning and it was a life buoy.

'Mr and Mrs Halston's son and daughter-in-law were both killed in the SVU 450,' John Stutton explained. 'Their three-month-old son survived only to die in a coma a week later. I believe the car design flaw described in your husband's file was directly responsible. We filed an action five years ago; we lost. On behalf of the Halstons and fifty other plaintives I have relodged a legal action, one that I am confident we can now win. I have also issued a press statement that will hit the stands tomorrow morning. Believe me, Mrs Gluckstein, this will be big news, very big news.'

Jerking her arms free from her handbag Mrs Halston suddenly grabbed Miriam's hands and squeezed them in gratitude.

'My wife says thank you. She hasn't spoken since the accident,' Mr Halston translated, turning his mournful bloodshot eyes to Miriam for the first time.

⤛⤜

Outside, the burly security guard insisted on walking the young widow back to the subway. It was cold but the faint hint of spring was buried deep under the chill.

'Mrs Gluckstein, you don't know the evil that is lurking in these streets,' Jesus Hosé explained. 'If they want to take you out they will take you out — but now ... now you have done the right thing; now they can't touch you.'

As they turned the corner Miriam saw O'Brien leaning up against a limousine. He seemed to be waiting for her. Jesus Hosé caught sight of him in the same instant. 'Keep walking,' he instructed, his hand tightening on the pistol hidden in his waistband.

But O'Brien didn't move. Miriam looked over and locked eyes with him. His steely blue stare displayed nothing but utter disdain. He spat slowly and deliberately into the gutter. But the young widow didn't care; she had broken her fear of him, she had won.

Shivering with this new sense of power she hurried along to the Fulton Street subway, her slim body bent against the icy wind as it blew straight off the Hudson. 'May the Rebbe save us all,' she said to herself as the ghost of Aaron rose up before her, smiling.

That night, in the tidied bedroom, she cleaned her face with cold cream and slipped on the heavy nightdress. It was a quarter to ten. A growing anxiety gnawed at her stomach as it had for the past few weeks at this time. 'Have faith,' she muttered to herself as she slipped between the chilly sheets. At three minutes to she could bear it no longer and leaned over to switch off the bedside lamp. She lay in the dark and waited. The silence was deafening.

At half past ten Myra knocked on the bedroom door and entered.

'It's gone,' she said, before sitting down on the bed. 'I can't believe it, it's gone.'

They both listened. Somewhere a dog barked; next door a baby started wailing. Then, suddenly, a distinctive, explosive sneeze sounded out from above Aaron's side of the bed.

'Myra, please tell me that was you.'

'It wasn't.'

235

Myra's voice sounded very small indeed. Again the sneeze echoed out, followed by several others, as loud and as identifiable as the first.

'Oi gevalt! Is it for this that I had a son?'

'And I a husband?'

It was then that the two women started laughing and weeping — just a little.

# Hair Shirt

I guess I never imagined I'd get so involved with a married man. I mean, it's not like I don't have options. Maybe it's this city: there doesn't seem to be a straight man who's not bad, sad or mad east of Parramatta. Maybe it's just the way I see things, but the bitter truth is that at the age of twenty-six I find myself deeply, undeniably and totally in love with my married lover of three years. Okay, this is going to sound really clichéd because, yes, he is my boss and yes, he is forty-seven, but I know we are meant to be together. It's an organic bonding I can't explain. He's my soulmate: we have the same energy, the same ambitions, the same sense of humour and the sex is transforming.

His name? Robert Tetherhook and we work for Pear Records. Actually Robert set up Pear Records in the late eighties; he was manager of a couple of really sick acts and one band went platinum internationally and the next thing Robert has his own company. But that's Robert — entrepreneurial.

He's good-looking, five foot ten, with hair, a little overweight but I like that, the way the curve of his belly fits around my back in bed — not that he ever sleeps the night, except when we're on tour with a band or at some marketing conference. When we're away together *legitimately*. I love those times, when I can pretend I'm his wife. He has hair on his shoulders and a long grey ponytail which he hasn't cut in years.

When we make love we have this ritual. I unplait his mane and brush it from the top of his head in long, luxurious strokes that reach all the way down to his waist. Yum. It's our special foreplay. I crouch over him with my breasts touching his back. As the hairbrush bites into his scalp tremors of ecstasy vibrate through his whole torso and he makes these little whimpers, purring noises in the back of his throat. I love brushing his hair; it's the only time I have power over him.

What Robert doesn't know is that I collect it. Tucked under my futon bed is a David Jones plastic shopping bag stuffed full. Three years' worth. Little grey clouds fragrant with aftershave, a faint whiff of semen and a particular underlay of fruitiness that is totally Robert. Sometimes after he's left, in those moments of abandonment sitting up in my bed with his seed dribbling down my thighs, the pillow roughed up and the doona still pungent, when the world's falling away and I'm thinking he'll never come back, he'll never sleep a full night with me and I will never have that luxury so many other women have of simply picking up the phone and dialling their man, and my fear begins to creep up from the floor, curling around the legs of the bed and crawling across the bedspread like a hideous slug leaving behind a thick slime of doubt, it's then that I reach down and pull out that bag to thrust my hands deep into the soft cloud of his fur. I love him. Did I say that before? Well, it's true; he's everything — my best friend, my mentor, my family. I wouldn't survive without him.

My shrink thinks he's my father substitute. I reckon that's simplistic; I can't remember ever fantasising about having sex with my father. In fact, I can hardly remember my father at all. He was killed in a train accident when I was eleven. I have a vague memory of his face if I really concentrate, and occasionally I dream I've met him again, only I'm my age now and he's his age when he died, which was thirty-six. Also, he was nothing like Robert. For a start, he was a weak man, a clerk in the City Council, whereas Robert is loud, very masculine and aggressive. Some people in the industry think he's a bully. The Bull from the North they call him because he's from Queensland. His brother was that well-known real estate developer who disappeared mysteriously a couple of years ago. Gavin Tetherhook. Robert's well known too but for different reasons.

Robert's younger than Gavin. He doesn't like to talk about his missing brother. Robert refuses to talk about a lot of things, though I've really helped him open up over the years. Now he actually tells me about his childhood. Like how awful it was when his father, a sugar cane farmer, went suddenly belly-up. That was a big change in Robert's life. It made a huge impression on him. I think that's what drives him now: a terrible fear of poverty.

I know he loves me because I'm the only person who really understands him. Robert's amazing. Underneath he's just a vulnerable little boy who's very very talented. The tragedy is that Robert really *is* creative. He should have pursued his own career as a composer — it's just that he's also a really good manager and he had to make money. But I know his true genius, unlike his wife. I know how to nurture him, like he's nurtured me.

It was Robert who taught me the biz, how to play off one magazine against another, how a smashed up hotel room with a singer and a hooker can engineer major CD sales. But most importantly, Robert was the first person to believe I had any talent at all.

Not like Mum. She always wanted me to be something solid like a nurse or a teacher. She lives by herself in a terrace near Summer Hill. She's pathetic really. She never remarried after my father's death and has been at the same job for twenty-five years. She works in a branch of the National Australia Bank. Sometimes I think she must be the only person in Australia who's been in the same job for twenty-five years. Just the thought of visiting her makes me feel nauseous. If there's anything I'm determined about, it's that I'm not going to end up like my mother. Ever. Oh, she still has sex. With this creepy guy she met through a singles website about four years ago. He had tea with us once and he couldn't stop staring at my tits the whole time. He's a Jehovah's Witness or something.

I think she's guessed about Robert. She's always on my case about not having a boyfriend and the dangers of married men. The weird thing is that they are the same age. She met him once at the office and she actually flirted with him, it was disgusting. Yeah, there is no way I'm going to end up like her.

Robert's wife doesn't understand him at all. I can tell from the way he talks about her. He's always complaining about how she's too busy whingeing about her health or planning renovations on the house to ask him about work or how he's feeling. Whereas when we're together we don't even have to talk, it's like we just sense when the other is in distress. That's how I know we're soulmates. I had our astrological charts done and his Mars is on my Venus — that's about as good as it gets. It's a psychic connection, truly. I even bought him a computer for his birthday so that he can compose his electronic music when he's at my place. He writes beautiful music, he really does. He's a genius. I think I said that before. He's going to leave her, I know it. It's just a question of finding the right time to tell her.

I've never met her. I've seen photos: she's about forty, pretty in a slim kind of way, with black hair she wears short and brown eyes. She looks as if she's Italian or something. Robert once said she had a French mother. They've got no children. She couldn't have them and they didn't want to adopt. She's nothing like me. I'm big and sprawly — I mean I have a comfortable body. Some might think I'm overweight but I like the way my hips have curves and my breasts are more than one handful. I used to be really hung up about being fat but Robert changed all that. He's taught me to be proud of my body. 'May thy cup spilleth over and your arse fill my hands for ever,' he used to whisper at the beginning. Let's face it: I'm big-boned. My father was Czech and my mother's Scottish-Australian. Dad was fat, lumpen and Slavic while my mother is angular and tall. When I stand naked in front of the mirror I can see both of them in me: the broadness of my father's cheekbones, his full mouth, my mother's heavy hips. Plus I'm blonde with blue eyes — the complete opposite of Robert's wife. At least you can say he hasn't got a type.

I could have met her by now if I'd wanted to. There was a stage when Robert decided that I should, as if an encounter between us would somehow absolve him of guilt. That's the generous analysis. The ungenerous one is that he'd get off on having the two women in his life in the same room. I refused. She doesn't know about me. She might sense something, but as far as I know Robert has never given her any reason to suspect and he certainly hasn't told her. He always makes sure she doesn't come to office parties or record launches if I'm going to be there. She loathes the industry so that isn't hard to arrange. I mean, why did she marry him in the first place if she doesn't enjoy what he does? Don't get me wrong, I consider myself a feminist, or at least a post-post-feminist. I mean, the word feminism was out of fashion by the time I was born. But I'm not a woman-hater and I know that if I met her I wouldn't be able to keep seeing Robert. It's easier to think of her as an abstract; an obstacle to be overcome, worn away by time like water eats into stone. And I'm succeeding, I know I am. It's just that Robert needs hurrying along.

The trouble is that she's always ill or too emotionally fragile for him to leave her. Robert's always trying to encourage her to get a full-time job and gain some financial independence. He's been saying that for three years now and I'm sick of it. I guess that's why I've decided to take things into my own hands.

Friday night and he's just left. It's raining outside. One of those Sydney nights when all the breeziness of the innocent sky is blown away and suddenly pelting rain traps us in our own nostalgia.

I keep a diary of our lovemaking because I like to look back at the entries and compare notes. I can see patterns. People think relationships are linear, that they progress. I don't think they do. I think they're shaped like metal springs, a spiral with decreasing circles. Lately Robert's gone quiet. I'm frightened he's going to leave me. Even tonight after we'd come, and he was lying curled up around me, there was this strange silence. He seemed to be whirling away from me like an astronaut who's severed the cord attaching him to the mother ship and is voluntarily floating into space, the universe reflected in his visor.

'This is ground control to Major Tom,' I whispered in his ear, knowing how much he likes that old Bowie reference, but he just made some excuse about being exhausted and how Georgina would be wondering why he was working so late at the office with his mobile off and how he should really go. And I let him. Because, my friends, I have stopped waiting. I have seized fate with both hands.

It was this *Vogue* article that really changed my life: *Pursuer or Distancer, Active or Passive — take control of your own life.* It was about co-dependent relationships and how they can hijack your life, your career and your biological clock. There was this paragraph about the tyranny of waiting for the phone to ring, about how 20 per cent of all women under the age of thirty-five spend 35.9 per cent of their time waiting for the phone to ring and 70 per cent of the time it's the wrong number which means they spend over 60 per cent of their lives waiting for something to happen that just isn't going to. Scary. That's me, I thought. The next night I stopped taking the pill.

It's no longer raining, but I can hear the water dripping off the gutter and onto the path below. It's cosy in here. I'm wrapped up in the doona and I think I can feel a tickle in my ovaries. Conception. At least I hope so.

≈

I suppose I reached some kind of decision driving home in that shocking rain. I like my car. Revise that: I love my fucking car. It is my metal skin, the extension of my own body heat teased out and stretched across its perfect steel chassis. You know why I love my car? Because I can climb in, switch it on, ride it hard and it doesn't ask any fucking questions. Which is why I fell in love with Madeleine in the first place, because she never asked any questions. Blind trust: there's no greater turn-on. I mean, she really believed in me. She'd look up at me with those big blue eyes, pure adulation shining out of them. It used to give me an instant erection. Used to.

You've got to understand: my wife is an intellectual. Yep, I married an intellectual with a rich daddy, because I could and because ... well, in truth, I suppose I thought some of it would rub off on me. Knock the rough edges off, take the country out of the boy and replace it with Hunters Hill. Fat fucking chance. If anything, despite *The Economist*, *The Guardian Weekly* and the Australian Chamber Orchestra subscription, I find myself becoming even more ocker, in reaction. I reckon it's Georgina's fault. Then again, it could be the influence of our wonderful prime minister Johnnie Howard. Since he got in, every redneck north of Cairns suddenly embodies the Great Australia we all know and love and — the radical minority anyway — escaped. I was that redneck pre-deconstruction. The big sullen oaf who hitched down from Tully around 1972, hit the Cross and the happenings at the Mandala Cinema and the boozy all-nighters at the Manzil Room, then one stoned night talked his way into being a roadie for Tamam Shud. That was my first break. The rest is history.

By the time I met Georgina I was managing three internationally successful bands and had my own office with fifteen employees. But secretly, between you and me, I still didn't feel legitimate. What I didn't realise then is that *you never do*. When I met this sophisticated ice queen with the degree in European Film, who'd lived in Paris, who had actually turned Mick Jagger down and was the first chick who didn't want to go to bed with me and hated rock music, I thought that if I could seduce her it would be the last piece of the puzzle. The final legitimacy. The finishing touch to this identity I had constructed for myself: Robert Tetherhook, head of Pear Records with an international reputation for all things cultural and discerning. In those days I really thought those things mattered. So I pursued and wooed with my rough-trade charm and, much to my amazement, Georgina married me.

I remember when I first fell in love with my wife. No, I didn't love her when I married her — in fact I spent most of the wedding fantasising about her sixteen-year-old niece who was one of the bridesmaids — but I did fall eventually. I recall it vividly. Georgina had been decorating our spanking new terrace in Paddington herself. It was about 1980 and she was wearing these really high shoes that were fashionable then. She was walking across the polished wooden floorboards carrying a vase of tulips when she slipped and fell, twisting her ankle. Glass, water and petals flew everywhere. Georgina lay in the centre of it in shocked silence, her legs splayed out, her skirt flung up exposing her little-girl knickers she liked to wear back then. All her neatness, her control, eradicated. Then, in this trembling vulnerable tone I'd never heard before, she calls out my name and I rush over. It was in that moment, in the sounding of her need for me, that I fell. Yep, every rational defence melted; it was like a flame-thrower shooting through permafrost. It was the first time I felt like her husband: needed, wanted, desired. Put the lead straight back into my pencil seeing her lying there. Fuck, things have changed since then. I've changed since then.

Now all she does is make me feel small, dickless, as if I don't earn enough, as if I haven't given her every bloody dream a chick could want, as if I haven't proven myself professionally. Like when I was awarded the Aria for best record producer in 2003 — only the highest accolade in the country for a man in my position. I've even got the silver pyramid sitting on my desk at home to prove it. You know what she said when I told her? 'Does this mean the Americans are finally going to start returning your calls?' In that bitch-butter-wouldn't-melt-in-your-arse voice of hers. As if she was terminally disappointed with me. Terminally.

Actually, at the time many things felt like they were terminal. You know that sensation when you've been running really hard for so long that you don't even notice the pace any more? It's only when you stop, your knees buckling, your head hanging down, your chest heaving for air as you retch with the effort, that you realise how fast you've been running — or living your life. Well, that's me, from the age of twenty-three through to now. Forty-fucking-seven.

This morning while I was shaving I found myself wondering what the point of it all is. There's that window of opportunity in shaving. You blokes would know what I'm talking about — when you wash the scrapings off with cold water and catch sight of yourself in the mirror. Nine times out of ten you barely register your own reflection, but there's that sneaking tenth time when, for a flash, you really see yourself — your creeping greyness, your ageing — and you find yourself thinking: who the fuck is that old codger and what's he doing in my bathroom?

Sorry, I always get morbid after sex. Post-coital depression, sort of a male PMT. Maybe it's the spilt seed factor. Always thought I didn't want children, and then when we found out Georgina's tubes were damaged the decision not to have them seemed easy. Don't get me wrong, I love children. I am, after all, a dedicated uncle, especially after my brother disappeared. When he went it was like a whole section of my childhood was torn out from inside me. Strange, because we never spoke much. But we were *connected*.

He's dead, I know it. I'm not religious but I can tell you the moment his soul left his body, because he *visited* me. It was in February, one of those stinking hot nights when you know it's a waste of time trying to sleep because the sheets stick to your body and the humidity sits on your chest like an outraged child. My recording company, Pear, is housed in this converted warehouse in Darlinghurst and I had all the windows wide open. There was this slight breeze that brought the smell of frangipani in from the street. It was past ten and the street below was alive with a flotsam of youth and energy. I remember leaning out, stretching my arms towards the shadowy limbs of the Moreton Bay fig and breathing in the air as if the perfume of all that life could erase my own aching cynicism. It was then that the fax machine suddenly kicked into action behind me. I remember thinking, that's weird, it's after hours, and I wasn't expecting anything from overseas. Expecting some illicit note from a lovesick kid to one of my trainees, I walked over. There, staring up at me in full colour, was my brother's face.

I nearly had a heart attack. I tore it off and walked over to the light. There he was: Gavin; more aged and worn than I'd ever seen him, with this smile — half-sardonic, half-triumphant — playing across his lips. As if he were saying, fuck you, fuck you all, I got away and I'm happy. Then, as I stared, the strangest thing happened. The photograph literally began to fade, these weird greenish patches bubbling up until nothing was left but his eyes staring out at me, then in an instant they disappeared too and I was left holding a blank piece of paper wondering if I'd imagined it all.

After that I started flying my nephews and niece down to Sydney for the occasional weekend. Maybe it was so I wouldn't feel so much of a prick for having lost contact with Gav the last few years of his life, or maybe it was about genetic continuity. I don't really know. Nowadays I try not to analyse things too much.

What about the girlfriend, you're thinking. Is he ever going to take moral responsibility for that? My friend, I'm a man, and we men have a distinct advantage over women. We stay desirable as we get older — shoot me down for saying it. But let's look at the plain facts. We're all animals when it comes to behaviour. You can impose as much cultural trappings, as much fancy psychology, economic reform, whatever you like on top, but when it gets down to the biological reality: we all think with our genitals. As simple as that. How do you think I sell records? What's a hit song consist of? Easy; it's either a chick singing

247

about how she wants her lover's penis to stay in her for the rest of her life, or it's a guy singing about how he wants to stick his penis in as many chicks as he can for the rest of his life. Excuse me for being so crude, but that's the way the world goes around. Georgina is past, Madeleine is future. When I'm with Georgina I am constantly reminded of my failings as a man. But with Madeleine I forget everything — work pressures, the fact that I'll need to get my teeth capped in the next year — and, most importantly, when I hold her smooth fleshy body I am suddenly back where she is in her life, with my future laid out in front of me, all the different pathways stretching forth like a myriad of golden opportunities. I'm an unabashed time vampire. She makes me young. Does that answer your question?

I can hear his car pulling into the garage. It's still comforting to me, the roar of confirmation that punctuates my day. The husband has returned. The ironic thing is that Robert would have no idea that I listen out for him, that I am secretly riddled with anxiety until I hear that familiar soft rumble as the BMW turns the corner into our street. I can't relax until I've heard it. There have been nights — we wives know them well — when I've lain there in our bed, pretending to myself and the rest of the world that I'm sleeping, when really I'm tottering on the edge of a half-dream, waiting for him to return. And as soon as the BMW drives around that bend, all the tension dissolves from my muscles like dew evaporating from the glistening threads of a spider's web in summer. Robert would laugh if I told him any of this. That bitter self-deprecating chortle of his, the one that says, I'd love to believe you, baby, but I know what you really think of me.

Yesterday I actually spent about twenty minutes trying to pinpoint the exact moment we stopped being emotionally honest with each other. I think it must have been sometime around the mid-eighties when I finally confessed that I'd known for about two years I was infertile but had failed to tell him. Or perhaps I'd merely failed to face up to the fact until then. But just because you stop being emotionally honest with someone doesn't mean you stop loving them. In my case, it has been the contrary. The longer the silence stretches between us, the more enigmatic Robert becomes and the more I want him. Some kind of perverse human psychology ... the fatal inaccessibility of desire.

The tragedy is that he thinks I think he was never good enough for me. I don't. I never have. He's always been good enough for me. I recognised all that turbulent shimmering potential the moment I met him; understood his fear and how it powered him, how it would propel him much further than the preppy private-school boys who were drifting through my life at the time. Why do you think I married him? But does Robert know how I feel? No. Because that isn't our *way*. Our way has become an intricate game of poker, of never letting the other know the true emotional stakes. This is what keeps us burning.

I'm sitting at my desk right now, staring down at this painting by Vermeer, *Woman in Blue Reading a Letter*. Did I forget to tell you? I'm a mature-age student doing a late-age Masters in seventeenth-century Dutch painting. Ridiculous really, but I have this dream of becoming a curator in my fifties. This painting will be the one I base my dissertation on. It's of a pregnant woman standing at a table entirely absorbed by a letter. There is a map of the Netherlands on the wall behind her and we can assume that her husband, the father of her unborn child, is away on travels. Her mouth is slightly open and her eyes are downcast. It is as if nothing exists for her in that room but the letter. A string of pearls sits on the table. You can only see part of the strand, but it fascinates me. Has she taken it out to fondle to remember him? Is she thinking of perhaps selling it? Does the letter contain some terrible news that she is just on the brink of responding to? We will never know.

I have a string of pearls. Robert gave them to me recently for our sixteenth wedding anniversary. An uncharacteristically beautiful choice for him. I suspect someone else helped him. No, not her. She wouldn't have the taste or the class.

Oh, I know. I've known from the beginning. From the moment he came back into this house with a lovebite on his neck. I've seen her from a distance, through the office windows, walking back and forth, sitting at her desk. A silly young creature with absolutely no physical grace whatsoever. I know why he chose her. There are two distinct reasons: she is the exact opposite of me and she will never challenge him on anything. The very same reasons he will never leave me for her.

～

I saw it at the laundromat pinned to one of those community boards — you know, one of those eclectic collections of diverse cards from *Vegan lesbian seeks like-minded soulmate* to Christian Help groups. I'd got bored waiting for the machine to stop spinning and I was scanning for possible band names — noticeboards are good for that — when this pink card with what looked like Russian lettering at the top caught my eye. In English underneath ran the phrase: *Old Wise Woman can spin something from nothing — knitwear is God.* I think 'god' was probably meant to read 'good' but there was something about the lettering that made me stare at it for a full five minutes. I didn't bother writing down the number, I just pulled the card off the wall and slipped it into my handbag.

Later at work I had a big fight with Robert over our latest act, Play 306, a teen boy band put together by an advertising company for Pepsi. I talked Robert into taking them on. Originally he'd been against it, calling the whole thing an exercise in crass commercialism and saying there was no way he was going to promote a bunch of wannabe talentless male fashion models. But when their first song became a hit — thanks to one of them impregnating a soap star and ending up on the front page of the *Daily Telegraph* under the immortal headline: UNDERAGE BOY TOY GETS OUR STACY UP THE DUFF — Robert suddenly lost his principles, and the next thing I know I'm at a photography shoot trying to talk the boys into dropping their undies and posing entirely naked except for fluffy toy rabbits covering their crotches. Robert's idea. He wants their new album to be titled *Bunny*. Over my dead body. I reckon we'll lose the grungier straight male demographic by being too

250

teenage girly and fluffy. I want *Rabbit* or better still *Hare-Gives-Lip* which has a sexier edge, right? Whatever.

We fought for an hour over it, in front of the whole office including the new intern who's way too attractive for my liking. It was really humiliating. In the end Robert pulled rank and that was when I rushed to the toilets. I was crying in one of the cubicles when the card with the Russian writing fell out of my pocket. It lay there staring up at me as if to say call me, call me.

The address was in one of those housing commission blocks — you know, the grimy sixties, a brick block with a few struggling trees bending exhausted over a concrete excuse for a playground. One windswept child on a swing screamed as she swung higher and higher in the sky. That was me once, I thought as I walked past.

The lift smelled of piss and marijuana while the corridor was an international but nauseating smorgasbord of curry, stew and frying fish.

The door was painted bright orange with a miniature Russian flag pinned above the knocker. I rapped tentatively. Immediately it was flung open by a woman not more than five foot tall, well over the age of eighty and dressed in a leather mini-skirt and ill-fitting blonde wig.

'Vat do you vant?' she asked in a heavy Russian accent. In lieu of a reply I held out the shopping bag full of Robert's hair. She peered in, sniffed then sneezed.

'Your man? Or maybe he belong to somevon else?' she muttered as she led me into the crowded lounge room.

Next to a garishly ornate three-piece suite covered in embroidered brocade stood a spinning wheel. It looked as if it had been teleported from another time. A state-of-the-art home movie unit with a seven-foot screen filled one wall. Perched on top of the screen were a dozen or so statuettes of various deities, from Buddha to Jesus to a lurid papier-mâché rendering of the goddess Kali.

251

'I am Madame Blonski, I am spinner. Vhat is your design?' Madame Blonski clutched at my arm.

Inwardly cursing myself for being such a gullible idiot, I reached into my handbag. The woman was obviously a fraud and the sight of a crystal ball sitting on top of the microwave beside a samovar did not increase my confidence.

'It's Ralph Lauren, you know, the Polo label. I think there's enough hair there,' I ventured, tentatively holding out the photo of a woollen shirt I'd torn out of a *GQ* magazine.

Madame Blonski glanced at it then peered dubiously at the hair. I waited nervously. Suddenly it seemed incredibly important that she confirmed there was enough there to knit the shirt to destroy the house that Robert built. With the nursery rhyme jangling around my head the three minutes she took to decide stretched into an eternity in which Robert left me, my publicity campaign failed entirely and I was without lover and job by the end of the month. Finally she put me out of my misery.

'Okay. I can make this. For you, fifty dollar.'

I nodded my head, incredulous at the instant relief that flooded my body. The old woman took the bag of hair and stuffed it unceremoniously under the couch; there were about a dozen other bags already shoved under there. Grabbing my arm she marched me back to the front door. She was so fragile she made me feel like a giantess, awkward in my suddenly massive ugh boots.

'Come back in a veek, Madeleine. Oh and I only take cash,' she announced.

She slammed the front door and left me standing on the doorstep wondering whether I'd imagined it all. It was only when I was in the lift that I realised she'd used my name without me telling her what it was.

～

I was halfway through my boxing session, my gloved fists pounding into the leather-clad palms of my long-suffering trainer, when I realised in an epiphany of guilt whose face was dancing in front of my eyes. Madeleine. That smug look that

252

glinted in her eyes as she said, 'Market forces.' Whack! 'The noughties generation.' Thud! 'Retro-Seventies.' Smack! How dare she? Who the fuck does she think she is challenging my judgement in front of my whole staff? We might be lovers but that doesn't mean we're equals!

Does she realise she's undermined my authority; worse still, made me look like some old fart in front of kids I'm old enough to have fathered, kids whose opinions actually matter, opinions that can seep through the walls of Pear and infiltrate the industry like a fatal rising damp? Does she know how many people want to see me fail? For fuck's sake, Play 360 are limited, they're this season's fourteen-year-old suburban chick's band, tomorrow's history. That's their market: short but truly profitable if milked in the right way — which is not to a bunch of inner-city, pot-smoking, neo-grunge male hippies who collectively amount to about a hundred sales and about two hundred illegally burnt CDs. Hare-Gives-Lip. Fuck that. Hasn't she taken in anything I've taught her?

I slam away until my tee-shirt is soaked, the internal soliloquy stops drumming against my temples and my knuckles begin to bruise up under my leather gloves. It's only walking back from the gym enveloped in that delicious vacant sensation one gets from strenuous exercise, watching bats engrave their way across the dusk, that I realise why I was so bloody furious. This is the first time she's ever disagreed with me. My Madeleine. After all, I created her, shaped her in the way I like, the perfect partner: amicable, mellow, a pillowy body of adoration I can sink my battleweary cock into. A highly crafted counterbalance to the constant barrage of criticism I go home to every night. And now my invention, my Eve, is rebelling. It's enough to make a man weep. The best I can hope for is that it's a temporary aberration — you know, one of those incomprehensible hormonal mists women often disappear into — and that my Madeleine will re-emerge like a freshly scrubbed car, glistening with unconditional admiration. She'd better fucking do.

I reach my beautiful house, with my beautiful wife framed by my beautiful pristine Federation shutters, and a wave of claustrophobia, the sense that this is my defined future for ever and ever, sweeps over me and almost knocks me to the dog-turd pavement. Because, as I'm sure a few of you habitually unfaithful husbands will understand, marriage is a delicate business. Like an intricate piece of machinery, it requires a sensitive balancing system. Real time with wife equals down time with mistress, the mathematical equation of which is something like four hours with the wife can be eradicated by half an hour with the mistress. I read that somewhere — was it Einstein? Like I said, marriage is a fragile equilibrium not to be recommended for the faint-hearted. And so, with that balance totally thrown, I pick myself up off the pavement and enter the house with unresolved fury buzzing around me like a swarm of irritated bush flies.

Women can be scary at the best of times, but they're most frightening when through some unfathomable alchemy they've somehow managed to work out what's going on. Personally I subscribe to the theory of alien abduction, only I think it was alien abandonment and women were introduced onto the planet as an extraterrestrial colonising species whose sole quest is to infect us all.

So there's my wife at the door, looking sexier than I've seen her in a long time, and my first thought is, shit, what anniversary have I forgotten? While I'm busy panicking she leads me to the dining room where she's actually laid the table and very nicely, thank you very much. Our best silverware, cloth napkins, even candles. Then she serves me my favourite — duck à l'orange with steamed snow peas and wild rice. Still suspicious I begin to eat, steeling myself for the moment she's going to ask me for something, like a holiday or some ridiculous new gadget we need like a hole in the head, but instead she says, 'Darling, how was work? Is everything okay?'

It's the sweetest voice I've heard out of her since we last had sex, which has got to be at least four months ago and, by coincidence, occurred on the night she asked me for a Mercedes SUV. So, gagging with suspicion and the parson's nose, I think, fuck it, I'll try the Play 360 dilemma on her, leaving the names out of course. And guess what? She agrees with me. She actually says she thinks my strategy, although short-term, is good.

I swear I harden up just hearing her say the words, 'Darling, your commerical nose is always right. Don't let anyone tell you otherwise.'

Pathetic, I know, but you've got to understand — this is beyond the Bay of Pigs, beyond Tehran, beyond East Timor. Our marriage is one of those entrenched guerrilla wars that drags on with each surprise attack from the undergrowth. This is Vietnam and, guys, she's the Viet Cong. So I'm still waiting for the innocent-looking veiled woman sitting in the corner to blow up when, smiling mysteriously, Georgina takes my hand and leads me upstairs.

I'm sitting beside the bed fully clothed, thinking what is wrong with this picture, when my wife drops to her knees and reaches for my fly.

Sometimes, when you've been with the one person for a very long time, you stop seeing them altogether. They blend in with the furniture, become an inanimate object that is entirely recognisable, entirely predictable. It becomes unimportant to hear them or see them clearly because you already know what they are going to say, where they are going to move to next. And you realise that a profound ennui has infiltrated every centimetre of your being and it will take a completely unexpected act to jolt yourself and your loved one out of such a predicament. I suspect that's how Surrealism was created — which happens to be the subject of the lecture I attended today and is a direct, or perhaps I should say lateral cause of why I am now kneeling in front of my husband in my very good Yves Saint Laurent suit about to take his penis into my mouth.

I blame Magritte, or should it be Dali? Whichever, there is definitely something surreal about the sight of my husband's erect member against the dark wool of the Paul Smith suit I made him buy that inspires me.

As you can tell by the objectivity of the thoughts running through my head, I'm not exactly emotionally engaged in the act of fellatio. Until, that is, the sound of Robert murmuring my name floats down in a loving, surprised and — I'm rather embarrassed to admit — thankful tone. Encouraged, I quicken my pace, tightening my grip as Robert groans and moans my name over and over. His fingers are winding through my hair, but not in that *I have control, I will push your head down* way, but tenderly, as if his amazement has made even his fingertips shy. As if all his normal defences have been breached by the audacity of my act.

And I love him then for his excitement. I love him for his vulnerability, for his cry as he buckles at the knees and shoots deep into my throat. I swallow with the panache of a whore and, in that same moment, find myself trying to banish the thought that yes, I can do it as well, maybe better, than her — the other woman, the *young blonde*, the invisible third party who is always between us.

But then as I stand I see that Robert, this great bear of a man, has turned scarlet with awkwardness as he stutters an apology. He kisses me with the hunger of youth, with the greed of old love that flares up in gratitude. And to my own amazement I believe him. I believe that he loves me. But before I can say anything he has me down on the bed, my panties yanked off, as if he is seeing me for the first time, as if we are a couple of clumsy virgin teenagers racing against our own inexperience. And he parts me to look at me. To study me.

'Beautiful,' he whispers as I fight to stop the bubble of tears that is rising like a disastrous hiccup from somewhere below my heart-line. And his mouth is on me, his tongue tracing a quivering path across the inside of my thighs. Unbearably tantalising, he teases me, circling around and around, his thumbs so gentle over my lips, over the tip of my clit which feels as if it is unfurling and craning its little head up to reach him like the tendril of a plant, screaming touch me, touch me. His mouth is moving slowly to the centre of my pleasure; parting my lips he blows for a second before flickering across the top of me, his tongue a hot probing rod now as he takes all of me between his lips, sucking, licking, pulling open my pleasure like a great secret shame until, clutching at his hair, I come screaming like never before.

256

And afterwards, his cheek a burning weight against my thigh, I can feel both of us wondering . . . what now?

&

It's exactly like the magazine illustration, only grey. Grey with a silver shimmer. Almost two-tone if you hold it up to the light. It has long sleeves and a collar open to the chest with three small pearl buttons to fasten it. The hair, now spun into a light wool, has the texture of cashmere but a little coarser. As I stroke it I imagine what people will think, what animal they might guess the wool came from — an Angora goat? Some obscure Tibetan sheep? A sheep dog? But they'll never think of human. I bury my nose in the soft folds and breathe deeply. Robert's scent has been almost eradicated, replaced by the faint scent of cheap soap. I imagine the tiny Russian woman at the sink, standing on a box to reach it, kneading all that hair with her minute hands. She's done a great job. At last I have something tangible, something actually made from his body.

I ring work to tell them I'll be in late, then I stretch the hair shirt out on the bed and wonder how it would look on him. Imagine his grey hair curling out at the collar, his fur that I love to sniff, to whirl around my fingers as I lay my head on his wide barrel of a chest, feeling safer than I ever do in the outside world. Daddy.

Shit! Did I just call Robert daddy? I twist the word around in my mind and change it to a Marilyn Monroe sexy sort of daddy. Daddy Sophisticate who picks you up in the BMW. Daddy Sophisticate who drives you to the Aria awards because you are his little girl ripe with cleavage and dripping in diamonds. Daddy Sophisticate who yanks your pants down and puts you across his knee to spank you ever so lightly. Yum. I'm wet between the legs.

Now I'm lying on top of the hair shirt. Close up I can see the forest of intricately woven hairs, each one plucked from a session of lovemaking, each one a chronicle of whispered promises — all of them broken. One loose thread sticks up like a deserting soldier. Without thinking I pull it out.

The accident happened suddenly, out of the blue. I was driving the Mercedes when the steering wheel jumped out of my hands and turned itself towards the oncoming traffic. Luckily it was in Paddington late on a Monday morning and everyone else seemed to be at work or looking at real estate, so all that happened was I slammed into the side of a Volvo in the oncoming lane which was travelling at about 15k. I think I must have passed out after that, because all I remember is coming to slumped over the steering wheel with a sharp pain shooting through my midriff. There was a tapping sound, and as my mind cleared the face of the Volvo driver — a young Greek incongruously wearing a fireman's uniform — came into focus as he knocked on the car window. I managed to unlock the door for him before the screaming siren announced the ambulance's arrival.

A shattered pelvis and one broken leg. Strangely, the Mercedes wasn't damaged much at all.

Robert was furious. I can only surmise it was a mixture of guilt and fear that somehow he might have been responsible for what he seemed to view as suicidal behaviour.

'Are you sure you didn't fall asleep at the wheel?'

'Robert, it was eleven in the morning!'

'Well, there has to be some rational reason. Mercedes are virtually accident-proof.'

'But not wife-proof evidently.'

'Georgina, I'm sorry you broke your pelvis and I'm sorry about the leg, but it isn't my fault. I'm just concerned that there might be some unconscious ...'

What a coward. He begins a sentence he can't finish. I deliberately let him struggle for a few more seconds.

'You think I want to kill myself?'

'I didn't say that. It's just that you're coming up to that time of life ...'

'Robert, I'm forty-two! I'm a good ten years off menopause.'

'Well, would you like to provide another reason why a perfectly healthy woman in full control of her faculties swings into oncoming traffic in broad daylight?'

'I told you, I don't know. It was like the steering wheel was operating independently.'

What could I say? It was the truth. Muttering something about losing his no-claims bonus he walked out, leaving a dozen roses and a box of candied fruit as consolation beside the bed. I hate candied fruit.

I lie back on the pillows now, gazing at the harness that holds my leg and pelvis in place. What *did* happen? Am I really suffering from some kind of unconscious self-destructiveness? But as I reconstruct the accident the memory of the steering wheel swinging around by itself as if powered by some invisible external force becomes increasingly clear.

I'm still lying on the bed with one hand on the hair shirt, the other between my thighs, when my mobile rings. I must have fallen asleep. Bleary-eyed I check the incoming number. Robert.

'Hey, babe, listen — I can't see you tonight, something's come up. Georgina's had an accident.'

'That's terrible.' Beat. Always play the sympathetic ear. Never display malice. 'Is she okay?'

'She'll live, but it's ugly — a broken pelvis and one busted leg. Weird thing is the car seems comparatively unscathed, although you should see the other guy's. It's gonna cost me my policy and some.'

'What happened?'

'She swerved into the opposite lane for no apparent reason. Crazy bitch.'

'What time?'

'About eleven this morning. Why?'

'No reason. Robert ... listen, I'm really sorry about the other morning. I had no right to question your judgement on Play 360. I've been thinking and you're totally right about them.'

Silence. I know he's melting at the other end of the line. Fluffing up with self-justification. I love it when he gets like that, all bristly like a tom cat.

'It's okay, baby. But next time just agree with me, okay?'

'From now on always. Hey, know what I'd do if you were lying right next to me this very moment . . . '

The great thing about phone sex is that you can be anyone, have anyone's body, fake the best orgasm you've ever had and the sheets stay clean. Plus you can embellish your lover's penis with a few extra inches and he need never know. The bad thing is that after you've put the phone down you suddenly feel very foolish and more than a little desperate.

Then I glance up at the clock and realise that I pulled the hair out of the shirt the very same moment Georgina swerved into the opposite lane. Suddenly I don't feel so desperate after all.

⁓

Fuck, I hate hospitals. I hate that non-descript colour scheme, the stench you can't help but associate with death and the ill-lit corridors that seem to wind on for ever. Maybe it's a flashback to a really bad acid trip that saw me in St Vincent's emergency ward fighting off a jungle of sprouting plastic chairs, or maybe it's because a hospital's where I think I'm going to end up dying. Either way, striding through some pus-green labyrinth trying to find my injured wife is not my idea of a happy Monday.

And when I did locate her it gave me a horrible shock to see her so fine-boned and white, her body strapped up in a pulley. Almost as bad as getting the call from the ambulance guys. For a second I wondered what I'd feel if she'd actually died. Lost would be the best way to describe it. I mean, how many times have I wished her dead in the last sixteen years, and yet if it happened I wouldn't know what to do with myself, wouldn't know how to deal with the sudden gaping abyss.

Oh, I'm not talking about lover stuff; that's for the mistress — the clandestine adrenaline kick you get as you use the excuse of going out to buy a paper or walk the dog, or nick down for a packet of fags, so you can make the call on your mobile and feel your cock harden at the thought of someone wanting you outside of the zone of the house, the comforting routine of it all. Something to sharpen the hunter. No, I'm talking about the shadow of marriage, the extra, irritating yet comforting limb that grows with cohabitation. The wife limb that you take completely for granted, until it is chopped off and you find yourself whirling uselessly like a broken gyroscope, trying to find your equilibrium all over again. Some blokes never do. Pathetic fuckers, you see them everywhere — at the pub chain-smoking in the corner, at the back of the cinema pretending they're waiting for a date — lurching around for the rest of their lives looking for that one piece of the machinery that will prop them up again. I'm telling you, Georgina's accident scared the shit out of me.

I'm not used to seeing my wife helpless. She's the kind of woman who's quite capable of setting up a stock portfolio on her own and only telling you about it five years later after you've stumbled upon some certificates.

My first thought was, I'll kill the bastard that did this to her, then I find out she was responsible for the accident. Suddenly I felt guilty, like she'd known about Madeleine all along and this was her perverse way of taking out her anger on me. Anyway, I had a word with the consultant and he agreed to quietly put her on some anti-depressants and get her home as soon as possible on the proviso that I hire a private nurse. He gave me a card with a number to ring and told me she was young but reliable and that on my health insurance state-registered nurses were covered.

I look down and see that the nurse has a Russian name. I smile. I'm partial to the Slavic aesthetic and I could do with some eye candy around the house, especially if poor Georgina is going to be landlocked for a few months. Feeling particularly benevolent I hire the nurse then ring Madeleine to cancel our rendezvous tonight. Fuck, it's hard being a man sometimes.

I haven't had any private time with him for over three weeks. Not even at work. Robert's been flying out to cover the tour of one of our major acts, but then when I try to hook up with him he's always rushing out for a meeting. I'm sure he's doing it on purpose. It's driving me crazy. At first he'd mutter stuff about being worried about Georgina, and how he has to stay home a lot to keep her company, and that he was really sorry but it'd all be over in a month or so when she was more mobile, then he stopped taking my calls. He has caller ID. I hate that, it's so rude. He's never done this before. He should be careful; I could cause a lot of trouble.

I vomited this morning. A great wave of nausea that had me running to the toilet before I'd even got up. I know why. As I stood there, my knees trembling, head hung over the toilet bowl, the heaving was followed by a huge surge of excitement.

Finally my life is going to change. We're going to change. We're going to become real. Legitimate, open, living together; me by his side at record launches, at concerts, standing at the door of our own townhouse, each with our own cars — his BMW, my Saab with the child's seat in the back. This will happen because I've decided it will happen. *Vogue* magazine: *Step 1 of self-redefinition — take control of your image, take control of your future, visualise what you want.*

I lift my nightdress now and stare at my breasts. I've never seen them so heavy. Taut. The nipples are darker and more prominent. Turning sideways I think I can see a slight bulge curving above my stomach: my womb. My fruitful womb.

The walking frame stands at the end of the bed like an overgrown crab waiting to hoist its legs over my body. It ages me just to look at it. Still, I should be thankful I can hobble to the toilet. I couldn't a week ago. I'd never realised how humiliating bedpans are. I have never been this helpless in my entire life.

Robert has had the spare bedroom converted into a sickroom. Fixed it up with a television, a table that swings over so I can eat in bed, and a stack of movies he rented so that I won't get too bored. He's even gone out of his way to find films that fit in with my degree, documentaries on the Dutch masters. He brought me a gift, a figurehead in the shape of a merman from some old ship they found off the Scottish coast a couple of years ago.

Robert has a real love of anything to do with shipwrecks; he's like one of those people who takes great delight in other people's misery — the Germans have a word for it: Schadenfreude. He had the figurehead erected over the bed. It's seventeenth century apparently; it must have cost him a fortune. We've argued about the gender. He's convinced it's a mermaid, but when I look at it I see a merman with a defined chest, noble suffering eyes and a carved ponytail hanging down his back.

Mermaids ... deviant mythical creatures that conjure up the notion of cunt as a briny, slimy, cold thing. Not the most attractive vision; still, whatever it is, male or female, it's mine and it watches over me. When I look up at it I imagine the figurehead carving a path through an uncertain future. Our future. Robert's and mine. For the first time I'm jealous. Isn't that unbelievable after three years? Suddenly the thought of him with her, of him kissing her, going down on her, makes me furious. I feel profoundly impotent lying here, pinned down by this great crushing weight across my pelvis.

I know he's taking advantage of my paralysis and spending hours over there with her. That's why he's so considerate, it has to be. Or this is the calm before the storm; there's some strange legal technicality to do with divorce that's making him invest in caring for me. God, I sound so cynical, but that's what sixteen years of cold war does to you. So what if we had sex a month ago and it was fantastic? That doesn't mean he's fallen back in love with me. I'm not that much of a romantic fool. Perhaps my infirmity has jolted him into a fear of his own mortality. Whatever, I've started to watch him closely.

He's hired a private nurse, a Russian woman who's been in Australia since she was about ten: Tania. She's really sweet, one of those younger women who have an emotional practicality about her. More endearing is the way her own beauty seems to be an irritant to her. Strikingly tall, a brunette with piercing green eyes, she does everything she can to diminish her physical presence. It's most amusing watching her deal with Robert, who stumbles around her completely intimidated. She's fiercely protective and wouldn't let him near me at first, insisting that she would be the only person to bathe me and change the dressings.

When Tania thinks I'm sleeping she gets on her mobile phone and has long conversations in Russian. I lie there drifting in and out of sleep, my dreams peppered with a floating hum of guttural Slavic. But sometimes she breaks into English. That's how I hear about her grandmother.

'Vali, you'd never imagine what babushka had to do the other day —spinning thread from human hair. Some young woman brings in a big bag full of her lover's hair, all grey. And you know what grandma did? She makes her a wool shirt. For what I don't know, but you can bet it will mean mischief for someone. Bad magic ... You know grandma, she just has to whisper your name and a tree will come crashing down ... Grandma said there was so much hair she reckon the poor guy must be bald by now ... She said the girl was young, not even thirty. Poor thing, she must have been desperate to go to babushka. Three years, she told her, there was three years' worth of hair in that big bag.'

My eyes flash open. Could it be? You know how it is: synchronicity. A snippet of gossip, a name that resonates, and in an instant you realise there's a web of fate linking houses, suburbs, even whole continents. A mesh that can destroy, misinform, create paranoia, make men rich, make women weep, start world wars. *Fear the imagined, not the truth*, my mother always used to say. Being a plain-speaking Presbyterian she believed in absolute truths and in her day absolute truths existed. Not like now.

That night when Robert collects my dinner tray I can't help noticing that he's thinning slightly on top. I haven't combed his hair in years; frankly I hate it. I've always considered long hair on men a statement of their lack of emotional development.

'Robert,' I say seductively. 'Would you like me to brush your hair tonight?'

Startled he actually blushes.

'Thanks, love, but nowadays I'm kind of weird about other people touching it,' he says, averting his eyes.

Liar, liar, with burning ears. Other people, except her. Determined to extend his discomfort I reach across and pluck a loose long silver hair off his shoulder.

'Has it always fallen out this much?'

'Georgina, you know I've always shed hair like an Old English sheepdog but fear not, this wolf isn't going to go bald yet.'

Once he's left I wrap the long hair around and around my finger until the tip bulges out red and painful.

⤛

The fucking bastard, I can't believe he just hung up on me. There's no point ringing again; he'll have registered the new number by now. I'd used my girlfriend's mobile because I knew he'd only pick up if he didn't recognise the caller.

'Robert,' I said triumphantly.

'Madeleine, are you okay? It's past nine. You know it's difficult for me to talk after nine.'

'I'm not okay. I need to see you; we need to see each other.'

'Oh, baby, I'd love to but it's really hard at the moment. Work's crazy as you know and Georgina's still housebound —'

'Fuck Georgina. I have needs too.'

'I know. I've been a real shit, I'm so sorry. But it'll all be back to normal in a couple of weeks.'

'And what's normal, Robert? Me hanging around waiting for the phone to ring? Meeting twice a week for a couple of hours so you can screw me and then go back to your wife?'

'Madeleine, I can't talk about this now, Georgina is in the other room. How about we do lunch tomorrow?'

'Lunch! I'll give you lunch —'

Bleep. The lonely sound of the hang-up.

I squeeze my eyes shut now and count slowly as the rage curdles into a bitter grief. This can't be good for the baby. Then, deliberately, I reach for the hair shirt.

⤛

It was ugly, asymmetrical, red with a darker spot in the middle and raised — just like a picture in one of those pamphlets — and it appeared, bang, just like that on my cheek, itching like mad, screaming out, scratch me, scratch me. Which I did, until it started bleeding. It was then that I drove straight to my dermatologist.

Melanoma. If you didn't know what it meant you could just about imagine it was the name of one of those dusky beauties with old-fashioned hips and melon breasts who used to hang, immortalised in fluorescent paint on velvet, over your bachelor uncle Jack's vinyl couch. I tried distracting myself with this vision until I realised I was speeding down Oxford Street and had forgotten to take the handbrake off. Not great for a fifty-thousand-dollar car.

My dermatologist stared at my face then, sighing heavily through the gap in his front teeth, hit the phone to ask his assistant to get a biopsy slide ready immediately. By that time I'm calculating the cost of my own funeral and wondering about life insurance.

'Mr Tetherhook, I have to confess I'm a bit perplexed. I've never seen a skin cancer so advanced pop up overnight like this.'

'How advanced?'

'For reasons of litigation I wouldn't like to hazard a guess. Are you sure you saw me last year?' he asked.

'Check your records if you doubt me.'

'It's not entirely unheard of; sometimes extreme stress can manifest in strange ways, like lesions on the skin.'

'Doctor, cut the polite subtext. Will I live?'

'Again, for reasons of potential litigation I can't really answer that, but it is safe to say that if the cancer is contained and hasn't spread to the lymph glands you have an excellent chance of survival. Of course, if the cancer has spread it's an entirely different scenario ... I'll ring you by tonight to let you know whether you will need further tests.'

Terror is not a fast-moving animal; it is a slow creep through the entrails up to the back of the throat where it repeats like bile through the waking day, eventually accumulating to a series of high-speed flashes of the phrase 'I'm going to die', blinking on and off like an epileptic fluorescent bulb.

By the time I got back to the car I was ready either to cry or crawl into a snug, warm, wet place where I could forget my own mortality.

'Hello? Madeleine?'

Pause; self-pity rattling down the line as I choke on my own grief.

'Can I come over?'

266

Cock, cunt, the thickness of him pounding inside me, wet tightness engulfing both of us, filling my very pores, as he loosens the fibres of my flesh. Oh yes, over and over, everything swelling, my labia, my lips, my nipples, my clit, deliciously shooting down the whole length of him as he, with the confidence of love, of time spent together, of knowing, enters me over and over until both of us scream out, first me and then him, shuddering together as life roars across us like a huge jet intent on its ascent.

'I love you,' I whisper afterwards into his chest. Robert says nothing, then hiccups loudly. A strange whimper from somewhere deep inside reverberates in the room. At first I think it might be the cat from next door, but as I lift my head I realise it is the sound of Robert weeping. I pull myself up and wrap my arms around him, cradling him to my breasts. My swollen, aching breasts.

'It's going to be all right. You're not going to die yet, Robert. Robert? Come back to me, baby . . .'

'Sorry. Just give me a minute to pull myself together.' He sits up and turns his back to me, ashamed.

'It's not that simple, Maddy, they're going to have to test the lymph nodes. The weird thing is, I didn't have the fucking thing yesterday morning. It just sprang up overnight. Funny how your whole life perspective can just change like that.'

'What do you mean overnight?'

'Just after you rang last night my face began to itch, then when I looked in the mirror . . . bang! Right there on my desk.'

The hair shirt was slung over the back of a chair at the end of the bed. It hung innocently, rippling slightly in the last of the evening sun. How powerful was it exactly? How much control did I have over whom it affected with its magic?

I was distracted by Robert cupping my breasts.

'You're larger, have you changed your pill or something?'

'Well, there have been some hormonal changes, but not quite the ones you might be expecting,' I said, smiling.

Robert fingered my nipples thoughtfully. 'You're not pregnant, are you?' he asked, almost casually.

267

I've just had the ten shittiest days of my life. One of those windows of time when God throws everything he's got at you, like your life is a skittle in some funfair sideshow, and the best you can hope for is that when the Supreme Clown Upstairs stops pelting you'll bounce back, preferably upright. Am I upright? I don't know any more. All that defined me, Robert Tetherhook, married man, successful record producer, has been bashed, shattered and finally softened beyond recognition.

I'm lying on a hospital trolley in a consultation room in the cancer ward of St Vincent's hospital. At this point in history I don't feel well. I am hoping this is psychological not physical, but frankly in the last few weeks the lines have completely blurred. In about five minutes the specialist is going to come in and tell me whether the cancer has spread to my lymph nodes. If it has, I have a forty per cent chance of surviving — with the help of radiation and any other treatment they can think of. Believe me, with my recent luck I'm not feeling very confident.

Georgina's with me. Ever since I had the biopsy she's developed this irritating optimism that reminds me of a born-again Christian and has taken to smiling banally 24/7. Which makes me feel like a dying child who's being lied to. Not a great sensation.

She's looking at me now, seriously overdressed in Chanel and the string of pearls I gave her for our anniversary which look incongruous with the walking frame. What is this — a funeral? But when I look closer I can see that she's scared too and just for a second I love her for it. Can I leave her? I don't know any more. All I know is that I've needed her more than anything the past few days and she's been there. I've even reached for her in the night and fallen asleep in her arms a few times; something I haven't done in years.

What the fuck am I going to do? I always thought it was an emotional cliché to say you could love two women, but here I am in that very predicament. For so long I've kept the two compartmentalised, neither impacting on the other. There was Georgina: the house, consistency, domestic intimacy. Then there was Madeleine: excitement, lust, youth, the clandestine. Like running two simultaneous acts, both so different they require entirely different skills. But then Madeleine had to go and get pregnant. More than four months pregnant.

God, I was furious when she told me. Shouting, jabbing my finger at her, furious, until I saw her face shrivel with grief and the sight of it brought back a picture of my father screaming at my mother. I stopped instantly, deflating with regret.

Four months. Me, a father. Inconceivable a month ago. Me, dead at forty-seven? Also inconceivable a month ago. If I were honest I'd tell you that a kernel of excitement flares up at the base of my belly when I say the word Daddy. What am I going to do? Will Georgina survive without me? Of course she will, she might even thrive, but will I? Am I ready to take on the responsibility of a child and a much younger wife? What about the divorce? I love my house; I love the life my wife has made for me. Madeleine is so gauche, so raw. But she's having my baby. My baby.

Okay, here it is: the verdict. Life or death? Father or corpse? The door's opening, the specialist steps inside, file in hand, and he's not smiling. And I decide there and then: if it's life, I will leave Georgina and parent my child properly. If it's death, I'll stay with Georgina until the end. Let fate and the schmuck upstairs with the bowling ball choose for me.

I've been thinking a lot about DNA recently, how vulnerable we all are if it gets into the wrong hands. I don't mean film stars worrying about being cloned from fragments left on a napkin in a restaurant; I'm talking about far more devious practices. You see, I believe that we leave particles of ourselves everywhere. Invisible shimmering dust paths that stretch through our days like undiscovered galaxies. And should someone want to harm us, or manipulate a piece of information to their own advantage, all they have to do is access a particle of our DNA. That's why we have to be very careful about who we let into our beds and into our hearts, and about where we leave fingernail clippings, flakes of dead skin and strands of hair. The naivety of love is no protection.

Naturally I've never bothered to explain my hypothesis to Robert. He thinks I'm mad as it is, but I'm a great believer in mixing feminine intuition with a smattering of scientific knowledge to make the kind of lateral leap that would, in another era, simply be labelled good sense. Don't get me wrong; I am protective of my husband. You don't live with someone for sixteen years without developing a strong sense of when they're in danger. The challenge is to make them discover that for themselves before it is too late.

Bizarre things have begun to happen to us and our marriage. Steering wheels don't just suddenly twist out of control and cancers don't just appear overnight without some external manipulation of the malevolent kind.

The door clicks open and I jolt back to the reality of clutching Robert's hand as he lies in a stunned paralysis that I suppose must set in when waiting to hear whether one is to live or die. The specialist is a smug man in jeans and Cuban heels who informs us that he was dragged away from his third honeymoon to operate on Robert. With the practised eye of the womaniser he assesses my face, cleavage and legs before he turns back to Robert who is now two shades paler than the wall behind him.

'Well, Mr Tetherhook, it looks as if you'll live to cause at least a few more decades of mischief,' the specialist announces as flippantly as if offering a coffee with milk and two sugars. Much to my amazement, Robert bursts into tears and collapses into my arms. Like I said — DNA.

'You look so ripe. It's kind of hard to believe — my child hiding in there.'

He stares at my belly, running his hands across its curve. I watch him, smiling. All is as it should be: Robert won't die, he will leave his wife, move in with me, we will have the baby in five months, it will be a boy.

The afternoon he was getting his result I was also in a hospital room, by myself, shivering as they ran that cold slippery thing across my skin and staring at the fuzzy outline of life floating defiantly on the ultrasound screen. An undeniable manifestation of our love. Thinking: whatever happens I will mother this child.

I prop myself up. We've just made love and he was gentle, too careful, as if he was frightened of hurting the baby. It's ironic: of the two of us I have the power now. No more waiting around for the phone to ring; no more clandestine meetings stolen between work and home.

'When are you going to tell her?'

'Today, as soon as I leave here. I mean it this time. I've made a pledge to God and that is my decision. I will be a good father.'

A pledge to God? I've never heard Robert talk like this before. I stare at him, unsure he isn't being sardonic.

'A pledge to God, Robert? Don't you just love me?'

'Of course I do. It's just that I feel I've been given a gift, the gift of life, and I mean to do something constructive with it.'

For a moment I wonder whether his dermatologist has put him on anti-depressants as he stands naked from the waist down in the middle of my bedroom, wearing a tee-shirt advertising an ancient AC/DC tour, his flaccid penis dangling comically under his belly, his face aflame with a fervour that would make even a Scientologist nervous.

'Robert, you sure you're all right?'

'I've never been clearer. Maddy, this is going to be a whole new start, for both of us. I'll buy Georgina out, get us a small townhouse with an extra bedroom — only what if it's twins?'

'It's not twins, don't worry.'

'You've had an ultrasound?'

I nod, feeling a little guilty about being so manipulative.

'And?'

'It's a boy.'

'A boy.' He gazes at my womb again, enraptured. He loves the idea that it will be a little clone of himself, I think slightly resentfully, but adore him for his excitement anyway. A flash of the future shoots through me: Robert pushing a stroller wearing board shorts and tee-shirt, looking fatter and older, me walking next to him, pregnant with our second child, his hand in mine.

'What's that?'

He walks over to the chair and picks up the hair shirt. For one terrible second I'm scared he'll recognise his own hair, his own smell. But no, he's examining it like it's just another shirt. Funny how we're so oblivious to our own debris, the pieces we leave behind, the emotional chaos that erupts when the door closes behind us.

'Just a top I had made.'

'It's beautiful, a really good weight. What's the fabric?'

'Oh, this new goat's hair that's become fashionable. I was thinking of giving it to you for your birthday.'

'That's so sweet.'

He holds it up against him. Naturally the colour of the hair shirt suits his eyes and skin tone perfectly. He stares at himself in the mirror as if he is seeing himself for the first time. A shiver runs through me; he's displaying an intense narcissism I've never seen in him before. It's almost as if the shirt has possessed him.

'Madeleine,' he murmurs in a low formal tone.

I stiffen. I hate it when he uses my full name, it usually means he's going to announce something portentous — like he's changed his mind and is going back to Georgina. But instead he takes my hands and kisses them.

'It's been a ride, the last few weeks, but I really feel like I've come out of the other side. This — us, you, the baby, the cancer — has forced me to a new level of maturity. Of responsibility. At forty-seven I feel like I'm really becoming a man.'

Well, fuck, what do you say to that? Naturally I'm touched and naturally I'm suspicious. This is the man who wasn't answering my calls three weeks ago. Beside this isn't the streetwise, emotionally burnt-out Robert I've known and loved for the past three years. The best I can hope for is that once he's got over the shock of surviving cancer and becoming a father he'll settle back into the cryptic pessimist I love sparring with intellectually as well as fucking.

'It's like I'm reborn,' he announces, his eyes wandering back to his own reflection as he smooths down the hair shirt, almost as if he's caressing himself.

'Can I take the shirt today? As a memento.'

'Sure, babe. Now, you are going to ring me the second you tell her? I've got the study ready for your things if you want to move out immediately.'

'Absolutely.'

He kisses me briefly on the lips, throws off his tee-shirt, slips the hair shirt over his head, then pulls on his trousers. A second later his pager goes off and he's out of there, leaving me glowing with post-coital victory.

Madeleine's shirt is kind of silky with a slight edge to it. It feels great on the skin, like someone's hugging me. The ideal weight for wool, whatever fucking old goat it was made from, perfect for a Sydney spring day. Walking away from her apartment I feel younger than I have in years. Like a great burden has been lifted off my shoulders and everything is possible. *Daddy, Papa, Da, Father*. The image of a miniature version of myself snuggling up to my bare chest plays pleasantly across the back of my eyes. My son. Aged two, aged four, aged nine, playing soccer as I stand on the sideline screaming support. First girlfriend, first rock concert, first car, wedding speeches, grandchildren, christening. Genetic infinity.

Suddenly nothing else seems important. So what if the next band makes platinum? So what if Play 360 signs to Sony US? What am I planning to become — a name on a plaque in the reception room of some recording agency? A footnote in some outdated history of Australian rock, total print run: ten thousand. Was that going to be my legacy? Not now. Now my life's taken a sharp left, is running off the tracks and heading for the forest, the deep impenetrable forest, and, my God, does it feel great.

As soon as I opened the door I knew. He had a blissed-out look in his eyes and yet, for the first time in our marriage, he was shut off. An invisible veil drawn between us. I'll remember that moment until the day I die. Tragedy is like that: it dresses down, hides itself in an arbitrary moment that suddenly spirals out into a drama that will haunt you for life.

He stood there dressed in that thing, that monstrous piece of theft, unable to look me in the eye.

'Georgina,' he stammered, 'I'm leaving you for Madeleine. I have to, she's having our baby.'

'Robert, for Christ's sake, come in,' I said, 'and have a cup of tea.'

We sat opposite each other, the kitchen table running between us like a no-man's land between enemy trenches. My grandmother's Victorian teapot stood in the middle like an aberrant watchtower, the sugar bowl a stationary tank that promised to take no prisoners. I kept sneaking glimpses at the shirt, that shimmering travesty that smelled of profound betrayal, of blood.

The grey-gunmetal tint gave it away immediately. I knew; how could I not? I've slept with him for sixteen years, saturated in his juices, breathing the shifting nuances of his pheromones as he matured beside me. How many times has his hair fallen across me as he held himself over me making love? How many times have I shut my eyes beneath that grey tent? How many times have I plucked a stray hair from the pillow, out of the plug-hole, from his shoulder as he left for work? Of course I knew.

I couldn't tell you what we said that afternoon. I vaguely remember talking about splitting the mortgage, sorting out the bank accounts, the stock portfolios. I remember him trying not to weep, his shoulders wrestling with painfully silent tears. But most of all I remember thinking that whatever I did I had to get my hands on that hair shirt.

This morning I put on my pearls, the strand he gave me for our wedding anniversary. It must have been a premonition, as if all the ghosts of all the abandoned wives of my family were guiding my hands to the necklace. Or was I inspired by

Vermeer's blue lady, also on the brink of receiving very bad news?

Whatever, the gesture crystallised into this moment, when I embrace my soon-to-be ex-husband. We move together, and as we do the catch on my pearl necklace snags on the hair shirt. As I step away, that tiny thread pulls a ladder down the fine weave — an innocent little descent into hell.

'Oops,' I say, smiling slightly.

⁓

The spasm is sudden, violent and excruciating. Like the worst period pain you could ever imagine. I'm on the balcony, watching the bats streaming across from the Botanical Gardens like they always do, umbrellas of black beating their way heroically against the fading light. I am thinking about Robert, the joy of trust, of being able to plan holidays together, of introducing him to my friends, being Mrs Tetherhook — when the pain strikes.

I double over immediately, grasping the rail to stop myself falling over. The contraction passes but before I can catch my breath another sharp jolt shoots through my body. I hobble to the bathroom; already I can feel the sticky gush between my legs. Out of my mind with agony I pull my pants down and place myself on the toilet, just as another heaving pain rips through my abdomen.

Ten minutes later, with tears streaming down my face, somehow I find the courage to stare down between my thighs. There it is: the shiny dome of its forehead showing through the mucus and blood, the tiny arms curled up towards its closed eyes. A perfectly formed male foetus.

⁓

Life's strange. Rephrase that: life's fucking out there. I used to think we had some control, that things happened for a reason, even the weirdest things, as if a sequence of events created a pattern that made sense. Now, looking back over the past few months, I think that's total bullshit. We know nothing. All we can hope for is that we survive this terrible getting of wisdom called life.

I still manage bands. Actually Pear Records got voted most innovative Australian record company last week, not that there was that much competition given that there are only two real players in the race. I guess what's really changed is that I've fallen in love for the second time in my life.

It's different this time round. At our age there's so much baggage that sometimes you have to be prepared to shove it all into an attic, throw away the key and then look for a new bed in which to hold, kiss and rediscover each other all over again. Just ask Georgina — I know she'll agree with me, she does that a lot these days. And we've started to laugh at ourselves. Fuck, it's good. Almost as good as the kissing.

As for Madeleine, I had to let her go. Don't get me wrong: I felt bad about it, really bad. I even went into therapy. But she'll bounce back; smart girls like her always do. It wasn't like I abandoned her. After the miscarriage I helped her get a new job, bought her a new car, even gave her money for a mortgage. Then I went out and got myself a haircut.

# Custodian

To look at him, you would think him an average elderly gentleman: that is to say, a seasoned individual of some two score and ten, with a generous but not ostentatious income of one hundred guineas or so per annum. A man of sound disposition.

His hat is tall and of French origin, a trifle youthful perhaps for his age; his suit is elegant, his pumps well-polished. His face is typical of a gentleman in his fifties: jowly, worn, with remnants of beauty still visible beneath the ruin. His hair is grey with streaks of silver, full tresses he wears to his shoulders — again, the affectation of a far younger man. Something of the cynic plays around his lips; it is a mouth that looks as if it might once have been given to humour, but has been tempered by some past humiliation. He is an upstanding citizen who exudes an air of casual indifference, but if you were to examine him closer you might notice that under the shiny hat rim his eyes are bright with suspicion. They dart about the fashionable tea-house as if he is frightened ... of what? Of recognition perhaps? Of somehow being exposed?

A young woman in a striped dress and bonnet enters, a parasol swinging off her belt. Her beau, a handsome swain, obviously a local merchant from the Haymarket, walks beside her, laughing. Except unto themselves they are not interesting, but the sight of the maiden with her air of *joie de vivre*, the very embodiment of youth, causes our gentleman's hand to suddenly tremble, spilling his coffee across the glass table and into the lap of his immaculate trousers.

A waiter immediately appears to sponge away the offending fluid but his customer pays no heed to his ministrations. He cannot tear his eyes away from the exuberant couple. Suddenly he grasps the sleeve of the waiter.

'How old do you take me for, boy?' he asks in a low gravelly bass.

'A mature gentleman, sir. A man of some standing, around five and fifty, I'd wager, sir.' The waiter hopes to receive a larger tip by dropping ten years off his honest estimation.

A great weariness settles upon our protagonist, melting his features into despondency.

'I was born in 1824, boy, which makes me, as of today, twenty-six years old — no older than the gentleman over there,' he states, pointing to the swain.

The waiter looks at him for a moment, his head cocked as if to question the man's sanity. 'In that case, a happy birthday to you, sir,' he replies a little too cheerfully then, bowing, rushes away to share the gentleman's eccentricities with the kitchen. The gentleman slumps back in his chair, tea forgotten, as he recalls the beginning of his strange story. Three years before in the year of our Lord 1851 on a wintry January afternoon in that bastion of English colonialism, the British Museum.

In a dreary office located in the bowels of the department of Greek and Roman antiquities a youth bent over a crumbling clay pot. With gloved hands, he carefully examined its markings through a magnifying glass. At twenty-three Alistair Sizzlehorn was of a delicate mien: his long wavy blond hair, his blue eyes and narrow face spoke of an aristocratic heritage, enhanced by his soft white hands and long fingers, all suggestive of a consumptive nature. In actuality, the archaeologist was of a far more robust disposition. The son of a Presbyterian minister and his dour unsentimental older wife, Alistair had grown up in the harsh Yorkshire dales. Isolated as a child and left to his own devices, he had developed a fascination for the primitive ruins the valleys held and his over-active imagination quickly plunged him into a mythical world of mysterious burial mounds and rings of archaic stones.

A scholarship to Cambridge cemented his interest in the past and, much to his father's chagrin (he had wanted his son to follow him into the church) Alistair immediately took up an offer from the British Museum on graduation — an apprenticeship to the legendary Dr Edward McPhee.

McPhee had been in the department of Roman and Greek antiquities since the turn of the nineteenth century, when he himself had started at the museum as a twenty year old. It was rumoured that the venerable archaeologist actually lived in one of the department's vast storage cupboards for it was certain that no one had ever seen him outside the building. Since his engagement, Alistair had never once managed to arrive before McPhee nor leave after him.

The aged professor of archaeology was a diminutive wizened man whose dress seemed not to have changed (nor been laundered) since the early 1800s, which gave him a somewhat foppish appearance in keeping with the dandies who flourished under King George IV. This demeanour was misleading, however: there was nothing the slightest bit decadent about the young archaeologist's employer; on the contrary McPhee was a puritan — a self-righteous zealot who revelled in the denial of other people's pleasures. In short: the most disagreeable and misanthropic individual Alistair Sizzlehorn had thus far encountered.

Alistair detested him. He found McPhee's constant lectures about the immorality of Ancient Greece and Rome entirely devoid of a sensual or even aesthetic understanding of the periods. Sometimes he wondered whether McPhee was human at all. He had certainly arrived at the conclusion that the man lacked a penis; he was an asexual creature who reminded Alistair (in his more generous moments) of some lesser species of mollusc.

In Alistair's darkest reveries — when the London fog encased the high windows of the museum in an impenetrable cloud, when time dripped down the walls like a creeping damp, when McPhee scuttled around him like a scaly louse, muttering in that nasal high-pitched squeak about how Roman hedonism led to decay then atrophy, and how England with its greedy colonists and now, horror of horrors, its worship of science over the high arts, was degenerating in the same way ('The triumph of Darwin!' he would exclaim) — the young archaeologist would suddenly find himself plunged into an abyss of despair for fear he too, in fifty years' time, would be transformed into such a desiccated miserable creature. For, to Alistair's profound embarrassment, he was still a virgin.

It was a difficult predicament. He had insufficient income to procure the services of some generous street girl (of which there were many, and many of them quite lovely). Besides, being of a romantic nature, he found the application of commerce to love abhorrent. To add to his chagrin, his paltry wage from the museum was not enough to entice any educated young lady of standing to consider him as a marriage prospect. The hope of any kind of sexual congress seemed to be floating further away from him by the day. He was frequently distracted from his work by the delicious vision of his thin but well-proportioned limbs wrapped around a buxom wench resembling the voluptuous marble Venuses who adorned many of the artifacts in his care. The vision would hover tantalisingly before him, yet every time Alistair racked his mind for a practical solution it ascended a few more feet out of his reach.

He was immersed in this particular quandary when McPhee burst into the room like a small but noisy explosion. 'Master Sizzlehorn!' he barked, in his harsh Glaswegian accent. 'Ye are needed in ma office on a matter o' the most confidential and private nature. And look smart, boy, a lady of aristocratic bearing is involved.'

As they hurried down the windowless corridor where gaslights flickered palely against the yellowed walls, Alistair had to lengthen his stride to keep up with the irrepressible McPhee, despite the octogenarian's silver-topped cane.

'Mr McPhee, may I remind you that I am twenty-three years of age and therefore entitled to be addressed as such,' he said in a peeved tone.

'Indeed, boy, indeed,' his employer responded distractedly, patting down his long silver curls, coat-tails flying behind him and a ridiculously high lacy collar framing his prune-like face like that of a demented bishop. Alistair despaired of ever receiving a modicum of respect from the octogenarian.

They arrived at a door marked, perplexingly, Office 142. McPhee swung around dramatically and stared for a moment at the young man's navel before casting his eyes upward, his employee being a good twelve inches taller than himself.

'Now I know ye think me a man incapable of any sentiment whatsoever ...' He hesitated hopefully, as if waiting for his apprentice to protest the statement, but to his secret disappointment Alistair held his silence. Sanguinely the professor continued, '... but I intend to surprise ye. I am about to offer ye the opportunity of a lifetime, a chance to distinguish yourself at an early age as an archaeologist and curator of the highest distinction. But be warned: I expect ye to make a good fist of it. Do we understand each other?'

Amazed by the curmudgeon's change of tone, and now bursting with curiosity as to what might lie inside the room, Alistair nodded with great solemnity. Satisfied, McPhee again smoothed down his greasy locks and opened the door.

A woman — clearly a lady — sat on a Windsor chair, her back held stiff, her bosom high. Her veil was down, her hands were covered by the finest kid gloves, and she wore a bustled coat of the latest fashion. Alistair had a strong sense that what lay beneath the veil could only be beautiful, for the woman held herself with the confidence of one who was completely conscious of the effect she had upon others: desire. A valet, smartly dressed in her colours, stood by her side awaiting instructions.

Alistair's eyes were next drawn to a long table covered with objects of varying sizes and shapes, each in turn covered by a silk kerchief. Thus were the artifacts beneath completely concealed.

'Your ladyship,' McPhee simpered. The woman, without standing, held out her gloved hand. 'McPhee,' she murmured in a velvety tone that immediately pricked at Alistair's crotch. McPhee grasped her hand eagerly and, much to Alistair's hidden disgust, planted a slobbering kiss upon the leather.

'Ever your faithful servant,' he replied in a docile but croaky voice. Then, straightening himself, he pushed Alistair before him.

'May I introduce the young man I made foremention of: Mr Alistair Sizzlehorn, formerly of Cambridge, a most talented archaeologist. Mr Sizzlehorn, meet Lady Whistle.'

Alistair, blushing now to the roots of his blond hair, bowed deeply, praying the aristocrat would not notice the cheap fabric of his breeches.

'Charmed, my lady.'

'Indeed.'

She flicked up her veil, causing the archaeologist to inhale involuntarily. She was a mature woman, of forty-six years or so, but she still held her beauty — a full handsomeness of wide cheekbones, a strong nose and a dangerous mouth. Her skin was impossibly pale and Alistair suspected the copious application of cosmetics. Her coiffured hair was raven black and her body of generous proportions, particularly her bosom. When she smiled he noticed that her pearly white teeth were perfect and ever so slightly predatory.

'Let us not indulge ourselves in subtle niceties, Mr Sizzlehorn. I need a curator of sorts. I need a discreet individual with excellent Latin and a good drawing hand to catalogue and translate for me. McPhee tells me you are that man.'

'Indeed, I hope to be, my lady.'

'In that case, before we begin let me ask you: are you familiar with the phrase *gabinetto degli oggetti riservati*, once known as *gabinetto degli oggetti osceni*?'

Her Italian was flawless and Alistair wondered whether she might not in fact be of Italian descent.

'The Cabinet of Restricted or Secret Objects, from Pompeii?' he replied, trying unsuccessfully to keep his nerves from showing in his trembling voice. He had heard rumour of the secret room in the Museum of Naples which was said to house a collection of erotic objects of explicit and magical nature. Objects that had been rescued from the doomed Roman city of Pompeii, infamous for its worship of Bacchus and love of carnality.

The legend of the secret cabinet had circulated the corridors of Cambridge in whispered conversations amongst his fellow students, the heirs of the landed gentry, many of whose families held similar erotic collections in their own vaults. Aware of his impoverished background and experience Alistair had always been too intimidated to pass comment, fearing he would be exposed and humiliated both as a virgin and a pauper. But the descriptions of grotesque but titillating ithyphallic statues and erotic murals had captivated him nevertheless.

'The very same.' Lady Whistle's velvet tones drew him sharply back to the present.

'The Italian archaeologist Antonio Bonucci is a close friend of mine. When the *Risorgimento* began in Italy last year he approached me with the idea of cataloguing and documenting some of the objects, in case that upstart Garibaldi destroyed the collection. I have brought you some of the objects entrusted to me — I have, of course, documentation to accompany each artifact. But before I reveal them, I should warn you that these are not for the eyes of the innocent or the puritan.'

Alistair blushed again, worried that his virginity might suddenly blossom on his skin like some hideous stigmata. His eyes slid sideways to McPhee, who stood stoically by the table, his hand absentmindedly stroking the top of his walking cane.

'If you don't mind, my lady, an upstanding gentleman of the Presbyterian persuasion such as myself would prefer to step outside to avoid the corrupting nature of such objects,' McPhee murmured, his voice thick with embarrassment.

Lady Whistle nodded, a glint of amusement playing in her eyes. Before the bantam octogenarian left the room he turned to his prodigy. 'Now, Mr Sizzlehorn, promise me that when you look upon these demonic items of worship you will view them with the cold eye of the archaeologist and dismiss all licentious thoughts.'

'I should never have the audacity to approach such antiquities otherwise, Dr McPhee,' Alistair replied, mustering all the sincerity he could.

After McPhee had left, Lady Whistle stood, a steam of perfume rising with her. She was even more statuesque standing and seemed to be only an inch or so shorter than Alistair who was a good six feet tall. She turned to her manservant. The archaeologist now noticed he was a remarkably handsome lad of no more than fifteen. Grinning mischievously like a dusky Puck who had just stepped from the shadows of a forest glade, the valet stared back brazenly. His gaze revealed a maturity far beyond his years; an observation that disturbed Alistair profoundly.

'Toby, I believe we are ready now,' Lady Whistle said a trifle impatiently.

With tantalising slowness the valet pulled away the silk kerchiefs one by one, as if conducting a peepshow.

285

The revealed items were extraordinary. Astonishing in their beauty, they also displayed a complete obscenity, a gleeful celebration of the pornographic.

The centrepiece was a marble statue some three feet in height: the figure of a beautiful youth, his arms raised up as if he had once clasped a water jug, his back arched. Extremely realistic, it was as if the boy had been turned into marble with the wave of some arch wizard's staff. One's eye was immediately drawn to the statue's huge semi-erect penis. It was impossibly thick, veined, the bulge of the head clearly visible under the foreskin which was still drawn over the tip. Its very tumescence was a pornographic celebration of existence, of life force itself. The startling contrast between the feminine beauty of the boy and his ultra-masculine organ created an erotic counterbalance which further enhanced the exquisite artistry of the statue.

If he followed the ways of the Latin poet Catullus, he could fall in love with such a youth, Alistair found himself thinking.

Lady Whistle's seductively deep voice broke his reverie. 'From the House of the Vettii. The statue would have been part of a fountain — the sex organ is, of course, a water spout.' Her tone was objective, as if she were describing a rare species of butterfly.

The young archaeologist, scarlet to the roots of his hair, had to force himself to look up; as he did, he had the distinct impression that the valet, Toby, was winking at him.

'And these?' Alistair asked, covering his embarrassment with a deep baritone timbre. He pointed to a series of bronzes of comical dwarves with satyr-like faces, each completely overshadowed by a humungous erect phallus taller than themselves.

'The Romans attributed magical powers to dwarves. These were powerful talismen — both for luck and virility. The phallus itself, as you can see by the carving on these small clay slabs —' she indicated squares of red travertine each with a crude bas-relief of an erect phallus with a Latin inscription — 'was considered to bring both happiness and good luck to a household, and a representation was often to be found hanging above the door. Hence the inscription: *Hic habitat felicitas*. I have no doubt that, with such plethora of penises available, happiness indeed dwelt therein. But I digress; it is this that I am most interested in.'

She indicated a scroll Alistair hadn't noticed. She pulled off her gloves to handle it and Alistair immediately observed that her hands belied her age, which he now realised was far closer to fifty. She unrolled the manuscript to reveal an elaborate sketch of what appeared to be an orgiastic rite. The participants were evidently followers of Pan: some of the women were half-goat and many of the men bearded satyrs — all engaged in a variety of sexual congress, from sodomy through to bestiality. Each face was etched with a strange bliss akin to religious ecstasy, as if they were striving for a higher goal than just carnal pleasure.

Struggling with his own tumescence, the courageous archaeologist attempted to adopt the detached professional air he had promised McPhee.

'I assume this is a bacchanalian ritual — the central figure looks like Bacchus or the Greek equivalent, Dionysus, with his beard and goblet. He appears to be the master of ceremonies.'

'Indeed. But the real fascination is the transcription of the text beneath this mural — found on the walls of the Villa of the Mysteries. Its Latin is too complex for my schoolgirl grasp, but I am told it suggests that this particular orgy was undertaken in the quest for eternal youth. A quest that was, so the inscription implies, successful in its outcome.'

Lady Whistle's gaze, although candid, held a far more salacious implication. The ghost of premonition passed over Alistair, causing him to shiver.

'My lady, you do realise that the mural would have been metaphoric — most likely a device to stimulate the clientele of a brothel or the staid marriage of a rich merchant?'

'Perhaps so, perhaps not. I have evidence that leads me to believe it is a literal explanation. But that does not concern us now — let us return to the matter at hand. I wish to employ you for two purposes: your official role will be as compiler of a catalogue of the collection, for the museum and for posterity. Your second, secret, task is to translate and break the riddle of this Dionysian rite. I will pay you well for the former, but for the latter I will reward you with riches undreamed of.'

*With riches undreamed of ...* her language was strangely old-fashioned, as if English were indeed her second tongue. The story of Faust and his pact with the devil floated up from the recesses of Alistair's memory.

Beneath the lace shawl he became aware of an ivory cleavage that plunged into tantalising shadow; lower down, her waist — pressed no doubt into such an impossibly narrow shape by a steely corset — looked as if he could encircle it with one hand. Even further down he caught a glimpse of her delicate ankles clad in pearly grey kid leather. She would be a seductive patron, of that he had no doubt. But it was the promise of freedom from poverty and the status he would achieve by having his name attached to such a catalogue, not to mention the appeal of breaking the terrible ennui of his current laborious and repetitious duties, that really fascinated him.

It was all too much for the archaeologist, who had supped on nothing but milk toast for two nights; Alistair found himself suddenly weak at the knees. Lady Whistle, noting his faintness, clicked her fingers. Immediately Toby slipped a chair beneath him, into which he collapsed thankfully.

'Take the offer, sir. You won't regret it ... trust me,' the valet whispered conspiratorially.

Smiling sardonically Lady Whistle addressed the hapless archaeologist. 'I ask only one condition: that you tell no one, not even your employer, of the second task. You must understand, the mural was copied illegally from the walls of the House of Mysteries itself — you are only the fifth person to see it in recent history. And, as you may appreciate, I have my reputation to consider.'

'And Madam's reputation is impeccable,' her servant piped up. The gentlewoman stroked her valet's cheek in a decidedly non-maternal fashion.

'Thank you, Toby. I am fortunate that Lord Whistle is such an understanding husband.' She turned back to Alistair, her fingers still caressing her valet. 'He is *so* fond of his horses. Why, his jockey hardly ever leaves his side. Isn't that right, Toby?'

'Indeed, my lady.'

'So, my dear archaeologist, have you reached a decision?'

'I will take the commission.'

'Both of them?'

'Both of them,' Alistair answered, swallowing nervously as the image of his father staring disapprovingly from the pulpit floated down before him.

~

That evening the young archaeologist returned to his boarding house by way of a hansom cab. As he parted with the shilling he could ill afford, Alistair consoled himself with the notion that the luxury was a celebration, a way of accustoming himself to his future prosperity. Therefore it was not without some satisfaction that he noticed his landlady, Mrs Jellicoe, spying from behind the dingy length of material she optimistically referred to as her curtains.

'In the money I see, Mr Sizzlehorn,' she remarked as Alistair entered the darkened hallway of the boarding house.

'A temporary aberration that I hope will soon become permanent,' he replied cheerily, smiling into the gloom of the spacious but sadly neglected terraced house.

Mrs Jellicoe clicked her dentures in disapproval, her jowly face framed by the yellowed bonnet she was never seen without. Gambling — the lad must have taken to the turf, she thought disapprovingly, already wondering what poor unfortunate she could replace him with if he should fall to rack and ruin. Ruminating over the possibilities, she returned to the parlour where she settled into her knitting like a fat spider content in her web.

At the top of the stairs Alistair opened the door to his garret room with the rusty key Mrs Jellicoe had entrusted to him with as much ceremony as if she were handing over the keys to the Royal Mint itself.

The garret was dark except for a strand of moonlight struggling to penetrate the dingy skylight set high in the slanting roof. The air was chilly. Shivering, Alistair scurried across the bare floor to light a mutton-fat candle on the three-legged desk propped up by a quantity of Latin texts.

The wick spluttered into flame, illuminating the room which was a mish-mash of strange angles and awkward beams running across the ceiling with no apparent logic. An oil painting of Dante's Inferno hung on one wall; an inferior piece reminiscent of the work of Hieronymus Bosch, Alistair had rescued it from a pawn shop on High Holborn. Attracted by the garishness of the writhing Dante besieged by temptations, he had tempered the dramatic effect of the canvas with a cheap lithograph entitled *The Elysian Fields* that hung opposite. In contrast this was a colourful rendition of Utopia, showing a meadow populated by angelic shepherdesses and cherubs playing lyres. The diaphanous nature of the maidens' garments had not been lost on the lonely youth, who often imagined himself lolling in such a field, his head in the lap of one of the nymphs.

There was little else in the garret apart from these two paintings: a rickety bed, with a painted brass headpiece his mother had insisted he transport from home; a pathetic hearth blackened with soot; and a chipped china washstand equipped with an enamel jug, the water in which was guaranteed to be freezing no matter the season. In the corner was his desk, with a miniature of his parents and his certificate of graduation attached to the wall above.

After poking the struggling fire until it ignited into some semblance of warmth, Alistair fell in exhaustion upon the bed. Suddenly the whole house shook as a train headed into nearby Euston station. It was an event which occurred every twenty minutes or so, day and night, adding to the atmosphere of uncertainty which permeated the rambling boarding house. Every week saw some tenant being evicted and a new one installed, for Mrs Jellicoe fancied herself a wronged woman and happily displayed a healthy lack of respect for the male of her species, particularly those who deluded themselves regarding the power of their charms. In Mrs Jellicoe's world, economy would always triumph over sentiment. 'I got no time for yer story-spinners and fly-by-nights. Forty long years I put with the gropings of an incontinent dipsomaniac and these four walls is all I have to show fer it, God curse Mr Jellicoe's drunken heart,' the landlady would often confide to no one in particular during one of her own inebriated moments.

Alistair listened to the last of the train's rattling fade with one final hoot into the distant clatter of the city, then glanced over to his Latin dictionaries. He had topped the subject at Cambridge — the legacy of his father who had insisted that if his child were to roam wild he should at least roam in Latin.

The vision of Lady Whistle's fine white hands drifted like a wisp of smoke across his thoughts, followed incongruously by a troop of whirling dwarfs, each encumbered by an inordinately colossal member. Disturbingly, many carried McPhee's grim visage upon their squat dancing bodies. Just as Alistair was despairing of exorcising the whimsy, Lady Whistle entered the scenario, clad in the garb of the goddess Venus, her generous bosom resplendently visible. Alistair relaxed into the delicious fecundity of the phantom's breasts and sex to lose himself in the insistent throbbing of his fantasy.

⌑

For the sake of discretion, Dr McPhee installed Alistair in an office which, unless one had prior knowledge of its hidden doorway, was impossible to locate — which was entirely McPhee's intention as he feared the intrusion of any other staff.

The room was freezing, heated only by the steam off a nearby water heater. Alistair bent over the desk, his icy hands clad in fingerless mittens, a threadbare scarf wound around his thin neck, painstakingly copying the shape of a bronze figure entitled *Priapus pouring*. The crowned god was standing with one hand on his hip, robed except for his naked erect phallus over which he appeared to be pouring holy oil. An expression of amused detachment adorned the deity's face, as if the tumescent organ might possibly belong to someone else.

The archaeologist's drawing was as good as his Latin, and he had accurately sketched in the details of the figure in Indian ink: the folds of the robe, the long wavy beard that suggested a Persian influence, the high crown perched on the figure's head. He was just about to begin sketching the erect member itself when McPhee burst through the door in his customary bombastic fashion.

'Lad, I think not!' he exclaimed, his voice tight with outrage, one long yellow fingernail pointing critically at the offending appendage. 'We at the BM have our standards. Standards we are obliged by Queen and State to uphold. I suggest either a reduction in size or, better still for the sake of modesty, a blank.'

Alistair looked at him, perplexed.

'A blank? You mean a cloud around the groin area?' he asked innocently, privately appalled by his employer's request, but at the same time considering the possibility that McPhee might have drawn such a cloud around his own genitals a good five decades earlier.

'A cloud? Tosh and poppycock! I said a blank and I mean a blank!'

The octogenarian looked as if he might explode with rage, but Alistair was not to be deterred.

'But Dr McPhee, that would not be historically accurate.'

'Mr Sizzlehorn, when you are as decrepit as I am, ye'll understand that history is a fluid concept, merely elastic reportage that is shaped and documented by the historian. We are not only archaeologists, we are also custodians — custodians of the Christian soul which is an impressionable and fragile thing. We cannot allow images of celestial beings with huge ...' At this point the man began to splutter, saliva flying as he tried to wrap his tongue around a word that had perhaps never before graced his mouth.

'Reproductive organs?' Alistair articulated helpfully which only irked the professor further.

'Precisely. Mothers and children might see such a thing and be greatly distressed or, worse, corrupted. The British Empire cannot have that, never mind the British Museum, not to mention the British Queen.'

'Quite; but this is a private commission and Lady Whistle has specifically requested that the depictions be accurate.'

'That might be the case, laddie, but I also know that Lady Whistle intends to donate the catalogues to the museum after her death, and if we are to display them at any time in the future they will require censorship.'

'But should I not consult with Lady Whistle first?'

McPhee paused, stared at the offending member with unbridled disgust, then sighed heavily.

'In that case, I suggest a compromise. Ye are to draw only the outline of these ... areas without filling them in in any manner whatsoever. This will greatly lessen the impact of such obscene realism.'

'Do I have a choice, Dr McPhee?'

'No, ye do not, Mr Sizzlehorn. Och, and by the way, this came for you, by way of Lady Whistle's valet.'

McPhee handed Alistair an envelope of the finest parchment and smelling faintly of vanilla. It was sealed with a crest depicting bagpipes crossed with what looked like a Corsican coat of arms, making Alistair wonder again as to the origins of his patroness. He opened the envelope cautiously: a five-guinea coin fell out. The invitation was written in an elegant hand that could only be female:

> *You are expected at Lady Whistle's town house at seven this evening, both to sup and commence work on a more private matter. Tardiness of any kind will not be tolerated.*

The address was scrawled on the back of the envelope. Alistair lifted it to his nose and breathed in the scent deeply. Behind him he heard McPhee sniff in disapproval.

'I'd be putting that coin away safely, if I were you, laddie. She'll be making you work hard for your money — believe me, I know,' the professor said, an odd smile playing across his lips, leaving Alistair with the uncomfortable impression that there might be more to McPhee's relationship with Lady Whistle than he had originally perceived.

❦

Number 36 The Strand was a Georgian townhouse of elegant classical proportions, opposite gardens and close to the Temple. The mock Grecian porticoes and arches above the windows delighted the aesthete in Alistair. The archaeologist, dressed in his best attire, paused before walking up the gravel path to pull down his tails and adjust his only tall hat. This was the life he aspired to, this was why he had fought so hard to escape the dreary rectory he had grown up in where his father's frugality had been constantly drummed into him. This was what his soul had yearned for: the effortless grace money brought, and with it the luxury of time to devote oneself to philosophical matters, to the pursuit of sensuality and the indulgence in all things wantonly human.

Already he saw himself escorting a beautiful sophisticate like Lady Whistle, riding with her in Hyde Park, sitting with her at the Opera, accompanying her to the theatre. His daydream was rudely interrupted by the bruised face of a street pauper, no more than eight years of age.

'Spare a ha'penny, mister, for an orphan of the gutter.'

Caught unawares and feeling guilty for the extravagance of his reverie, Alistair threw the boy a penny — something he would never normally do.

'Thank ye kindly and God bless,' the child called out, running off down the street before Alistair changed his mind.

In two strides the youth arrived at the imposing door. Through a window he thought he detected the flurry of a movement before he pulled the cord of the door bell.

&gt;

Alistair leaned back in the cushioned armchair, repressing the desire to belch. Before him sat a supper tray still laden with plates.

To his immense disappointment he had been welcomed not by Lady Whistle but by a maid who had ushered him into a study off the spacious reception area which was dominated by a sweeping marble staircase.

'Madam is occupied with an unexpected visitor,' the maid had explained. 'But she wished for you to sup and said you would understand the work she has left for you here.'

The study contained a bookcase filled with what appeared to be leatherbound travel diaries — secured behind a locked glass door, to Alistair's frustration — maps of antiquity on the walls, and a walnut desk upon which lay the section of the scroll he had viewed earlier with four stanzas in Latin beneath it.

Almost immediately the maid returned with a supper tray. After she had left Alistair uncovered the dinner: a steaming feast of succulent roast pork, apple sauce, roast potatoes, stewed swede and a side of marinated quinces, followed by a rice pudding drenched in a butterscotch sauce. The meal was accompanied by a mellow claret of some vintage. Alistair could not remember supping so well in his life.

As he ate he fancied he heard the low murmuring of a male voice in the room next door, followed by the staccato of a woman laughing. Torn between satiating his appetite and satisfying his voracious curiosity, he hastily finished the dessert and tiptoed to the wall to press his ear against the fabric of the wallpaper.

'It is a ridiculous and preposterously carnal idea, Elendora, an alchemy of the absurd. It simply won't work,' the male voice announced in an amused tone. It was a voice rich with wit and irony and Alistair recognised it immediately. He had met its owner on one unforgettable occasion, when he made a state visit to the museum to indulge a well-known (and diverse) interest in the antiquities of the Mediterranean.

'But, Dizzy, think of the fun I shall have along the way!' Lady Whistle laughed in such an intimate way that Alistair was convinced Disraeli must count her amongst his many conquests.

'I have heard nothing,' the Chancellor of the Exchequer declared. 'My ears remain unsullied and, if anyone should ask, I shall declare my absolute ignorance!'

''Tis a pity we should become so rigid and fidelity should take on such ridiculous importance as we get older. You used to be such a delightful distraction in your younger days.'

'That, my dear, is the penalty of hindsight and wisdom.'

'And ambition perhaps,' Lady Whistle replied, her voice dripping with sarcasm.

At this the voices faded, as if the speakers had moved to another part of the room. Abashed at his eavesdropping, and with his heart thudding at being in such close proximity to a man he greatly admired, Alistair returned to the desk, wondering how on earth Mr Disraeli might be connected to Lady Whistle and her commission.

It was with this thought foremost in his mind that he began the painstaking task of translating the Latin text.

Each stanza ran under a different section of the mural. As Alistair stared at the semi-naked figures twisting in a variety of embraces, it became clear to him that the orgy itself was in fact a sequence: four phases of activity clearly linked to the verse accompanying it. He read over the first stanza again.

> *Gather together boy, girl or priest (scholar?)*
> *Create a celebration (or feast)*
> *Revelries to toast the God himself*
> *Lord of the Harvest, make the dance (orgy?) complete*
> *And immortal joy, eternal youth, shall be thy wealth.*

Her scent betrayed her first. Realising that she stood behind him, a shiver ran down the back of Alistair's neck then turned into pinpricks along his spine. It was the combination of her perfume and the warmth of her body and, under it, something else that teased at his virginal senses. The hidden matrix of woman, the odour of sex still lingering. But more disturbing was the realisation that he had not heard her entry into the room nor her footsteps upon the polished floor. It was as if she had appeared behind him magically and it was this uncomfortable sensation that kept him frozen to his seat, eyes forward.

She spoke and the warmth of her breath tickled his ears.

'Well, my young man,' — he thrilled at her use of *my* — 'what mysteries have you unveiled for me?'

She moved around the desk to face him. She wore a lilac satin ball gown pleated into a thousand shimmering folds at the waist, the bodice as tight as a second skin, its dangerously low décolletage edged in black lace. The sleeves were ornate and unusual: their long cuffs of matching black lace finished well past her hands and were reminiscent of the medieval era. Her neckline was naked except for a choker of ornate jet. The spiky pieces so resembled shards of broken glass that Alistair found himself wondering how the stones did not cut into her flesh. A shiny band of black against the dazzling whiteness of her skin, which was as smooth as a girl's, the choker seemed to separate her head from the rest of her body, her face floating above it.

Her ebony hair was swept up to reveal a deliciously long neck and rather large unadorned ears. These appeared to be her only flaw and, like the deliberate fault woven into a Persian carpet, merely displayed her other perfections to greater advantage. Her cheeks were flushed and Alistair was convinced he could see the outline of a love rose — the imprint of teeth just visible — fading from her neck. Again he wondered about her relationship with the Jewish statesman.

He pushed his scribbled notes towards her.

'It is a ballad, a narrative explaining the actions within the mural.'

'Now tell me something I do not already know.' She smiled and leaned towards him, perfectly aware that by doing so she revealed more of her breasts. Alistair, cursing his impetuous hormones, crossed his legs and examined the document in a vain attempt to control the dancing hieroglyphics his own words had suddenly transformed into.

'Well, madam,' he played for time, 'the text appears to be an instruction manual divided into four stanzas. As you will observe, the ... the ...' He struggled for an appropriate word that would not be deemed disrespectful, '... revelry is in fact a narration itself. We see the same thirteen participants throughout the mural, each time engaged in an entirely different set of actions. As far as I can tell, there are four separate dances or choreographs to the ...'

'Orgy, Mr Sizzlehorn. We are adults; I think we may speak plainly.'

'Quite; orgy. So the four stanzas are a means of explanation for the different stages.'

'And you have translated the first, I see?'

'I have begun, although there is some confusion as to the exact translation for each of the participants. For example, the first line may be translated both as scholar or preacher, although the word "purity" in relation to this particular individual is

297

entirely unambiguous. In contrast, the use of "girl" or "young woman" here suggests an individual who is not chaste because it could be translated both as wife or female slave.'

'You mean to say there is a prescriptive aspect to the description of the individuals involved?'

'Indeed. The first stanza is a general summary of the ... orgy and its intention; the next three appear to give specific instructions, including the astrological timing of the event which seems to be of paramount importance. This is linked to the placement of Jupiter, the planet, and to the geometric symbolism of the positioning of the figures, which is extraordinary because the mural itself is an illusion.'

'In what way, Mr Sizzlehorn?'

'Well, at first glance one believes oneself to be viewing a chaos of wild abandonment, of spontaneous desires, but in fact it is anything but. Rather it is a highly coordinated and extremely controlled sequence of poses.'

'Therein lies Eros.'

'I'm sorry, I don't follow ...'

'You are young, Mr Sizzlehorn, and the young are romantic. They believe in the natural impulses, in the unfettered spontaneity of love. But believe me, when one has a wealth of experience a certain jadedness sets in, and one finds oneself searching for sophistication, for a civilisation of desire. Refinement and restriction become erotic.'

'But what of the heart?' Alistair couldn't refrain from blurting out, strangely worried for the soul of the woman standing before him. She smiled in a bemused fashion; a less generous person might have called it condescending.

'Mr Sizzlehorn, I am rich, very rich, and the very rich are very different. We leave matters of the heart to the lower classes, because *we* can afford to.'

A chill swept over the archaeologist as, for a fleeting moment, he caught a glimpse of how she might observe him through such a prism. The view was not pretty.

'But back to the task at hand. Please translate for me the final two lines of the first stanza, which I believe might contain the overall conclusion.' She waited, her face impassive.

'*Lord of the Harvest, make the dance (orgy?) complete / And immortal joy, eternal youth, shall be thy wealth,*' he read aloud as undramatically as he could.

'Then it is *fatum*. You must transcribe the last three stanzas as accurately as possible so the real dance can begin.'

'The real dance, Lady Whistle?'

'The re-enactment, Mr Sizzlehorn. The re-enactment.'

As January exhaled its frosty breath, giving way to the slightly more hopeful month of February, Alistair finished the sketching of ten objects: three small bronzes, three plates with erotic scenes painted upon them, one hand mirror, two lamps (the wick emerging from the tip of the phallus) and one Hellenistic herm with the obligatory erection. Each drawing took several days and at the end of each week he visited Lady Whistle's townhouse to hand his work over to Toby. The valet would then gleefully fill in the blank areas McPhee had insisted upon. The first time he saw Toby sketching in an enormous phallus with dismaying expertise, the archaeologist had protested, shocked that Lady Whistle should be so flippant regarding the explicit commands of his employer.

'Dr McPhee was most adamant,' he exclaimed. 'He assured me that if the depictions were literal they would never be exhibited at the museum. He was concerned about their impact upon the Christian soul, Lady Whistle.'

The aristocrat merely laughed.

'Does the Christian soul lack the facility for Eros, sir? I think not. And as Eros lives within the body, as does the soul, I would argue that both are God-given and thereby equally deserve celebration.'

'Perhaps. But do you not want the catalogue to be displayed?'

'Naturally. And one day it shall be, in all its full glory, to be looked upon by eyes far less prejudiced and more enlightened than our own. Besides, to allow such omissions is to undermine the intention of the objects themselves.'

'But what shall I say to Dr McPhee?' Alistair's heart sank; in his mind's eye he could already see his diminutive employer imploding with rage.

'Say nothing. I shall tell him I am keeping each completed drawing to be bound in a set, and when he wishes to look upon it I shall have a plethora of excuses to take us into eternity.'

'But that would be a lie, my lady.'

'Not a lie but a strategy. You would do well to learn the craft, Alistair,' she retorted, her black eyes shining. The archaeologist couldn't help but grow heady at her use of his Christian name.

He had also finished the translation of a second stanza and was working on the third. The second verse sat beneath a scenario in which thirteen participants were arranged in a star formation, fornicating in ways Alistair had never imagined possible. Several times he had to turn the scroll upside-down to work out which organ was entering which orifice — always keeping in mind McPhee's instruction to maintain a scientific perspective at all times.

There were six chimeras of goat and human — three female, three male — and six humans. The thirteenth figure was an enigma. Alistair had studied the bearded youthful figure over and over. He was the only fully clad person in the entire mural and the archaeologist couldn't work out whether he was victim or victor, priest or god. The figure had a feminine beauty, even bearded, and wore a wreath of vine leaves. He was the pivotal element in each tableau. Alistair could only assume that it was Dionysus himself. Whatever the case, it was clear that the thirteenth figure was an observer of the orgy, not a participant — that was, until the fourth tableau.

∽

One evening Lady Whistle joined him in the study. Demurely dressed in grey jersey, her hair coiled in a fine net, she came armed with tracing paper and a set of fine pencils wrapped in a roll of linen.

'Please excuse my intrusion, Mr Sizzlehorn. I have an astrological intuition I wish to act upon. I hope I will not disturb you.'

Disturb him? She distracted him to the point of despair, he thought, trying hard not to stare at her ankles or bosom.

'Of course not, my lady,' he replied curtly as she settled herself on the other side of the desk and pulled the drawing of the first tableau towards her.

Alistair watched surreptitiously as she placed the tracing paper over the figures sprawled in a starfish configuration, a tangle of vaginal, oral and anal stimulation. She traced their outlines then, with a ruler, joined them with straight lines. A set of points began to emerge.

Fascinated, Alistair abandoned all pretence of his own work and watched as she reached up to the bookcase and pulled down a large manual entitled *Astrological and Astral Formations of the Northern Skies*. She opened it to an entry marked Jupiter in the sign of Sagittarius in the fifth house. It showed an illustration of the placement of the planets joined by a series of lines. Carefully she placed the tracing over it. The orgiastic formation almost exactly matched the placement of the stars. Shaken, Alistair dropped his pen.

'As I thought,' Lady Whistle murmured, 'the mural is a depiction of a spring rite. The thirteenth figure is the young Dionysus, *Dendrites*, a manifestation which translates as tree-youth — to burst into leaf or blossom — a representation of the spring equinox. Now, I wager that if I trace the next three segments of the mural they will move progressively closer to the exact position of the first day of the astrological year.'

Carefully her hand, its long pale fingers grasped around the pencil, sketched in the figures. She had the dispassion of a mathematician, Alistair noted, marvelling at the scientific precision she displayed as she bit her lower lip in concentration.

The tracing of the fourth segment proved to be not quite a match for the correct star formation. Alistair looked at the fourth stanza which he had just finished translating. A hypothesis that had been forming in his subconsciousness suddenly articulated itself.

'There's a fifth segment missing. I'm sure of it!' he blurted out.

'A fifth section of the mural?' Lady Whistle asked cautiously.

'And with it the fifth stanza. Look carefully ...' His excitement caused him to dispense with the etiquette of formal address.

He pointed to the outer edge of the scroll. On close inspection the margin between it and the fourth tableau did seem unnaturally wide. Lady Whistle followed his gesture but did not appear as perturbed by the idea as Alistair imagined she would be.

'This is wishful thinking,' she said. 'The priest, who is the embodiment of Dionysus, is seduced in the fourth stanza. There is nowhere further for the narrative to go.'

'Perhaps, but something seems incomplete in the verse. Besides, shouldn't the final position of the figures match the transition from the old year into the new?'

For the first time in their acquaintance Lady Whistle looked anxious, a mere glimmer before she resumed her usual unfathomable demeanour.

'I suspect the discrepancy results from the shifting of the skies since the second century AD. Believe me, if there were a missing fifth tableau and stanza, I would know.'

A twitch pulled at her lower eyelid and instinctively Alistair sensed she was lying. She pulled his notes towards her.

'This is the translation of the fourth stanza?'

'Indeed, my lady. Completed a moment before you entered the room.' He gazed again at the transcription — it certainly sounded final, but he was sure there was something still to come.

*Worship me in sensual abandonment*
*But forget not the rites of Spring*
*Nor the moment my bountiful arms spread*
    *across the sky.*
*Thirteen revellers in symmetry should lie*
*Four times from womb to tomb from mother to whore,*
*Only then shall my powers be lent.*

She walked around the desk and stood behind him, her proximity eclipsing him like a dangerous proposition.

'In that case your task is almost done.'

He could feel her breath teasing his ear. 'What is it like to stare at these figures night after night? Does it not excite you, Mr Sizzlehorn?'

Alistair breathed in sharply, sensing a trap.

'Naturally, Lady Whistle: I am a man. But I view the mural as a work of art, as a metaphor not an actuality.'

'But if it were an actuality — if I could promise to recreate the temple, the identical furnishings of the Villa of the Mysteries, the exact incense burning, the hypnotic pounding of the drums, the priestesses and the satyrs — would you participate, Mr Sizzlehorn? Would you help to conjure the great, trembling life force?'

By this time she had made her way around the desk again and stood before him, unflinching in her intention. Alistair wondered whether he had misheard: the wild statement did not fit with what he thought he knew of Lady Whistle and her station. For one disjointed moment he had the distinct sensation that someone, or something, else had spoken from deep within her. He tore himself away from her eyes. Of course he had fantasised about such carnality while working on the translation. Having never known a woman, the notion of sensual abandonment on such a scale was completely abstract, but the idea of framing such behaviour with religion and ritual excited him immensely. It appealed to both the archaeologist and the romantic.

'But you cannot do that, my lady,' he stuttered. 'It would be against the law and God.'

'I can do what I like. There will be no murder, no blood sacrifice. And we are all of age, sir.'

'We?'

'I have twelve willing participants who fit the requirements of the rite.'

The air between them thickened like a velvety skin that shimmered with sexual possibility.

'But who would be involved in such a thing?' Desire dried his mouth.

'Sophisticated individuals who have been tainted by power, fame, wealth — creatures who seek risk, seek escape from the tedium of conventional life. Some you might recognise; others will be there because I have chosen them for their beauty. But I promise, all will be masked. These are influential people, Alistair, but they are also people who believe in the force of Eros. Not the Eros confined by the limitations of romantic love or the repetitious machinery of procreation, but an Eros to be elegantly and coherently worshipped. A ritual to be re-ignited by the knowledge contained in your translation.' She placed her hands dramatically upon the drawing. 'The beauty of body sliding across body — gestures unseen for thousands of years.'

'But such a thing would be a fantasy,' Alistair protested. 'The amount of research, of re-construction involved, is inconceivable.'

'I have achieved it. I have rebuilt the interior of the temple from the House of Mysteries as accurately as possible. It lies hidden on my country estate, Whistlewaite. We are ready, Alistair. All we are missing is the thirteenth participant.'

She leaned across and ran her finger along Alistair's jaw line, arriving at the edge of his lips. With exquisite lightness, she caressed them, sending tremors throughout his entire body. They exploded in delicious finality somewhere in the back of his brain as her fingertip pushed its way into his mouth. Alistair was convinced he was about to swoon. To complicate the matter further Lady Whistle sat on the desk and pressed against him. It was the nearest Alistair had ever been to a woman and the soft pillow of her breast felt as though it were burning a circle through his threadbare coat.

'The thirteen member is the priest — the pure scholar,' she murmured, her breath licking the side of his face. 'The cerebral virgin. Virgo. He is you.'

Alistair had the strong impression that reality had departed at some juncture and the room, himself and the woman before him had seamlessly entered a dream world. A world where his preconceived notions of how women behaved — particularly those who were far above one's station and therefore unattainable — had been turned topsy-turvy.

'You are a virgin, are you not?' she whispered, rolling her tongue around the word as if it were an exotic fruit.

Unable to speak, he nodded dumbly. She smiled and eased her finger out of his mouth. 'Wonderful. The ritual must take place at the exact moment when the old astrological year passes into the new. From the wisdom of Pisces into the energetic child of the Ram, Aries. Midday on the spring equinox, the twenty-first of March.'

She caught up a shawl of heavy silk and swung it around her shoulders with a flourish. 'That allows you six weeks to make a decision, Alistair. For, trust me, the ritual *will* take place.'

⁓

Sleep fled his tormented body and flapped around the bedroom like a trapped bird. Resigned, Alistair sat up to light a candle. He was still wondering whether his feverish imagination hadn't conjured up the whole encounter. If Lady Whistle hadn't scrawled the date and time she intended to conduct her bizarre rite on a slip of paper and fastened it to his lapel like a railway ticket pinned to a lost child, he might be inclined to believe that carnal frustration had indeed addled his brain. But no: there was the paper, as real as the moonlight creeping under the grimy curtain.

But what of his soul, Alistair thought; furthermore what of love? Or had that emotion become completely redundant amongst the aristocracy? He tried to rationalise but his logic was fuzzy with exhaustion. He had always imagined his first encounter would be of a passionate nature. A tender consummation of desire shared by common intellectual spirits. The image of the thirteenth participant, the priest, his bearded face infused with religious ecstasy appeared before the insomniac.

'You will experience a greater love than mere romance,' Lady Whistle had promised. 'We thirteen shall form a human link to the cosmos. For a brief moment we too shall be gods.'

Was Lady Whistle's sanity entirely whole, he wondered. But to see what she had built, to go back in time . . . ? He had dreamed of this all his life: to walk with the Romans, to be worshipped like a deity, to be seduced like an emperor. He fell back against the pillow, sleep claiming him at last.

He was woken two hours later by a loud knocking.

'Mr Sizzlehorn, there's a servant 'ere for you — a whippersnapper from Lady Whistle, so 'e reckons. Wants words with you, he does, at this ungodly hour!' Mrs Jellicoe bellowed through the door.

Alistair groaned. Throwing a worn silk dressing gown over his nightshirt, he ran across the freezing floorboards to open the door before Mrs Jellicoe broke it down with her pounding.

Toby, immaculate in his uniform, his youthful face impossibly fresh for six in the morning, stood grinning on the other side. Mrs Jellicoe, clad in a nightgown covered with a ridiculous number of satin bows, quilted roses and other frivolities, peered fascinated over the valet's shoulder.

'Thank you, Mrs Jellicoe, I'll deal with the matter now.'

'And make sure you keep your voices down — there's folks still sleeping, Mr Sizzlehorn. Lucky you're one of me favourites, getting me up at this time and in winter too,' she muttered grumpily, pushing aside a mouse trap set upon the landing as she made her way heavily down the stairs.

Unperturbed, Toby turned to Alistair. 'Lady Whistle wishes to know your answer,' he announced, one eyebrow raised critically as he caught a glimpse of the stark garret room.

'At this time of the morning? I thought I had six weeks.'

'My mistress keeps her own hours and waits for no one,' the valet replied, a sudden seriousness ageing his face immediately.

Something snapped on the landing behind them. They both looked down; a mouse, its spine broken, thrashed its way to a slow death.

'Your answer, Mr Sizzlehorn?'

'Tell her I say yes,' Alistair replied, his own world lurching into a myriad of new possibilities.

⤚

February rolled into March and spring began to lace the cold winds with hope. Across the Channel, Louis Napoleon declared himself Emperor Napoleon III; further afield Englishmen flocked to the colony of New South Wales drawn by the discovery of gold; while at home the poet Tennyson continued his comfortable post as Poet Laureate.

Alistair had not seen his mysterious patroness after that fateful night. Ever since then she had insisted her valet collect the drawings directly from the museum. For the archaeologist, life reverted back to its normal drudgery, leavened only by the anticipation that began to grow like a canker deep within him as the spring equinox approached. He was both terrified and exhilarated. He felt like a man awaiting his own execution. Desperate to distract himself, he tried spending some of the new-found wealth Lady Whistle's stipend had given him. Fighting against his inherent frugality he even attended the opera, but found that without a companion the experience merely highlighted his loneliness.

At one point he thought about seeking absolution and determined to confess the demonic arrangement to his one friend, a merchant from the Haymarket, Harry Holworthy. But when it came to it, he found himself telling the easy-going capitalist that he had received an unexpected inheritance from a maiden aunt. Harry urged him to invest the money in stocks — shares in the East India Company and a malt house in North Cumbria — rather than fritter it away. After purchasing a new suit, hat, gloves and riding boots, Alistair took Harry's advice and was delighted with the profit he accrued in a matter of weeks.

'This will see you through to an early retirement,' Harry had promised. 'We shall make you a gentleman of leisure yet.'

As the third week of March drew near Alistair found himself wondering if he would be transformed; whether such deviancy would leave him jaded and incapable of any future love. But the vision of the pencilled strokes he had copied so faithfully being brought to life — the quivering limbs, lithe flesh wound around flesh, breasts, buttocks, sex sliding into sex, with himself at the centre, being caressed, stroked and worshipped — quickly dispelled any ethical dilemma. He had made a promise, a contract that could not be broken, he reminded himself piously, secretly thrilled to find a moral justification.

The nineteenth of March arrived. On his customary walk to work Alistair noticed that already the daffodils and crocuses were poking bright green shoots through the black soil of the flowerbeds. Sparrows had begun to collect twigs and the delirium of courtship seemed to be increasing everywhere, except in his own life. Fear not, my man, he said to himself, in three days' time you shall be a changed creature, a debonair blade able to boast of such sophisticated, sensual delights as most men will never experience in a lifetime. After that you will be able to have whomever you choose. The soliloquy was consoling, and his pace picked up. With a whistle he strolled through the park towards the museum, now oblivious to the courting couples around him.

He had almost completed the final drawing for the catalogue — an erotic scene painted on a mirror showing a woman mounting the loins of her lover, one hand tenderly stretched out over his chest. In the background the faint outline of a male slave of the bedroom, a *cubicularius*, hovered discreetly. Alistair was just finishing the curves of the woman's breasts with the most delicate of strokes when he became aware of the presence of someone else in the room.

'It must be an entirely absorbing task,' said a sweet, high female voice, followed by a short peal of laughter which cascaded incongruously through the dreary room. Alistair, completely taken by surprise, looked up.

Standing before him, wearing a pale yellow silk dress, a damp furled umbrella by her side, her friendly face framed by a bonnet that was neither frivolous nor severe but spoke of a slightly audacious nature, was a woman who looked only a few years younger than himself. Alistair sprang to his feet, knocking over a bronze of a dwarf, who fell onto the tip of his ridiculously huge penis and balanced there precariously. Alistair, in a feeble attempt to conceal such obscenity, stood before the table his arms spread wide.

'How did you get in?' he demanded, feeling intruded upon. After all, only three people had entered the room since he had begun the catalogue — McPhee, Toby and Lady Whistle. The girl laughed again, although Alistair noticed she was also blushing. With a cheeky air she held out her hand.

'Margaret McPhee. Amused to make your acquaintance, especially surrounded by such *quaint* depictions of *l'amour* ...'

'McPhee! McPhee has a daughter?'

'As far as I know, Uncle has not duplicated himself in any shape, size or form. We must thank God for this miracle. Uncle has always appeared to show little interest in human relations — unless, of course, they are several thousand years old.'

'You are his niece?'

'Precisely, just as you are his apprentice.'

'Assistant, actually.' Here Alistair bristled with self-importance. 'Working on a very important and secret commission.'

'Evidently,' Margaret McPhee responded, a wry smile playing around her wide mouth.

The archaeologist spread his coat-tails in a feeble attempt to obscure her view further. 'These works of art are not for the eyes of respectable young women.'

'Oh, and I suppose they are perfectly respectable for the eyes of young men? Or are you not a respectable young man?'

'That is entirely different. The male eye has the ability to discern, whereas the female is far more susceptible.'

'Are you suggesting the female sex is the weaker gender or the more sinful?'

Her feisty retort caught Alistair by surprise. Stammering furiously he suddenly felt little more than a whirling scarecrow caught in a gust of wind.

'I mean merely to defend you from the more animalistic side of mankind.'

'I thank you for the sentiment. But I don't require defending, although, of course, you might if Uncle discovers I am here. He would probably explode in outrage and end up splattered on the ceiling like a tapioca pudding.'

She laughed again. Alistair struggled to keep his grave demeanour.

'He would indeed, and then he would terminate my employment immediately which is not a frivolous matter, Miss McPhee,' he replied soberly.

'I wouldn't let him. I have never seen anything so ... explicit,' she said, her eyes widening as she glimpsed his current sketch. Alistair stood frozen, still holding out his coat-tails, unsure about the social conduct the situation demanded. Ignoring him entirely, Margaret McPhee stood on tiptoe and actually peeped over his shoulder.

'But there is a beauty,' she murmured.

'Miss McPhee, I demand that you leave this office immediately, before my position is morally compromised. Besides, where is your escort?'

'Escort? Phooey! I am a governess, Mr ... ?'

'Sizzlehorn. Alistair Sizzlehorn.'

'Mr Sizzlehorn. I have also attended Miss La Monte's art classes so I *have* seen the naked human form before.'

'But not in this state I should hope.'

She blushed again, violently, and turned away from the table. Taking off her bonnet she revealed a pretty neck and long fair hair. She was no great beauty like Lady Whistle but there was something very appealing about the daintiness of her features and the candour behind which she tried to hide her innocence.

'Do you mean to insult me, sir?' she demanded in a peevish but endearing tone.

'I mean to protect you. This ancient culture is to be studied with an educated eye, one that has a comprehension of the religious significance of such artifacts. This is not pornography, but works of worship, Miss McPhee.'

She looked at him, deeply intrigued but also quizzical, as if she might have misjudged the awkward youth standing before her, his arms still flung askew, his pale face with its burning eyes animated with a feverish passion.

'You draw well, Mr Sizzlehorn. You have a deft hand, almost as deft as my own.'

'I do?'

Outside both of them heard the distinctive thump of Dr McPhee's footsteps approaching. But neither seemed to care, held as if in a spell by the attraction between them. Margaret, seeing that Alistair was hampered by protocol, took the initiative.

'Perhaps one day you might escort me to the show of the Pre-Raphaelite Brotherhood at the National Gallery. They are controversial but quite brilliant artists, I believe.' Quickly she thrust her card into Alistair's waistcoat pocket, a moment before McPhee burst through the door.

'Margaret! What is the meaning of this?' McPhee stood in the doorway, bristling with outrage. His niece immediately ran over and embraced him, which softened his fury considerably.

'Uncle! I grew tired of waiting for you in the lobby so I found my way here.'

'And how was that?' McPhee demanded, glaring at Alistair accusingly.

'A very nice lady at the entrance desk told me you might be found in this office.'

'Alistair, is this true?'

'Absolutely; your niece found her own way here.'

'Well, now she is leaving,' McPhee announced, taking the girl by the arm.

'Delighted to make your acquaintance, Mr Sizzlehorn,' Margaret managed before she was propelled back out into the corridor.

Five minutes later McPhee returned.

'I see ye have almost completed the catalogue, boy. As of tomorrow ye'll be moved back downstairs where ye can compile a set of illustrations of Grecian vases from the first century AD. I'm happy to report that the pastoral scenes painted upon these vessels are banal in the extreme. And, Master Sizzlehorn, if I should hear any rumour that ye are playing court to my niece, your employment will cease immediately. I hope, as a gentleman, I have made myself clear on this issue?'

'Perfectly,' his assistant responded, the throb of disappointment in his breast.

The clocks chimed five and Toby arrived as punctual as ever, wearing a festive frock coat of pastoral green rimmed with yellow velvet.

'These are my country rags,' he announced cheerfully. 'I am to Whistlewaite this evening — my lady has begun the final preparations for the spring rite. She has told me you are to be collected on the eve of the twentieth, which is tomorrow, and driven to the estate, where you shall be washed and fed. The ritual itself is to take place at midday on the twenty-first. Are you prepared, sir?'

Alistair again wondered how much of a confidant Toby was for Lady Whistle. The juxtaposition of his extreme youth and savoir-faire deterred the archaeologist who always felt hopelessly naive alongside the valet's cocky worldliness.

'I am ready,' he replied faintly.

'Then put a smile on, sir, it should be an adventure. Most men would give their left testicle to be in your position. You're a lucky man, sir, a lucky man.' The valet winked. His words shocked Alistair.

'But what am I sacrificing? Answer me that,' he responded, articulating his fears out loud. The valet smiled, then did a dance shuffle in his buckled shoes.

'Nothing you wouldn't have sacrificed sooner or later, believe me.'

'Does Lady Whistle share all her secrets with you, Toby?'

'Me and Lady Whistle go back a few centuries. She trusts me and I trust her.'

'A few centuries?'

'A figure of speech, sir,' the valet finished mysteriously, then left carrying the last illustration for the catalogue.

There are times in a man's life when his destiny takes on the form of a pendulum, swinging precariously between two directions; times when the normal constraints and social mores by which one lives are rendered as meaningless as melting snow. This was such a time for our protagonist.

As Alistair cleaned the shavings of charcoal from his desk, warmed his hands on the water heater, and looked one last time out of the barred window clouded by the shadows of nesting pigeons, he couldn't help but feel a sense of doom. Sighing deeply he glanced about the office. On the one hand his senses were stretched as thin as a drumskin upon which excitement had begun its relentless beat; on the other, he felt paralysed by the intuition that his life was about to change irredeemably. The question was: how?

Outside the museum, instead of turning left — his usual direction home — the apprehensive youth turned right and made his way across High Holborn, down Drury Lane and towards the river. The waxing moon shone, making shadow-witches of the trees and turning every iron railing into the turrets of a magical castle. Alistair was lost, not in thought, but in a rare fog of sensations; a harking back to a more primitive reasoning as something other than logic guided his feet.

What was his fear? He tried to rationalise his emotions. Was it the loss of innocence? It is merely a physical transition, another voice answered, a carnal voice bristling with impending adventure. Don't worry, you will remain unchanged in essence. You will just gain experience, knowledge of how to pleasure another, it continued seductively.

The image of Margaret McPhee, her face flushed with sensuality, her fair hair loosened, suddenly stared up from the glistening surface of a puddle.

Alistair reached into his waistcoat pocket and pulled out her card. To his astonishment he was just three streets away from her. With the urgency of a man seeking salvation, Alistair began to run.

⇌

It was a large red-brick terraced house, with a straggling cherry tree at the front. A modest dwelling in a prestigious street; a typical residence of the nouveau riche, the merchant class that had made their money through the manufacturing mills of the north. Alistair bounded up the granite steps and rang the bell.

'The mister and missus ain't in.' A buxom housekeeper, one hand still grasping a feather duster, stood at the open door, glaring hostilely.

'I'm here to see the governess, Miss McPhee?'

'She don't take gentlemen callers after six.'

'I am her cousin from the country. It's urgent.'

'In that case, I suppose you could wait in the pantry.'

Staring aimlessly at a hock of ham that lay on a side table next to a cabinet of fine Dutch china, Alistair suddenly felt like a complete jackdaw. What presumption he had displayed. What if she wasn't the slightest bit interested in his company? What if she had just been playing him for a fool? Crippled with self-consciousness, he noticed a smear of soot upon his jacket sleeve which he was busy rubbing off when Margaret McPhee entered. 'Coz!' she cried out, startling him.

Margaret turned to the corpulent housekeeper squeezed up behind her in the doorway. 'That will be all, Mrs Porter. I'm certain my cousin wishes for some private words with me.'

After a suspicious look at Alistair, the housekeeper nodded curtly and took her leave. Margaret softly closed the door.

She was more beautiful than he had remembered, but her beauty lay in her ordinariness. She did not have the refined aristocratic cheekbones, patrician nose or full mouth of Lady Whistle, nor the lushness of her complexion; instead it was the neat symmetry of her form, the animation of her bright, green eyes, her enthusiasm that made her radiant. She smiled at him.

'Why, Mr Sizzlehorn, you have displayed an ingenious audacity I would not have attributed to one previously so censorious.'

'I had to see you.' His words tumbled out in a clumsy rush.

'Are you ill? You look so pale.'

'I have to go away the day after tomorrow. I have an engagement ...' he trailed off, wondering why the proximity of this young woman threw what had seemed so important into irrelevancy.

'An engagement — that sounds mysterious.'

'Just promise me you will come to the gallery tomorrow, to the exhibition you wished to see?'

He moved closer and stood inches from her, drinking in the fall of her hair, the emerald streak that was her eyes, the sheen of her pearl buttons, and found himself wondering if, some time in the future, she would ever reach out to him naked, call him her own.

314

'Such urgency is unconventional. Are you here to court me, sir?'

Her sudden formality made him smile, it sat so uncomfortably upon her quaint figure. Seeing his smile, she frowned. He feared he had been misunderstood and took her hand.

'Forgive my impatience, Miss McPhee, but I find myself at a strange crossroads in my life, the outcome of which is uncertain. But to answer your question: yes, I believe I am.'

'In that case, Mr Sizzlehorn, I shall meet you tomorrow at the doors of the National Gallery at two o'clock sharp. And now I must return to my wards. Good night to you, sir.'

Before he had a chance to respond she was out the door. He stared at a giant copper tureen, which mockingly reflected back his wan, confused face.

'Thank you, Margaret, thank you,' he whispered, drowning.

That night Alistair stoked the fire as high as he could, then dragged the looking glass over and propped it against the mantelpiece. After locking the door, he stripped off his garments and stood entirely naked before the glass.

Was he a well-made man?

His torso was long and pale, his shoulders a good width but already afflicted with the stoop of the scholar. He was slender, his legs tapered and muscled. A thick bush of golden hair crept across his loins and travelled up to his chest. His yard was of a decent size, he presumed, thinking back to the fellows he had seen naked at boarding school. There was still the shadow of boyhood upon his physique, as if his torso hadn't yet thickened fully. His hips were slim, his buttocks high and firm, his waist strong. No other eye has seen my body, he thought, wondering whether he would be considered handsome or plain. It was a curious, furtive sensation to be examining himself so coldly.

Running his hands down his flanks he tried to imagine they were a stranger's hands. How would he surrender himself? *Would* he surrender himself? He did not know how to behave in such a circumstance — or could he trust to instinct? And afterwards, would she, Margaret, desire such debased leavings? His thickening sex answered all his queries. As he caught the shadow of his profile — the curve of his body, the arc of his organ, his hands resting defiantly on his hips — he could have sworn he saw the sinister silhouette of the twin horns of Pan rising up behind his head.

∼

The mermaid was painted in the romantic style of the Pre-Raphaelites, but the realism of the scales, the white skin, the pensive but utterly self-absorbed look on the sea-woman's face as she gazed down at the water, her long red hair trailing into the sea, was shocking. It was a totally credible fusion of fish and flesh.

'I think she would be cold and clammy to touch, like the slimy skin of an ocean trout,' Margaret said, facing the painting. She was dressed in a blue calico gown with ruffles down the front and a straw hat trimmed with matching ribbon. She dared not look at him for fear he would see the rose of excitement creeping across her own fair skin.

'Without a human heart,' Alistair continued, thinking about another woman altogether, 'and yet it is her very beauty, her inaccessibility that shimmers so seductively, that creates the fatal trap into which all sailors fall ...'

'... to be pulled down to the bottom of the ocean by her clinging arms ...'

'... the poor man gasping as he tries desperately to sprout gills instead of lungs,' Alistair concluded wryly.

Margaret laughed, a gleeful child-like sound, her head thrown back, all artifice leaving her. The archaeologist watched her enchanted, his arms aching with the compulsion to pull her to him. Everything she said and did fascinated him, yet if he were to look unemotionally upon her he would have to conclude that there was nothing extraordinary about her. She was well-mannered, displaying the grooming of her position as a governess; she was neat in her appearance, pretty rather than beautiful, shrewd within the realm of her experience with a wit tempered by an acceptable amount of curiosity. But, most importantly, she listened to him intensely, as if all he had to impart was of the utmost intelligence and import. No one had ever before treated him with such reverence; it was dangerously intoxicating.

She turned to him and, with an air she imagined to be seductive but in fact was a little clumsy, she asked, 'Have you fallen prey to such a Medusa?'

'Maybe; maybe not.'

An ambiguous answer that immediately made the young woman desire him more.

Had he, Alistair wondered, trying to concentrate on the next painting: a portrait of drowned Ophelia floating down the river, surrounded by copious auburn hair tangled in water lilies and river reeds. The expression of tranquil resignation on the suicide's face made him ponder his own destiny: was he too about to voluntarily end his life as he knew it? Would a part of him — the romantic who aspired to higher spiritual values — perish?

Somewhere in the gallery a clock chimed three. The apex of his dilemma drew nearer. Again he felt as if his destiny was split into two clear choices. Margaret could be his salvation; all he had to do was stay here, by her side.

The exotic musk of a passing woman wafted across the room and drew Alistair back into contemplation of the orgy that awaited him. This was his opportunity to be transported back into a time he had dreamed of inhabiting, a chance to taste hedonism. He could have both; why not? He would have Margaret as his future, his life companion, and he would have Lady Whistle as his guide into a realm of money, power and fantasy. One woman would be his spiritual anchor; the other his sensual liberator.

'Margaret,' he blurted, 'please excuse my presumption but I have little time. I am to go away tonight for a short while and I fear I shall return changed. How, I cannot tell. I know our acquaintance has been extremely brief, but I believe that time is not linear in such circumstances . . .'

'What circumstances, Alistair?' she asked, trembling.

'I feel a strong affinity for you. When I am with you I am strengthened; your presence, your words, cause a kind of alchemy in me. One I wish to explore deeply and for quite some time, with your consent.'

He took her hand; it was the first time he had touched her. Gloved, it felt tiny in his own but even through the kid leather he could feel her quiver.

'How long are you gone for?'

'I do not know, but I would like to call for you upon my return. Do you understand the seriousness of my intent?'

'I think I do,' she replied blushing.

Margaret realised she was ignoring all the advice her mother had imbued her with. Could she trust him? She hardly knew him, and yet she had never felt so stimulated by a man. It was as if he were able to appreciate the qualities in her other men had found precocious: her desire to paint, her interest in politics. But most importantly, despite her average attractiveness (for she knew the limitations of her beauty) he desired her.

'I shall wait for a message,' she said firmly, gazing again at the mermaid. It came to her that she should be as mysterious, as alluring as the sea maiden, and so, after allowing him to kiss her hand, she left.

Alistair stood by the window dressed in his new and uncomfortably tight French frock-coat, clutching the matching tall hat, feeling like an entirely different man — an individual he suspected he might not like.

Outside, the afternoon sun struggled to penetrate a mass of cumuli. Alistair thought the clouds resembled a pompous judge, his wig tumbling about him in rolls of silver-grey. A brand new travelling bag sat at his feet. He had borrowed a hunting jacket of the finest sharkskin from Harry, but wondered whether he would actually need it. This attention to the details of his forthcoming country visit was a futile attempt to subdue the anticipation that threatened to subsume him.

The distant peal of church bells rang in four o'clock. It began to drizzle. He looked down at the street three storeys below; it appeared unchanged. Urchins, ragged in bare feet, yelled excitedly at each other as they ran by. On the corner two women, still dressed for market, gossiped while nearby a chimney sweep and his lad, both blacked by soot, hitched up his bone-thin nag ready for the weary journey home.

Alistair watched anxiously. Sure enough, at the last peal of the fourth bell Lady Whistle's carriage swung around the corner. It was unmistakable with its sinister black polished veneer and gold trim. Two coachmen in the Whistle livery drove the two black horses, which pranced and chafed restlessly like overbred aristocrats.

Before it had even pulled up, Alistair was running down the stairs.

'Mr Alistair Sizzlehorn?' The man at the door was ruddy and saturnine with a dour sensibility and a heavy Cornish accent. Alistair nodded. The coachman picked up his bag and passed it up to his companion. 'It's a good four hours' hard drive to Whistlewaite, weather and horses depending, sir. I suggest you rug up and garner your strength for the ceremonies ahead.'

The servant opened the door of the sprung carriage to reveal a luxurious interior with satin padding and cushions. It was furnished with a side table holding a hamper of food and a bottle.

'Are there to be no others?' Alistair enquired, wondering at the extravagance of sending such a vehicle to collect just one individual.

'The rest of Lady Whistle's guests are to be making their own way to the estate, sir. Climb in, sir, and make yourself comfortable. Dinner's in the basket and the wine is of good vintage. God willing, we'll make Colchester before seven.'

The archaeologist, who had never travelled in such magnificence in his life, tried to look nonchalant as he clambered in.

Sinking into the satiny cushions that smelled faintly of rosewater, he looked through the pleated silk curtains, each bearing ribbons in the colours of his patroness, at the grim boarding house. All manner of debris — rags, empty bottles and human waste — was piled up against the iron railings and

Alistair felt that the carriage was a magic carpet finally whisking him away from poverty and into a world of unimaginable ease and splendour.

~

'Wake up, sir, wake up!' The coachman's voice penetrated his sleep like a fog-horn. Alistair pulled himself out of the rocking arms of his dream and forced his eyes to open. The coachman stood at the carriage door, a blast of cold air streaming in. Beyond lay the shimmering outline of a large country mansion, its windows beacons of golden light.

'We are here, sir!' the servant shouted unnecessarily, as if the diminished light might have affected Alistair's hearing.

'Do I smell salt?'

'Aye, sir, the sea's over them cliffs. It's all Whistle land, right down to the beach. Make yourself smart, sir — we'll be at the door in five minutes.'

A moment later the carriage began winding its way along the crunchy gravel driveway, the horses' breath two jets of steam spurting into the cold night.

The house itself looked to be recently built. Majestic, of pale stone, it was in the Regency style, the portico lined with white mock Grecian columns. The grounds (from what Alistair could see from the coach) appeared to be immaculately landscaped — a controlled panorama of topiary, ponds and lawns. A number of avenues lined with tall elms branched out in various directions.

Alistair, anticipating his first encounter with Lady Whistle in over two months, found to his irritation that his heart was leaping around like an over-eager puppy as the coach pulled up in front of the massive oak doors. Two footmen and two maids stood on either side of the entrance, alongside glowing braziers.

The archaeologist climbed out, expecting Lady Whistle to appear to greet him personally. Instead the older woman servant — the housekeeper Alistair assumed, for she was dressed immaculately in spotless linen — moved towards him, gesturing for the footman to take his bag (which was beginning to look increasingly pathetic next to such grandeur). She beckoned him towards the mansion. 'Her ladyship is unavailable for the present, sir. She sends her sincere apologies and hopes you will not mind being escorted immediately to your sleeping quarters. She will call upon you later.'

As Alistair walked through the huge double doors he couldn't help noticing the replica of the travertine bas-relief of the phallus hanging above the door, with *Hic habitat felicitas* — Here dwells happiness — written beneath.

Alistair was led through room after room, each seeming to open into a larger version of the previous one. Much of the furnishings were eclectic, a strange combination of antiques and the Oriental — here a King Louis XIV gilt table, two Ming vases atop it; there, the massive head of a water buffalo beside a medieval suit of armour.

'Is Lord Whistle in residence?' Alistair asked, curious to meet the patriarch of the household.

'His lordship is in the Orient on business,' the housekeeper replied curtly, the keys at her hip swinging as she marched him swiftly through the labyrinth of chambers.

'And the other guests?'

'Retired for the night. My lady likes to keep a strict eye on her visitors. She has a very heightened sense of the proper, particularly when her guests are here for a very particular purpose.'

Her gaze, seemingly devoid of irony, settled on him as they arrived at a door after climbing what seemed endless flights of stairs.

'Well, Mr Sizzlehorn, I am sure you will enjoy your stay here.'

She gestured to the footman who opened the bedroom door then carried in Alistair's bag. After curtseying formally, the housekeeper retreated back into the shadows.

It was a spacious room with curiously circular walls — the walls of a turret, he guessed, wondering why he hadn't noticed this architectural feature from the exterior of the building. The walls were painted a light lilac. In the centre stood a four-poster bed with a high mattress covered in a matching lilac quilt. The bed had heavy drapes, presently pulled back, which Alistair knew would serve nicely to prevent draughts. A curious crossbow hung on one wall: inscribed with Arabic, its bow tipped by horn, it appeared to be made of a copper-coloured ore he had not seen before.

On the opposite wall was a long plait of black hair tied at the bottom by a single lilac bow. Much surprised, the archaeologist stared at it, wondering what on earth the symbolism of such a curious wall hanging could be.

'My lady's, sir, from when she was a child. She's got a strange sense of humour, Lady Whistle has,' the footman volunteered, then gratefully pocketed the threepenny tip Alistair gave him and departed.

∽

Alistair rested on the bed. As the rocking sensation of the coach journey faded from his limbs, the atmosphere of the mansion wrapped itself around him, a susurration of sounds. The howling wind outside he imagined came off the turbulent ocean; then there was the dulled rhythm of servants running up and down various staircases, carrying irons and other warming nocturnal paraphernalia to petulant guests, and a trickle from the water closet. As Alistair sat there, the condensation still drying on his boots, he realised that he had never felt so alive, as if the dreary half-life he had lived since his college days, the drudgery of London town with its beggars, rakes and hussies, was all finally behind him. Everything seemed brighter, infinitely more vivid.

He pulled off a glove and stared at the pulse in his wrist where the life force pumped incessantly. This is what I am surrendering to, he thought, blind impulse, a deeper existential joy.

'Alistair?'

Lady Whistle's alto voice was unmistakable. Embarrassed to be caught in a vulnerable moment of introspection he stood up.

'I trust the room is to your satisfaction?'

She was at the door, dressed in an evening gown of burgundy crepe. The twin mounds of her breasts were visible through the purple lace that finished in a high collar framing her face, thus giving her the appearance of being ornately dressed and yet somehow naked. Around her neck glittered another choker only this one was of diamonds: four impressive crystals set into a black

322

velvet ribbon. Priceless no doubt, Alistair thought; if he were to live three lifetimes he would never be able to purchase such an item.

Lady Whistle moved forward, her dress swishing against the floor.

'This was my bedroom as a girl.' She smiled at Alistair's perplexed expression. 'I was Lord Whistle's ward before he married me. He is a good twenty years older than I and prefers the company of men to women.'

'I'm sorry.'

'Do not be; it is a perfectly amiable arrangement. We share trust, companionship and, most importantly, freedom.'

She sat on the bed beside him and ran her hand along the counterpane. 'To think that I slept here too, in this bed, when I was as innocent and as pure as you,' she said, smiling again.

Nothing deflates the ego more than a patronising woman, Alistair thought, his confidence collapsing like a tower of stacked playing cards. As if she could read his thoughts, Lady Whistle lifted his hand and placed it in her lap. Despite his anxiety the archaeologist hardened instantly.

'Trust me, there is nothing more alluring to a libertine than innocence. Now come, I wish to show you my temple. It will be a tantalising prelude to the fully orchestrated work tomorrow.'

She led him by the hand down a plain back staircase, obviously used exclusively by the servants. It ran through the mansion like the hidden backbone of some huge animal, the rest of its body — the rooms — pulsating with invisible intrigue behind the wood panelling.

Lady Whistle held a candlestick high above her head as they passed landing after landing, each with a barely noticeable door set into the wall. They had descended five flights when the stairwell opened out into the dark cavern of an underground cellar.

'Wait here,' she murmured, plunging him into darkness as she disappeared behind a door with the candle. A second later she pulled him into the chamber.

He stood there shivering slightly, the scent of wine hanging heavy in the air. Suddenly the room was illuminated as Lady Whistle lit a candelabra. A vaulted ceiling suggested it might once have been a crypt long ago, the remnants of an earlier building. Now it was clearly used as a cellar: one half was filled with wine racks holding row upon row of dusty bottles.

'As you will appreciate, I had to construct the temple far away from prying eyes,' she laughed. 'Come.'

She pointed towards a door on the far side of the chamber. Alistair followed her across the stone floor. The door was ornately decorated with copperplate and embossed with a series of hieroglyphs which Alistair recognised as Sanskrit and some Latin.

'Within lies the temple of Dionysus. May all who enter feel joy in their souls and bodies,' he translated. 'But why the Sanskrit?'

'The Pompeiians were also worshippers of the goddess Isis. Such writings were found in the Villa of Mysteries — of which this room is an exact duplicate.'

She pulled out a key, its handle phallus-shaped, and unlocked the door.

It swung open to reveal a large chamber that was octagonal in shape. Lady Whistle lit eight torches, one in the centre of each wall. Their wicks were encased in bronze statues of stunning nude youths with erect penises — Alistair instantly recognised them as duplicates of the ithyphallic figure he had documented for the catalogue.

The floor was a tiled mosaic showing the bearded figure of Dionysus. On his head sat a wreath of snakes intertwined around vines and he stood upon a bull and a lion, one foot planted firmly on each beast's back.

'He is standing over the planetary formation for the spring equinox.' Lady Whistle lowered her voice in reverence, as if she were standing at a sacred altar.

In the centre of the room were twelve stands, each holding a yellow robe and a gilded mask. Some had goat horns, some had bull horns — Alistair imagined the masks would cover half of the wearer's face.

'These are the masks all the worshippers will be wearing, except for the thirteenth participant — you.'

'I will be unmasked? What about my reputation, my anonymity?'

'Trust me, Alistair, after this you will be part of a secret but powerful sect; one which will facilitate great opportunity, I promise.'

Uncertain, the archaeologist studied the painted walls. If it were not for their contemporary dress, he might have been transported entirely back to first century Pompeii. The satyrs — half-goat half-man — seemed to leer at him as they thrust into an abundance of succulent flesh. It was an amazing sight: the mural he had been staring at for all those months on the scroll, now recreated with astonishing accuracy in this chamber — all except one wall which was mysteriously blank.

'Why is that panel empty?'

'It represents the unknown future; a depiction of the philosophy that although our actions might influence our destiny, nothing is ever truly fixed.'

'You have the correct configuration of worshippers?' he asked, his voice now throaty with desire.

'Seven men and six women. We will begin and you will watch. You will only be drawn into the formation for the fourth stanza — the climax is clearly marked upon the floor; my people know exactly the position to take. Eros shall flow in a slow, controlled ecstasy. And I promise, it *will be* ecstasy.'

She took his arm and walked him to the fourth panel. He stared at the mural. The priest lay in the centre of the orgy mounted by a goat woman, her breasts thrust forward, her head thrown back in bliss, as she was simultaneously taken by a bacchant from behind.

'This will be you tomorrow,' Lady Whistle whispered, pointing to the priest. She placed her hand firmly on Alistair's tumescent organ bulging under his breeches. 'Until then you must save yourself.'

She turned swiftly and walked away, disappearing behind a panel that vanished as mysteriously as it had appeared. Toby stepped out of the shadows.

'Good evening, sir. I have the last of your instructions. Firstly, if you care to look above you, you will notice a skylight set into the ceiling. This is placed so the sun's rays will hit the ritual at the exact moment Pisces moves into Aries, when Dionysus will be reborn as the New Year. You are to time your climax to that moment.'

The valet grinned at Alistair's worried expression. 'Don't concern yourself, sir, Lady Whistle is an expert at such matters. There is a herbal concoction by your bed to ensure that you get a good night's sleep. Tomorrow a maid shall come to you at eleven o'clock. She will bathe you and anoint you — an initiation during which you are to remain chaste. At quarter past eleven you shall be dressed in your costume and brought to this room, where all shall drink a ceremonial goblet of wine. Then the ritual will begin. And, sir, a tip from an expert: try to banish all intellectual thought from that point on. You are here to live completely within your skin, to harness a power that stretches far beyond the civilised mind.'

The archaeologist woke the next day to a room flooded by a mauve luminosity. His head wasn't as cloudy as he had expected after the sleeping draught. Before he could climb out of the high bed a pretty maid hurried in and pulled open the curtains. She was dressed in a tight pinafore, a crisp white apron stretched over her voluptuous hips. Was this his test, he wondered, as she instructed him to strip entirely while she ran a hot bath for him in the adjoining bathroom.

She emerged ten minutes later, her face flushed from the steam. Alistair stood there shivering, his dressing gown clutched to his groin. The maid, smiling mischievously, walked across the room and pulled the gown away from him.

'My lady was right,' she murmured, glancing at his quivering yard.

In the bath he lay like a child while she washed him, running the sponge over every curve, into every crevice. Alistair shut his eyes and concentrated on declining every irregular Latin verb he could think of. He must not spill his seed, he must not — the phrase ran like a chant through his head as the maid's hand tracked its seductive path across his skin.

Afterwards he stood, legs apart, while she dried him, running the towel between his buttocks, patting him dry under the scrotum, exquisitely encircling his erect organ. He caught sight of himself in the looking glass. There was something sacrificial about his nudity: his pale body with the golden hair running down between his nipples to his groin, his yard maintaining its proud stance as the maid delicately continued her task.

When he stepped out of the bathroom a saffron silk robe lay on the bed. The maid slipped it over his shoulders. It fell in pleats to the ground, loose around his naked torso. She fastened it with a cord of plaited silk then, standing on tiptoe, blindfolded him.

Despite the daylight outside, the temple had been transformed into twilight by three blazing oil lamps, held by glinting bronzes of male nudes. The flickering flames illuminated the painted walls and the heady scent of smouldering spikenard, myrrh and ambergris filled the air. Alistair was led to the centre of the dome. Fingertips brushed his face as the blindfold was pulled off.

He stood in the centre of a circle of twelve people, each masked, each one's body oiled and adorned with a girdle of leather. The men's shoulders were draped in purple silk — the royal colour. There were, as promised, six men and six women; he was the seventh man. Through the glow of the flames he saw that the men varied in age. Three seemed of middle years, their torsos solid and covered in the body hair of the mature man. One, over six foot in height, looked as if he might be an athlete, his muscled belly and chest a progression of cambers, his penis lolling heavily under a short fringe of goat skin.

Another Alistair recognised as Toby; he was wearing the half-head of a goat's mask and his oiled flesh was nude except for two anklets of gold chain. His body was as beautiful as his face; his tumescent yard, delicate in shape, a stark contrast to the rest of him which still held the physique of a youth with narrow shoulders, smooth buttocks and slim hips.

But it was the women towards whom Alistair's eye was naturally most drawn. Three of them were young, very young, no more than eighteen he guessed — one was a petite blonde, her long hair cascading over the mask of a lioness, her breasts small and round with large pink nipples, her hips wide and full, her sex a golden bush. Beside her stood a tall brunette with olive skin, older, her physique a stark contrast to the girl with full high breasts and impossibly slender hips. Her sex appeared naked, without hair at all. On the other side of the circle stood a Negress, her skin a glistening polished ebony over abundant curves. It was as if her flesh cascaded down from her neck, breasts trumbling down onto an ample belly and full hips. Her eroticism lay in the very bountifulness of her.

Lady Whistle herself wore a silk robe of gold, naked underneath except for a single gold chain that looped around the top of both thighs then encircled her waist, there breaking into a fine lace mesh which ran across her upper torso, encircling but not covering her breasts, to finish at a choker around her neck.

She was crowned by a wreath of vine leaves and a feathered mask covered her eyes. Athene, the owl, Alistair thought, the goddess of wisdom. She held two goblets of wine: golden vessels in the shape of a goat's horn. It was then that Alistair noticed that the eleven other participants held such a goblet in their hands.

A servant slipped through the circle, her nude body glistening with reddish ochre. She held out a wreath of vine leaves intertwined with live, writhing snakes. Horrified, Alistair stepped back.

'Fear not, they are drugged and harmless,' Lady Whistle whispered. Tentatively Alistair allowed the wreath to be placed upon his head.

Lady Whistle stepped forward ceremoniously and handed one of the goblets to Alistair, indicating that he should drink. Heart pounding, his cock thickened already, Alistair gulped the liquid — it was a sweetish mead overlaid with spices, with another, unknown flavour which resonated on his palate.

'Let the ceremonies begin,' Lady Whistle announced in Latin. As the others drained their goblets, music began playing — a strange cacophony of lute and drums with a thin reed instrument dancing over the top. Alistair strained his eyes to see a quartet standing in the shadowy corner of the room, dressed as musicians of the era would have been.

Lady Whistle clapped suddenly. The brunette began to run; two of the men followed her and caught her roughly by each arm. She struggled — oversized dramatic gestures that Alistair realised were deliberately theatrical. With a jolt he recognised the scenario: the rape of the Titian representing the formation of Rome. The men carried her back to Lady Whistle who was still standing beside Alistair in the centre of the circle. Taking an arm and a leg each they hoisted her up and parted her so that her sex was raised up in mid-air.

Alistair was transfixed: he had never seen a woman's sex thus displayed. The labia and clitoris were a glistening ruby, beyond which lay the hills and furrows of her body. Lady Whistle lifted her goblet and poured the rest of her wine over the woman, who wriggled and gasped in the men's strong hands. Toby then stepped from the circle and, with the woman still held high, took her sex into his mouth, pleasuring her with his tongue, fingers and lips. The others followed, turning upon each other as they slowly caressed breast, buttock, oiled flesh under fingers, lip upon lip. It was not the impersonal physical taking Alistair had imagined it would be; instead there was a deep sensuality as bodies merged, man and woman, man and man, woman and woman, kissing deeply with tongues lingering, backs arched, arms encircling waists and shoulders. Dreamily he wondered whether they had known each other before to inspire such intimacy.

Lady Whistle herself had two men pleasuring her, one kneeling behind her and one before. The first buried his face between her ample buttocks; the other — in clear view of Alistair — used his fingers to stretch wide her labia, his tongue a flickering lizard between her legs. Two women faced one another, each sucking the other's nipple as they were both taken from behind, their buttocks held high. One of the men towered over his female companion as his large yard slid in and out of her; the other man, topped with the mask of a bull, was a lot shorter, his fingers pressed into the flesh of the girl's buttocks.

The music grew louder, the drumming an ancient thumping beat that resounded off the walls. The revelry that encircled him was a gleaming mass of limb wrapped around limb. Overwhelmed, Alistair sank to the ground, his head spinning. One man's legs and buttocks transformed into the form of a hairy goat; another's feet split into the cloven hoof of a ram. Hair ridged along the spine of one young girl and a lion's tail sprouted between her buttocks, shaking wildly into the air. Had he been drugged, the archaeologist wondered as a liquid fire coursed through his veins, drawing all sensations to one point: his loins.

As his vision blurred and then refocused he dimly realised that the orgy had arranged itself into the formation of the second illustration. Lady Whistle was in the centre, her thighs held open by the man whose yard she sucked while another thrust into her as he himself was being taken by a half-bull, half-man. Was it Toby, Alistair wondered foggily. The negress caressed the valet while the man beneath her buried his head between her massive breasts. Twelve bodies forming a single connection through lip on lip, hand on breast, organ buried in organ.

Alistair lay on his side untouched, delirious with desire, each glistening nipple, cock and labia dancing like delicious fruit before his own mouth. He reached out but no sooner had his fingers achieved a caress than the object of his desire evaporated like a mirage as each participant deliberately moved away.

A drum roll and the orgy metamorphosed into the third stanza, moving closer to the diagram of the stars embedded in the mosaic floor. Around the nucleus of Lady Whistle and her two partners, three other couples arranged themselves to make up the tail and hooves of the ram.

Out of the corner of his eye Alistair could see the brunette on her knees, sucking the yard of one man while another took her from behind, both their legs spread. Another woman, her head between both sets of buttocks, licked wildly at the brunette's clitoris while she herself was being taken from the front.

Alistair rolled over onto his front, every nerve ending tingling with bliss, his senses sharpening with the mounting effect of the Spanish fly lacing the mead. His heart began to pound wildly as he realised his moment was drawing nearer.

Three drum beats sounded out. Above, he saw the curtain covering the skylight being slowly pulled across, like the lid of a massive eye opening.

The drums stopped suddenly and the shimmering of a thousand bells rang out. Hands pulled Alistair into a spread-eagled position, pinning down his arms and legs. His silk robe was torn away. Every mouth descended upon him — male and female — travelling over his body, sucking, licking, kissing. Struggling to hold himself back, Alistair shut his eyes. Against his lids danced an image — a flushed face of a beautiful man in his mid-thirties, bearded, a mysterious smile playing across his full mouth. *Burst, burst into leaf*, he whispered in Latin. Recognising the god Dionysus, Alistair's eyes flew open.

The mouths left his flesh and Lady Whistle took his yard into her mouth, encircling him slowly with her tongue, cupping his balls in her hand, his arse, penetrating him with her fingers. *Not yet, not yet*, Dionysus whispered into the scholar's ear as Alistair reached up and drew the plump buttocks of the young blonde girl onto his face. The rich scent of her filled his nostrils as his fingers wound their way across her sticky labia and then into her while his tongue flicked across the erect bud of her clitoris. She guided his blind hands to full breasts that he knew must be Lady Whistle's as the aristocrat lowered herself onto his rock-hard cock.

The blonde moved away. Now Alistair could see Lady Whistle riding him, her breasts bouncing gently. Behind her, Toby knelt and eased himself into her nether entrance. An expression of both ecstasy and pain came across her features. Above Alistair's head another man thrust out his penis, the goat fur on his thighs and his cloven hooves vividly realistic to Alistair's befuddled mind, which was now entirely transported back to a mythological time of satyrs and fauns.

Lady Whistle leaned forward and took the goat-man's cock into her mouth, sucking greedily. Alistair squeezed down hard on her nipples. The man being sucked began to caress the breasts of the girl on his left as she parted her legs for another man's organ. Alistair was dimly aware that the formation was being completed through touch and intercourse — each body linking with the others to form the backbone, flanks and legs of the Ram.

Alistair felt his spirit rise from his body and float to the roof. It hovered there and he looked down upon the revelry. A couple covered each of the stars, limbs stretched out to complete the outline. He could see himself beneath Lady Whistle, the only unmasked person, his lips pulled back in bliss as she rode him over and over. The figure of the bearded priest on the mural began to glow as a shaft of sunlight travelled across the room, illuminating one by one the figures undulating in their strange dance. Finally it reached the central nucleus of Lady Whistle and Alistair. *Whoosh*: Alistair was sucked straight back into his body. He felt the tight, burning ring of Lady Whistle's sex sliding up and down his cock and the mounting pressure of orgasm building at the back of his head, deep in his balls, as every nerve ending tensed in preparation to blast forth in a shuddering propulsion of energy.

*Now!* Dionysus whispered, *now!*

'Now!' screamed Lady Whistle. 'Now!' Her vagina began to clench and, blinded suddenly by the passing sunlight, Alistair exploded, his seed shooting forth in a great shuddering of white-hot pleasure. All around him orgasmed in unison and he felt his life energy ejecting itself away from his body, leaving him suddenly drained.

As the screams and groans subsided, with Lady Whistle still sitting astride him, Alistair opened his eyes and found himself staring at the blank fifth panel. To his horror, it magically began to form a tableau — the missing section he had always suspected existed. He saw the orgy, moments after completion, the spent satyrs lying across their nymphs, emperor across priestess, empress across gladiator, all still masked. In the centre, the priest lay spread-eagled as if sacrificed. His face was now a mass of wrinkles, the visage of the old Dionysus, the gnarled vine waiting to be cut down to make way for the new.

Alistair touched his own face. Rough and wrinkled, it did not feel like his skin as he knew it. Lady Whistle slid off her mask. Smiling down at him was the face of a beautiful young woman; herself at twenty-three. Alistair pushed the aristocrat off and began to scream.

⌦

The elderly man sitting alone, obviously shaken, catches the attention of the young woman. She crosses the room to his table and offers a polite curtsy.

'Excuse me for interrupting, sir, but I was wondering whether you might be a relative of a dear friend of mine whom I have not seen for some three years — a Mr Alistair Sizzlehorn. You bear a strong resemblance to him. He was a most promising archaeologist with the British Museum at the time of his disappearance. We were intimates; indeed, I waited a good year for him before I considered other suitors.'

Alistair stares fully into Margaret's face until the scrutiny moves from impolite to plain alarming. As the older man's countenance gathers intensity, Harry, the young merchant, fearing for his fiancée, places his arm across her shoulders, as if to protect her.

The elderly gentleman stands suddenly, breaking the moment. 'I am sorry, I have never heard of him. Now, if you will excuse me there is someone I have to meet.'

Alistair Sizzlehorn makes his way around the street corner and out of sight of the tea house. There he leans heavily against the wall, emotion shaking his aged body.

# Bat

The signals had gone up and the Lord Admiral's immortal words — 'England expects that every living man will do his duty', followed by the more pointed message, 'Engage the enemy more closely' — had been read eagerly by every sailor, from the midshipmen to the gunners. Nelson's direct appeal had spread through the men like a virus, infecting them with a heart-pumping patriotism mixed with something far sweeter: the love of a great commander and the soaring sensation of being part of a momentous occasion which everyone knew would change both history and the fate of England itself.

'Damn Bony, and damn the French and the Spanish,' whispered Norwich Pebblesmith, an eleven-year-old drummer, to his companion but his words were lost as the instruments began their frenetic beat. Ahead, the massive Spanish three-decker, the *Santa Ana*, seemed almost within arm's reach. It towered over the *Royal Sovereign* but already the English cannonballs had smashed into the hull of the flagship and shattered the beaked bow. All around the small boy lay the injured and the dying. Somewhere there was screaming, but the drummer held firm, focusing on nothing but the motion of his wrists which now seemed to be thrashing through treacle. In front of him, Vice-Admiral Collingwood stood defiantly dressed in his epaulettes shouting orders, exhilarated by the stench of gunpowder and blood, his face flushed, his eyes glittering dangerously.

Suddenly the deck shuddered and there came a massive crunch and the sound of splintering iron and wood as the *Royal Sovereign* rammed the crippled *Santa Ana*.

Norwich was thrown to the deck. As he lay there dazed, staring up at the billowing smoke that scarred the otherwise perfect blue sky, he noticed a whitish creature lazily flapping its way towards the Spanish vessel. As first he took it to be a bird, but there was something unnatural about the manner in which its wings lifted and descended. Rolling onto his side Norwich crossed himself, believing he might have seen the manifestation of a dying man's spirit or, worse still, Old Nick himself.

## Falkland Islands, 20 May 1982

It was white and covered in fine pale hair that looked translucent in the light. Red beady eyes swivelled around in a head that was delicate, almost noble in its structure. The nose — an organ dedicated to the invisible art of scent detection (Nature had cared little for its external appeal during its evolution) — was an intricate labyrinth of folded skin and quivering tissue shot with a lattice of minute veins. The two oversized ears covered most of the small domed head and were similarly complex organs that seemed to promise a view right into the creature's skull should one be so brave as to peer inside. Its wings, when spread, were a startling ashen hue and reminiscent of the battered fabric of a beach umbrella. The mouse-like torso boasted two bright pink nipples — a rude reminder that the animal was a fellow mammal. Two claws, seemingly grafted carelessly at the end of each wing, looked like a mistake in design. Its minuscule penis (hidden beneath a fold of grey skin most of the time) and furry scrotum hung upside down against the animal's body along with everything else. The creature lived in Chaplain Murphy's quarters, its wooden perch located in the corner of the crowded cabin, next to his missal and a large bottle of whisky.

The bat had been HMS *Ardent*'s mascot for as long as the current captain could remember — and he had been with the Royal Navy for a good thirty years. The tradition was that the creature's welfare was entrusted to the chaplain in residence, which was how Father Murphy had acquired the animal, inheriting it from Chaplain McDougal upon his retirement.

It was easy to keep, requiring little food except pieces of fruit from the galley and the occasional bowl of milk which it would drink delicately, balancing like a trapeze artist from its perch, furry white neck stretched out, the inverted snout dipping down to the creamy surface and its long pink tongue steadily scooping the liquid up into its hairy mouth. It had no name except Bat, and had been on the ship for so long that only new recruits ever noticed it.

Father Murphy had once tried to identify the exact species the animal belonged to, but had been forced to give up as its albino appearance had proved a source of confusion. It most closely resembled the fruit-eating bats of the Amazon, but its snout was longer, its teeth sharper and its wing span proportionally longer than the miniature bats in the tattered copy of *National Geographic* he had found in the library. It squeaked only very occasionally and its droppings were dry and pellet-like — easy to sweep up. Perhaps the strangest thing was that the bat had no scent whatsoever. This disturbing characteristic seemed to contribute to its invisibility and it was easy to forget that it existed at all.

Father Murphy, a corpulent man in his late sixties, had nevertheless grown fond of the creature and had taken to reading his favourite psalms aloud to it. The bat would hang quietly from its perch, occasionally lifting its head in the chaplain's direction, a quizzical expression on its mouse-like face. After moving on to the New Testament the cleric noticed that the animal responded particularly well to the parable of Saint Francis of Assisi, thus convincing him that it possessed an intelligence. In his more inebriated moments, Father Murphy imagined its brain would be a grid, like you might see peering through a gun sight, made up of muffled sounds, its dimensions divided by echo and the scent of heat. Very different from his own brain, but possessing an intelligence nevertheless.

A closet animal liberationist who felt morally conflicted over the imprisonment of the creature, the cleric had persuaded himself that the animal was happy. Being albino it would never have survived in the natural world anyhow — an observation Father Murphy found comforting whenever the bat shook its waxen wings restlessly, as if the distant memory of flight had suddenly fallen upon it like a shadow.

But today the bat was not happy, it wasn't even content. The thud of rocket fire vibrated through the metal hull of the ship and the animal could smell the acrid scent of battle permeating the musty confined air of the cabin. With one claw the bat preened behind its left ear, then hopped along the perch to peer haplessly at the empty food bowl below. It hadn't eaten in over four days. Swivelling its head around, it stared at the bunk where Father Murphy — an amorphous miasmatic collection of scents and movement to the bat — usually lay. The bunk too had been empty for several days.

The screech of an overhead jet cut through the cabin, disorienting the bat which flew upwards and knocked itself blindly against the ceiling, then fell down onto the soft mattress where it lay like a crumpled rag.

'You poor thing.' Reginald Smithers, twenty-six and on his first commission as a ship's chaplain, and in the middle of his first war, stared down at the dishevelled animal. Then he gingerly picked it up with one hand. The furry creature stirred into life, one questioning eye cocked up at the clean-shaven cleric.

'He's dead is old Father Murphy. Killed in action administering the last rites. Rotten bad luck,' the priest told the bat as he carried it to the perch. Carefully stretching out a claw, the bat grasped the wood and swung itself back into position. It swayed slightly, as if rocking itself in mourning, all the while staring at the empty bunk.

'No need to grieve too hard — he lived a full life and went down like a soldier. He's bound to get a DCM posthumously,' the chaplain continued with forced cheerfulness while filling the food dish with pieces of chopped apple and orange from the ship's cook.

'So it's just me and you from now on,' he finished, wondering what kind of affection he would get from a bat. Still, it was better than no companionship and Father Smithers, afflicted with acne and an unfortunate effeminate manner, had been having trouble developing any camaraderie at all with the seasoned paratroopers eager for combat.

Resolutely he swung his kit onto the bunk and sniffed. They had removed Father Murphy's clothes several days before but had left a rusting chest of possessions beneath the bed, assuming that the church would claim responsibility for them. The bed had been stripped but still held the musky smell of the dead cleric: moth balls and an old-fashioned sweetish aftershave.

Reginald knew that the night air was freezing but he also knew it was icy fresh and full of sea salt. He wrenched the porthole open and retired to the en suite bathroom — a luxury afforded only to the clergy. Stooping to step through the low metal doorway, Reginald sighed deeply then shut the door.

The bat cocked its head and gazed at the porthole. Beyond, the black sky was alight with the dramatic phosphorus trails of missiles and the smouldering lights of the starlight shells as they floated towards the ground with a deceptively benign beauty. The spectacle stirred something in the very depths of the bat's primordial psyche. This was its domain, the kaleidoscopic burning landscape a trigger that ignited all of its instincts.

The creature edged its way to the far end of the perch then opened its wings fully. Flapping wildly it made a straight path for the open porthole and, after hovering for a second, was swallowed by the night.

~

The paratrooper hunkered in a ditch contemplating the vividness of everything around him. Fear had heightened his senses; he had seen action in Northern Ireland and knew the difference between the exhilaration of adrenaline and the nauseating sweep of fear — the feeling that your eyelids were pinned to your head, all senses pulled tense, as open as they could be, drinking in every second, every slight flutter in the grey panorama as you waited for death to spring out at you. The deadly jack-in-the-box, the one second element you hadn't calculated on that got you every time. This was war, the butting up of the pig's head of Life and its convulsing end, the pounding minute in which all your memories collided violently into a dangerous clarity where limbs moved before thought or morality.

A fighter jet screamed overhead. Five seconds later a nearby explosion turned the sky a bright white-yellow and they were showered with dirt. Crouching, Lieutenant Clive Scarsgard

341

checked himself. Fine, all in one piece, amazing. The luck of the Irish, you might say, except he wasn't Irish.

As his ears stopped ringing he realised his feet were starting to freeze. The icy water that filled the bottom of the trench was seeping into the shitty puttees he had been forced to wrap around his ankles because the second-rate DM boots they'd been issued with were too short. Fucking crappy English design, Clive thought for the hundredth time in the last twenty-four hours, wondering whether the Argies crouching in their tents on the other side of no-man's-land had better boots. Probably. Next kill he made he was going to take the boots he promised himself.

Bullets whistled overhead and the dull thud of distant explosions peppered the air. He leaned back against the frozen mud and stared up at the sky. It was fucking amazing, he reflected, marvelling at the iridescent streaks of phosphorus hanging like rips in a canvas, seeming to promise a luminous heaven behind the velvet skin of the night. The absurd thought that the army might include in their recruitment campaigns the idea of war as scenic occurred to him. He wanted to laugh out loud. Gallows humour; the hysteria of the man awaiting execution.

Since arriving by landing craft near Port San Carlos a day ago his life had veered between the strange tedium of waiting in very uncomfortable places and rushing into combat — a flurry of flying bullets, screaming commands and plunging bayonets. It had been nothing like they had described at training camp; then again, what was the point of trying to convey a realistic picture, he thought dreamily, it would be like recounting the loss of virginity — an entirely different experience for each individual.

He had discovered several interesting things when pushed to extremes: firstly, that he found killing exhilarating; and secondly, it was far more difficult to shoot a man dead than he had assumed. Even riddled with bullets they still kept running at you stupidly, as if they hadn't yet realised it was all over. The third thing was the indescribable stench of hand-to-hand combat. The smell of terror mixed in with shit, piss, blood and steaming entrails combined with the smell of damp, dirty clothing. It was so foul Clive was forced to breathe through his mouth to exorcise the taste that clung to his nostrils.

He touched the *kukri* — the eighteen-inch curved Gurkha fighting knife — on his belt. He'd had to use it to finish off a soldier at the last Argentine bunker after plunging his bayonet into the sleeping teenager. He touched the blade for good luck. It was a bad habit he'd got into. His officer in command — an irritating public school boy who was barely older than himself and already a proven coward in combat — glared at him for making a noise. The enemy — an Argentine machine-gun post — was barely a hundred metres away. But despite radioed commands to advance, the platoon had done nothing but crouch in the ditch for the last two hours.

*It is not death*
*Without hereafter*
*To one in dearth*
*Of life and its laughter,*

*Nor the sweet murder*
*Dealt slow and even*
*Unto the martyr*
*Smiling at heaven:*

*It is the smile*
*Faint as a (waning) myth,*
*Faint, and exceeding small*
*On a boy's murdered mouth.*

Wilfred Owen's poem rattled around Clive's brain. He had remembered it suddenly on coming across his first corpse — a young guardsman, not more than nineteen, stretched out as if in sleep, his face wax-white, his lips pulled back as if in dream. Only the open mouth of his wound obscene against the stained snow gave him away — the back half of his head was missing. Clive had stared at the body, marvelling at how empty it looked. Was that death — the skin discarded by the soul? The squadron had pushed on before he had time to think about it. But the kid's face kept floating back to him at odd moments. He looked like someone Clive might have picked up if they had met in civvies at some bar in a back street of Soho. In another time, in another kind of struggle.

The boy might have been a younger version of himself: closet poetry reader, overt narcissist, likes to live a little dangerously, fucks men but falls in love with women. Would that be his epitaph? Don't think too much, Clive, don't. Too much thought and you're a goner.

Not that he didn't expect to survive. He'd known since he was a kid that he was lucky — touched by the angels, his mother used to say — shimmering with a kind of handsome ease that made others instantly jealous. Fate kept him safe. Maybe that was why he sought out risk — to test the gods. He liked to push his luck. When he was ten he'd had a sledging accident; his best friend had broken a leg but Clive had got away with barely a scratch. At twenty, a car accident — the driver was killed, the passenger behind him paralysed for life, but Clive had emerged from the wreck with a bruised cheek and whiplash. In Northern Ireland he'd been driving behind a car that was ambushed, avoiding death by a matter of seconds. The luck of a fallen angel walking unscathed through a collapsing world.

He shifted his weight now, feeling around with one frozen foot for a ledge to lift himself out of the slush. Apart from the commanding officer three other soldiers squatted in the ditch with him: Cedric, a heavy Welshman in his thirties with a wicked sense of humour, who shared Clive's dislike for their officer; a young cockney who appeared to have stumbled into the army without much understanding of how he'd got there; and a seasoned sergeant who'd seen operations both in the Middle East and West Africa — a man of few words and much action. Clive had followed him through several advances already, trusting his aptitude far more than that of the bristling CO.

Cedric was busy checking his weapons over and over, the young cockney kept untying and retying his boot laces — a reaction to shock, Clive guessed — while the sergeant glared at the commanding officer as if he was thinking of saving the Argentines the effort of killing him and was about to do it himself. It promised to be a long night.

The bat flew quickly, propelled by the glacial wind that came off the choppy waters of the South Atlantic and rushed inland. It was flying over San Carlos water, known as 'bomb alley'. Impervious to the icy temperatures the animal was in its element, dipping low as it glided over the mountainous waves and through their spray. Its fur stood on end over every part of its body, the wings of skin stretched out to scoop up each gush of air.

A Harrier jet zoomed past. The vortices trailing off each wing momentarily knocked the bat off course, transforming its path into a crazy zigzag.

It flew over HMS *Antelope*. Below, the crew ran across the deck like crazy ants, scrabbling to fire anti-aircraft missiles at the Argentine fighters that were screeching down like angry wasps. One missile hit the water and exploded prematurely, sending a spray of shrapnel and sea up like a sudden tornado. Indifferent, the bat soared through it.

The animal was excited now; for the first time in thirty-seven years the reason for its existence had been reignited, and the calling which had played through the creature for centuries drummed wildly in its blood. It existed for one destination only — the battlefield.

It hovered in mid-air above a discarded buoy covered by several sea lions huddling together for warmth. The bat shook off the sea spray that had stuck to its hair and wings. Sensing the creature's presence, the sea lions took fright and dived off the buoy like panicked shipwreck survivors. Drawn by the streaks of light and the roar of distant guns the bat flew on towards the island, hazy memories of other battles, the thunder of fire and flame, pulsing through its brain.

Juan Martinez pushed his night-sight goggles up to his forehead, swore then spat. He hadn't seen a British soldier for over an hour and yet the tracer bullets continued. He couldn't tell whether they had spotted the machine-gun post dug into the side of the mountain or not. What was this crazy war for anyway, he wondered, a fucking PR operation for a dictator. A bogey man whose thugs came in the middle of the night to steal people. Was he now one of Galtieri's hooligans?

Although he didn't agree with the regime, he wanted order, but when they had dragged away the long-haired primary school teacher in his village he had begun to have doubts. The newspapers were screaming that inflation was over 600 per cent and many of the farmers were suffering, really suffering. Still he'd got out. To here. This shitty piece of nothing. Three weeks he'd been on the island — two weeks occupying the territory and putting up with the resentful English residents, and one week of fierce fighting — and he was beginning to think that maybe the Brits should have this miserable piece of land after all. It was too cold, and too far away to serve Argentina. What had General Galtieri been thinking? That it would make some great holiday destination, the next Club Med perhaps? Fucking stupid. Almost as ridiculous as squatting in a tent for four days wrapped in state-of-the-art US-issued parkas. It was a travesty; they were better prepared for the weather than combat. He felt like some extra in a B-grade war movie waiting for the director to yell *Action!* He was eighteen years old and only joined up because his older brother was already in the army and had boasted of all the opportunities — the good uniform, opportunities for promotion, travel, women — everything Juan had dreamed of back in Cordoba. He knew that if he didn't get out he would end up just a cattle hand like his father.

But there was another reason why he couldn't stay in the village. He was a lover of men. At least he thought he was a lover of men. He didn't know for sure; he just knew that when he looked at women he didn't feel the way he should. They didn't get him hard, not like men did.

Sweet Mary, Mother of Christ, he prayed, protect me now and I promise I will be a transformed man when I get home. He only knew of one man in the village who was like that. The unhappy goat herder had been so ridiculed and persecuted that one day after church they found him hanging from a beam in his hut, his body already a week old. That wasn't going to happen to him, that wasn't going to happen to Juan Martinez.

Juan unzipped his parka and, with fingers that were trembling with the cold despite woollen gloves, he rolled himself a cigarette and lit up. No, he was going to get himself some help, he was going to change. He'd find some girl he could at least talk to and pretend. Maybe he'd even marry. He was going to change, for Jesus and God.

But being in the army, now that was different. Back at the base, Juan had loved the packed-in bunks, the proximity of all those bodies, the maleness, the camaraderie and joking around, the way the young soldiers would walk around naked, showing off but never admitting it, almost as if they knew. They'd even made jokes about sucking each other off it was so fucking lonely. The comment had made Juan instantly hard just imagining it. It was dangerous. He had to watch himself all the time, play tougher than the rest, be more macho. But he was good, the best actor he knew.

He touched the seeping scratch that ran across one cheekbone — his first war wound from a bayonet five days ago in hand-to-hand combat. He'd killed a Scots Guard with his own bayonet one night. The fight had made him a hero and had instantly secured his reputation as *un hombre con huevos*. Homosexual, Juan Martinez? Not him.

So where were the pale-skinned *ingéles* hiding now? Peering out again at the bleak horizon dotted with the gnarled skeletons of burnt-out shrubs, he wondered how long it would be before the next wave of soldiers wielding bayonets, their backs criss-crossed with ammunition, swooped out of the dark, their faces smeared with camouflage cream. At first Juan had thought they were Gurkhas because they were so fucking short. But after seeing the blue eyes rolling back on the soldier he'd killed, he knew they were *gringos*. Boys like themselves, just better trained.

Behind him, the lights of Stanley still burned like some floating fairy satellite. For a moment Juan wished he was back home in the village, at his mother's, a mug of strong chocolate warming his hands while the women muttered their endless mantra of births, marriages, infidelities and deaths. *Remember my son Juan, killed in battle like a true hero, God rest his soul.* The premonition of his mother, dressed in black, whispering into the ear of Julietta, the oldest widow of the village, made him shiver. Butting out his cigarette he promptly dismissed it from his mind. Stupid superstition. He was going to live. He was going to go home, help with the calving for one more season, then he would hitch a ride to Buenos Aires and make some money in the nightclubs as a bouncer like his cousin Enrico.

'Get down, you idiot,' one of his companions hissed as an RAF army helicopter flew over, its search-beam travelling across the battlefield like a great white eye. The soldiers fired off a couple of rounds of ammunition before it flew off, swaying dramatically like an overburdened bumblebee.

'*Adios, gringos.* May you rot in hell.'

'Hey, Dario, when are we gonna get out of this shit-hole?'

'When I get orders. Until then you have my permission to continue to compose love letters to that sweet-arsed mother of yours.'

'Fuck you,' Juan responded affectionately.

'Fuck you too. And send my love to Cordoba.'

It was a programmed knowledge that drew the animal to its prey. A sensibility wired into it thousands of moons before. Was it vulnerability, a certain doubting nature, that the bat craved? Or perhaps its motivation was more incidental than that — an unusually high temperature, a racing heart, a certain plasma type. Whatever the characteristic, it had existed in mankind from the moment the first *homo sapiens* had drawn breath in an African cave and a small bat, nesting above the primitive family, had opened its hooded eyes, disturbed by the bawling infant. War and blood, pounding fear and sheer terror — they all had a smell.

The bat swooped low over the moon-drenched beach, a bluish pebbled strip against which the ocean beat endlessly as it had for millennia, oblivious to the burnt-out landing craft lying like an upturned beetle in the surf.

The animal flew over the curve of the harbour then, using its sonar, hugged the cliff face as it swept down towards battle.

❦

'Jimmy five over to base, request permission to advance, over, request permission to advance.'

'Permission granted, suggest three degrees north to join left flank.'

The radio operator pulled off his headphones and gestured to the commanding officer. Finally some action, Clive thought, and not a moment too soon — his toes felt as if frostbite had set in and his numbed brain couldn't imagine anything worse than staying there a minute longer, not even hand-to-hand combat.

'Prepare bayonets,' the CO whispered. Grimly the four men reached for the scabbards fastened neatly to their belts, each praying the enemy wouldn't hear the telltale click as they fixed the blades to the rifles. Clive swung the weapon up to hip height, ready to spring over the ridge. He loosened his chin straps in case he received a head injury and braced himself for the command that would send them running over the lip of the trench and straight towards the line of battle.

'Advance.' The commanding officer threw his arm forward. All four men scrambled up over the icy mud and ran full pelt towards the wasteland that suddenly yawned in front of them.

Immediately there was a series of flashes to Clive's left. He realised it was machine-gun fire coming at them from a hidden Argie dugout. Clive fired back then dropped to the ground. In that second there was a thud then a blinding explosion. Phosphorus lit up the area and the man running in front fell, taking Clive with him.

He lay face down as pieces of shrapnel, flesh and earth rained down, praying as the futility of his life passed through him like a night sweat. Not me, not me, not now, please God not me ... The chant went on until the thudding in his eardrums subsided and the external world rushed back, and with it an acceleration of time. Survival. A possible future. Check your limbs, eyesight, weapons.

Everything seemed intact. Sound returning first, as a distant wailing that disorientated him, taking him back to the police sirens of Northern Ireland — the first thing you'd hear after a bomb attack — then the wailing intensified into screaming.

Clive lifted his face. It was the soldier next to him, the cockney, his ashen face rolled towards Clive's, eyes popping in terror. Blood spurted out of the stump where his leg should have been onto the snow. The Welshman ran over. Crouching, he pulled a torque tight around the wound and screamed for a medic. Clive reached for the headset Cedric had thrown down next to the dying soldier then something hit him in the back of the neck. A bullet or a piece of flying shrapnel in the narrow strip of exposed flesh between his collar and helmet. The force of it knocked him back to the ground.

Unsteadily he raised himself to his knees and touched his neck, terrified that it might be a serious injury and it was only shock keeping him alive. There was blood on his fingers. A bullet graze it had to be, a near hit by some invisible sniper.

Something pale flickered at the perimeter of his vision; it looked like a piece of torn sail cloth rising and falling on the night wind, strangely incongruous over a battlefield. It disappeared into the hazy horizon and Clive forgot it.

The bat licked the blood from its stained muzzle. The taste was a resounding medley of colour fusing into harmony but there was a note missing, a complementary underpinning, high-pitched, pure and soulful. The animal's sonar moved forward over the rocky terrain, reading, searching.

The landscape was rendered a smoky red with boulders translating as large dark stationary masses against the silhouette of a crimson sky. That was the trouble with these night-sight goggles, Juan thought, his head unnaturally heavy from the equipment, you couldn't tell lumps of rock from abandoned tanks. Suddenly one of the masses began to move, running from one edge of his night sight to the other. Lifting the machine gun, he aimed and fired. The movement of the gun ratcheted up his arm. A howitzer to his right burst into action a second later, firing in the same direction. Gustavo. The mass stopped then dropped to the ground.

'Have we got them?' Juan screamed, pushing the goggles to his forehead. Gustavo joined him. Very cautiously Juan moved his head to the gap between the mounds of earth so he could peer out of the buried post. A tracer bullet whistled past, narrowly missing him, and buried itself into a sack in the opposite wall. Immediately sand began to trickle out.

'Where are the bastards hidden? In the mud like fucking lizards?' Gustavo hissed behind him. Juan crossed himself, thanking Jesus for his survival.

'If they know where we are, we are sitting ducks!'

'How can they know? No one can see a fucking thing through that mist.'

'Then how could they know where to fire?'

'Some gringo got lucky, that's all, relax.'

The others began to argue about whether to abandon the post or not. Juan leaned against the freezing wall and felt for his rosary tucked safely into an inner pocket. Another four hours in this hell-hole and he'd go crazy.

'We'll die of cold or boredom, or maybe both.'

'So? It might be a better way than being sliced to pieces by some mad fat Englishman.'

They laughed, but the youngest amongst them — Carlos, barely seventeen — looked frightened. 'Listen, you guys, I have a fiancée, she's expecting me home.'

'You, a fiancée? You haven't even popped your cherry yet!'

'I don't care what you say, I think we should cut our losses and fall back. We've been here for two days and what have we done? Nothing.'

Arguing broke out again. The kid had a point: apart from a few sporadic bursts of gunfire and a few casualties, the post felt obsolete, like some forgotten island in the middle of a vast stormy sea. It wasn't a reassuring feeling.

When Juan turned to the others, everyone looked up to listen — even his superior officer — because the soldier was famous for speaking only when it was important. He paused for a second, secretly thrilling at the anticipation on the eager faces. Leadership suited him, he knew it; it heated his blood.

'We should radio to see whether they have a position on the advancing troops and then make a decision.' He addressed the commanding officer directly, then, for the sake of decency, added a questioning 'No?' so the man wouldn't feel as if his authority was being threatened.

'I was just going to suggest that myself,' the officer replied, glancing furtively at the expectant soldiers. Immediately the radio operator got to work.

Satisfied, Juan reached into his rations and began to chew on some beef hash, the salt flooding his body with renewed energy. It was good to know he still had his sense of taste; hunger made him human again.

'They have a position on advancing troops — five miles north of us. Base says they will have back-up here within the day.'

'Bullshit, they said that yesterday.'

'I say we stay.'

'Doesn't our opinion count?'

'This is the army, not a fucking democracy. I'm the highest-ranking officer here and when I say we stay, we stay.'

Juan looked back at the terrain — it was eerily quiet, unnaturally so. Something had to give and that meant movement. He was almost looking forward to it, the waiting was worse than anything.

'Relax, you guys, we'll see action before dawn. I know it, I can feel it in my cock.' He grabbed his crotch for emphasis and the others laughed, the tension briefly dissipating then crystallised as thickly as before. Somewhere nearby an owl hooted, startling a couple of the soldiers who, after realising it was a false alarm, laughed again. Juan slipped off his helmet and lifted his balaclava to scratch his scalp which was itchy from days of dust and filth. A sharp blow knocked him against the wall and something flashed past his face and out over the trench beyond. He crouched, dazed.

'What was that?' Dario asked. 'White shrapnel?'

'From what? There was no explosion,' Carlos piped up as he knelt beside Juan. 'You okay, my friend?'

Juan reached up to the back of his neck: it felt like a bullet graze, he was bleeding slightly.

'I'll live.'

'Maybe it was an angel.'

'Sure, where I come from angels don't have fucking teeth. You're fucking crazy.'

'We're all fucking crazy to be in this war.'

'Hey, maybe I'll just catch some sleep — you guys can take over for an hour or so. Wake me when the marines come.'

'Sure, Mr Smart arse.'

Juan curled up, pulled his parka hood over his head and fell instantly asleep.

Five miles north Clive crawled into the Argentine tent they'd commandeered. He wanted to see if he could find new boots his size. There was nothing but a couple of sleeping bags and some rations. Inside a biscuit tin Clive found some chocolate. He stuffed the dark bitter pieces into his mouth. He'd never tasted anything so delicious. He sat on one of the sleeping bags. The Argies must have abandoned the tent in a blind panic, there were still socks strewn across the bottom. He leaned back and, closing his eyes, slipped into a deep dream.

He is sitting in a crowded bar. There is a drink in his hand: whiskey, Jameson's, he can smell it. The place is noisy — he recognises it vaguely as a bar in Soho he used to go to, tucked behind the theatre district. He liked it because it was like a Dickensian tea-house — there was even a portrait of Disraeli on the wall. He also liked it because, although the clientele was mainly heterosexual, it was a discreet pick-up for men.

Clive looks around. The crowd is mixed: young couples meeting after work, suits, secretaries, advertising geeks in denim, women in tailored elegance spelling money. Tourists stand out amongst the English with their suntanned blondeness and beige leather. From the clothes and the rosy faces Clive guesses that it is winter outside. As the voices pull into an articulated focus he steps into the throng and immediately forgets that he was dreaming.

There is a man sitting at the bar, his back to him. An empty stool stands to the right of him, almost as if people are afraid to sit next to him. On his other side two women chat loudly together. One, a vivacious blonde in her early forties, attractive and confident, gestures dramatically with her hands, as if she hopes to catch the attention of the dark silent man.

Clive doesn't need to see his face, he can read the signs: the way the youth sits, his broad back tapering to his waist, below which his hard, round arse juts out over the wooden seat, smugly waiting to be fucked, to be toppled from all its glory; the way the women keep glancing furtively; the body language of the men, either puffed up or leaning slightly in that direction, as if they too would like to be looked at, or at least acknowledged by the mysterious stranger. It is the aura of the famous or the extremely handsome — Clive knows it is the latter.

He pushes his way through the crowd. People keep turning to him, acknowledging him. They all look vaguely like people he knows, their features a composite of characteristics of friends, family, ex-girlfriends, even teachers from his primary school. As he passes amongst them, somewhere in his unconscious comes the dull revelation that these chimeras are composed of people who have played a significant part in his life, who have loved him in one way or another.

He sits down on the vacant bar stool. The bartender, an uncanny mixture of his father and his maternal grandfather, immediately places another Jameson's in front of him, as if he knows exactly what Clive drinks. The dark man continues to look directly ahead. Clive glances across — the stranger's thighs are muscular and long under tight jeans, the legs of a working man or athlete. A fold of his white shirt exposes a glimpse of stomach, and the olive skin, taunting in its muscled, rippling perfection, fascinates him. It is an oasis of sex, a chink in the enigma into which he could slip his fingers and break the surface of aching desire. But he doesn't. He plays the moment, eyes down — the stranger's prick thickening under his stare, pushing the denim up into a solid curve below the belt.

He can feel the heat of the youth rising off him even from where he is sitting; his aroma is rich, a sweet musk. Without saying a word the boy turns. Clive stays still, eyes averted, relishing the feel of the gaze travelling across his skin. Finally he looks up and smiles to himself.

The boy is stunning, striking in the way of a roughly hewn sculpture, as if the artist, having carved such classical beauty, had been loathe to complete the task for fear the face would be too gorgeous, too perfect in its symmetry. Therefore his splendour lies in the infinitesimal imperfections: the nose, aquiline and noble, looks as if it might once have been broken; the strong chin — intensely masculine — is split by a deep dimple; the eyes, almond and almost lidless with golden irises flecked with green, are, at second glance, placed slightly at an angle, the right being fractionally higher than the left; but the mouth ... the mouth is faultless.

Just staring at it gives Clive an instant erection. Placed in a narrow face with very high cheekbones that hint at some distant Indian heritage, the lips are almost an obscenity. Curved and impossibly full they jut out from the boy's face as if they had been painted on at the last minute. It is the mouth of a far older and far more experienced man; a wry knowing plays at its corners, suggesting that the boy is acutely aware of his own beauty and finds its existence in such a body ironic. It is not the mouth of a boy but rather the mouth of a libertine, the lips of someone who, despite his intelligence, can't control his own inherent carnality.

The balance of his beauty is offset by a scar that runs from the top of one cheek towards the corner of his mouth. It only adds to the flawed edginess Clive finds so erotic; it is a mark of aggression, of experience which sits like a paradox on one so young. The scar, Clive notes, is a deep mauve and looks as if it is still healing, the flesh beaded like the uneven lip of a vagina. He can almost taste it.

They lock eyes and the youth's desire cuts like a blade. Shaken, he stands. The boy follows and Clive is surprised to discover that the youth is taller than himself, his shoulders not yet settled into their adult width, his hips and buttocks a too narrow basket for the heavy cock, now a stiff rod pushing against the blue denim. They say nothing. Clive, knowing that the boy will follow, allows his dreaming to take him back through the crowded room towards a door with a neon Exit sign.

The door leads into a stairwell, the kind that might exist in any building, the concrete spiral that always leads to a roof. Clive begins to climb, vaguely aware of the incongruity of walking out of a bar with the atmosphere of a Victorian pub and into a stairwell that belongs to a sixties' office block. He doesn't care; everything feels right, feels as if it has fallen into place, destiny running to course. The boy behind him shadows his steps, echoing his gestures, his breath, his heat, on the back of his neck.

He begins to climb faster until he is running full pelt as the stairs wind up flight after flight. Finally, at the top, the stairwell finishes with a door marked Authorised Persons Only. Without hesitation, and without turning around, Clive pushes it open.

He is on a roof high over a city he doesn't recognise. Instead of the freezing English winter the temperature is balmy, the view below a bustling hornets' nest of lights, cars, sirens blasting out, waves of music, exotic, thudding, floating up like translucent bubbles. Behind him he hears the sound of the door closing and the panting of the boy as he catches his breath.

He closes his eyes. Waiting. That dangerous, accelerating eternity before the first caress. Heart pounding like a frenzied drummer. Cock bursting. Skin a thousand sensors bursting with expectant desire. He could come right now, without a single touch. The boy's breath is warm on the skin of his cheek as one hand pushes over his flat stomach, reaching down for his cock which is like hard steel, and begging for freedom.

The kid bites the back of his neck — pleasure bordering on pain as, in the same instant, his fingers unzip Clive's fly and pull out his prick. Hands grip him firmly, encircling the tip, stroking him, pressing himself into Clive's back, his own penis pushing against Clive's buttocks. Clive — always the Top — struggles for a second, aware of the power of those muscled arms that are thicker than his own yet holding back their full strength. He twists in the youth's embrace and, opening his eyes, takes that mouth into his own, hungrily kissing the fruit of his lips, his tongue probing, wanting all of him, now and for ever. Hungrily the boy responds, hands everywhere, frantic under his shirt, around his arse, squeezing him, probing him. Clive, sucking at his tongue, wonders at the impossible sweetness of him. Am I dreaming? I am dreaming ... so I am dreaming ... let this be real, he thinks. Curling his fingers through the thick black hair, he jerks the youth's head back suddenly, enjoying the surge of power, the fight. He pushes the boy down to his knees. The youth plays along, taking Clive's cock with both hands, paying homage, running the tip across his cheeks, slowly over his mouth, over those lips (pleasure pounding dimly at the back of Clive's sleeping mind), teasing, tonguing the eye, his hands encircling Clive's arse, playing him as if he's fucking him.

Unable to bear any more Clive grabs the back of his head, pushing him hard towards his groin — the boy takes all of Clive's prick deep into his throat without gagging. His tongue circling around and around, his rhythm increasing faster and faster, stopping only to suck Clive's balls, then run his tongue down the length of his shaft before those lips eat their aching way over him again.

Clive watches the beauty of the boy, his swollen mouth riding him. His orgasm sharpens and mounts suddenly, shooting from somewhere deep inside his body, and he comes with a profundity that shakes deep within him, the boy swallowing all.

They stay there for a moment, the city noise swelling in the silence. The boy, after wiping his mouth, grins and stands, towering over Clive. He kisses him briefly on the mouth then, taking hold of his hips, turns him around roughly, pushing one knee between his legs, forcing him to widen his stance. For a moment Clive wrestles with him, trying to twist away, but the youth overpowers him. Twisting one arm up behind his back, he forces Clive to bend over. It is strangely exciting, this moment before surrender — the boy's cock a thickness blindly pushing against his buttocks. Clive shivers. He's never been taken by a man and yet this time he wants it. He wants the feel of him inside, to be split like a peach. To be filled, rammed, to feel his shuddering violence. The youth spits into his hand, moistens Clive, then enters with a sharp thrust. Clive freezes, trembling with the novel sensation of being possessed, yet still in control. In control of his own pleasure and that of this youth's. Feeling him tighten the boy pauses, then reaching around starts to caress him again. Clive hardens and slowly the boy begins again, this time pushing gently then becoming faster; he presses Clive's buttocks wide apart, squeezing his flesh, now thrusting deeply. Clive gasps as the pain and pleasure fuse into one ecstatic understanding of being taken. This is abandonment, he thinks, this is how it is to be taken and to be the taker. The youth's panting mixes with the cries of the city below, the screech of a night bird and Clive's own cry of ecstasy as the thundering of the boy's orgasm releases his own — more intense than ever before.

'What is your name?' The young stranger's voice is more mature than Clive had imagined. He waits for a moment before answering.

'Clive,' he says softly. 'Clive.'

He woke.

'Scarsgard, look sharp!' his commanding officer barked in his ear. For a second he lay there trying to remember where he was and who he was. The dream came flooding back and, terrified that he might have a telltale semen stain down his trousers, he sat up. The CO pressed his rifle into his hand. 'Get the fuck up. We attack in ten.'

The moving shadows of the other men fell across the canvas as Clive checked his clothes. He had come. He cleaned himself up with a tissue, thanking God that the standard-issue parka was a dark wool, then stepped out into the chilly dawn.

Juan woke up with a crick in his neck and cramped limbs. He'd been curled against the wall. How long he'd been asleep he wasn't sure. But he had had the strangest dream. A dream of desire. A phantasm, a warning that he must stop the hypocrisy of his existence or else he wouldn't survive. Not whole. Not as a complete man. The dream had been so vivid he could almost taste the semen at the back of his throat.

After checking his comrades weren't looking he cautiously ran a hand down the front of his pants. He was wet. He had come. Jesus, in the middle of a war, in the middle of a battlefield, he thought, wondering whether to do such a thing was disrespectful to the dead. He crossed himself just in case, then realised his bladder was bursting.

'Look who's risen from the grave,' joked Gustavo.

'Anything happening out there?' Juan gazed bleakly at the stretch of scrubland; beyond, the sea was a dull grey streak on the horizon.

'Nothing, not even a vulture. Hopefully they've all run home to their queen.'

Juan stretched, then, hoisting his rifle over his shoulder, walked to the back of the trench, to the wall facing away from the front line.

'Where are you going?'

'To piss. Think you can hold the fort without me?'

'No problem! Watch out for snakes.'

Juan stepped out of the dugout and, after glancing around, cautiously walked a few steps away and, his back to the trench, began to urinate.

Clive dropped to a crouching position, the other three soldiers fanning out beside him. All of them had sighted the gun post at the same moment — an ordinary-looking bank of mud almost indistinguishable from the surrounding scrubland, except for the tiny black ring of a machine-gun nozzle staring straight out from a small hole in the mound. The dawn light painted the whole terrain with a rose wash as pink rays began to creep up into the sky. Sunrise just like any other day in any other part of the world, Clive thought, aware that his back teeth had begun to rattle. Excitement? Fear? He peered back at the gun post. He knew that beyond the façade the wall would be open at the top. It was a vulnerability, one he could exploit. Gesturing to the others, he crawled forward on his belly, conscious of the eye of the gun barrel staring out blindly.

He moved another five feet, the barrel didn't move. Praying there was no one behind it, he reached down to his belt and unclipped a locked hand grenade. Holding it between his knees, he pulled at the pin with both hands; after several hard tugs it came out. Using his best bowling style he lobbed it into the gun post.

Juan was just shaking himself dry when the explosion knocked him to the ground. He lay there for a moment as the panorama tilted on its edge then swayed back to horizontal. Then he hauled himself up, dimly aware of a throbbing in his left side. Through a film of blood he saw smoke streaming out of the gun post and heard an eerie screaming coming from within. His comrades. Juan ran, legs pounding against the scrubland, and dived into the flames and smoke.

One half of the gun post was a smouldering mass of twisted metal fused with human flesh: two of the soldiers were dead. Juan recognised Dario's torso from the heavy gold chain around his neck, normally hidden under his army vest — the blast had stripped him naked. The screaming came from Gustavo. His body had been thrown against the far wall; he was missing an arm and a leg. He was still clutching his rifle. As Juan approached, the screaming stopped. Juan stared down at his dead friend.

Clive saw the outline of the man's head before the man spotted him. He dropped out of sight then, crouching, made his way over the broken wall of the smouldering dugout. The soldier was standing over a corpse; there was something about him that Clive recognised — his stance, the width of his shoulders. Bizarrely he had taken his helmet off, his long black hair fell to his shoulders. Clive could tell that he was handsome, and perhaps it was this and the vulnerability of his naked head that made the paratrooper falter for a second before lifting his rifle to his shoulder. One swift bullet in the back of the head, that's all, he thought as he peered through the sight then squeezed the trigger. It jammed. Knowing he had no time, Clive jumped on the youth, pushing him down to the ground. Locked together they wrestled in the smoke and burning embers.

Clive fought against the boy's weight to raise his bayonet to kill him. The youth twisted around, throwing him onto his back, struggling to reach the long dagger attached to his belt. As he did, the two men finally saw each other's face.

Clive recognised him instantly: the full mouth, the scar running from cheek to lip.

'Clive,' Juan whispered before running his dagger deep within the Englishman's body. In the same moment Clive's bayonet came plunging down into Juan's chest.

# Diver

I'd never openly describe myself as a recluse, but I guess that's what most people would call me. The bitter truth of it is that I'm only ever truly comfortable in isolated locations, like the windy stretches of Dartmoor, or Iceland, or the Gobi Desert. I don't like human beings very much at all. I would have made a fantastic astronaut, except there wasn't much training for that in the working-class Liverpudlian suburb where I grew up. Instead I was drawn to the docklands and the wild grey Irish Sea; more importantly, to what lies beneath it.

The first time I dived I immediately knew that I had found my element at last. Don't get me wrong, it's just as crowded underwater, but it's a non-human, tremulous, shimmering busyness that defies time and place and the pettiness of our own primate species. There's the well of darkness beneath you, the horizon of light above, and the orb — a cascading blue as you descend to nowhere and everywhere. I loved it from the very first: the way the suit wraps around you like an amniotic sac, the pressure demarcating your every move in syrupy-slow responsibility. But before I go any further, I'd better introduce myself.

My name is Seamus O'Connor and at the time of this whispered confession I am thirty-two years old, six foot two and of not bad complexion. I have my father's thick black bog-Irish hair, which I sometimes wear in a ponytail, and my ma's brown eyes. And I'd been divorced six months by the time I found myself on oil rig 2564.

It was a colossal dinosaur of a thing, built back in the early 1970s during the time of the North Sea oil boom. The oil company that owned it had been making a tidy profit ever since. Oil rigs are manned twenty-four hours of the day, each man working six hours on, six hours off. As diving engineer my job was the underwater maintenance of the massive concrete pylons; two of them driven into the sea bed at the shallower end, two of them floating held by pins. I checked for fallen pipes, cracks in the coring and any other potential problems. It was a dangerous job that involved spending three days in a decompression chamber after the dive and the heavy accountability for the souls of four other divers beneath me in rank.

The rest of the time was spent above water: playing cards, exercising, watching porn, helping with mechanical operations and reading. A twenty-four-hour operation, come sun, rain or tempest. One week the night shift, a howling gothic world where you battled the wind from cabin to cabin; the next week the day shift, a relentless stream of endless light, with no time between the two to adjust your body clock. Three months on the rig, three months off. But they paid you like a millionaire for putting up with the isolation and a yawning tedium that would transform the sanest man. And I had fought hard to get my industrial diving rating.

I was there to forget. My wife had run off with my best and only friend, Hanif, back in Liverpool. I married Meredith when I was in my early twenties. It wasn't a whirlwind romance but a calculated relationship. Even then I knew that if I didn't marry I'd end up calcified in my own misanthropy and Meredith, not much more than a girl, mistook my cynicism for intellectual sophistication.

In those days I liked to delude myself that my attitude was poetic; now I see it as downright selfish. I wish I'd loved Meredith better, and I wish that Hanif had loved me more, but my wife was beautiful and in need and Hanif had a Middle Eastern pragmatism I had always lacked. He made sure he was there when I was not.

Strangely enough, my anger wasn't directed towards them but at myself. I guess that's why I signed on for the gig in the first place. A year to stew in my guilt and abandonment. How many evenings I wasted on that oil rig, lying on my bunk, listening to the rig creak, turning over the last days of my marriage, looking for a telltale fault line that I might have addressed — the only conclusion I ever reached was amazement that they hadn't run off together sooner. I had not been an easy person to live with, just as I knew I was not an easy person to work with.

'Eh, Seamus! You coming with us on the dip-the-wick excursion?' Jimmy, the rig's chief maintenance officer, a short cockney with an even shorter temper, stuck his head into the room. The men, all twenty of them, visited the nearest brothel on the last Thursday of every month. It was a ritual; those men attended the whorehouse like they were going to church, I'm telling you. I'd been with them once before, and once was enough.

The brothel, located in the windswept harbour town of Lerwick in the Shetland Islands, was above a fish and chip shop with a red light shining bravely over the door. The smell of cooking grease hung in the air and the five 'ladies' who worked there were all fifteen stone or more, hefty Scottish lasses with the vernacular and the hair on their legs to prove it.

My co-workers tricked me into accompanying them by telling me they were going to see a great floor show. I've always like those clubs because, under the coloured lights and mirror balls, the strippers remind me of waving forests of seaweed. Those places were a fantasy underwater palace for me, and many was the time I'd escaped into some dive in old Liverpool town. I'm a watcher not a toucher and the lads knew it.

But after a hellish helicopter ride through whipping winds, we arrived at the tiny port and there was no show. Instead I found myself staring at the massive thighs of a fifty year old named Mary MacDougal who cooed over my thick black hair and the muscles in my arms then offered to go down on me. I declined politely, saying I would be just as content with half an hour of female conversation and, after rolling herself a cigarette, Mary was more than happy to oblige. I never found out if she was a fantastic lay but I'll say this much: those whores of Lerwick have the trick of opening a man up and listening as he spills his heart. Then again, being the only available women for a hundred nautical miles in either direction means they'd get plenty of practice.

Before I knew it I was telling Mary about the divorce and the terrible loss of my wife and best friend. It was the first time I'd talked to anyone about it and it was comforting and easy for she was a stranger. Now that sex was out of the equation we both relaxed and Mary pulled a bottle of excellent Scotch malt from under the rickety fold-out bed.

'Aye, there's many a damaged man that ends up on the rig. It has a calling for the masochists amongst us. But the isolation can destroy a good brain,' she concluded, knocking back the whisky, her massive breasts straining against her fluorescent pink nylon teddy.

'I'm no masochist, but I suppose you could say I'm paying some kind of emotional penance. It was my own negligence that lost me my wife, after all,' I answered, joining Mary in a second glass.

Outside it had begun to snow and I was thankful for the gas fire's dancing blue flames. Mary belched and smoothed down her greasy hair with the gesture of a coquette half her age.

'I had a client once, years ago,' she said, 'maybe even twenty years. Of course I was a real looker in those days. You wouldn't be sitting there drinking that whisky if you'd seen me then. Anyways, he was from the rig too. Real sharp he was and regular with the cash. A wee lad, couldn't have been more than five foot, but feisty.'

'And?'

'Well, one month he didn't visit, or the next either, and then the next thing I know the insurance company is all over the town asking questions.'

'Questions?'

'They'd found him floating in a small raft. Dead he was, with his eyes scratched out. Turned out he'd gone stark raving mad. Tattle, that was his name — Jim Tattle. He had some marital problems, just like you. The sea's got a voice, she'll taut you with your history at the best of times. You should be careful,' she finished, leaning forward dramatically. The sound of the howling wind and the soft patter of snow filled the room.

I realise now that she was trying to warn me, but at the time it was easy to dismiss the story as the starved imaginings of a town gossip. I should have known better.

Mary must have said something to the other lads because the next thing I knew they'd dubbed me Seamus the Puritan. Not that I cared. If anything it gave me an excuse to withdraw further into my own company. But that wasn't good for the job. The men like to have a diving engineer they can trust, not only with their lives but with their personal problems as well.

I know I'm a cold man, but knowing something doesn't mean you can change it, and I was painfully aware of how false I sounded when I tried to engage them in talk about their girlfriends or how awkward I looked playing soccer with them on the pitch marked out on the wooden deck. I'm just not a social animal by nature and I have always found it impossible not to be true to myself. Then they decided I was making a moral stand with my voluntarily celibacy and they took every opportunity to remind me of it.

'Eh, Seamus! Are you training for the priesthood or is it that our fine Scottish women aren't good enough for your bastard Irish loins?'

'Seamus, I was going to invite you to me cabin to watch the porn film with the other lads then I remembered that you were dickless.'

> *'Seamus the puritan went to sea,*
> *Not a muff-diver he would be,*
> *Not a leg or tit man either,*
> *Just worked himself into a dickless fever.'*

One day they nailed a used condom on my cabin door. Another time I found a blow-up sex doll hanging in the shower unit. It got worse as the next visit to the brothel drew nearer. I suppose I could have stopped them but in a perverse way I think their ridicule fuelled my own sense of martyrdom. I'm a self-righteous bastard at the best of times but give me something to be indignant about and I become impossible. It's in the blood.

I became monosyllabic, spending my hours checking my apparatus over and over, as if somehow the decline of my marriage could be reversed by the maintenance of my equipment. I greased the lines, cleaned my masks, pored over my diving tables again and again, replaying all the arguments, all the heartbreak, trying to arrive at a point where I could forgive. Jesus, I missed them both.

Pay day came and most of the crew left for Lerwick. As the clouds swallowed up the faint bee-speck of the helicopter I relaxed for the first time in weeks and began walking around the deck, pacing my territory like a dog.

It was a wonderful feeling, the purity of solitude swelling my soul like a benediction. It felt fucking great. All I could hear was the screaming sea and the seagulls. Salt drying on my skin.

Knowing that the skeleton crew were all below, I actually took all my clothes off and whirled around like a demented dervish. The huge gas flame of the rig roaring above me, the struggling sun catching in my hair, painting me with a rare northern heat. And for the first time in six months I felt the terrible grief of the divorce losing its grip.

That evening I decided to eat in the chief engineer's private office. It was a formal room set high above the control room with a 360-degree view of the ocean. On a clear day, if you squinted, you could just see the tip of Peterhead on the Scottish mainland. It was like being on top of the world, as if you were steering the entire globe through time and space. I loved it up there.

I got myself a nice piece of local salmon from the massive freezer and some excellent hollandaise sauce the chief prepared regularly and froze. I cooked the fish then washed it down with some vintage sauvignon blanc I'd sneaked on board. I sat at the oak desk, crystal glass in hand. I felt like a king. Slowly my euphoria leaked away. A king of what? What was there for me back in Liverpool? A phone number I'd be frightened to ring and a house I was being forced to sell.

As night wrapped itself around the windows I stared out at the blooming stars and tried to think of nothing. Absentmindedly my fingers crept across the desk surface and began to stroke some marks that had been carved into the wood. I peered down at them. *Tattle* had been scratched out in thick clumsy lettering.

Suddenly a faint cry made me jerk up my head. I froze; realised it was just the seagulls and the roar of the flame. I relaxed but then there was another shout, this time louder. A man was screaming somewhere out there on the ocean.

I rushed to one of the windows. Outside, wavering bands of captured light rolled across the sea like a drowning sunset but it was an empty shimmering. There was no one to be seen. Then the distant but unmistakeable sound of a voice crying, 'Help me! Help me!' floated across the water.

This time I ran to the deck. I steadied myself against one of the metal struts and stared into the strip of illuminated water. Again I heard the plea but saw nothing. I reached for one of the flare guns strapped to the side of the life rafts. Holding it high I fired it into the night sky.

It burned brightly, a comet scattering crimson fog. For a split second, I saw the ghostly outline of a life raft, the silhouette of a man standing up in it, arms held to the sky as if he were commanding the heavens. His words were clear above the wind: 'I see! I see!'

Then he vanished, just like that; the man, the boat, his shadow against the horizon. It was then that the story of Jim Tattle, the eyeless madman, came flooding back.

Needless to say I had trouble sleeping, but after pushing my travel trunk up against the door of my cabin I forced fear out of my head and drifted into oblivion.

The next morning I woke early. I got up to douse my face with my customary wake-up call of freezing water. One side of my neck felt peculiarly bruised. I pulled my shaving mirror from the wall. A blue-black track of lovebites ran from just under my chin to my collar bone. I gazed at them blankly. It was so bizarre I didn't realise what they were at first. Confused, I touched them carefully. My neck was definitely bruised as if whoever or whatever had sucked and bitten me deeply. I sat back on the bunk. I couldn't remember anything about the night except that I had slept far more soundly than usual. I was pretty sure I hadn't dreamed. I smelled my fingers; they had a curiously sweet fishy scent. And it wasn't just on my hands. Sniffing the air I followed the scent; it led to my pillow.

I buried my nose in the rough cotton; the whole bed stank. Suddenly I noticed something glinting and I peered down. Nestled on my pillow was a small pile of translucent fish scales.

I scooped them up and carried them to the desk in the corner. Under the lamp I examined them with a magnifying lens I keep for looking at shells and sea specimens.

The fish scales were pearly and larger than I'd ever seen. There were over ten of them and each was around half a centimetre across. They had a bronze hue and looked a little like crystal snowflakes. I placed them under a stronger lens and was shocked to see that each scale had distinctly individual patterns, very similar to the swirls of fingerprints. I'd never seen that before in any known species.

I sat back, trying to assimilate the facts. Was it possible that some bizarre fish species had crawled into the cabin and attacked me while I was sleeping? I knew that sometimes the wind will pick up a flying fish and throw the writhing creature onto the deck of a ship or oil rig. But flying fish belong in tropical waters, and besides, what kind of flying fish would crawl across the floor of a cabin and leave lovebites on its human occupant?

The curious and sometimes obscene relationships fishermen have with sea creatures floated through my mind: tales about dugongs being courted as sea-maidens because of their breast-like teats and near-human proportions; the more graphic stories I'd heard of men fucking skates because their vertical mouths were vagina-like. I cursed my Irish imagination and resolved to ignore the mystery and focus on prosaic matters. I tossed my bed sheets into the laundry. But somehow, later that day, I found myself outside the administration office determined to find out more about Tattle.

I switched the light on and the fluorescent tubes sputtered into life, creating a bluish underworld. There was a computer on the desk, a short-wave radio and several metal filing cabinets pushed up against the back wall. Feeling horribly furtive I walked over to them. Harris, the administration officer, a fastidious man in his late sixties, had been working for the oil company for the past thirty years. He was overweight and had trouble squeezing his flesh into the undersized suits he insisted on wearing. I'd often wondered whether his preoccupation with detail and tidiness was a reaction to the war he obviously fought with his body. Whatever the cause, Harris was meticulous and obsessive — if Tattle had actually existed Harris would have filed all the details of his case for sure.

The first cabinet was marked 'Personnel Files: 1975–85', the second cabinet contained 1985–95. I knew the rig had been in operation since 1974, although it had gone through several overhauls since then. Mary the prostitute said the Tattle incident happened about twenty years before. I reached for the first drawer.

The main files were arranged chronologically and then within each year personnel were filed alphabetically. I found a Taylor who had worked the rig from 1978 through to '82, a Thomas who was the electrician from 1980–81. There were several other Ts but no Tattle.

I scanned the files again. Time had shaded the tops of the main files with dust and grime. It was then that I noticed the clearly delineated outline of a file that had been removed from between Tass and Topper. Okay, suppose it was Tattle's file — where would have Harris hidden it? I was sure someone as bloody anal as Harris wouldn't have thrown it away, especially if there'd been a legal case attached.

I looked around the room. Harris's desk was bare except for a curious photo of an albino bat torn out from a magazine and stuck on the wall above the computer screen. The man must be some kind of animal nut, I reasoned. I tried the drawers; one was locked. I knelt on the floor and meticulously began to pick the lock.

Inside was a *Playboy* issue July 1982, a framed photograph of a woman I could only assume was Harris's mother, an electric alarm clock engraved with the immortal words, *To E. M. Harris, for twenty years of loyal service*. Under all of this lay a large package. I pulled it out and dusted it off; it was sealed with thick sticky tape. I switched on the kettle in the corner, waited for it to boil and steamed it open carefully. Then I tipped the contents out onto Harris's desk.

First item: a newspaper clipping from the *Aberdeen Evening Express* dated 16 June 1975. It read:

> *Last night the body of an oil-rig worker, Jim Tattle, twenty-six, was found floating in a life raft fifty miles north of Aberdeen. Tattle, a diving engineer, had been suffering from a mental disorder for some time. No foul play is suspected.*

Clipped to this was another article, this time from the *Edinburgh Echo*:

> *The horrible sight of an eyeless corpse floating in a life raft shocked fishermen working off the east coast of Scotland early this morning. The victim, identified as Jim Tattle, an oil-rig diver, was found stark naked and sprawled across the inflatable life raft. Mr Tuttle, who had just undergone a marital break-up and a nervous breakdown, had gouged out his own eyes. The oil company had no comment.*

I leaned back in the chair; I could feel the gorge rising in my throat. So Tattle had been a diving engineer like myself and, also like myself, had suffered a recent separation. Under the clippings was a file: the insurance company's report, addressed to both the oil company and Tattle's family. The final verdict was that all evidence pointed to death by self-inflicted wounds, therefore defined as suicide. Poor bastards, I thought, they wouldn't have got a penny from the company then. We all had to sign a disclaimer regarding mental illness as a condition of employment. I found myself feeling some affinity for the anguished phantom I'd seen the night before.

Beneath the file, slipped between two blank sheets of aged yellow paper was a slim notebook covered in a deep blue satiny fabric. I opened it and was immediately transfixed by the spidery handwriting that slanted upwards at the end of each line. A title was scribbled across the first page: *Here is the journal of Jim Tattle*. I began to read.

*16 May 1975*

*Another grey day, sometimes I wonder why I bother to write in this journal at all. I think it's because the discipline is stopping me from going crazy. It's been six months now and I've started to forget what Vauxhall looks like. Isn't that pathetic? I checked all the drill's fuses twice over tonight. Anything to avoid talking with my so-called co-workers. Bunch of total morons. If I hear another knock-knock joke I'll puke. They don't seem to care about anything except making money and the see-through blouse Cilla Black wore on 'Top of the Pops' last night. I could scream. There's one man I get on with — Harris. He's older, reminds me of my dad. He's got the same old-fashioned gruffness. Maybe I'm just more comfortable with rude people.*

*He sat next to me at dinner, which was brave considering how the rest of the crew ridicule me. We had a smoke in his office later. He told me he saw an albino bat once on some war ship he served on. That would be fantastic, to see something as weird as that.*

*Later I smoked some pot and listened to Pink Floyd's Dark Side of the Moon — again! What a truly amazing album. It felt like the music was playing every secret emotion I had. At about 1 a.m. I had one of those revelations you get with really good grass. For a moment I thought I was in telepathic communication with Eddy. He was telling me that it was okay I didn't go to his funeral.*

*17 May 1975*

*I just woke up and there was that odour again, all over my cabin and bed. A weird musky smell. This is the fifth morning in a row. Maybe I should tell whoever's on cleaning duty about it. Then as I was dressing I noticed a couple of puncture marks in my arm. Just like someone had bitten me. This is beginning to really spook me.*

I stared out the window at the lightening sky. So Tattle had experienced something similar. I flicked forward through the diary, my hand trembling. His handwriting got wilder and wilder. The last entry was marked 9 June, a week before he was found floating in the raft. It was as if he had scribbled it in a mad hurry — the lines ran diagonally across the page and finished hanging in mid-air, like a series of mini cliff-edges.

*9 June 1975*
*It's here, screaming, like hooks in my skin, like the rush from a razor-sharp climax. Surrender. Don't fight it, not any more. Eddy, I'm going to be with you. Like we were, playing soccer on the field outside the house. Boys, we were boys, possibility screeching in every train whistle, in the London fog, in the dreams of our grandfather. We were going to be millionaires, artists, rock stars, chasing life itself. Taste, taste summer, the chilly smoke, frost on the grass and hot tarmac. Sirens. The song of the siren. She's coming for me. Guess this is goodbye. Sucking sleep from the sky and shitting out the moon. Eddy, my brother, my shadow half . . .*

There was nothing else. I suppose he finally wanted to be with his dead brother. The prostitute was right: the sea can throw up memories like seaweed after a storm. It's that vast glassy surface — a fucking mirror for the soul. Me, in my darkest moments. I related to poor Tattle — the shadowy outline of that eyeless figure drifted back into my mind.

I don't know what made me take the file, but I did. Somehow, its existence made his suicide and burial feel incomplete. Some South American tribes refuse to be photographed because they believe the camera steals the soul; and Australian Aborigines don't allow their people to be named after their death. Perhaps it was the sense that as long as the file existed Tattle would remain floating out there on that glassy surface screaming, 'I see, I see'.

Out on the lower deck I placed the file in a rubbish bin and torched it. The flames danced up through the wire, vivid against the colourless vista. Grey sea, grey sky. I squatted, warming my hands, staring into the fire, the heat a glorious contrast to my freezing ears. I felt like the last man on earth. And you know what? It wasn't that bad.

As the last of the paper crinkled up I made a vow to bury my grief and Tattle's ghost together. Then I heard the whirring blades of the returning helicopter.

The next couple of days passed in a blur, just the eternal routine of checking equipment. One of the workers discovered a broken cable and I had to radio the main office to order a replacement. The men were jovial — empty balls will do that. Their conviviality would last a week and then they'd slip back into sullen acceptance of the monotony of the endless little tasks that go into maintaining the rig. Personally I've always liked routine, it takes the edge off time, blunts its teeth. Day became night became morning became afternoon ...

Besides, being young, I didn't yet feel that galloping fear some of the older men experienced who knew the rig was their last chance to make some real money. Yeah, I was naive enough to think I had all the time in the world. And I'd tricked myself into thinking I'd forgotten all about Tattle and his mysterious death.

Until one of the men pushed an envelope into my hand.

'A love letter from your Mary. The old cow insisted I give it to you. I would have forgotten but I found it in me back pocket.'

I stepped into my cabin and reluctantly tore open the cheap pink paper.

*Dear Mr Seamus, after you left I remembered something about Tattle. Something strange I have not told anyone else. The last time he visited me there were funny marks on his body. I see a lot in my industry but I ain't seen nothing like this before. Like a sucking or a beating perhaps. I remembered my first thought was whether he had been hurt by the other men. Bored men can get*

377

*cruel. But to my eyes it looked like animal tracks of some
kind. I didn't ask Tattle because he was quite distressed
by this time and not entirely in his right mind.
Hope this helps. Yours, Mary MacDougal.*

Helps what, I thought. Why should I care about Tattle? A man's
problems can hang around a rig like a ghost for years, even after
the man himself is long gone. Every off-shore worker knows
that. The secret is to walk through that haunting as if you
haven't a care in the world. Otherwise the negative energy will
stick to you like metal filings to a magnet.

⤚

The weather was changing; warmth floated in on the breezes
that came from the land. It made the men restless and set the
cook humming. It usually made me dream, but for the last week
I'd found myself plunging into a deep imageless slumber each
time I laid down my head. Perhaps it was the switch over to
night shift; whatever it was it disturbed me.

This particular evening I woke up with a pounding at my
temples. The air was stuffy with a rich animal smell I couldn't
identify. For a moment I wondered if a mouse had died behind
one of the walls. With my head still pulsing I yawned and reached
under my pillow. My hand touched something unfamiliar. A blue-
black pearl, left there like some sort of message.

It was large and misshapen, not perfectly spherical like a
cultured pearl. There was something alien about the way it
shone in the light, as if it had come from an entirely different
terrain.

I ran it across my skin; it was sticky, as if it had only just been
removed from the oyster. Then I sniffed it. A familiar salty musk.
I'm telling you, as a good Catholic I blushed when I remembered
where I had smelled the scent before. I lay there struggling with
my erection, before my alarm went off indicating my shift had
begun. It had to be a prank the lads were playing on me.

I waited until the last meal of the shift then confronted the
crew.

'Which one of you jokers thought this would be funny?' I held up the pearl.

They looked at me blankly. Then Nick the navigator, a bit of a showman, held out his hand. I dropped the gem into the centre of his palm. He studied it as if he were a jeweller examining the Queen's crown; the others watching, fascinated. Finally he looked up with a mock-serious look plastered across his long face.

'What the fuck are you on about, Seamus? This is a fucking pearl. A valuable one at that. What's this got to do with us?'

'Someone left it under my pillow.'

There was an awkward silence. Then Nick spoke up again.

'Okay, fess up, you mob, which of you lads is in love with this here Irishman?' At that they all cracked up.

'Come on, who left the love note?' Nick yelled over the laughter, which only sent them into louder peals of hysterics. I sat there, face burning, not moving an inch.

'Mate, you're losing it. You should get over to the knocking shop before your balls ferment the rest of your brain,' Nick added.

∽

I spent the rest of the night alone in the library. I couldn't find a reference to anything as big or the same colour as my pearl. It really was exotic. I'd placed it on the flat top of a desk barometer and it stared back at me, almost as if daring me to give it definition.

By the time dawn started to creep in under my blinds I'd decided it was one of the most beautiful things I'd ever seen. I settled under the eiderdown and switched off the lamp, hoping that this time I might actually dream. Of what I don't know — giant oysters?

I started to doze off but was suddenly flooded with the sensation that I was slipping underwater without my diving mask. I sat up, struggling to draw breath; coughed, almost expecting my lungs to bring up water. But nothing came. 'It's an anxiety attack, that's all,' I said to myself. 'Breathe deeply and it will go away.' I relaxed then lay down. Again I felt as if I were drowning. Finally, dosed up with sleeping pills, I fell asleep only to wake an hour later. This went on throughout my rest time.

I moved through my next shift with limbs as heavy as lead, a slow dread growing in my guts — the terror of falling asleep. At dawn I approached my bunk like it was an electric chair. This time I had drunk the best part of a whisky bottle and taken two Valium on top of that, but the fear was still upon me. I lay there, eyelids wide, my heart rattling like a stone in a tin despite the drink and the drugs. Each time my eyes started to droop and exhaustion eased its way through my muscle tissue it felt as if my lungs were filling with water and I was being pulled down into liquid suffocation.

The next day I propped myself up with caffeine and some No Doz pills the cook gave me. I had no choice: I had a job to do. The new cable had arrived that morning and, as chief diver, I knew it was I who had to go down and weld the new section to the old. I was inspecting the cable when one of the crew put his head around the door to tell me there was a phone call for me.

There was only one phone on the rig and usage was restricted to one call per man per week, incoming or outgoing. I'd never had reason to use it and I couldn't think who'd be ringing me now. The extraordinary notion that it could be Jim Tattle himself calling from the underworld occurred to me as I walked swiftly to the communications cabin.

'Seamus?'

Her voice brought an avalanche of memories, a past I had tried to smother with rationality; but now, hearing that familiar soft tentative tone of hers echoing down the line, I realised I loved her yet. My heart lurched as I wondered whether maybe, just maybe, she was coming back.

'Meredith? Are you okay?'

'Of course.'

A yawning silence; I free-fell through it, limbs twitching in anticipation.

'And you?' she said eventually.

'I've been better.'

380

'Seamus ...'

Oh, please don't use my name unless you mean it.

'Seamus, I'm pregnant. I thought it best if you heard it from me ... and well, we're getting married. Seamus ...'

But I'd already put the phone down, shaking.

❧

The doctor unwrapped the blood pressure band from my arm. The reading was slightly high but nothing to stop me making the dive. It was my silence that disturbed him.

'Are you okay?'

'Fine, doc, fine. I'd just like to get on with it,' I snapped.

Scribbling on my chart, he gave me clearance.

The computers had mapped out my descent and the diving tables had told me the exact mixture needed for my body weight at that depth. The Heliox had to be exact to avoid narcosis — the rapture of the blue, Jacques Cousteau called it. This dive was particularly dangerous as the rusting cable was right near the bottom of the rig, a good sixty metres down. Every move was a mathematical calculation. Aside from the tremendous water pressure pressing down on me the whole time, the other big problem with these oil rig dives was the possibility of getting lost in the murky waters of the North Sea and panicking. Elements that have a rational man talking gibberish in a matter of seconds. I know because I've seen it myself.

Personally, the more dangerous a dive the more I like it. Visibility is limited to the narrow beam shining from the lamp clamped to your mask, illuminating a black and white murky world, while at that depth the air you're breathing becomes thick like molasses. But I loved the solitary atmosphere. The sense of possibility in the total silence, the unknown, the feeling of being suspended in eternity.

I climbed into the dry suit required for deep dives and put on a full helmet with built-in radio and a light. There was not an inch of my skin exposed. I always imagined this was what it would be like back in the embryonic sac. Floating, fully protected, fully insulated.

Then they lowered me into the freezing waters of the North Sea. Clutching the welding equipment attached to a separate cable, I began to slide down the shotline.

❧

It only took a few minutes to reach the break in the cable. On the way down I passed through shoals of fish darting around the clumps of mussels, oysters and molluscs that had grown around the pylons of the rig. The struts created a false reef which the sea creatures were happy to colonise and the divers happy to harvest.

Thirty metres deeper and I finally saw the cable through the misty waters. The broken line lashed slowly in the current like a sleepy sea snake. I caught hold of it; a section of about eighteen feet was missing, broken off due to rust. I radioed the information to the surface and was cheered to hear Nick's voice radioing back down as clear as if he were standing right next to me.

I had almost finished the repair welding when I first saw it — a glint of silvery-bronze caught in the luminous hexagon of my light. My first thought was that it was the tail of some large fish. I ignored it and continued welding, the dull glow lighting up the area. The creature swam through the beam again and this time I saw enough to make me drop the welding torch.

Long tendrils of red hair drifted through the water like seaweed; the copper of a sea perch, light fragmenting off the scales and illuminating the white-blue skin. At the top of the tail, where the body of a fish would naturally widen out, were the unmistakeable broad hips of a woman. Her sex, neatly located in the centre of the tail, was hairless. She had no thighs, just a crevice where evolution had fused land legs together. Nauseous with shock, I dived after the descending welding torch, catching it just in time. I returned to the shotline, hanging on for dear life as I collected my wits.

'Seamus, what was that noise? Are you all right?' Nick's voice echoed in my head.

'It was nothing, I dropped the welding torch, that's all. Had to get it back.'

She was floating at the edge of the beam, dipping in and out of shadow. There was just enough light for me to see the full breasts tipped with mauve nipples like those I'd seen on sea cows and the delicate bone of her neck, more pronounced than a human's, arching out like white coral. Her face had broad cheekbones that were almost Asiatic only more pronounced, a nose that I suspected was decorative rather than functional, and lips that were the same colour as her nipples. Her eyes, which appeared to have no pupil or iris but were entirely blue from lid to lid, stared straight at me displaying an intelligence that was so other I had absolutely no way of reading her.

Even more frightening was her size; she looked to be taller than myself, which made her about seven foot in length.

'Seamus?' Nick's voice pulled me back to the reality of the luminous world above. But *she* was still there, swaying with the current as naturally as a dolphin.

'Seamus, you sure you're all right? You sound a little strange.'

'There's something down here, something wonderful . . .'

As I spoke, still locked on those incandescent blue eyes, she opened her mouth and blew out a large air bubble which shimmered and danced like a silver balloon before ascending out of sight. Then, with a twitch of her tail, she disappeared into shadow.

Without thinking I broke free of the surface supply of Heliox and turned on my emergency supply cylinder.

'Seamus, you're not making sense. I suggest you begin your ascent as soon as possible. Do you hear me?'

'Later, Nick, I have to follow . . . I've got to . . .'

'Seamus!'

I dropped the welding torch again and, now breathing air from my bail-out cylinder, freed myself from the shotline. The decision surged through my body like liberation. A fine red hair trailed across the glass of my mask and I was off, following the glint of her tail, pinning her with my light. The line above me drifted loose — a broken umbilical cord to the humanity I had abandoned. Or had it abandoned me?

Nick's voice faded as we swam deeper and deeper into great billowy clouds of seaweed. Startled fish darted past. I should have been frightened. I should have realised what was happening, but instead I felt remarkably tranquil, as if I'd finally arrived at the pinnacle to which intuitively I knew all the events in my life had been leading.

Even through my suit I could feel the water getting colder and my ears began to pound as we swam to greater depth. Always before me the tantalising silvery curves, the wondrous magic of her, and every time I told myself she could not possibly exist she would turn around and hover with a solemn gaze, her hair a floating storm, her pale arms stretched out against the green-black vegetation, her webbed fingers extended, as if to say, 'No, I am as real as you are, as visceral as the trickling beads of condensation on your mask.' Then without warning, she would be off again, a twist of silver in a swirl of water.

We must have swum for a good half-hour, until we reached an underwater cliff-face, a ridge of caves and crevices over which schools of fish zigzagged furiously. It was monumental. Dimly I tried to squeeze a possible location from my befuddled mind but I couldn't remember any such markings on the map I'd seen of the local sea bed.

The creature was closer now, only about three feet away from me. I could see the markings on her tail clearly: large scales reminiscent of ocean fish found at higher depths. Ridges ran down either side of the tail suggesting a piscine skeleton beneath. Swimming behind, I could see her buttocks protruding above the area where the tail finished. Again here were signs of being human: the cleft between her buttocks was clearly delineated. There was no doubt, mermaid or not, fish or flesh, she was highly desirable.

She finally stopped at the entrance of a dark tunnel under an overhanging lip of rock. The huge tentacles of an octopus curled out, partly camouflaged against the rock surface. I reeled back; a nesting octopus could be ferocious when disturbed. But she didn't hesitate, fearlessly ducking down and disappearing into the tunnel mouth. A second later the octopus shot out, propelling itself furiously through the water like an outraged water-spout, a jet of black ink spilling behind it. A moment later the mermaid re-emerged and gestured for me to follow her into the tunnel.

I glanced at the meter on my air tank; it indicated that I had only about an hour's worth of oxygen left. I would barely make it to the surface if I left now, and not without the risk of ascending too fast and getting the bends. To follow the mermaid seemed certain suicide. Just then my light captured the glint of something metal. I turned it fully on the object: it was an old mask, clouded up with algae and weed, caught on a rock just at the edge of the tunnel's mouth.

The mermaid smiled; at least, her mouth formed the shape of a smile. Whether there was any human perspicacity behind it or whether it was the dumb mimicry of an animal that had once been smiled at and had remembered the shape of such expression I couldn't tell you. But it was the smile that drew me, against my better judgement as a man, a diver and a Catholic, into that tunnel.

The opening was covered with coral and all manner of weed; it was so narrow and dark that I feared I would knock my cylinder and lose what precious Heliox I had left. I was just beginning to despair when the tunnel broadened out into an underwater cave.

Something was shining above me. Peering up I thought I must be hallucinating as a glimmering indicating the surface of the water seemed to loom up suddenly. To my amazement the head and shoulders of the creature just a few feet in front of me disappeared as she broke the surface. I followed, my mask misting up as soon as I hit air.

It was an underground air pocket — a cavern of about twelve feet across and seven feet wide. I'd heard about such things but had taken the stories as myth, the kind of tales that giant squids and ghost ships belonged to. But I had to believe that other divers must have been there before me, releasing their air into the cave to create such an unnatural environment.

I sat resting against a stone bank for a moment, wondering whether I had now completely surrendered to a world of delusion and, if so, would I survive if I took off my helmet and breathed in air that could be noxious.

Staring up I realised that the ceiling was covered with stalactites that glowed in the dark, giving off enough phosphorescence to illuminate the whole cave with a soft greenish light. I could only assume that the rock was alive with a kind of organism that had evolved to produce light as a survival mechanism.

Several strange white crabs scuttled sideways into the shadows, pincers waving madly — a species I'd never seen before. Tilting my head I saw the mermaid. Through the misted-up mask she was just a tantalising outline of shimmering curves and tail, but she was close, close enough for me to touch. I peered at the dial showing the amount left in my tank: thirty minutes' worth. Without stopping to analyse my choices I unstrapped my helmet and pulled it off.

The air was surprisingly clean. I had thought it might be foul but instead it was mysteriously sharp, with a higher oxygen content than I'd imagined.

I lay there for a moment before turning in her direction. Part of me expected her to vanish, melt away like a mirage. Part of me expected to wake up drowning.

She was lying propped against a shelf of coral, the whole glorious length of her now out of the water, and she was staring at me with as much amazed curiosity as I was showing at her. I placed the helmet on a stone shelf above me so that it illuminated both of us. My heart racing, I cautiously moved towards her, half-anticipating her to dive back into the water and disappear for ever like some frightened wild beast. She didn't move, just stared back candidly, no fear in her eyes. Encouraged, I stopped about a foot away from her and let my fascinated gaze travel her whole physique.

Her wet hair streamed down one side of her face, leaving the other side of her head visible. Where there should have been an ear was a gill like that of an amphibian, rippling as if sucking in air. The rest of her facial features appeared to be human-like, as I'd noticed before. Her nose was sharp and upturned, the nostrils teardrops which I now suspected operated as a secondary breathing device. The shape of her face was triangular, probably smoothed down by evolution to make her more streamlined. Her lips obtruded more than a human's, as if they might serve to gasp air from the water's surface. She appeared to have teeth. Her shoulders were narrow but the bones in her neck protruded gracefully above heavy breasts that lolled tantalisingly on a narrow chest.

Below her stomach was a soft curve and, apart from the fact that she lacked a belly button and that she was hairless, her sex appeared convincingly human. Confrontingly naked, it sat on a pubis that jutted out further than on a human woman — I suppose because of the lack of legs. The labia and clitoris were clearly visible and directly beneath them began the fish part of her in a long sweep of scales and fin.

Terrified that I had conjured up my own succubus through thwarted desire, months of celibacy and grief, I lay down on my back again and shut my eyes, hoping to will myself back to some kind of sanity.

I felt her lay her hand over my cock through my dry suit. I opened my eyes. She was leaning over me, watching as I grew beneath her webbed fingers, her breasts falling over my face. It was too much for any grown male — human or otherwise — I'm telling you.

I pulled off my suit and lay there as naked as the day I was born. Then I touched her for the first time. She was surprisingly warm and as smooth as silk. There was no hair nor even evidence of any follicles under my touch and her skin was so thin that I could feel the blood pulsing beneath it. She seemed to tremble, a shiver that rippled right down to the end of her tail which flapped gently against the rock. She was about a foot taller than myself and as broad across the shoulders and hips. The size of her was as exciting as the utter strangeness. Deciding I would have to take the initiative I placed both hands around her waist and pulled her down so that she was lying beside me. Then, leaning over her, too excited to wonder about the danger of it, I began to explore her anatomy.

I carefully pushed back her hair and touched her lips; she sucked at my fingers like a fish, her mouth warm and soft as any woman's. I traced the sweep of her neck bone, as beautiful as a bow of ivory, then covered her two breasts with my palms. Firm and pendulous, they had all the fecundity of a woman in her prime, a woman aching with the ripeness of maturity. She was not young, that much I could tell — perhaps in what she measured time, about the same age as myself.

Her nipples — the areolae covering most of the breast — rose in response and her fish tail began drumming with a restless excitement. I squeezed her nipples, my own erection now pressing against the slippery surface of her belly, her labia stuck to my thigh like a limpet.

I could have taken her then. There was something incredibly erotic about the way we were examining each other objectively, her cool gaze as she stared at my flesh as if I too were some fantastical creature in her eyes. Instead I ran my tongue down the centre of her torso, tasting salt, sea water, all the way down to her vagina. Unlike a human, her outer labia were thinner than her inner lips, it was as if the vagina itself had become a seal against water. Her clitoris was larger than any woman's, almost penis-like. It hardened under my fingers and it was then that she uttered her first sound — a strange croaking that sounded like a seal.

I watched fascinated as the tip became swollen then I tasted her with my tongue. Again the crystallised salt of the ocean, but sweeter. Curious, I lifted my face, the tip of her clitoris was identical to the blue-black pearl I had found under my pillow, only as soft as flesh.

I felt her fingers in my hair; she dragged me up to her lips and, curiously, rubbed noses. The kiss of a mermaid, I thought absurdly, until the sensation of her breasts against my chest brought me back to the moment. Straddling her tail with my knees, I paused before entering her. The memory of losing my virginity swept through me suddenly — the same sense of excitement and trepidation born of the ignorance of a Catholic schoolboy as I started at the sacred sex of the town whore. A citadel of furled, sticky flesh, gates of Heaven against which I tentatively pushed my adolescent cock. Overwhelmed and humbled before the Fuck God pushed me hard to feel so oh so right, and now here I was again: virgin of sorts, about to commit a transgression that would take me to the edge of paradise. Or would it be Hell? My cock now resting between her thick inner lips, thicker than any woman's, her skin colder than any human's. Pulling me in, sucking me in, and then I was there. Tight, wet silken glove, a web that slipped over me, a hangman's noose of illicit pleasure and I was a goner, so help me God. All thought convulsing into a hot joy as I took her over and over. She, wrapping her arms around my shoulders, her mouth sucking my neck greedily as her tail drummed madly against the rock. Like any woman lost in the moment.

I slowed my pace. She felt so good I thought I would come there and then, and somehow the idea of that was frightening as if climax would chase the mirage away, would bring death.

Steadying myself against her breasts, I took one nipple into my mouth as I teased the edge of her with my cock. One blue eye, immense, pressed up against my cheek swallowing my whole horizon. The musk of her filling everything, the wetness, stickiness. The sense of her squeezing down hard on my flesh. Faster and faster, her webbed fingers pressing into my back, her claws scratching at me wildly, and Oh Mary, sweet mother of God, the pleasure staggering me, it shook the very base of me, every inch of me blossoming and swelling and bursting up, all the months of loneliness, of anger, of grief, of aching for a woman, thirsting for touch, mounting like a burning ball of joy that gathered speed faster, faster, from deep in my body to blast a path right through me in a shooting kaleidoscope of shrieking ecstasy. The shrieking — was it mine or hers? She arched with me, her voice clicking with my cries, her orgasm rippling like any woman's as she contracted around my exploding cock.

As I lay there, resting my head on those great breasts of hers, I prayed, 'Lord, save me now, for I have lost both my humanity and my soul.'

It could have finished there; in a way it should have — I would have been left with my illusions and my dreams. The satiated misanthrope, the spent sailor collapsed upon his mermaid like some Pre-Raphaelite painting, except I was a man with penis and testicles and she was a fish with a vagina. But for all of that I knew we had made love, had enjoyed a communion between species. I had to believe that; I was staking my soul on it.

I slid off her exhausted. The air was thinning out — I'd used a fair amount of it with the exertion. I reached across and kissed her, the azure of those eyes piercing me like faith. She smiled beneath my lips, then moved her mouth up.

At first I thought she was going to lick my eyelids — you know, how some women like that. But then her mouth fastened down over my eyeball like a suction cap, sending a brilliant white flash across my closed retina. I waited a split second, wondering if I was being paranoid, but she didn't let go. The image of the sightless Tattle suddenly shot through my mind. Terrified, I tried to push her off but she had me pinned, her great tail weighted across my thighs. I struggled wildly and my arm touched the side of my helmet. Clawing at it blindly, I swung it hard and hit the side of her head.

Reeling, she let go. A streak of blood appeared at her temple and her face turned several shades paler. She looked at me, as if to say that she couldn't help what was an animal impulse. Then, without a sound, she slid off the rock and disappeared into the black water.

Rocking myself I nursed my swelling eye, my lungs heaving as the air thinned. I was growing sleepy with the lack of oxygen. I pulled my cylinder over and let the remaining gas out into the cave. It wasn't an unpleasant place to die. The beautiful phosphorescent light danced on the rock face like a pantomime in silhouette. I lay back and stared at it. I thought I saw all my life pictured there: Meredith, Hanif, the day we'd all gone boating together and caught a crab; my first communion; my parents; the small cottage on the west coast of Cork where my grandfather lived; all of it, the good and the irredeemable. Then suddenly, between the shadows, I see a phrase carved into the rock.

*I found my brother here and we were happy. JT*

Tattle. Poor Tattle. With one last supreme effort I pulled a large empty sea shell towards me and began to whisper into it all that had happened . . .

# Acknowledgments

I would like to thank the following individuals for their contribution to the crafting of this book: Belinda Balding, Sue Berger, Gavin Brennen, Rabbi Burger, Michael Donohue, Scott Hocknull (of the Queensland Museum), William Eiseman, Lesabelle Furhaven, Jane Gleeson-White, Katja Handt, Darren Holt, David Knibbs, Adam Learner, Adam Long, Simon Mark-Isaacs, Francis Oeser, Leo Raftos, Moshe Rosenzveig, Paul Schütze, Victoria Thaine and Des Walters of the Descend Underwater training centre.

Also on the editing front, Linda Funnell and Nicola O'Shea for their usual brilliance; my Australian agent Rachel Skinner; and my mother Eva Learner for her ongoing unconditional support.

For an extra short story, go to
www.tobshaseroticfiction.com,
hit on the link to a free download
and subscribe to Tobsha Learner's
free quarterly newsletter . . .

Also available by Tobsha Learner

## *Quiver*

*Quiver*'s twelve interlinked short stories explore
desire and transport us into a world of love, power,
pain, pleasure and obsession. Experience the
excitement of lust at its most primal . . .

978-0-7499-5904-3

## *Yearn*

A Sydney sculptor wonders whether a lover can
be summoned by the act of artistic creation.

A London weatherman inspires both obsessive
lust and devastating storms.

An eighteenth-century biographer discovers
a magic, erotic ritual that will change his life
for ever . . .

978-0-7499-5906-7